"Please, my lord, you should go. It would not do for us to be found here."

"Very well," he said, "I will look to see you tonight at the embassy reception. Goodbye, my—" He turned away before he could say more than was wise, and took a step toward the door.

Then, just as quickly, he turned back and closed the distance between them. Without a word, he took her in his arms and kissed her, quite thoroughly. She melted against him for a moment, returning his kiss with sudden passion of her own. But then she stiffened. He released her at once, of course, though he could not quite regret his action.

"Footsteps," she hissed. A measured tread was heard outside the library, and then up the stairs.

Peter stood motionless, his hand still on her shoulder. "My apologies again," he murmured, as the front door opened and closed below. "Clearly it is not safe for me to be alone with you."

Though she blushed charmingly, her expression was by no means condemning. "So it would seem, my lord."

Other **AVON ROMANCES**

BRENDA HIATT

WICKEDLY YOURS

AVON BOOKS
An Imprint of HarperCollinsPublishers

This is a work of fiction. Names, characters, places, and incidents are products of the author's imagination or are used fictitiously and are not to be construed as real. Any resemblance to actual events, locales, organizations, or persons, living or dead, is entirely coincidental.

AVON BOOKS
An Imprint of HarperCollins*Publishers*
10 East 53rd Street
New York, New York 10022-5299

Copyright © 2003 by Brenda Hiatt Barber
ISBN: 0-06-050759-4
www.avonromance.com

First Avon Books paperback printing: November 2003

Avon Trademark Reg. U.S. Pat. Off. and in Other Countries, Marca Registrada, Hecho en U.S.A.
HarperCollins® is a registered trademark of HarperCollins Publishers Inc.

Printed in the U.S.A.

10 9 8 7 6 5 4 3 2 1

For Keith,
the inspiration for all of my heroes

Prologue

London
September, 1808

"**P**romise me you'll do your best, William, and mind your teachers." Twelve-year-old Sarah Killian pressed her lips together as soon as she finished speaking, determined not to cry in front of her little brother.

"I said I would, didn't I?" he replied with a scowl that made him look fiercer than any eight-year-old should look. "And don't call me William."

Sarah gave him a quick hug, careful not to crush either her new clothes or his, the first they'd had since running away from the workhouse two years ago. He endured it without squirming, which told her he wasn't as confident as he pretended.

1

"Flute, then," she amended.

Though the nickname had begun as teasing—the older lads making fun of young William's high, piping voice—he'd adopted it as his own after proving his worth by fighting—and beating—his tormentors, most of them nearly twice his size. Surely such a scrappy boy would be able to fend for himself at boarding school.

"An' you take care o' yourself, too," he said when she released him, his eyes suspiciously bright. "I still think it's a stupid idea, y'know, goin' to school when we're making a good living here."

Sarah set her jaw stubbornly in anticipation of yet another argument over the decision she'd made last week. "You won't be able to work as a climbing boy much longer—you're gettin' too big. And won't you like never having burns on your feet again?" His chimney-sweep master often used hot irons to prod the boys more quickly through the narrow flues they squeezed through.

"I s'pose. But I been talking to Twitchell's lads, and they say I'd make a bang-up pickpocket with a bit o' training, and—"

"No!" Sarah cut him off. "That'd be dishonest—and dangerous." She'd picked her own share of pockets for Twitchell, in fact, but she refused to let her brother follow that path. He was her responsibility, had been since their parents died within a week of each other almost three years ago.

"Besides," she continued, "if you don't go to school, I won't—and I'm really wanting to. 'Specially after Mrs. Hounslow was kind enough to make the arrangements and all."

Flute nodded, though he still looked skeptical.

"Long as this so-called grandfather of ours don't change his mind about paying, I'll go. For a while, anyways."

Sarah wasn't sure he'd fully understood Mrs. Hounslow's hints of what would happen if she stayed with Twitchell's gang—what happened to most comely young girls on the streets once they reached a certain age.

"A pretty thing like you?" the charitable woman had said, tears standing in her eyes. "In a year or less, you'd be forced to trade your virtue for your keep. I want to spare you that, my dear."

It had been enough to convince her to accept the woman's help, and even Flute agreed that Sarah must leave London. In a few minutes she would board the mail coach for Cumberland, in the far North of England, to attend Miss Pritchard's Seminary for Young Ladies. Two hours later, Flute was to board another, bound southward to Westerham School in Kent.

At the insistence of Mrs. Hounslow, who was known about the streets of London for her charity to orphans, a grandfather they'd never seen had agreed to pay for their schooling—even though he'd cast off their mother and wanted nothing else to do with them. Sarah didn't much care, as long as the man's money got her brother and herself off the dangerous London streets. Since escaping the brutal workhouse, she'd seen more than a dozen children die of want, violence, or at the hands of the so-called law.

With a rumble and a clatter, the mail coach rounded the corner of the inn yard where they waited. Quickly, Sarah grasped her brother's shoulders, forcing him to look her in the eye.

"I'm goin' to be the best student Miss Pritchard ever had," she assured both him and herself. "They'll turn me into a real lady there. Then I c'n get me a good job, send you to university—make a real life for the both of us. I promise."

She prayed he'd believe it, despite the fact that their mother, a "real lady," had failed to provide much of anything for them. To her relief, he nodded, his eyes glistening again.

"C'mon, lass, we've a schedule to keep," barked the coachman, tossing her small valise into the boot of the coach and opening the door to the already-crowded interior.

Sarah gave her brother one last hug. "Be good, William. I'll write you!"

Before she could cry, she clambered into the mail coach and wedged herself between a fat farm wife and an elderly parson in rusty black. As the coach rattled away, she felt a sharp pang of loss at leaving the only person in the world who mattered to her.

As London streets gave way to the unfamiliar green of the countryside, however, melancholy gave way to determination. They'd survived this long with nothing but their wits, she and William. Surely, with enough hard work, anything was possible. She *would* keep the promise she'd just made, or die trying.

Chapter 1

London
October, 1816

"**G**one?" Sarah Killian asked in disbelief. "How can William be gone?"

Mrs. Hounslow, smaller than Sarah remembered, and a little bit grayer, looked as though she might cry. "Believe me, I had no idea. I sent word that your grandfather had died, as I wrote to you, and only then did the headmaster inform me that he'd run away from Westerham."

"But . . . all of those letters you sent me. You assured me William was doing well." Sarah followed Mrs. Hounslow into the tiny but very clean parlor of the little house on Gracechurch Street, where she had arrived after three grueling days on the south-bound mail coach.

"I fear I was sadly deceived by the headmaster," Mrs. Hounslow replied. "I presume he did not wish to lose your brother's annual tuition. Not until the source of that tuition disappeared did he tell me the truth. I have requested an inquiry by the board of directors, you may be sure."

"Then . . . did William receive none of my letters?" Sarah couldn't quite grasp the enormity of what had happened. "He never answered them, but I attributed that to his youth—and gender."

The older woman nodded sagely. "Men, and particularly boys, do tend to be dreadful correspondents. But no, it appears William left the school before the end of his first year. I have not yet managed to locate him, as I only discovered it yesterday."

"His first—. He's been missing for *seven years*?" Sarah gasped, a hand going to her throat. "Anything might have happened to him!"

Horrible visions rose before her eyes. Little William, at the mercy of far worse than his old climbing master, beaten, forced to . . . "He—he could be anywhere by now," she whispered as tears threatened to choke her. "He could even be dead."

For eight long years, Sarah's one goal had been to fulfill the promise she'd made her brother the day she had left London. That goal had supported her through her first months at what had turned out to be a harsh school in a harsh climate, established solely to educate orphans lucky enough to have benefactors.

That goal had continued to sustain her as she stubbornly learned everything possible from those teachers willing to work in that environment. Finally, that goal had driven her to apply for a teaching post upon graduation, so that she could earn both the money and experience necessary to return to London and seek gainful employment.

Now she was here, but her goal was farther away than ever—perhaps even unattainable. She took a deep breath, trying to keep panic at bay. "What of a position? Were you able to find one for me?"

"Ah, here's Maggie with our tea. Do have a bit," Mrs. Hounslow urged, taking the tray from the middle-aged maid. She poured a cup for each of them before answering Sarah's question.

"I *am* sorry, my dear, but governess positions are not so easy to come by as all that. First, you must establish yourself, demonstrate that you have respectable connections. Indeed, now I see your face again, I fear it may be a trifle, ah, difficult to secure such a post."

Sarah set down her cup, untouched. "I should perhaps tell you that I spent every bit of money I had on my fare to London, and on this dress." She fingered the brown-checked country gingham, the best she'd been able to afford after paying for her journey from Cumberland. "If not a governess position, I can work as a seamstress, or even a lady's maid—or in a shop somewhere."

"Oh, no, my dear." Mrs. Hounslow appeared shocked. "You come of a good family, whether they choose to acknowledge you or not. You are too young to be a lady's companion, so governessing is your only option. That—or marriage." She regarded Sarah speculatively. "In fact, I should say—"

Sarah interrupted this flight of fancy with a blunt

question. "Then how am I to live while I search for William?"

"Search—? My dear, you mustn't do any such thing. It would be most dangerous. I shall make inquiries, and I doubt not we'll discover something of your brother's whereabouts soon enough."

"Of course I must search for him." How could Mrs. Hounslow imagine otherwise? To prevent further argument, she reverted to the other topic. "You were discussing my options for survival?"

"Oh! Yes. As it happens, I have found you a respectable place to stay—a most respectable place. One that may offer far better opportunities than a governess post."

Mrs. Hounslow's hands fluttered about her as she spoke, betraying her nervousness. "I have discovered a cousin of your mother's here in Town, and I'm certain she will allow you to stay at her home until we can get you settled more, ah, permanently. When we finish our tea, I shall walk you to Berkley Square. Lady Mountheath will no doubt be delighted to meet you."

Lord Peter Northrup drained the last of a well-earned pint of ale and stood. After a fortnight away, he'd had a productive morning catching up on the news, political and social. His talk with a clerk or two at the War Office was most rewarding, and now he'd concluded with a pleasant hour among friends at the Guards' Club.

"Leaving us, Colonel?" asked Tom Pynchney, a talkative fellow who still wore his regimentals despite the fact he'd done no soldiering since Paris more than two years ago—any more than had Peter himself.

Peter hid a wince at the designation. "Aye, I've a thing or two to do at home before readying myself for the evening," he replied, twitching the fit of his coat back to its customary perfection. The news he'd heard this morning had brought back enough unpleasant memories without additional reminders.

Lord Fernworth, already well into his third bottle of wine, guffawed from a nearby table. "Have to change to yet brighter colors, you mean? But I believe you may be losing your edge, Pete. Didn't you wear that same orange waistcoat only last month?"

Peter smiled indulgently and shook his head. "You should know me better than that, Ferny. That one was peach. This one is apricot." This drew a general chuckle, to which Peter graciously inclined his head before picking up his hat and walking stick and taking his leave.

He was used to his cronies' ribbing about his flamboyant collection of waistcoats, which defied the current fashion for sober blacks and blues. In fact, he prided himself on his unruffled calm in the face of their ridicule. This was who he was now: frivolous man of fashion, genial party guest, caretaker and conscience of his more dissipated friends.

Besides, deviating from the norm was no bad thing. He was all too aware of what atrocities were possible under the guise of conformity. This morning's conversation with Mr. Thripp at the War Office had brought back far too much, briefly cracking his carefully maintained veneer.

"Word is, the Black Bishop is due to hang by the end of the year," the clerk had told him.

Peter had felt a surge of satisfaction, as that traitor had been directly responsible for the incident Peter had tried hardest to forget from the war. "When was he caught? And by whom?"

Mr. Thripp shrugged. "The Foreign Office keeps to itself, so we don't get much beyond the bare facts. He was taken almost two months since, and I heard that a Mr. Paxton, a fellow working for the Bow Street Runners of all things, brought him in. Charlton saw it. Keep it under your hat, though. Everything's supposed to stay quiet until after the trial."

Peter had agreed, of course, but the conversation had given him much food for thought.

Before his marriage in August, Noel Paxton had been hot on the trail of the Saint of Seven Dials, that legendary thief who'd been stealing from London's rich and giving to the poor—and who had ceased operations precisely when the Black Bishop was arrested.

During the Congress of Vienna, Peter had suspected Noel acted as far more than a mere courier for Wellington. Therefore, he'd thought it odd that Noel would be working for the Bow Street Runners. If the Saint was actually the Black Bishop, however, it all made perfect sense.

While it was disappointing to realize that the Saint's vaunted "heroism" had merely been a ruse by a vicious traitor, Peter felt a sense of satisfaction as the missing pieces of the puzzle fell into place. Certainly, no punishment could be harsh enough to atone for the deaths the Black Bishop had caused. A vision of young Billy Winton's face swam before him—a private under Peter's command, not yet out of his teens, cut down before he'd lived his life. The long-suppressed rage stirred again, but Peter quickly subdued it.

No, he would think only of the future—in particular, this week's social calendar.

Tonight he would wear his scarlet-and-gold waistcoat, he decided, with the embroidered gold coat. His colorful wardrobe was one of the few indulgences Peter permitted himself, though in fact he could afford far greater ones. Amazing what careful investments could achieve in a relatively short time.

Walking briskly up Dover Street toward Grosvenor, where he was temporarily staying at his brother Marcus's house, he reflected that it was just as well his friends remained in ignorance of his assets. Ferny, for one, would be continuously hounding him for money. He would refuse, of course, but others might be harder to deny. His best friend, Harry, for instance.

"Pardon, guv'nor, 'ave ye a penny to spare?" a bedraggled urchin broke into his musings.

Smiling down at the lad, Peter reached into his pocket and flipped him a shilling. "Put it to good use, now," he admonished the delighted child.

"Aye, guv, I will, guv!" the lad exclaimed, then scurried off, no doubt to boast to his mates about his successful begging.

Peter sighed. Yes, he was far too soft a touch. Still, it wasn't something he wished to change about himself. Not after—again his thoughts shied away from the past.

Life was good now, and he was more than content to play the gallant dandy with a reputation for knowing everything about everyone. His time—and thoughts—were well occupied looking out for his friends and for any unfortunates who crossed his path.

He rounded the corner to Hay Hill and nearly collided with a trio of women near the railings, two of them hovering over the third, who appeared to be in some distress.

"My pardon, ladies!" He swept off his hat and bowed. "May I be of some assistance?"

The youngest lady looked up and he was forcibly struck by the beauty of her wide blue eyes and heart-shaped face, only partially obscured by her close-fitting bonnet. "Thank you, sir," she said in a cultured voice that belied her rustic clothing. "Maggie here appears to have strained her ankle."

With an effort, Peter turned his attention to the injured woman, clearly a servant by her dress. "Let's have a look."

"Come, Maggie, have a seat on the stoop here and let the gentleman help you," urged the older woman, no doubt the beauty's mother. "I told you it was too far for you to walk so soon after that nasty sprain you had last month. Perhaps you'll listen to my advice in the future."

While she lectured on, Peter managed a quick examination of the affected ankle. He'd had far too much experience with injury during the war, but this one, thankfully, was minimal.

"It's a bit swollen, but nothing a day or two of rest won't cure," he said after a moment's probing. "I'll get you a hackney."

This effectively stopped the older woman's chatter. "Oh! Thank you, sir, but I fear a hackney is a bit beyond our means."

The younger woman nodded. "Indeed, there is no need, sir, though we thank you. I was just offering to walk back to Gracechurch Street and send someone—a neighbor—for Maggie. It's only three miles each way."

Peter's eyebrows rose, though he refrained from commenting on the novelty of such an undertaking for the sake of a mere servant. Instead, he raised a hand to hail a passing cab. "Pray allow me this small indulgence. It's not often I get to play the hero."

He smiled at the daughter as he spoke. Working class or not, no healthy male could fail to enjoy having such a pretty face regard him with gratitude. Besides, he could never resist helping damsels in distress.

He assisted the injured maid into the hackney, then turned to the others and held out his hand. To his surprise, the beauty shook her head.

"I thank you, sir, for your kindness to poor Maggie, but Mrs. Hounslow and I have business to conduct in this part of Town."

Not the older woman's daughter after all, then. As he paid the coachman the fare to Gracechurch Street, he reordered his original assumptions and made a few new ones. For the first time, he noticed that the younger girl clutched a small valise.

"Anything with which I can be of help?" he asked, reluctant to leave them. Peter loved a puzzle as much as he enjoyed playing the rescuer. "May I offer my escort, at least?"

He reached out to take her burden from her, but

she backed away, glancing at the older woman, who said, "You are very kind, sir, but it is only a step. However, I do thank you again—I thank you very much indeed!"

Though he would very much have liked to fill in the blanks of what appeared to be an intriguing story, he could hardly insist in light of this dismissal. He therefore bowed, murmured that he would always be at their service, and took his leave of them.

Glancing over his shoulder as he continued on his way, he saw the two women turning onto Berkley Square. For a moment he debated following at a distance, but regretfully decided it would be unwise. The nameless beauty was almost certainly not of his world, so what could he do beyond persuading an impoverished but respectable young woman to trade her virtue for his protection? Not his style at all.

Firmly putting the girl from his thoughts, he headed toward Grosvenor Street, and Marcus's townhouse. He had more pressing matters to consider just now—such as which cravat would best complement the ensemble he meant to wear to Lady Driscoll's ridotto tonight.

Sarah gazed around Berkley Square with barely concealed awe. Never during her youthful years in London had she ventured into Mayfair, instead making her living, such as it was, selling flowers and trinkets to the theatergoers in and about Covent Garden and Drury Lane. That, and picking the occasional pocket when opportunity presented.

Nor had eight years at Miss Pritchard's prepared her for the opulence she now saw about her. The school had been utilitarian and drab—and so had the teachers, come to think of it. But there was nothing either utilitarian or drab about Berkley Square! Tall, gracious houses surrounded a central garden dominated by graceful plane trees and a sort of miniature Chinese pagoda.

The houses themselves were more elegant than anything Sarah had ever seen, with their beautiful brickwork, immaculately painted facades and imposing portals. The thought of actually living in one of them, even temporarily, seemed almost laughable—like a pig taking up residence in a royal palace.

And the people! Resplendant ladies walked here and there, holding delicate parasols and accompanied by distinguished-looking gentlemen in black, or by smartly dressed maids.

Sarah glanced down at her new brown frock, the prettiest she'd ever owned, and realized that even the maids were more modishly dressed than she. No wonder that handsome gentleman who'd aided poor Maggie had looked at her so strangely! How foolish she'd been to imagine admiration in his expression.

Mrs. Hounslow seemed to share none of her reservations, however, for she walked right up the front steps of the third house on the right and boldly plied the door knocker. Determinedly gathering her courage, Sarah hurried to stand beside her.

The impeccably imposing door opened to reveal an even more impeccably imposing butler, clad in black. "Yes?" he asked in icy tones.

"Good afternoon," Mrs. Hounslow said briskly. "Might I know your name?"

If anything, the butler's expression became even

more supercilious. "I am Hodge, madam. Your name and business?"

"I am Mrs. Hounslow, Hodge, and this is Miss Sarah Killian. We should like to speak with Lady Mountheath."

Hodge actually curled his lip, in a manner Sarah had heretofore only read about in novels. "I think not. Perhaps, if you go to the rear entrance, the housekeeper might be able to assist you."

Sarah took a half step back, prepared to comply, but Mrs. Hounslow was not so easily deterred. "I assure you, Hodge, that we are not tradespeople, nor back-door people at all. In fact, Miss Killian is a relation of Lady Mountheath's—the daughter of her cousin Mary. Pray inform her that we are here."

Though he looked profoundly skeptical, the butler bowed—then closed the door in their faces. Sarah blinked, then glanced questioningly at her companion.

"Odious man! No, Sarah, don't retreat. I don't believe Lady Mountheath will dare to let us leave without first investigating my claim."

Apparently she was correct, for a minute or two later the door reopened and the butler, as starchy as ever, motioned them into the marble-floored front hall. Sarah gazed, wide-eyed, at the gilt tables, richly upholstered chairs and numerous objects of art scattered about, illuminated by an extravagant number of candles.

"Wait here," the butler said, showing them into an anteroom near the back of the house. In contrast to the ostentatious ornamentation of the main hall, this room was simply and sparsely furnished, no doubt for the reception of "back-door people."

"Do you think—?" Sarah began, but Mrs. Hounslow shushed her, nodding her head toward the open doorway. An instant later, a large, turbaned woman in yellow satin swept through it, her expression every bit as disdainful as the butler's had been.

"So. You are Miss Sarah Killian?" Her voice was both strident and haughty.

Painfully aware of her outmoded gown and worn valise, Sarah nodded. "I am . . . my lady?"

The woman bobbed her turban. "Yes, I am Lady Mountheath. Now, what is this wild story about your being some sort of relation?" Her gaze slid to Mrs. Hounslow, who stepped forward eagerly.

"Yes indeed, my lady. Sarah here is the daughter of your own cousin Mary, who was daughter to Lord Wragby, your uncle. She only arrived in Town today, and as you are now her nearest living relation, it seemed fitting that I bring her to you."

Lady Mountheath raised an eyebrow. "And how do you come into the business, Mrs.—?"

"Hounslow, my lady. Esther Hounslow, of the Bettering Society. I make it my business to see to the welfare of poor orphans like Miss Killian here. It was I who, ah, suggested to your uncle that he subsidize her schooling at Miss Pritchard's Seminary for Young Ladies. And indeed, she proved both an exemplary student and teacher there."

Sarah felt that it was time she entered the conversation. "I have come to London to seek employment, my lady, not charity," she said, forcing an authority she did not feel into her voice, just as she'd had to do when teaching her first class of unruly girls.

Lady Mountheath raked her with a critical gaze.

"And what has that to do with me? My daughters are long past the age of needing a governess."

Mrs. Hounslow spoke up again. "She will need to live somewhere until she obtains a position, my lady. Your, ah, charity is quite famous—I read of it in the *Political Register* only a few weeks since. Once it is known Sarah is your cousin, you must agree it would look rather odd if she were not under your protection."

To Sarah's surprise, Lady Mountheath flushed an unattractive shade of puce. "Very well," she snapped, glaring at Mrs. Hounslow before turning to Sarah. "I do remember your mother—*and* how she disgraced the family. See you do not make me regret my generosity."

"I doubt I will have to impose upon you for long," Sarah said, stung. "I am well qualified for a governess post and have brought references from Miss Pritchard and two of the teachers."

Lady Mountheath sniffed. "You may find a post more difficult to obtain than you expect, young woman. For *honest* employment, it is no asset to be so—that is—"

She seemed to falter for a moment, but recovered at once. "I will have the housekeeper find you a room and inform you of your duties while you make your home with us. Charitable I may be, but I'll not keep you in idleness."

"Well, that's settled then," exclaimed Mrs. Hounslow delightedly. "You see, Sarah? I told you it would all work out. And never fear, my lady. Even if she cannot obtain a position as governess somewhere, she may well make a match, which will take her off your hands just as effectively."

An odd grimace twisted Lady Mountheath's mouth. "As her mother did? This way, Miss Killian."

After returning Mrs. Hounslow's parting kiss, Sarah obediently followed her new benefactress from the room, marveling at the abrupt change in her physical circumstances even as she braced herself for whatever verbal barbs might come her way.

It afforded her no satisfaction to realize that Lady Mountheath had likely been referring to her looks earlier. Hadn't Miss Pritchard also warned that her pale gold curls and wide blue eyes would hinder rather than help her on her chosen path?

"A governess in a noble household is a nobody," she'd said. "The men of the household will take liberties and the women will turn you out for it. You'd be advised to stay here, safe from the depravity so prevalent among our so-called upper classes."

At the time Sarah had assumed that venerable woman's misgivings stemmed largely from her unwillingness to lose her best—and lowest-paid—teacher. Surely, that gentleman who had helped poor Maggie proved that some members of the *ton* were decent, compassionate people.

"Grimble, this is Miss Killian, a kinswoman of sorts," Lady Mountheath informed the large, black-clad woman supervising two ill-favored maids as they polished plates in the dining room. "She will be with us for a week or two—*perhaps* longer." Her tone made it clear she hoped that would not be the case. "I leave it to you to find a place for her in the household." Without another word to Sarah, she left them.

Mrs. Grimble, a plain woman well past middle age, swept Sarah with as critical an eye as her mistress had done. "Not been much used to work, have you?" she asked after a moment.

Sarah blinked. "Indeed I have, ma'am. For the past two years I have taught four classes a day, six days a week, to two dozen girls of various ages."

"Educated, are you?" The housekeeper seemed to regard this as a drawback rather than a benefit. "I'd advise you not to put on airs, Missie. Her ladyship won't abide it. Maisie," she said to one of the maids, "see you and Betsy finish quickly—it's near time for the table to be set."

With a jerk of her head, she indicated that Sarah was to follow her, but as they were crossing the front hall, a top-hatted gentleman entered the house. Mrs. Grimble bobbed a curtsey, verifying Sarah's guess that this must be Lord Mountheath.

He nodded absently at the housekeeper, then glanced at Sarah. Then lifted his quizzing glass for a better look. "Well, well. And who might this be?"

"Sarah Killian, milord," Sarah replied, dropping a curtsey. "My mother was cousin to Lady Mountheath's mother, and she has agreed to let me stay here for the present."

"Indeed!" Lord Mountheath continued to gaze at Sarah in a way she didn't entirely care for. "As a member of the family, you will dine with us tonight, will you not?"

Sarah glanced at the housekeeper, who quickly smoothed a frown and gave her an almost imperceptible nod.

"Of . . . of course, my lord, if you wish it."

He smiled broadly, large teeth showing through thick lips. "Excellent. I'll see you again soon, then."

Finally taking his eyes from her face, he turned and headed up the stairs.

"If you're dining with the family, you'll need to freshen up." Mrs. Grimble's voice dripped disapproval. She led Sarah, still carrying her valise, up three flights of stairs to a tiny room under the eaves.

"I'll have the extra bed moved out before nightfall so you can have this room to yourself," Mrs. Grimble said grudgingly. "You can change without help?" Her tone implied she didn't have much choice.

"Of course. Thank you." Sarah saw no point in telling the housekeeper that she was already wearing her best dress, her only others being a pair of school uniforms. She owned nothing remotely suitable for dinner with a peer and his family.

Once alone, she took stock of her surroundings. The deep-set dormered window let in a dusty shaft of sunlight, revealing two narrow beds, a single chair, a washstand, and a few hooks on the wall in lieu of a clothes press.

At school she'd shared a dormitory with eleven other girls, and even as a teacher she'd had to room with another woman in a chamber not much larger than this one. To have this room to herself was an unexpected luxury. And she was in London again, surely that much closer to William! She was determined to find him as quickly as possible.

With that settled in her mind, she gave some thought to her own situation, which was far from hopeless. True, she had no money, but employment would soon change that. She'd left London eight years ago, a frightened, ignorant girl with street smarts and little else. Now she was a well-educated woman with skills that should allow her to move on the fringes, at least, of Society.

She allowed her imagination a brief ramble, spurred by something Mrs. Hounslow had said. For years, her dream had been to provide a home, perhaps a three-room flat, for William and herself. In her more optimistic moments, she'd even imagined a small cottage in the country, complete with chickens and a milk cow. Now, however, she flirted with a grander idea.

Though governesses rarely interacted with their employers, surely there was a remote chance that some tradesman—or even a gentleman!—might catch sight of her, might fall instantly in love with her, marry her, and provide handsomely for her. It happened in her favorite novels.

Her thoughts strayed again to the handsome gentleman who had hailed the hackney. To be loved by someone like that—She fingered a curl that had escaped its confining bun. Her appearance, which some seemed to think beyond the ordinary, might not help her find respectable employment, but if Mrs. Hounslow was to be believed, it might help her to find a husband—and marriage would be more secure than any hired position.

A maid entered then with a ewer of water, dispelling such fanciful musings—for that was all they were. With a fleeting wish for a bit of looking glass, Sarah tried to make herself presentable for dinner.

Chapter 2

Four elegantly dressed people turned to regard Sarah when she entered the dining room—Lord and Lady Mountheath, whom she'd already met, and two young women perhaps a few years older than herself. Only Lord Mountheath smiled.

"I apologize for my tardiness," Sarah said. "I, ah, neglected to ask what time you would be dining."

The younger ladies only stared, but Lady Mountheath's eyebrows rose into her turban. "And why, pray, should it matter to you when we dine, Miss Killian?"

Sarah opened and closed her mouth, looking to Lord Mountheath for support. In response, he rose and extended a hand to her.

"I invited her to dine with us," he informed his wife. "As she is a cousin, it seemed appropriate. No

doubt Fanny and Lucy will enjoy her company as
well. Welcome to the family, Miss Killian."

Though Lady Mountheath looked outraged and
her daughters tittered, he led Sarah to the empty
chair next to his own and motioned for a footman to
serve her.

"So, my dear, tell us about yourself," he said solic-
itously, filling a wine glass for her. "What are your
plans?"

Sarah smiled at his kindness, hoping that was all it
was. "I intend to find a position as a governess. Mrs.
Hounslow has promised to help me do so. I hope not
to impose on your hospitality for more than a few
days."

"Very commendable," Lady Mountheath said
coldly before her husband could respond, then
turned pointedly to her daughters. "Surely you do
not intend to wear that to Lady Driscoll's ridotto tonight, Lucy? You wore it only last week to the Stan-
hope ball."

Lucy, a tall, pallid young woman with small blue
eyes and flyaway brown hair, shrugged. "Mr. Galloway said I looked well in it—that the color matched
my eyes. It's a perfectly nice gown, unlike—" Her
eyes strayed to Sarah with a barely concealed sneer.

Her mother frowned. "I told you to keep your distance from that young man, did I not? Everyone
knows he is naught but a fortune hunter. My lord,
you will need to warn him off, should he approach
Lucy tonight," she told her husband.

But Lord Mountheath was still looking at Sarah,
with an intensity that made her more than a bit uncomfortable. "I thought I'd stay home tonight," he
said. "Seems impolite to leave our new addition all

on her own, her first night in Town." Sarah could not misunderstand the suggestiveness of his smile now.

Nor could his wife, it seemed. "You'll do no such thing," she said sharply, and to Sarah's relief. If all the family went out tonight, she would be able to begin her search for William.

But Lord Mountheath did not give up so easily. "I'll do as I please," he retorted. "I don't care for such entertainments anyway—not likely to be a smoking room, knowing the Driscolls."

"Very well. Stay home if you like," Lady Mountheath responded with a slight shrug. "However, I have decided to bring Miss Killian with us to the ridotto."

It would have been difficult to say who at the table was more startled at this declaration. Fanny and Lucy stared open-mouthed, Lord Mountheath's eyes widened with surprise, and Sarah was aware that she herself was gaping.

"I—ah—I fear I have nothing suitable to wear, my lady," she finally confessed, though with a pang, for she would dearly have loved, just once, to attend a grand Society function.

"Of course not," agreed Lord Mountheath. "No matter. You can stay home and tell me all about yourself."

Lady Mountheath glared at her husband—and at Sarah. "Fanny, your old rose and white gown should fit Miss Killian well enough—you're much of a height. As soon as we finish eating, have your maid pin her into it. And you, miss, mind you say nothing about your parents to anyone. Leave all explanations to me."

An hour and a half later, Sarah regarded herself in Fanny's looking glass with something like awe. She scarcely noticed the mended tear under the left arm, nor the stain near the hem in front. This was far and away the finest gown she had ever worn, and it made her look almost a different person.

"It seems to suit you," said Fanny peevishly before turning back to her dressing table, where her maid was attempting to style her thin brown hair into ringlets.

"Aye, miss, it does indeed," agreed the rotund maid with an enthusiasm that earned her a glare from her mistress. She quickly turned back to the business at hand.

Sarah smiled into the mirror, for they were right. The pink of the bodice flattered her pale skin and hair, and the high waist showed off her ample bosom to advantage. It was a far cry from the black-and-gray high-necked uniform she'd worn for the past eight years, or even the brown-checked frock she'd thought so fine when she'd left for London.

"Thank you so much for lending this to me," she said to Fanny, who shrugged.

"Libby here is too fat to wear my castoffs, so you may as well have it," replied the other girl ungraciously.

Sarah glanced anxiously at the maid, feeling sorry for her after such an ill-natured outburst. But Libby, struggling with Fanny's string-straight tresses, appeared not to have noticed.

Though she knew she wasn't nearly so well turned out as the Mountheath ladies, and though they completely ignored her, Sarah couldn't help feeling a bit like a princess as they all set off in the elegant carriage.

The delay in her search for William gnawed at her a bit, but excitement helped to keep her impatience at bay. This would surely be the most magical night of her life!

Lord Peter winced as Harry Thatcher downed his third glass of champagne.

"We've not been here half an hour yet, Harry," he admonished, knowing it would do no good, but obliged by concern for his oldest friend to make the effort. "Do you want Lord Driscoll to have you forcibly removed?"

Harry snorted. "Don't much care, to tell the truth. This party is boring as hell. Besides, I need some fortification after a fortnight of witnessing Jack's domestication. Poor bastard."

The pair of them had returned only the day before from a visit with their old friend and wartime crony, Jack Ashecroft—Marquis of Foxhaven these past two years.

"Can't imagine why you're pitying Jack," Peter said. "He and Lady Foxhaven quite obviously dote upon each other, as well as on little Geoffrey. He's happier than I've ever seen him, and that's saying a lot."

Two weeks visiting their longtime friend at his estate in Kent, where he'd retired shortly after his marriage, had left Peter rather envying Jack his present happiness, in fact.

Harry clearly did not share his sentiments. "Jack *thinks* he's happy now, but once the novelty wears

off, he'll realize what he's done—shackled himself to
a life of duty and domesticity, routine and responsibility." He shuddered visibly and signaled a passing
footman for another glass.

Peter managed not to frown. "You don't think
your lifestyle will pall eventually? It must get old to
wake up every morning—afternoon, I should say—
too muzzy-headed to dress yourself."

"That's what Brewster is for," said Harry with a
shrug.

Peter didn't pursue that topic, knowing that his
friend would have difficulty dressing himself without his valet's help even if he weren't hungover, as
Harry had lost his left arm during the war. Of
course, now he used that as one more excuse for getting foxed every day of his life.

Though he'd never admit it, Harry needed a good
woman—a wife—to keep him in line and give him
new purpose. In fact, Peter was half tempted to make
that his project for the autumn Season. Not that
such a task would be easy. Harry would have to be
head-over-ears in love to overcome his deep-seated
aversion to matrimony. Still, with that in mind,
Peter looked over the ladies assembled at tonight's
ridotto—a fair sampling of what was available.

Miss Cheevers, standing near an archway, was
pretty enough with her dark hair and eyes, but she
had a streak of pettiness he couldn't like. Lady Min-
erva Chatham was both beautiful and properly behaved, and Peter had never known her to be unkind.
She was a bit flighty, but Harry might not mind that.
His friend would certainly consider her above his
touch, however.

"Lord Peter! How nice to see you again," came a feminine voice at his elbow.

Turning, he managed an outwardly pleasant smile. "Good evening, Miss Mountheath. The pleasure is mine, of course."

The Mountheath sisters represented the worst of all possible worlds. He could have overlooked their lack of beauty easily enough if their characters had compensated. Alas, they did not. Both sisters were self-important, tediously banal, and undeniably ill-natured—as vindictive as their mother, who was legendary in her penchant for shredding reputations.

He spared a quick thought that here was yet another reason to keep his investments a secret. As fourth son of the Duke of Marland, Peter was considered a respectable catch. Were it known he was rich besides, he'd likely top many matchmaking mamas' lists of eligible bachelors, inviting attention from some quarters he'd prefer to avoid.

"Do you know whether Mr. Galloway is here tonight?" Lucy Mountheath asked now, while Fanny batted her pale, watery eyes at Harry, who managed a half smile in return.

"I believe he may be in the card room," Peter offered, hoping he didn't sound as eager as he felt to have the sisters move on.

"Now, Lucy, remember what Mama said," Fanny admonished. "I certainly won't go chasing off to the card room with you, and you can't go alone." But then she smiled unpleasantly. "You can always take Miss Killian with you, however."

With a start, Peter noticed the young lady hovering behind the Mountheath sisters—the same young lady he had encountered that afternoon, his beautiful puzzle. Clad in a fashionable gown, she was even more beautiful than he remembered—and more puzzling.

Lucy Mountheath, however, regarded her with open disfavor. "I think not. I have no intention of going to the card room anyway."

She turned with a sniff but before they could leave, Peter said, "Won't you do us the honor of introducing your friend, Miss Mountheath?" He noticed Harry was staring at Miss Killian in bemusement and belatedly realized that this was an opportunity to further his new plan.

Lucy grimaced but turned back. "Oh, Miss Killian is merely a connection of my mother's," she said ungraciously. "She is staying with us temporarily, until . . . that is . . . Lord Peter Northrup and Mr. Thatcher."

The lovely Miss Killian drew her startled gaze away from Peter and bobbed a curtsey while the two sisters looked on in amusement. "I'm pleased to make your acquaintance, gentlemen," she said, her voice as low and pleasing as Peter remembered.

Concealing his surprise that this vision was a member of the Mountheath clan, he bowed. "Charmed, Miss Killian. I take it you are but recently arrived in Town?" He had the distinct impression that she preferred not to acknowledge their earlier meeting.

"Yes, my lord. In fact, I arrived only today."

Harry stepped forward with an elegant bow and took her hand. "Then let us be among the first to welcome you, Miss Killian. May I offer you some refreshment?" He seemed not at all put off by her connection to the Mountheaths. A good sign, Peter thought. Or was it?

She looked uncertainly at the Mountheath sisters, who were both glaring in outrage. "I . . . That might be nice," she said.

"Come, Lucy," Fanny said, turning with a sniff. "I see Miss Spence, and I simply must know whether that story about her brother and her mother's abigail is true." Without a backward glance, the Misses Mountheath abandoned their young companion.

"Is this your first visit to London?" Harry was asking her, apparently oblivious to her startled glance after the sisters.

"Not exactly," she replied. "I lived here as a child, but I have not been back since."

Stepping to her left side, Harry extended his right arm with a courtly gesture. "I see. Where have you lived in the meantime?"

After a moment's hesitation, she took the proffered arm. "In Cumberland. A few miles from Penrith."

Peter accompanied them to the refreshment table, trying to divine whether Harry's attention to Miss Killian went beyond mere admiration for a pretty face. He was also trying to figure out her relationship to Lady Mountheath. Peter prided himself on knowing the family background of nearly everyone in the Upper Ten Thousand, but he knew nothing of this girl whatsoever. Yet.

"Are your parents in Cumberland as well?" Peter asked.

She shook her head. "My parents died several years ago, my lord. I merely attended school there."

"But you're here now, and that's what matters,"

said Harry, with a frown at Peter's inquisitiveness. Peter frowned back.

"Yes, it is," she said with surprising firmness. "The past is the past."

Harry blinked, and Peter raised a brow. So, she didn't wish to talk about herself. Did she have something to hide, then? His interest quickened at this additional evidence of a mystery.

While Harry procured her a glass of ratafia, Peter took the opportunity to examine Miss Killian more closely. That gown—it was by no means new. In fact, hadn't Fanny Mountheath worn it last winter, to the Plumfield do? Yes, and to the Chesterfield ball, as well. She must be some sort of poor relation, then.

He recalled a recent article in the *Political Register*, a small but incisive newspaper, which criticized certain members of the *ton* for their notable lack of charity. The Mountheaths had been pilloried by the anonymous author, a regular contributor who signed his essays "MRR." Had they taken in this girl in an effort to counteract the ensuing gossip? It seemed likely.

But who *was* she? He was determined to find out. After all, he could scarcely promote a match between Harry and an unknown quantity. Besides, he needed a challenge to occupy his mind. Peter was certain those were his only motives.

Well, almost certain.

Sarah accepted the glass of ratafia from the charming Mr. Thatcher with a smile, grateful that he and Lord Peter—the helpful, handsome gentleman who had intruded on her thoughts since that afternoon— had ceased their probing for the moment.

She was also grateful that Lord Peter had not referred to their earlier meeting, particularly in front of the Mountheath sisters. They would have been certain to misinterpret it, to her detriment, and to inform their mother, who might use it as an excuse to eject the already unwelcome Sarah from her home.

Until she found William, or at least a position somewhere that afforded her another place to live while she searched, she couldn't allow that to happen.

Though she'd meant to halt Lord Peter's questions about her background with her last comment, the silence now threatened to become awkward. Feeling that she couldn't afford to alienate anyone else in Society, as tenuous as her position with the Mountheaths was, she cast about for something conciliatory to say.

"That's a very striking waistcoat," was the first thing that occurred to her.

Lord Peter glanced down at the gold-embroidered scarlet with a smile, though Mr. Thatcher stifled what sounded like a laugh. "Thank you, Miss Killian," Lord Peter said. "It's one of my favorites."

Now there was no mistaking Mr. Thatcher's amusement. "What, you're actually admitting you've worn it before? You must know, Miss Killian, that Pete here is renowned for his unending succession of gaudy garments. His clothes press looks like a tropical garden."

Sarah now recalled that this afternoon Lord Peter had been wearing a pale orange waistcoat. At the time, she'd had no idea it was not in keeping with current fashion, but now she realized that the other gentlemen present were all clad in shades of blue, brown and black. Lord Peter seemed not at all put out by his friend's teasing, however.

"I find it rather refreshing," she offered.

"Again, I thank you, Miss Killian," Lord Peter said with a half bow. "It's true that I try not to repeat myself too often, but I haven't worn this since June. Three months seems a reasonable interval."

"How do you keep track?" Mr. Thatcher asked with a chuckle. "An elaborate cataloguing system, no doubt. I prefer to spend my time on more pleasurable pursuits." He winked at Sarah, and she smiled back uncertainly.

But Lord Peter shook his head. "I've no need for a system. I keep it all in my head. In fact," he said, with a glance at Sarah, "I have a tendency to remember everything anyone has worn to any function I've attended over the past year or more. A waste of brain space, I suppose, but there it is."

Sarah felt the color creeping up her neck at this oblique reference to the old gown of Fanny's she wore, which he clearly remembered. But then she realized that every lady here tonight doubtless knew her gown was not in the latest stare of fashion. She surely had less to fear from Lord Peter than most of them.

"A formidable talent indeed," she said now. "Surely, such a memory for detail is something to be envied, not disparaged."

"You've found yourself a champion, Pete!" Mr. Thatcher exclaimed before Lord Peter could respond. "A moment." He paused to exchange his empty glass for a full one as a footman passed with a tray. After a long draught, he continued.

"Aye, Peter here is a walking *Debrett's*, Miss Killian—remembers everything about everybody. A memory like no one I've ever known, except perhaps Wellington himself. In fact, the Iron Duke put Peter's abilities to good use in the Peninsula, and again in Vienna."

Sarah looked at Lord Peter with new respect, only to discover him frowning at his friend. "Do stopper it, Harry. We don't want to bore Miss Killian with war stories her first evening in Town."

"I'm not bored in the least," she assured him, wondering why he appeared so ill at ease. "Did you both fight in the wars, then?" She would never have guessed that the dandyish Lord Peter had been a soldier. How interesting.

Mr. Thatcher grinned broadly. "War heroes, the pair of us," he assured her. "I lost my arm at Salamanca, then went on to fight another year on the Peninsula. The gratitude of those we fought to defend makes it all worthwhile, however." He gave an exaggerated sigh and waggled his eyebrows.

Sarah had to laugh at this obvious bid for sympathy and adulation. "Very commendable, Mr. Thatcher. You see me duly impressed—and grateful."

"Ah, but how grateful?" he asked, sidling closer.

She was fairly certain he was teasing, but said, "I see you are quite adept at parlaying your heroism into an advantage with the ladies. I am not so easily manipulated, however." She glanced at Lord Peter and found him grinning at her response.

Mr. Thatcher chuckled as well, clearly not the least bit upset. Following her gaze, he clapped his friend on the shoulder. "Now Pete, here, can claim even greater deeds, though he hasn't my badge of honor to show for them. Why at Vittoria—" he began, but Lord Peter cut him off.

"That's enough, Harry," he said with an authority that startled Sarah. "Miss Killian, it's time we restored you to the Mountheaths. It won't do for Lady Mountheath to see you spending your evening with the likes of us."

Mr. Thatcher frowned, but on encountering Lord Peter's eye, he stifled whatever protest he might have made—rather to Sarah's surprise. Lord Peter extended his arm and she gingerly took it, acutely aware that it was the first time in her life she'd been escorted by a lord—even if it was only across the room.

"My apologies for Harry," her companion said with another quelling glance at his friend. "When encouraged by a lovely lady's smiles, he has a tendency to run on, though he knows I prefer not to dwell on the past—any more than you do, Miss Killian."

Sarah looked up at him curiously, struck by the anomaly of his strong, handsome profile and almost foppish attire. "I should think most war heroes would enjoy reliving the days of their glory."

For the barest moment a grimace of what might have been pain crossed Lord Peter's face, but he converted it so quickly to a smile that she thought she must have imagined it. "Far better to live in the present, in my view," he declared lightly. "Give me fashionable London any day over the blood and mud of war."

Before she could voice her agreement, they reached Lady Mountheath.

"Good evening, my lady." Lord Peter swept her a

bow that contrived to be both respectful and flamboyant. "I thought you might wish to have Miss Killian restored to your care."

As Sarah had feared, Lady Mountheath spared barely a glance for Lord Peter before turning a censorious gaze on her ward. "Thank you, my lord," she said, glaring at Sarah. "My apologies if Miss Killian has made a nuisance of herself. She has yet to learn how to go on in polite society."

"Nuisance!" Lord Peter exclaimed. "Not a bit of it. In fact, Mr. Thatcher here was hoping for your permission to take Miss Killian driving tomorrow. Weren't you, Harry?"

If Mr. Thatcher was startled, he hid it admirably. He had been lagging behind, but now stepped forward. "Indeed I was, my lady. I would be honored to show Miss Killian the Park and other sights."

Lady Mountheath's eyebrows ascended into her turban. "I should say not, Mr. Thatcher! Your reputation precedes you, though I will *assume* Miss Killian is too new to Town to know of it—or how improper it was of her to speak with you gentlemen at all." The look she sent Sarah implied she believed her quite capable of deliberately inviting the attentions of a rake.

"We were quite properly introduced by your daughters, my lady," Lord Peter told her. "Indeed, I thought Miss Mountheath and I might make it a foursome tomorrow," he added.

"Oh? Oh!" As if by magic, Lady Mountheath thawed. "I'm certain Lucy would like that very much, Lord Peter. And with *you* along, I need have no fear that Miss Killian's reputation will be at any risk. Oh, Lucy!" She beckoned to her daughters.

Sarah shot a grateful glance at Lord Peter, wondering whether he were making a sacrifice for her sake or if he actually wished to spend time with Lucy Mountheath. Not that it mattered. It would get her out of the house, perhaps affording her an opportunity to make a discreet inquiry or two about William.

He returned her glance with a slight smile that told her nothing, though it caused her heart to flutter slightly. Really, she was being most foolish, she chided herself. This man was a lord and a war hero. She mustn't misinterpret his kindness as any sort of *romantic* interest. He'd only just met her.

"Yes, Mama?" Lucy Mountheath came up to them just then, her sister in tow.

"Lord Peter has invited you for a drive tomorrow," her mother informed her. "I wished you to assure him yourself that you have no other plans."

Lucy flushed an unbecoming shade of red but turned at once to Lord Peter with a simpering smile. "Of course, my lord, I should love to drive out with you!" She shot a triumphant glance at Fanny, who managed to pout and cast flirtatious eyes at Mr. Thatcher simultaneously.

"Until tomorrow, then." Lord Peter bowed briefly over Lucy's hand, then he and Mr. Thatcher moved away.

"I don't see why I can't go too," Fanny said before they were quite out of earshot. "His friend could come along and we could all be quite cozy together."

"Mr. Thatcher and Miss Killian will be going," her mother told her. "I hope *you* have not been romanticizing that man's reputation, Fanny! He's the veriest scoundrel, not to mention maimed by the war. I would never allow a daughter of mine to receive his attentions."

Though Fanny still pouted, Lucy smirked. Clearly she had caught the implication that such a man was good enough for their poor relation. Sarah barely noticed the insult, trying to conceal her outrage that Lady Mountheath should hold Mr. Thatcher's heroic injury against him.

"Shall I wear this dress again, my lady, or the one I arrived in this afternoon?" she asked, rather than voice her thoughts.

Lady Mountheath turned an irritated gaze on her. "Neither will do, of course. My girls will have to see what other castoffs they have that you might use for the duration of your stay with us. I refuse to allow you to embarrass this family. I trust Mrs. Hounslow is actively pursuing that governess position you mentioned?"

"I believe so, my lady." Sarah carefully kept her tone polite, mindful of her goal. "I will send a note to her tomorrow, if you'd like, asking her to redouble her efforts."

"Yes, please do." Turning her back to Sarah, Lady Mountheath began instructing Lucy on how she was to behave on the morrow if she hoped to bring Lord Peter up to scratch.

"But I don't particularly want to marry him, Mama," Lucy protested, "though it will be nice to have him dancing attendance on me. He is too far down the line to inherit, nor is he very rich. He hasn't even his own estate or town house!"

"When a girl reaches six and twenty, she can't afford to be so choosy," her mother bluntly informed her. Now it was the younger Fanny's turn to smirk. "The son of a duke is nothing to sneeze at, even if his fortune isn't all we could wish."

Sarah tried to ignore the unpleasant byplay, but couldn't help wondering why the thought of Lucy marrying Lord Peter sent her spirits into her shoes. To distract herself, she focused on what she hoped to accomplish tomorrow, though in truth she could think of little besides seeing Lord Peter again.

Chapter 3

❝I don't know why you're still grousing," Peter said as he and Harry settled themselves into the comfortable wing chairs in Marcus's library. "I'm the one who'll have to put up with Lucy Mountheath's inane chatter while you admire Miss Killian's lovely face."

"I'll have to listen to that shrew's chatter as well, as we'll all be in the carriage together," Harry pointed out, reaching for the port bottle on the nearby table to refill the glass he'd already emptied.

Peter moved the bottle out of his reach. "Marcus offered me the use of his house, not his cellars," he said mildly. "My brother will undoubtedly expect to find a few bottles left on his return."

Lord Marcus Northrup, Peter's younger brother, was away on a belated wedding trip with his new bride, visiting a property to the north they had recently purchased. Until Marcus's marriage, Peter and his older brother, Andrew, had shared this house with him. As Peter had yet to find new lodgings, Marcus had suggested he stay here, rather than at their father's ducal mansion, while Marcus was gone.

"Can't think why you brought me into this at all," Harry protested. "If you wanted to drive out with Miss Killian, why not ask to do just that?"

Peter debated for a moment before answering. "I had the impression you rather . . . admired Miss Killian. Thought you might like the chance to spend some time with her," he said casually.

Not casually enough.

"Damn it, Pete, is that what this is about?" Harry demanded, sitting upright. "You've hinted I should go the same route as poor Jack, and I've told you in no uncertain terms what my feelings are on the matter. It's bad enough you abetted Jack's marriage, and your brother's. Don't aim any of your damned matchmaking at *me*!" He pulled the port bottle out of Peter's hand.

Peter let him have it. "Sorry, old boy, you're right. It's not my business." He, of all people, should have remembered that no amount of drink seemed to cloud Harry's perceptions when it came to important matters.

"Glad you realize that." Harry drained another glass. "Can't deny Miss Killian is a taking thing, but I can't see that harridan Mountheath letting her out for a tumble, and I'm not interested in anything more, I assure you."

Peter abruptly abandoned his half-formed plan. Harry and Miss Killian clearly would not suit. "In that case, I apologize for speaking for you. It's just a drive, however. An hour of your life. Once it's over, you need think no more of the matter—or of Miss Killian."

Harry regarded him shrewdly. "So, I wasn't far wrong to begin with. You're rather taken with the new beauty's charms yourself."

Damn Harry's perceptiveness! "I won't deny she's the prettiest thing I've seen this year, and quick-witted besides," he confessed, "but I wouldn't have suggested the drive had I not thought you interested as well."

"I abandon the field to you," said Harry with a wave of his hand. "Dare I hope this means you've finally realized you can't keep meddling in your friends' lives to avoid living your own?"

Peter frowned and looked away. "I don't know what you mean."

"The devil you don't," Harry retorted, making Peter wince. "Ever since the mop-up at Toulouse, you've been a different man—this frivolous dandy you affect. You cluck over trivia while ignoring everything that makes life worth living—including women. Anything that might make you remember what you once were."

"What I once was is overrated," Peter snapped. "The blood of two hundred young—"

"Not your fault, Pete, and you know it," Harry insisted, cutting him off. "It was an ambush. There was a traitor."

A traitor indeed, Peter thought—one who would now face justice. But what of his accomplices? He'd heard the Saint of Seven Dials had a small army of street urchins helping him. They must be guilty of treason as well.

"Besides," Harry continued, as though echoing his thoughts, "you made them pay for it. I never saw such—"

"That's enough! I went too far." With an effort, he forced the ugly memory from his mind. "Let's talk about something else."

Harry shrugged. "As you wish. Miss Killian, perhaps?"

"I'm curious about her, that's all," Peter said. Though she would be a pleasant distraction, he realized that he was still not ready to risk any sort of involvement—anything that might pierce the careful armor he'd built around his emotions.

"Doubt you'd be so curious if she were an antidote," Harry replied, grinning. "But call it what you like. As you say, it's but an hour out of my life to watch you at your wooing."

"I'm not—" Peter broke off at Harry's grin and shook his head. "Very well, I deserved that. But it's only an hour out of my life, as well. Then we can *both* turn our minds to other things."

He rather doubted an hour in Miss Killian's company would allow him to solve the mystery she represented, however. And risky as it might be to spend too much time with her, her mystery was surely safer than the other one that beckoned. For he itched to know the whole story of the Black Bishop, erstwhile Saint of Seven Dials—and his accomplices.

By five o'clock the next day, Sarah was beyond eager for her promised drive in the Park.

A half-formed plan of slipping out of the house once everyone was abed the night before had been foiled on discovering the door to her attic room locked from the outside, with no key in evidence. It had been but poor consolation to realize that Lady Mountheath had likely taken that precaution against her husband creeping into Sarah's chamber during the night.

When released from her chamber, Sarah had noted with interest that all of the attic rooms appeared to have identical locks on the doors. On returning upstairs after breakfast, she had pilfered a key from an open, empty room. A quick test confirmed that it would indeed operate her own lock, solving that particular problem for the future.

So far, however, she'd been given no opportunity to escape the house. The housekeeper had questioned her thoroughly about her skills, then put her to work in the stillroom, infusing tisanes and measuring out herbs. The last stillroom maid had been fired for idleness months before, so the family store of physics had grown dangerously low.

Now she was dressed in another old gown of Fanny's, this one an unattractive shade of dull green with yellow trim. She didn't care. In a few minutes she would be out of the house—and she would see Lord Peter again.

Even as she reminded herself not to nurse foolish hopes, a knock came at the door, and a moment later Hodge, the butler, announced Lord Peter and Mr. Thatcher. Lucy and her mother hurried forward at once, while Sarah merely stood, waiting.

"Good afternoon, my lord," Lady Mountheath exclaimed. "May I offer you some refreshment before you set out? And you too, of course, Mr. Thatcher," she added as such an obvious afterthought that it bordered on insult.

"Thank you, no," Lord Peter replied. Sarah thought she discerned a faint frown at his hostess's rudeness, though Mr. Thatcher took no notice. "We are eager to take advantage of the fine weather."

"Of course, of course." Lady Mountheath gave her daughter a fond glance. "Your eagerness is most commendable. Have you your parasol, Lucy? You don't want to spoil your complexion."

Though Sarah was a good deal fairer than her cousin, her lack of any shade beyond her bonnet was not deemed worthy of comment. Lucy displayed the required item, and the group headed outdoors to the waiting curricle, Fanny lamenting audibly as they went.

The gentlemen helped the ladies up, then seated themselves, Mr. Thatcher next to Sarah and Lord Peter next to Lucy, directly facing Sarah. At a word from Lord Peter, the coachman whipped up the horses and they trotted off.

"It is ever so nice a day for a drive, don't you agree?" Lucy asked with what was no doubt intended as a flirtatious smile for Lord Peter.

He assented, then turned to Sarah. "Is the sun too bright for you, Miss Killian?"

"Not at all, thank you, my lord. It is quite late in the day, after all." She was grateful he refrained from mentioning her missing parasol, as she did not own one.

"Late in the day?" Mr. Thatcher echoed with a yawn. "Why, I've only been awake three hours. The day has scarcely begun."

Lucy primmed up her mouth at this evidence of Mr. Thatcher's debauchery and turned again to Lord Peter. "Surely *you* do not keep such hours, my lord?"

He shook his head. "I'm generally up well before noon, Miss Mountheath. Today I was awake by nine."

"I'm glad to hear it." She then proceeded to describe a shopping trip she and her sister had taken the morning before and Sarah was able to turn her attention to their surroundings, examining the grand houses, manicured gardens and clean streets of Mayfair with interest.

She found herself glancing eagerly at every boy they passed, and had to remind herself that William was no longer a lad of eight, but would have just turned sixteen. Sixteen! He was nearly a man. Would she even recognize him now? He must have been working at something all these years, and she feared it might be thievery. But then a worse possibility occurred to her.

"At what age can boys enlist in the army?" she asked, interrupting a detailed description of a bonnet Lucy had bought.

The gentlemen glanced at her in surprise, while Lucy looked outraged. "I beg your pardon," Lucy began, but then Lord Peter interrupted her, earning him a glare of his own.

"Sixteen," he said, "though well-grown lads of as young as thirteen or fourteen have been known to falsify their ages to join the fighting. Why?"

Sarah relaxed marginally, feeling a bit foolish. "I was merely curious," she said. "I was thinking about the war, about all of the lives lost, and how dreadful it was for the . . . mothers who lost sons." Lord Peter regarded her with open curiosity.

"An interesting, if melancholy, train of thought. Did you know someone who lost a son to the war?"

"Melancholy indeed!" Lucy exclaimed before Sarah could answer. "Might we please talk of more cheerful things? The war has been over this year and more, after all."

Sarah was quite happy to drop the subject. "My apologies. By all means, resume your riveting tale."

Though she frowned suspiciously, Lucy resumed her monologue after only the barest hesitation. As before, Lord Peter seemed politely attentive, but his occasional glances at Sarah made her wonder just what he was thinking. Mr. Thatcher appeared to be dozing.

They had entered the Park now, and as it was the fashionable hour, the paths were thronged with pedestrians, riders and carriages. This was another part of London new to Sarah—and one she realized she could learn to enjoy.

Suddenly, her gaze sharpened. That boy, there, throwing stones into the Serpentine . . . Could it possibly be? Fair, unkempt hair, threadbare clothes, and a certain familiar cockiness to the way he held himself . . . Her heart began to race.

The boy looked to be about the right age, she thought, particularly if he hadn't been eating well all this time. As the carriage continued on, she craned her neck to keep the boy in view. If only he would turn, so she could see his face—

"Something of interest, Miss Killian?" asked Mr. Thatcher, apparently not asleep after all.

Though it tore at her heart to do so, Sarah pulled

her gaze from the boy and forced a smile. "Everything, actually. I've never been to the Park before."

Mr. Thatcher glanced around, then shrugged. "I suppose novelty can add interest to anything."

She was glad he seemed disinclined to probe further—but then she encountered Lord Peter's eye again. For a long moment, he held her gaze, one eyebrow raised, before turning back to Lucy, who nattered on, oblivious.

After a moment, Sarah risked a glance over her shoulder, but she could no longer see the boy she had marked. Somehow, tonight, she *must* find a way to begin her search for William.

"No matter I owe you my life twice over," Harry said as he and Peter drove away from the Mountheath house. "This past hour should have discharged my obligation and put you in my debt. I've never been so bored in my life."

Peter sent his friend a crooked smile. "I'll not ask you to make such a sacrifice again, though I confess I found our drive . . . intriguing."

"Intriguing? I trust you don't mean Miss Mountheath's conversation, since I doubt a thought ever enters her empty head without escaping through her mouth."

"I noticed," Peter agreed with a chuckle. "No, I was referring to Miss Killian. There's more there than meets the eye, I'm convinced."

Harry shrugged. "What meets the eye is enough for me. She's a deuced pretty thing, even in such an ugly dress. Presented properly, she'd take the town by storm."

Peter thought the same, but wasn't particularly

gratified to know that Harry shared his sentiments. "Indeed. But I was noticing something else. I believe she may be looking for something—or someone."

"Think she had an assignation in the Park, then? Quick work, if she only arrived in Town yesterday."

"Not an assignation, no." At least, Peter preferred not to think so. "She did seem preoccupied, however."

"Can't say I blame her," Harry said. "No one could be expected to concentrate on Miss Mountheath's blatherings—though you appeared to give it a noble effort."

"I try to avoid being rude." Peter wondered if he wouldn't live to regret this particular act of gallantry, however. Judging by Miss Mountheath's self-satisfied triumph upon saying her goodbyes, she no doubt expected an offer within days.

Much as he'd have preferred to avoid all of the Mountheaths, Peter saw no way to pursue the mystery that was Miss Killian without calling at their house again. He hadn't missed Miss Killian's bereft look when her attention had been called away from whatever she was staring at.

What was her purpose in coming to London, really? Anyone would need a powerful inducement to stay with the Mountheaths. Perhaps it was time he made a few inquiries.

Dinner seemed to drag on interminably. The Mountheaths were engaged to go to the theater after the meal, and as Lord Mountheath said nothing about staying behind, Lady Mountheath was happy to exclude Sarah from the outing. Much as she'd have liked to see a theatrical performance, Sarah was relieved. This would finally be the opportunity she needed.

"Goodness, look at the time," Lady Mountheath exclaimed, finally rising. "Girls, run upstairs for your wraps while we call for the carriage. You," she said, turning to Sarah, "may start on that mending Mrs. Grimble set out for you in the maids' cupboard."

"Very well." Sarah tried to sound disappointed, not wanting the others to suspect how little she wished to accompany them. Not that the ladies were paying attention to her anyway. Lord Mountheath's eyes lingered on her for a long moment, but then he followed his wife from the dining room.

Sarah waited until she heard Lord Mountheath's heavy tread on the stairs, then headed to the maids' cupboard, a small room beneath the servants' stairs at the rear of the house. The stack of mending wasn't as high as she'd feared—she should be able to complete it in an hour or so. She carried it up to her room and barely noticed when the family left for the theater.

On finishing the sewing, she went to her door and listened. The house was quiet—no doubt the staff were relaxing in the kitchens. Already she'd noticed the grimaces the maids and footmen made behind their employers' backs. The servants doubtless took advantage of every opportunity to leave off work and share their latest grievances.

Quickly, Sarah changed from her ugly borrowed finery into one of her old gray school gowns and snatched up the mobcap she had worn in the stillroom earlier that day. Stopping frequently to listen for anyone who might see or interrupt her, she slipped down the servants' stairs and out the back door, then across the garden and out the gate, into the mews. She was free.

Stuffing her flaxen hair into the mobcap, she hurried along the alleyway behind the great houses. Not until she was two streets away did she slow her pace and take stock of her surroundings. At this hour, there was more carriage than foot traffic in Mayfair, and the majority of pedestrians appeared to be footmen running errands or tradesmen and laborers heading home to less exalted parts of the city.

She headed in that direction herself, for if William had returned to London, it seemed likely he'd have gone back to their old haunts near Drury Lane, where he had friends. Several times she stopped lads near William's age to ask if they knew him, but none did, not surprisingly.

After an hour she turned back, afraid her absence might be marked if she stayed away too long. Reentering Mayfair, she finally admitted to herself that she had likely set herself an impossible task. Approaching a broad intersection, Sarah saw a crossing sweeper, shouldering his broom as he abandoned his post for the night, and resolved to try one last time.

"Excuse me," she called to the boy. "Yes, you there! May I ask you a question?"

The lad came forward slowly as Sarah approached, until they met in the pool of light cast by one of the numerous streetlamps on Mount Street. He looked up at her with a scowl, but then his expression changed to something like wonder and he swept off his cap and executed an awkward bow.

"Evenin' miss. Did you need summat?"

"Just information," Sarah replied with a smile at his eagerness. The boy's eyes widened further. "I'm looking for someone, and I hope you can help me find him."

"I'll do what I can, miss," he assured her fervently.

"Thank you. Do you by any chance know a boy by the name of William Killian? He'd be just sixteen, and fair."

The lad's face lost some of its eagerness. "Can't say I do, miss, but I c'n ask around. Might he go by Will, or Bill?"

Sarah tried to swallow her disappointment. William might not be in London at all, for all she knew. "He might. I haven't seen him in some years. He used to go by the nickname Flute when he was younger."

She hadn't given that name before, thinking it impossible that William would still be using it—but now the boy was nodding.

"That's a name I've heard, right enough. Flute. Don't know 'im meself, but Renny's mentioned him once or twice."

"Really?" Sarah tried to contain her excitement. Surely there could be other boys using that nickname. Eight years was such a long time. Still . . . "Can you tell me where to find this Renny?"

The lad nodded again. "I c'n show you." He looked up at her expectantly and Sarah bit her lip.

"I have no money, I'm afraid, or I'd pay you for your trouble. I'm new to London and haven't found employment yet, but—do you work this crossing regularly?"

"Aye."

"Then I promise, as soon as I find a position, I'll come back with a few pennies. What is your name?"

"Paddy. But that's okay, miss. I'll be passing close by where Renny lives on my way home anyway." He headed north, motioning for her to follow him.

It was possible, of course, that young Paddy would take her to someone with evil designs in hope of a reward, but his eagerness to help seemed genuine. Besides, what choice did she have? Her trust was rewarded when he stopped across from a fashionable—and therefore probably safe—house, in the heart of Mayfair, on Grosvenor Street.

"It's that one there, miss." Paddy pointed. "These days, Renny works for a proper swell what lives there."

Sarah looked at the tall town house and nodded. "Thank you, Paddy. I'll go speak with him. And I'll pay you for your help as soon as I can, I promise."

Paddy grinned. "I don't doubt you'll find a job soon enough, miss," he told her. "Pretty as you are, you'll have the gents tossing you gold guineas, mark my words."

Though she feared Paddy thoroughly misunderstood the sort of employment she was seeking, Sarah only smiled rather than attempt to explain to a ten- or eleven-year-old boy. Heading across Grosvenor Street, she veered off to the side to find her way to the back entrance of the indicated house, as the front door was obviously out of the question.

A narrow alley led to the mews, housing the stables for each house along the row. Grooms hitched horses to carriages and coachmen prepared to take their masters to late entertainments, but no one took any notice of the nondescript gray figure slipping through the garden gate halfway down the row.

The house sported a small ornamental garden and a rather larger kitchen patch. Sarah made her way along a narrow path winding between rows of cabbages and carrots to tap at the kitchen door. A kind-faced woman opened it, wiping flour from her hands onto her broad white apron.

"Yes, miss? May I help you?"

"Yes, please. I'm looking for a boy named Renny. I'm told he has a position here."

"Come in, do."

The cook stood aside to allow Sarah to enter the brightly lit kitchen. Maids bustled about, washing up dishes and pots from dinner and putting them away. It seemed a cheerful place, and Sarah was conscious of a fleeting wish that the Mountheath household were more like this one.

"Is Renny here?" she asked. "I have a . . . a message for him, from my brother."

"He's likely out in the stables, though he may be off running errands or such. I'll send someone to see." The cook beckoned to a young maid. "Polly, do run out to the stables and see if Renny is still there. He has a visitor."

The redheaded maid bobbed a quick curtsey and hurried out the back door, leaving Sarah no option but to wait where she was, despite her impatience to find William.

"Have a sit-down, miss, do," the cook invited her, indicating a chair at the big kitchen table. Sarah's agitation must have shown, for the woman then said, "Polly won't be a moment, and if Renny's not there you can leave a message for him."

Sarah nodded, forcing herself to relax, and moved to the table. Just as she took a seat, however, she heard a disconcertingly familiar voice on the kitchen stairs at the opposite end of the room.

"—just nip down to request a late supper for our return, then we'll be off," the voice was saying, growing in volume as its owner approached.

Alarmed, Sarah stood just as the gentleman who had been speaking entered the kitchen. Surely he would never recognize her dressed like this, she told herself, trying to turn away before he caught a glimpse of her face.

Too late.

With a start of surprise, Lord Peter Northrup came toward her. "Miss Killian?"

Chapter 4

For an instant, Peter thought he must be mistaken, that it must be a chance resemblance, but the alarm on Miss Killian's face as she turned back to face him proved her identity, apart from those memorable blue eyes.

"What are you—that is, is something wrong?" he asked when she did not reply.

Mrs. MacKay, the cook, looked from Peter to Miss Killian, then quickly busied herself rummaging in a cupboard. The maids, after a few curious stares, followed her lead, pretending to ignore the interesting tableau.

"Lord Peter!" Miss Killian finally said, rather breathlessly. "Is . . . is this your home? I had no idea, I assure you."

Startled as she obviously was, he had no trouble

believing her. "My brother's home, actually, but as he is away, he's given me the run of it at present." He paused, questioningly.

She dropped her gaze for a moment, then took a deep breath and met his eyes again. "I was looking for a servant I was told works here—a boy named Renny. I, ah, promised a friend from school that I would try to find her brother while I was in London, and this Renny may know something of him."

"How commendable," Peter said, just as though he believed every word. "I fear, however, that I gave Renny the evening off, half an hour since, and he's not likely to be back for some time. Come, let me escort you home, while you tell me about your friend's brother. Perhaps I can be of some assistance."

Coming forward, he extended his arm and Miss Killian tentatively placed her hand upon it. "Will it not look odd, a gentleman like yourself escorting an apparent maid through the streets of Mayfair?" He was pleased to see a trace of amusement in her eyes.

"I'm considered an oddity already," he said with a shrug and a smile. "Mrs. MacKay, please tell Mr. Thatcher that I've had to run an errand, but that we'll go out as soon as I return. Have another bottle sent up if he wishes it." Then, turning back to Miss Killian: "Shall we?"

Heedless of the curious looks from the kitchen maids, he led her out into the kitchen garden with as much aplomb as though he were leading her onto the floor of a grand ball. Glancing down, he saw her lips twitching, but she remained silent.

"I don't suppose you'd care to tell me why you're dressed as a maid?" he asked as they exited into the mews. There was something decidedly pleasant about the feel of her small hand on his arm. "Could you not have simply sent a message, asking Renny to come to you at the Mountheaths' house?"

She shook her head. "I didn't know anything about Renny until this evening. I, ah, slipped out of the house after the family left for the evening, in hopes of finding some clue to my . . . friend's brother's whereabouts, but I had no idea where to start. I was exceedingly fortunate to chance upon a crossing sweeper who was able to direct me here."

"Ah." If anything, the mystery had deepened—Peter would lay odds it was Sarah's own brother—or lover?—she was seeking. The latter possibility caused an unpleasant lurch in his stomach. "What is her brother's name? Perhaps I've heard of the boy."

She was silent for so long that he thought she might not answer. Finally, as they turned onto Grosvenor Street, she spoke. "His name is William, though he apparently goes by the nickname Flute. I, ah, don't believe he uses his surname."

Brother, then, he thought with a surprisingly strong sense of relief. That surname was undoubtedly Killian. But—"Flute? That name *is* familiar." He thought for a moment, then it came to him.

"Yes! A boy called Flute was valet-in-training to a friend of my brother's, when he stayed with us briefly last spring. Scrawny lad, as I recall. I shouldn't have guessed him as more than fourteen."

"He's sixteen, actually." She forgot to disguise the eagerness in her voice, Peter noticed, hiding his smile. "Do you know where he is now?"

Regretfully, he shook his head. "I'm afraid not.

Last I knew, Lord Hardwyck had a different valet. He might know, but I fear he is in the country with Marcus—my brother—to advise him on the estate Marcus has just purchased."

Miss Killian's face fell. "I see." But then she seemed to rally—and to remember her fiction about the boy. "Still, that is more than I knew before, and I can write to my friend and tell her that her brother was doing well as recently as last spring."

"Of course." They had reached the edge of Berkley Square. "I presume you would prefer to go in by the back door?" he asked.

"Yes, I would prefer my absence not be noted. I would have to explain, and . . . my friend would not want it known that her brother may be living rather, ah, irregularly. Though if he was training to be a valet, he must be doing quite well for himself."

It was a question, and Peter felt obliged to reassure her.

"I'm certain that he is. Miss Killian, we can't have you wandering the streets of London like this, so I'll take this investigation upon myself, with your permission. When Renny returns, I'll see if he knows this Flute's current whereabouts, and I'll report back to you the moment I discover anything. What say you?"

Her shining eyes were answer enough, making her lovely face fairly glow. "*Would* you? That would be splendid. My friend will be so grateful, I know. And so am I."

"Your gratitude is all the reward I need, Miss Killian." Looking down at her upturned face, Peter was seized by an almost overwhelming urge to kiss her.

He took a quick step back before he could give in to an impulse that would surely lead to trouble—for both of them.

If she noticed his sudden change of manner, she gave no sign of it. "Thank you, Lord Peter," she said, referring, he was certain, only to his offer of help. "I will await your report."

"Good night, Miss Killian." He firmly resisted the temptation to close the distance between them. "I'd best leave you here, as two are more likely to be noticed than one."

"Yes. Yes, of course." With a last dazzling smile that left him breathless, she turned away and hurried to the Mountheaths' back door, entering without another backward glance.

Peter lingered, just to be sure she had roused no alarm, then slowly walked back to Grosvenor Street. He couldn't deny being a bit disturbed at how easily Miss Killian had slipped into the role of maid for her foray into the streets. If her brother was who he thought he was, could she possibly be of his own class?

The Mountheaths must believe her to be, he reminded himself. They were by no means known for their charity, as MRR's wickedly amusing essay in the *Political Register* had pointed out, and Lady Mountheath had an absolute horror of scandal. She would never have taken in a girl of dubious antecedents.

And why did he find that so reassuring? Class mattered not at all if he were merely going to help the girl—an admirably plucky girl!—find her brother. Besides, Miss Killian had given him no particular indication that she had any romantic interest in him.

And if she did, would he dare to trust it, when so much about her was a mystery? She was clearly as poor as a churchmouse, whatever else she might be. Though she could have no clue as to the extent of his fortune, his very status among the nobility might tempt her to feign affection should she believe him attracted to her. Which he could not deny he was.

He would simply have to be on his guard. Not only against Miss Killian, but against his own inclinations as well.

So eager was Sarah to hear news of her brother, it was all she could do to hide her excitement when Lord Peter came to call the next day. Lucy Mountheath went to no such effort.

"See, Fanny, what did I tell you?" she hissed triumphantly when he was announced. Then, turning a simpering smile on their guest, "How *very* delightful to see you again so soon, Lord Peter! Mama predicted you would not be able to stay away, but I scarcely dared believe her." She went off into a peal of affected laughter.

"How very perceptive, my lady," he said, bowing first over Lady Mountheath's hand, then Lucy's, then Fanny's.

He took a step toward Sarah, who had glanced up from the corner where she sat retrimming a bonnet, but Lady Mountheath stopped him, saying sharply, "Pray do not bother Miss Killian, my lord. She needs to finish her sewing so that Lucy may wear that bonnet this afternoon. Come sit between Lucy and me while I ring for a fresh pot of tea."

Lady Mountheath sent Sarah a quelling glance,

but the moment she turned away, Sarah looked again at Lord Peter, hoping he might give her some sign of whether he'd been successful in locating William. Nor did he disappoint her.

Though clearly not daring to say anything under the watchful eyes of the female Mountheaths, he managed to catch Sarah's eye for an instant and send her a quick smile and nod. Her heart soared—with relief, of course. Only with relief.

For the remainder of his quarter hour, he kept his attention strictly on his hostesses, listening politely to their gossip even when it bordered on the vicious. He never agreed with their assessments of their victims' character, Sarah noted, merely nodding and making noncommittal noises when some response was required. Finally, he stood.

"I must take my leave, ladies. I trust I will see you at Lord and Lady Plumfield's ball tonight?"

Lucy tittered. "Of course. I have kept the first dance free for you, my lord."

"And I the second," Fanny put in, earning a glare from her sister.

Sarah thought Lord Peter's smile looked rather forced. "I am all impatience." Then he looked pointedly toward her. "Mr. Thatcher has expressed a wish to dance with Miss Killian tonight. I assume she will be one of your party?"

Though Lady Mountheath's smile faltered, she quickly concealed her obvious displeasure. "Certainly. Certainly, my lord. You may assure Mr. Thatcher that she will attend."

"He will be delighted, I know." With a collective bow to the room that Sarah fancied had included her, he left them.

She assuaged her disappointment at receiving no real news of William by telling herself that surely, over the course of a ball, Lord Peter would find some opportunity to tell her what he had discovered. He had appeared quite cheerful, which must mean—

"So!" Lady Mountheath's indignant exclamation broke into her hopeful thoughts. "You must have used your wiles quite effectively yesterday, to have ensnared Mr. Thatcher so quickly. I hope you said nothing unseemly."

"Of course not, my lady," Sarah replied. "I said very little, in fact." She did not add that Lucy had scarcely given any of them a chance to squeeze in a word.

Lady Mountheath looked from Sarah to Lucy for confirmation.

"I did not *hear* her say anything *outré*, Mama, though she did try to turn the conversation to political matters."

Lady Mountheath rounded on Sarah at once. "Politics! I thought you had been properly schooled, miss, but I see it is not so. If there's one topic a lady should studiously avoid, it is politics. Shame on you!"

Sarah opened her mouth to protest, but then closed it, realizing that nothing she said would be believed. "Of course, my lady." Perhaps William had a position in a house that needed a governess, she thought hopefully, refusing to allow her benefactress's unpleasantness to spoil her buoyant mood.

"Hurry up with that bonnet," Lady Mountheath said after glaring at her suspiciously for another long moment. "Then, since you've shown yourself so handy with a needle, you can make the necessary alterations to the gown you'll wear tonight. It will be an old one of Lucy's this time, which will require a bit more work as she is statuesque and you are not."

Sarah merely nodded, careful not to let the corners of her mouth turn up. William was surely in Town, and tonight she would discover where! Seeing Lord Peter again was merely a means to that end, of course. She mustn't let her excitement over finding William spill over into eagerness to see—and perhaps dance with?—Lord Peter. That would never do.

Still, she could hardly wait.

"Oh, buck up, Harry," Peter admonished his friend as they left Grosvenor Street. "It's just one dance, and with the fetching Miss Killian. I'm not asking you to spend any time with the Mountheath sisters this time."

"You swore not to do any more matchmaking there," Harry reminded him. "I thought you wanted Miss Killian for yourself, in any event."

"I do. That is . . . I never said any such thing. Damn you, Harry!"

His friend was laughing now, and Peter had to grin in response. "Don't know why I still rise to your bait. You know I've no need to wed. One of the nice things about being fourth in the succession."

"Need and inclination are two different things," Harry pointed out, watching him closely.

But Peter wasn't about to give him more ammunition. "No inclination, either. As I said before, I'm merely curious about her. I'm hoping tonight I'll get to the bottom of her mystery, and that will be the end of it."

They'd been walking briskly as they talked, and now approached the grand entrance of the Plumfield mansion.

"Hope so, for your sake, Pete," Harry said with every appearance of sincerity. "Too much time in Miss Killian's company could well overset a man's reason. And too much time in Miss Mountheath's would be enough to make one leave Town entirely!"

Peter could not disagree with either sentiment.

Due to Harry's earlier heel-dragging, the orchestra was already tuning their instruments by the time he and Peter were announced. The dancing would be starting momentarily.

"There you are, my lord!" Lady Mountheath exclaimed, hurrying forward with her daughters in tow. "Poor Lucy was all a-twitter, fearing you would not arrive in time for her dance."

"I am wounded that you would think me capable of disappointing her, my lady," he replied automatically, trying to ignore the spastic fluttering of Miss Mountheath's lashes for fear he might disgrace himself utterly by laughing.

Just as well that he would begin the evening with the Mountheath sisters, Peter reflected with an inward sigh. He'd get it over early, then be able to turn his attention to more pleasant—no, more interesting—matters. The music began and he held out his arm to his simpering partner. "Shall we?"

Not until the opening minuet was under way did Peter spot Miss Killian, halfway down the line of dancers. She was more becomingly attired than he'd yet seen her, in a white gown with a sash of azure satin that matched her eyes—not that he could see her eyes from here. A froth of lace about the low neckline matched that at the hem and the wide sash emphasized her slender waist.

He apparently stared too long, for Lucy Mountheath followed his gaze and remarked, "That old rag of mine looks better on my cousin than I thought it would. I all but wore it to death two seasons ago, as white and blue have always been my best colors." She fluttered her lashes again.

Peter resisted the temptation to ask whether she had something in her eye. "That yellow is very nice as well," he said instead, indicating Lucy's beribboned silk concoction.

"Thank you, my lord," she simpered. "Mama thought it too highly ornamented, but I think all the pink and blue bows bring out my cheeks and eyes, don't you?"

The dance parted them then, and Peter was, thankfully, spared from replying, as he'd have been forced to be less than truthful or hurt Lucy's feelings. Between her height and the cascading ribbons, she looked like nothing so much as a Maypole.

A country dance followed, in which Peter partnered Fanny Mountheath and Harry partnered Miss Killian, though in different sets. Peter approached Miss Killian for the next dance, but she regretfully informed him that she was engaged for it—in fact, Mr. Pottinger was already at hand to claim her.

"Have you a waltz free, by chance?" Peter asked then. "I should like a chance for some conversation." He dared say nothing clearer with Mr. Pottinger hovering, but her eyes brightened with comprehension.

"Indeed, I have every waltz free, as Lady Mountheath has forbidden me to dance it," she said with a rueful smile. "Perhaps we might sit one out together, however?"

The music began again as she spoke, and Peter bowed. "I will look forward to it." He resolutely turned away rather than watch Pottinger lead her into the dance. It wouldn't do for anyone other than Harry to imagine he had an interest in that direction.

Would the orchestra never play a waltz? Sarah wondered impatiently. Enjoyable as it was to have men clamoring to partner her, she would gladly have skipped the intervening dances to hear what Lord Peter had to say.

"Do you know, Miss Killian, that sash exactly matches your eyes? The loveliest eyes I've ever beheld, I might add," Mr. Galloway, her current partner, said as the dance brought them together briefly.

"I thank you sir," she replied, though he was the fourth gentleman to say something similar.

Sarah was aware that she looked her best—indeed, the best she'd ever looked in her life. Not only had her alterations turned a dress that was ready for the dustbin into something quite fetching, but Libby, Fanny's rotund little maid, had slipped up to Sarah's room before dinner to style her hair.

"It's a fair treat to work with hair like yours," she'd said, by way of explanation for the favor. "Plus, I knew you would appreciate it."

And appreciate it Sarah did, for now her pale gold curls were as stylishly arranged as any lady's here. And her dress—

She glanced down at her handiwork with a certain amount of pride. Lucy stood a full head taller than she, so she'd removed one lace flounce, cut several inches off of the hem and worked the lace of the flounce into the neckline, which had been sadly frayed. She had then fashioned the fabric from the hem of the blue satin underskirt into a sash, effectively concealing a nasty port wine stain near the waistline.

Still, she must not let the compliments go to her head. Just as well Miss Pritchard had cautioned her charges against silver-tongued men. Take Mr. Galloway, for example. Once he'd learned she had no fortune, his comments—and glances—had subtly changed from respectful to suggestive. Clearly, he now saw her as an object of something less than matrimony but continued his pursuit.

"May I get you a glass of something?" he said now. "We can go onto the terrace to admire the moon while we refresh ourselves."

To her vast relief, just then the orchestra played the opening strains of a waltz. *Finally!* "I'm sorry, Mr. Galloway, but I've already promised this dance to Lord Peter Northrup. Here he comes now, to claim it."

"My dance, I believe, Miss Killian?"

Lord Peter was resplendent tonight in sapphire blue, with a matching waistcoat richly embroidered in silver, making him several shades more colorful than the other gentlemen present. Sarah decided she quite admired his independence in matters of dress.

Taking polite leave of Mr. Galloway, she allowed Lord Peter to lead her to the very terrace she had eschewed a moment earlier. It was all she could do to wait until they were out of earshot of other guests to ask, "Well? What did you discover?"

Lord Peter's smile warned her to mute her eagerness if she wanted to keep her secret. "I did indeed obtain news of your friend's brother, though I have not spoken with him myself." He gestured to a stone bench and they both sat down.

"He is well, then? My friend will be relieved." The brief delay allowed Sarah to inject what she felt was a commendable detachment into her tone. "Have you his direction, so that she may write him?"

To her disappointment, Lord Peter shook his head. "If he has a fixed address, Renny either didn't know it or was unwilling to disclose it. According to him, this Flute has taken over the leadership of a group of boys in Seven Dials. It seems the boys were thieves and pickpockets under a master of some notoriety, but that master was recently forced to leave England."

"Twitchell?" Sarah asked without thinking, then wished she'd bitten her tongue instead.

Lord Peter, however, only raised a brow. "Your friend must have followed her brother's career more closely than you first indicated. Yes, that was the name. Flute is now attempting to find the boys more, ah, legitimate employment."

Though she had a hard time imagining her little brother in such a leadership role, she couldn't help but be proud of him. "Very commendable, to be sure," she said with forced lightness.

"Would you like me to try to speak with him, let him know his sister is concerned, or perhaps take a message?"

Sarah hesitated. Though that would undoubtedly be the safest way for her to communicate with her brother, she worried that William might give her away to Lord Peter before reading any note she sent. What might this fine gentleman think if he learned she herself had once been an urchin of the streets?

Gazing at Lord Peter's kind, handsome face, she knew instinctively that he wouldn't condemn her. Still, she couldn't quite bear to have his opinion of her so radically altered—nor would it be safe for a gentleman like him to venture into Seven Dials.

"Not yet," she finally said. "Let me write to my friend and discover what she wishes to do. She may well send me a message that you—or Renny—can pass along to him."

He regarded her for a long moment before nodding. "As you wish. But now, what can you tell me of this friend of yours? How does it happen that she is in a school for young ladies while her brother roams the streets of London?"

At Sarah's glance of surprise, he smiled apologetically. "I thought you might appease my curiosity in repayment for my finding the lad, that's all."

"That is more than fair, my lord," she admitted, wondering frantically how much she could safely tell him. He was no fool, and would spot any falsehood unless she was extremely careful. "I will tell you what I can, without betraying my friend's confidence."

"I would not wish you to do that, of course," he said. "I won't ask her name. Puzzles always intrigue me, however, and this one has been preying on my mind."

Something in his gaze hinted at a deeper meaning, and for a moment Sarah wavered. Did he suspect—? But surely he wouldn't be regarding her so kindly if he thought she had been lying to him all along. She wished she dared to tell him the whole truth.

"When my friend left London to come to school, her brother went to school as well. However, it seems he ran away from his school shortly thereafter, and my friend only recently discovered it. As you may imagine, she has been anxious to know what became of him."

"Of course. Is she, like yourself, without parents?"

Sarah nodded. "Our school is partly supported by charity. Most of the girls there are orphans." Was that telling him too much? Lady Mountheath had insisted that Sarah conceal her parentage because of the scandal her mother's elopement had caused all those years ago.

"You say she went to the school from London. I take it she knew of this Twitchell fellow then?"

"I, ah, yes, I suppose so. She told me once about a thief-master who preyed upon London orphans, and the name stuck in my memory." They were on dangerous ground now, but she forged ahead. "She feared her brother might fall under his power if he returned to London after running away from school."

"A reasonable worry. Did your friend have contact with this Twitchell herself, then?"

Sarah fought down her sudden alarm, striving to keep her voice calm. "I don't believe so, though perhaps she would not have told me if she had."

Lord Peter nodded. "No, perhaps not. I can see where she might want to conceal such a thing, though if she were but a child at the time, it should be no source of shame to her."

Was this for her? Should she tell him—? No, safer

to play it through. "Perhaps it is a memory she would as soon forget," she suggested.

"Understandable." He stood, holding out a hand to help her to her feet. "I perceive that our waltz is ending, and no doubt you have some gallant waiting to claim you for the next dance. It was unsporting of Lady Mountheath to forbid you to waltz, though it worked to our advantage in this case."

Sarah couldn't suppress a grin. "I let her think I was disappointed, but in fact I couldn't have waltzed anyway. It was not taught at school, as our headmistress deemed it scandalous."

"So you ceded a point already lost," he said with a chuckle. "Well done, as Lady Mountheath strikes me as the sort who must always have the last word."

"Indeed she is. Nor will she appreciate me depriving her daughters of the chance of a waltz with you, my lord, should she learn of it." She paused on the threshold of the ballroom, scanning for that lady's chartreuse turban.

"Not to worry. I called in a couple of favors to ensure that both sisters had partners for this particular dance."

Sarah looked up at him in wonder. "Did you? That was quite foresighted, my lord, and very kind—though perhaps not to your friends." That was uncharitable, but Fanny and Lucy had been extremely unpleasant to her at dinner.

"They owed me," he said with an answering grin. "There. Lady Mountheath has her back to us, so let us slip into the crowd before she turns."

They did so, walking quickly, but not so quickly that they would be marked. Sarah turned to thank him again, only to see Sir Lawrence Winslow approaching to claim her for the cotillion just forming.

"You'll let me know if your friend wishes me to take a message to her brother?" Lord Peter whispered.

She nodded, then turned to face Sir Lawrence. It would be all she could do to keep her mind on the dance for the remainder of the evening, she knew. For as soon as the Mountheaths were abed this night, she intended to venture out again, this time to visit Seven Dials—and William himself.

Chapter 5

❧❧❧

This, surely, was the riskiest thing she had ever attempted, Sarah thought as she again slipped out of the Mountheaths' garden gate, a threadbare gray cloak and shawl over her old gray dress.

Stealing food from the kitchens at school to supplement her and her classmates' too-meager diet had been nothing to this. Nor was her last escape from the house, when she had barely left the safe confines of fashionable Mayfair. Tonight she was heading for one of the most dangerous areas of London: the notorious Seven Dials, home to beggars, thieves and worse.

Home to Sarah herself, eight years ago.

At first she worried that after so many years she might have forgotten the way, but as she hurried along the nearly deserted streets she recognized one familiar landmark after another. There was the old pump at the corner of Golden Square, on Silver Street, where she and her friends had washed grubby faces and hands. Farther along she saw the same narrow archway where she'd picked her first pocket. Oddly, the memory of how frightened she'd been then gave her confidence now.

She hurried along Litchfield to St. Martin's Lane, then turned north. The last semblances of gentility fell away as she entered Seven Dials proper, with its narrow, dirty streets and alleyways. Now what?

She looked apprehensively at a pair of beggars leaning against a tumbledown wall, at another man in rags shuffling out of a nearby doorway, at the heaps of refuse giving out that foul smell she'd managed to forget over the years. How was she ever to find William? Her only safety lay in remaining inconspicuous, in appearing as poor as the others here.

Poor she certainly was, but even her old school things were far too fine for this setting, she now realized. And she'd spent eight years cultivating her accent—now the wrong accent. To survive this night, she needed to unlearn much of what she'd learned— and quickly.

A boisterous group of men and women spilled out of a doorway a short way ahead. Sarah shrank against the wall of the closest building, listening carefully to their speech. Yes, she could still do this.

Hurrying forward, holding her shawl so that it concealed part of her face and all of her hair, she approached one of the women. " 'Scuse me, mum," she said.

The woman turned to look at her. "Well?" she said impatiently.

"I be lookin' for me brother, mum. Ha' ye seen a lad name o' Flute hereabouts?"

"Brother, eh?" The woman gave a vulgar laugh. "Oh, aye, and I'm 'is granny." She glanced after her companions, who were continuing on their way, no doubt to another drunken revel.

"Do ye know where he be?" Sarah asked again, afraid the woman would grow bored and leave without giving her the information she needed.

"Back over that way." The woman pointed down a narrow alley. "Up the stairs on yer left." She squinted at Sarah's face. "Aye, he'll thank me for sendin' ye on, I'm thinkin'. Tell 'im Maudie sent ye."

"Thankee, Maudie, I will."

Sarah waited until the woman had hurried after her friends before turning down the alley, her heart pounding. She'd been so afraid she'd give herself away—

"What 'ave we 'ere, now?" A rough voice shattered her relief. "I ain't seen you about these parts afore."

Pulling her shawl even closer, Sarah glanced frantically at the stairs Maudie had mentioned, and half turned toward the voice. "Give ower—I'm in a 'urry," she said, but instead of the gruffness she'd tried for, the last word came out as a squeak.

The man stepped out of the shadows, grinning. He seemed enormous in the dim light. "I'll make it quick, then. Flip up yer skirts, gi' me what I want, an' you can be on yer way."

Sarah backed away, swallowing. She didn't dare scream. Not only would it bring more ruffians, her brother might hear her. She would not be responsible for getting him hurt.

"I'm afraid you don't understand," she stammered, forgetting to use street cant. "I'm on my way to visit a . . . a sick friend."

"Yer friend'll still be sick when I'm done." Leering, the man lunged for her.

Sarah ducked, narrowly evading him. "Leave me alone!" She infused her voice with every ounce of authority she could muster, but it had no effect. The man lunged again.

Abruptly losing her nerve, Sarah turned and ran, only to trip over an upturned bucket. Her attacker was on top of her at once, pinioning her arms behind her.

"Stop it! Don't!" she cried, forgetting her earlier concerns as the man began fumbling under her skirts. "Let me go!"

"C'mon, missie, I ain't—"

"The lady said to stop, Bert," came a cold voice from above them. "I suggest you do so."

Bert scrambled to his feet, hauling Sarah up with him. "An' 'oo are you to suggest anythin' to me? The lads hereabouts may answer to ye, but I don't."

He started to turn back to Sarah with a gap-toothed grin that disappeared abruptly when the other man's fist struck him full in the face.

"Blimey! Ye've broke me nose!" Shoving Sarah back to the ground, he swung at her rescuer.

Scrambling backward, Sarah was able to see that the newcomer was much smaller than Bert. That didn't seem to hinder him, however. Nimbly he ducked under Bert's large paw and swung a leg around behind the big man's knees. Bert fell heavily, hitting his head on the cobblestones with a re-

sounding crack that appeared to knock him sense-
less.

"Are ye all right, miss?" the victor asked, extend-
ing a hand to help her up.

Shakily, Sarah took it and he pulled her to her feet.
"Th—thank you." Finally getting a good look at
him, she realized that though he stood a full head
taller than she, he could not be out of his teens. In
fact, there was something markedly familiar about
him. . . .

"William?" she gasped.

Releasing her hand as though it burned him, he
took a step back. "What—? Nobody . . . Who are
you?" he demanded.

"You don't recognize me, William?" Sarah asked,
stepping into a thin shaft of moonlight so that he
could see her better.

He stared, frowning. "No one has called me
William in . . . Sarah?" Blank astonishment replaced
the frown.

Sarah thought her heart might overflow with love
and relief. "I said I'd come back for you, didn't I?"

"Aye. Aye, you did, but—" He shook his head in
wonder. "How did you find me?"

"I won't say it was easy. Oh, William!" She flung
herself at her brother, hugging him tightly. "You
can't imagine—" Then she released him, unexpected
anger abruptly replacing euphoria. "Why didn't
you stay at school? I only discovered you'd run
away this week, when I arrived in London."

"Did you, then? That's good, I suppose. Saved
you years of worry. Felt bad about that, I did, but I
didn't dare write—not that I was quite lettered back

then." Suddenly, he grinned. "It's grand to see you, Sarah! Come, let's get indoors."

Though bursting with questions, she waited until she'd followed him up the rickety staircase and into a second-story room already lit with several candles—a room that was surprisingly well furnished.

"Is this where you live?" she asked as he closed the door behind them.

"Aye. Lord . . . that is, I'm staying here for now, anyways."

Sarah removed her shawl as he spoke and his eyes widened. "Blimey! I always said you were a pretty girl, but you've growed up into—well—a real beauty. And you're book learned, too?"

She nodded. "And you, William, you've grown so tall. Perhaps—perhaps I shouldn't have worried so. But what have you been doing all of this time?"

"Eh, where to start?" He sat down on an over-stuffed sofa and motioned for her to join him. "School was even worse than I expected. Knew I wasn't cut out for that, but you were so keen . . . Anyway, I nipped back to London first chance I had."

Seizing his hand, Sarah sat next to him, trying to imagine him as a boy of eight or nine, making his way back to the metropolis alone. "Oh, William, I'm so sorry—" she began, but he shook his head and grinned.

"Nay, it was just as well. I joined up with Twitchell's lads and did right well for myself until the Saint come along."

"The Saint?"

"I guess if you've just come back to Town you won't have heard of him, but he's a legend here—

abouts. Helps folks what need it by taking from them what don't."

"Like Robin Hood? But he's real, this Saint?"

"The Saint o' Seven Dials. Aye, he's real. I spent more than two years as his right-hand man," he said proudly.

She released his hand. "You mean . . . he had you stealing for him?" Sarah wasn't sure this Saint sounded like much of a hero after all.

But her brother shook his head. "Nay, he never let me so much as pick a pocket once I started helping him. I was his go-between, tellin' him which folks needed help, fencing his loot for him, that sort o' thing."

"I see." Sarah wasn't sure she did, entirely, however. "But you're not doing that anymore?"

He shrugged. "He got hisself married and retired. Couple other chaps had a go at it, but did the same, after only a month or two each. Ain't no Saint now, but I'm aiming to fix that."

"Fix it? What do you mean?"

"Folks hereabouts need the Saint," he said seriously. "These gentry morts mean well, but they've got other concerns. I figure I c'n do the job myself, with no more need of a go-between."

"Become the Saint yourself, you mean?" asked Sarah, alarmed. "William, you can't! I forbid it. Breaking into houses, stealing—it's far too dangerous. I've only just found you and I mean to take care of you now."

He looked more amused than chastened. "A bit late for that, ain't it? I been takin' care o' myself just fine all this time."

"With help from this Saint," she pointed out, but he only shrugged.

"I'm growed up now—even he admits it. It was his idea for me to take over here when Twitchell got transported. But most o' the lads have real jobs now, so it just makes sense for me to help out in other ways."

Though she couldn't deny being proud of him, Sarah was determined to keep him from such a risk. "Surely there's someone else, someone older . . . Who is this Saint, anyway?" Perhaps if she spoke to the man, told him what her brother was planning—

But William was shaking his head. "Can't tell you that, Sarah, I'm sorry. Took my oath and I'm not about to break it. Besides, he's left Town," he added, with a look that said he knew what she'd intended.

"And the other two you mentioned?"

He shrugged, but made no reply.

Sarah recognized that stubborn set to his jaw. Even as a small boy, it had meant he wouldn't be swayed. But she could be just as determined.

"At least promise you won't do anything rash," she pleaded.

He scowled at her, but then his expression softened. "It's good having you back, Sarah. I wasn't going to do anything this week, anyways. But the Heinrichs, they're in a bad way. They'll need summat by the end o' the month."

It wasn't much of a reprieve, but she'd take it. "I can't tell you how happy I am to see you again, William—er, Flute." He grinned at her correction. "I hope to find a governess position soon. If both of us have employment, surely we can help those who need it with no need for thievery?"

"Maybe," he said with a shrug, then asked, "Where are you staying? How can I reach you?"

"I'm with the Mountheaths, in one of the big mansions on Berkley Square, if you can believe it. They are relations of our mother's—but it would be best if you not visit there. Lady Mountheath would be only too happy of an excuse to turn me out. I'll come again, or send word, once I've found a position."

"Send word," he said firmly. "You must remember, after your run-in with Bert, how dangerous it is here, 'specially for a girl like you."

She refrained from pointing out that it was dangerous for him, too. "Very well. But don't mention I'm your sister to anyone I send. I'll say you're the brother of a friend from school."

Though she was afraid he'd be offended, he nodded sagely. "Aye, if you want to fit in with the nobs, you can't be associatin' with the likes o' me. With your looks and learning, you might well land yourself one of them fine gents as a husband. That would set us up right pretty."

Though Mrs. Hounslow had said much the same thing, Sarah shook her head. "Even if I can keep my past a secret, that's unlikely. Position and wealth are everything in that world, I'm learning. Gentlemen look for more than beauty in a wife."

Even Lord Peter? a small voice asked, but she quelled it at once. It would be especially true of a fourth son, with no prospects to inherit a fortune or estate.

"Don't sell yourself short. You're more than a pretty face, y'know. How many girls would have the gumption to come to Seven Dials alone, at night, just to see what become of their runaway brother?"

Sarah threw herself into his arms again. "Oh, William, I've missed you so," she said, her voice breaking on a sob.

He hugged her back, then set her away from him. "Enough o' that," he said, a slight catch in his voice. "Come on. I'll walk you back to Mayfair."

Though he knew it was unwise, Peter could not resist calling at the Mountheath house the next day. Far from being solved, the puzzle that was Miss Sarah Killian tantalized him more than ever.

"Welcome, my lord. How good of you to call." Lady Mountheath greeted him. She had a distinct edge to her voice, and as he progressed into the parlor, he understood why.

No fewer than half a dozen gentlemen were present, and every one of them appeared focused on Miss Killian, seated off to one side, while the Mountheath girls sat outside the circle, pouting. Numerous bouquets crowded a nearby table, and he had no difficulty guessing to which lady they'd been sent.

At the sight of Miss Killian's sweet face bracketed by a leering Lord Ribbleton on one side and the fatuous Mr. Pottinger on the other, Peter was conscious of a degree of vexation that rivaled Lady Mountheath's, though he was careful not to let it show. The object of his visit glanced up just then and pinkened slightly as he caught her eye and smiled.

"Ah, Lord Peter! I knew you would come," Lucy Mountheath exclaimed, her pout transforming into a smirk. "Did I not say so, Fanny? Come, my lord, sit by me, do."

Knowing that to refuse would wound her feelings, Peter complied as pleasantly as his impatience would allow. "Good day, Miss Mountheath, Miss Fanny. I trust I find you well."

"Much better, now that you're here," replied Lucy with a simpering smile. "It's been rather a trying morning. Poor Mama has had to bring extra chairs in from the breakfast room."

"Aye, gentlemen are so shallow," Fanny declared, "losing their wits over a pretty face. They care not whether there is anything of substance beneath."

She did not bother to lower her voice, and Peter glanced at Miss Killian with concern. But though one or two of her gallants frowned in Fanny's direction, the object of the ill-natured attack appeared unmoved, though she must have heard.

"Not all gentlemen," Lucy reproved her sister. "Lord Peter clearly has not had his head turned by our cousin. He is able to see past such *obvious* charms—are you not, my lord?"

"I prefer to think so," he responded with perfect truth, for more than mere beauty drew him to Miss Killian.

Lucy preened, taking his words as a compliment to herself. "You are wise, my lord, as surface beauty always fades." She pursed her lips in an attempt at seductiveness that made her look as though she had bitten into a lemon.

Peter was spared from replying when three gentlemen rose to take their leave and two others were announced. Lady Mountheath seized the opportunity to put her own daughters in the way of so many eligible men by beckoning them over to take two of the chairs just vacated near Sarah. Peter followed more slowly, along with the new arrivals, Mr. Galloway and his cousin, Mr. Orrin.

"—I had no idea," Sarah was saying as Lord Peter took a seat at the edge of the circle about her. Though her spirits had risen at his entrance, she knew she would have to be more careful now. "As you can see, I'm not at all up on the latest news," she continued, ready to introduce the topic that most interested her.

At least three gentlemen instantly put themselves at her service, offering to tell her whatever she wished. She smiled, avoiding Lord Peter's eye.

"I scarcely know where to start," she said. "There are so many things of which I have heard only the merest mention. For example, this Saint of Seven Dials." She kept her voice light, as though she had picked the topic at random. "Who, or what, is he?"

"Some say a hero, others say a rogue," Mr. Galloway offered, moving his chair closer to her.

Sir Lawrence nodded. "A most mysterious thief, Miss Killian. The poor people idolize him, but he's been terrorizing the Upper Ten Thousand for two or three years now."

"He's a common criminal, if you ask me," Lord Ribbleton put in with a frown. "Stole a few rather valuable trinkets from me this summer past, in fact."

"Really? Did you catch a glimpse of him, my lord?" Sarah asked with what she hoped appeared only polite interest.

But to her disappointment, he shook his head. "Got clean away, as he always seems to do."

Lady Mountheath, her color high, declared, "He'll be caught eventually, mark my words. I can't think why you would be interested in such a low, vicious person, Miss Killian. I'll have you know he has robbed this house twice. Twice!" She fairly quivered with indignation.

Though startled, Sarah was reluctant to let the subject drop, now she had successfully introduced it. "Why, that's terrible, my lady," she exclaimed. "Can those in authority do nothing?"

Her ladyship sniffed. "It would appear not, despite the inducements we have offered them. At one point last spring, the Runners nearly had him. They traced some plate—*our* plate, mind you!—to a boy who was helping him. He was caught and imprisoned, but then he escaped. Escaped! From Newgate!"

"I heard that the Saint himself broke the boy out," Sir Lawrence said. "Disguised himself as a guard or some such. They say he can change his appearance to almost anything—like magic."

Lady Mountheath glared at him. "Pish! Bribed the guards, more like. Corruption is rampant among those sworn to uphold our laws and keep the citizenry safe, I have discovered. If the Saint is a nobleman, as some have postulated, I've no doubt he is paying the Runners off himself."

From what little her brother had told her about the Saint, Sarah was fairly certain he *was* a nobleman. But who? It was imperative she find out, so she could convince him to speak with William and keep him from attempting thievery on his own. Even more imperative than she'd realized, if William was already a suspect! Why had he said nothing about having been imprisoned?

"Surely, with so many clamoring for his capture, there must be rumors, at least, of his identity?" Sarah ventured.

"There have been several." Lord Peter spoke for the first time. "At one point last summer, even my own brother Marcus was under suspicion, absurd as it seems. At least, that was the only reason I could see for Mr. Paxton's inordinate interest in him. Clearly that came to nothing, however."

Sarah caught an edge to his voice, but if he'd thought his brother at risk, that would surely account for it.

"Interesting that the thefts stopped when your brother left London, however," Lord Ribbleton said, frowning. "How can you be so sure—?"

"Among numerous other reasons, because Marcus and his wife were with me when the last robbery was perpetrated," Lord Peter said sharply. "And though I grant you he's become more responsible since his marriage, I can't imagine he ever possessed the, ah, dedication attributed to the Saint."

Lady Mountheath made a rude noise. "Dedication, indeed! That last robbery you mention, my lord, took place in my very bedchamber!" She paused for dramatic effect. "The blackguard stole some very expensive jewelry right off of my dressing table as I slept. It's a wonder I wasn't murdered in my sleep."

Sarah gasped, her horror only partially assumed for Lady Mountheath's benefit. What daring the man must possess! "When was this, my lady?" she asked.

"Nearly two months since, but I declare my nerves

have yet to recover." Lady Mountheath put a trembling hand to her throat while her daughters clucked over her.

"Then I should think a change of subject is in order," Lord Peter suggested.

Sarah glanced at him with some irritation, but on seeing his stiff expression she realized belatedly that he was right. It would not do to have her particular interest in the Saint noted—not that he could know that, of course.

"Yes, of course," she said. "What can you tell me of bonnets? I perceive that the brims worn in Town are not so deep as I observed in the country."

The others obediently turned the talk to matters of fashion, with the Mountheath ladies making frequent pronouncements that admitted of no argument. Lord Ribbleton and Sir Lawrence took their leave, while Mr. Galloway, Mr. Orrin and Lord Peter continued the conversation, all doing a much better job of including Lucy and Fanny than the others had done.

Sarah tried to listen, as it was quite true that she had much to learn about current fashions, but her attention was still on the earlier topic.

It appeared her brother was right that the Saint had ceased his operations, whether temporarily or permanently. Had he left London entirely? Not that it mattered, she realized. What was important was that William believe that the Saint meant to resume his activities. It was the only thing likely to keep him from attempting thievery himself.

But how to convince him of that, when she had no idea who the Saint of Seven Dials was?

She must discover more about the Saint, she decided—enough that she could concoct a believable story about having met the man. Perhaps she could even send a message to William, claiming it was from the Saint himself. . . .

"—do you, Miss Killian?" Mr. Galloway was asking.

Sarah blinked. "I beg your pardon?" she asked, feeling stupid. That her cousins shared that opinion was evident from their smirks and giggles.

"I was commenting that you don't appear to consider yourself an arbiter of fashion, as Lord Peter here does," Mr. Galloway explained. "I'm certain he—and your fair cousins—will be able to bring you bang up to the nines in no time, however."

Though Sarah did not like to agree with something that was clearly intended as both a dig at Lord Peter and a compliment to the Mountheath sisters, she could only nod. "No doubt," she said vaguely, earning another snigger from her cousins.

Rather than take offense, Lord Peter smiled. "With that view in mind, Miss Killian, might I persuade you to walk out with me this afternoon? I would be delighted to instruct you on the intricacies of fashion."

"And my cousin and I would be most happy of an opportunity to walk out with *you*, Miss Mountheath and Miss Fanny," said Mr. Galloway quickly, with a glance at Lady Mountheath's gathering frown. "If that would be acceptable, my lady?"

Though she appeared not at all pleased with these arrangements, she gave a stiff nod. "Very well. You may all call at five. But you'll have them out no more than an hour."

All three gentlemen then took their leave with promises to return in a few hours. The moment they were gone, Lady Mountheath lectured her daughters on the imprudence of encouraging fortune hunters, then turned to Sarah.

"And you, miss, will only look foolish by setting your sights too high. Never forget that your noble grandfather cast your mother off when she eloped, making her as much a nobody as your father was. No gentleman of standing will consider you eligible, and the other sort will be interested in something quite apart from matrimony."

"Of course, my lady," Sarah replied, though her cheeks burned. "I'm certain Lord Peter has only your interests in mind, that I might not embarrass you or my cousins by my dress."

"Yes, Mama, that is surely it," Lucy agreed. "Lord Peter made it quite plain earlier that he has no designs upon Miss Killian. In fact, he was quite attentive to me, was he not, Fanny?"

Her sister nodded, but added, "I still find Mr. Galloway more charming, Lucy. He and Mr. Orrin both have a very pretty way with words, don't you think?"

The sisters went off into whispers and giggles until their mother resumed her diatribe on fortune hunters.

Sarah paid none of them any attention, her mind already on her upcoming walk with Lord Peter. She must somehow guide their conversation back to the Saint of Seven Dials. He seemed remarkably well informed, and could very likely tell her all she needed to know to dissuade William from his dangerous plan.

Most important, she would *not* allow herself to weave any silly hopes about Lord Peter's invitation, for to do so would only be to court disappointment, as Lady Mountheath said. He was kind—and curious about her—but nothing more.

She was almost certain of it.

Chapter 6

"**Y**es, Holmes, I'm sure that's it. Thank you."
Peter added the name of Miss Pritchard's
Seminary for Young Ladies to his page of notes.
"Nothing in *Debrett's Peerage* links the name Killian
to that of Mountheath, however. How go your in-
quiries?"

His valet, whose service had long extended beyond mere matters of dress, shook his head. "Nothing yet, my lord. It's such a common Irish name,
ferreting out this particular branch is proving difficult. Give me time, however."

"You have my complete confidence, as always.
The bottle green, I think," Peter added as his man
held up two coats for his inspection. He turned so
that Holmes could help him into the tight-fitting
coat, then smoothed it over his gold-on-gold waist-

coat. "Have you tried Doctor's Commons or Somerset House?"

"I have an appointment at the former and intend to make one at the latter in the morning," Holmes replied with a bow.

"Good man. I'll be off, then." Picking up his hat and stick, Peter headed out for his walk with the mysterious Miss Killian—whom he hoped would not be a mystery much longer.

Though Miss Killian was ready when Peter arrived, Lady Mountheath insisted that they wait until her daughters came down.

"Mr. Galloway and Mr. Orrin will be here momentarily, and it will arouse less . . . talk . . . if all of you walk out together." She sent a sharp glance Miss Killian's way, making Peter wonder what sort of lecture the poor girl had already been subjected to.

The "poor girl" merely smiled, however, and set her parasol aside. Remembering that she had lacked one during their drive, Peter glanced at the parasol and noticed that its lacy folds had been mended in spots. Another hand-me-down. Had Miss Killian come to London with nothing of her own?

The bell sounded then, and the other two gentlemen were announced. After pleasantries and a few minutes of idle conversation, the Mountheath sisters made their appearance.

"Ah, Fanny, how well that gown becomes you!" Lady Mountheath exclaimed. "And Lucy, that blue piping brightens your eyes beautifully. Do you not agree, gentlemen?"

All made murmurs of agreement, then Peter held out his arm to Miss Killian. "Shall we go, then?"

A moment later, the six of them were walking

down the pavement in the direction of Hyde Park. As usual, Lucy Mountheath took control of the conversation, this time with a detailed critique of what every woman had worn to last night's ball. She and Mr. Galloway were in the lead, followed by Fanny and Mr. Orrin, with Peter and Miss Killian bringing up the rear. After listening to Lucy's monologue for half a block, Peter slowed his steps slightly and leaned his head toward his partner.

"It is a fine afternoon for a walk, is it not?" he asked softly, so as not to draw the attention of the others.

"Indeed," she agreed, glancing ahead at her cousins. "And for my promised lesson on fashion."

Her look told him she knew perfectly well that was not his true reason for inviting her out, and he grinned down at her, tacitly admitting she was right. "I believe there is nothing wrong with your fashion sense that better funding would not remedy," he said. "Judging by the alterations you have made to gowns that were undoubtedly hopeless when new, I should say you have a good eye."

She pinkened slightly and fixed her gaze on the street ahead. "Necessity is an excellent teacher, my lord."

Peter cursed his clumsiness. "I meant that entirely as a compliment, Miss Killian. As your circumstances are clearly beyond your control, I cannot imagine reproaching you with them."

Though she smiled, she still did not meet his eye. "I fear not many in Society share your forbearance. However, as Society was never my aim, I should not let that bother me unduly."

He could see, however, that it did indeed bother

her more than she would admit. "And what is your aim, Miss Killian?" he asked even more softly.

"Employment," she replied after the barest hesitation. "I came to London in hopes of a governess post. Pray let me know if you hear of any openings, my lord."

Peter looked down at her upturned face, regarding him almost defiantly. Only the fact that they were in full public view prevented him from kissing her thoroughly on the spot.

"I'll keep my ears open." The thought of her immured in some schoolroom until her beauty faded and her disposition soured bothered him more than he cared to admit. If he learned more of her, perhaps he could help her. Before he could broach the topic of her background, however, she asked a question of her own.

"Earlier, I had the impression that you were well acquainted with the rumors surrounding the Saint of Seven Dials. Can you tell me more? I find myself quite curious about him."

Peter stiffened, then forced himself to relax before she could notice. Almost every lady he knew was fascinated by the Saint, after all. In fact, he himself had rather admired the man's daring until recently learning he was a traitor.

Miss Killian had most likely changed the subject to deflect any further inquiry about herself anyway, so he obliged her with an answer. "Indeed, I have followed his career with interest from the start. I do love a mystery, you know."

Was he unwise to put her on notice that he meant to solve hers? He was fairly sure she'd guessed that already—and his words were perfectly true.

"How long has he been operating?" she asked then. "And how did he come by his nickname?"

They turned from Mount Street onto Park Lane as she spoke and, while waiting to cross it, were forced to stand too near the others to continue their conversation unmarked. Not until they continued on toward the Park did Peter reply, his words masked by an argument that had broken out between the Mountheath sisters as to whether Miss Partridge's or Lady Durkle's gown had been an uglier shade of green.

"The beginning of the Saint's career is a bit murky," Peter said as they approached the Park gates. "His increasing audacity finally brought him to the attention of the authorities—and the newspapers. An enterprising journalist, struck by the Robin Hood parallel, dubbed him the Saint of Seven Dials, and the name stuck."

"And how long ago was that?"

Peter knew the exact date of that column, but he only said, "About two years since, though I did not pay close attention until the following summer."

In fact, he had left for the Congress of Vienna only a few weeks after that article had appeared. Not until his return, desperately needing new distraction from his memories of the war, had he turned his attention to the mystery of the Saint. It had diverted his mind—for a while—but he would have worked more diligently to solve the puzzle had he guessed the truth.

"I take it he had already become a celebrity of sorts by then?" she prompted when his silence lengthened.

"What? Oh, yes, quite. The cartoonists had a hey-

day depicting ladies—even the royal duchesses—
swooning over a masked bandit as he picked the
pockets of their husbands. His calling card became
such a byword for daring that reproductions were
sold in shops for a while, until Bow Street put a stop
to it. The Saint was enough of an embarrassment to
them already."

"Calling card? He uses a calling card? My, that *is*
bold of him," Miss Killian said. "What does it look
like—or does he no longer use it?"

"He was still using it two months ago, when he
terrorized Lady Mountheath. She found one in her
ribbon box."

"As I'm sure she told anyone who would listen."

"Indeed." Peter smiled in spite of himself. "It was
a simple card, really—a black numeral seven topped
by a golden oval—a halo. So easy to reproduce that
I'd be surprised if every theft attributed to the Saint
was really committed by him."

Could it be, he suddenly wondered, that the Black
Bishop was not the original Saint? Perhaps he had
murdered or bribed the legendary thief, then taken
over his role in order to continue his treasonous activities right here in London.

As Lord Peter paused, Sarah stared into space, a
completely outrageous idea seizing her brain. No,
no, surely it would not be possible—

"Miss Killian?"

With a start, she realized she had stopped walking; the others were now some way ahead. "Oh! Pardon me. It's just . . . I have never seen swans so large
before," she said, gesturing vaguely toward a
nearby pond. "They are beautiful, are they not?"

"I've always thought so," Lord Peter agreed, regarding her curiously. Not surprising, as her excuse had sounded feeble even to her own ears.

Moving forward again, she tried to pick up the thread of their conversation about the Saint. She would need more information, if she came up with no better idea. "So, my lord, were you never robbed by the Saint? You seem more amused than affronted by his exploits."

He frowned. "I wouldn't say that. But I am not rich enough to offer a tempting target, nor, I hope, do I possess the other attributes that distinguished his victims."

"What attributes to you mean?"

"One thing that made the Saint seem so heroic was how he selected his targets," he explained. "To the best of my knowledge, he never robbed anyone I would care to call a friend."

Sarah was still confused. "Do you mean he only steals from those of lower class? But I thought . . . the Mountheaths—"

"No, no, you mistake me. In fact, rather the opposite. He only stole from those who could afford the loss, and from those who, well, seemed to deserve it."

A light broke upon her. "Oh, I see! Then . . . the more unpleasant a person is—a rich person, of course—the more likely he is to be a victim of the Saint? That certainly explains why Lady Mountheath has been robbed twice!" She couldn't help laughing, though she glanced ahead to make certain the sisters were still out of earshot.

"Precisely." His mouth twisted with something that might have been amusement. "That's one reason so many people believed the Saint must be a member of the *ton*, though of course servants have a gossip network quite as extensive as their employers do. Still, it's easier for a gentleman to ape a servant than the reverse, and the Saint appears to have taken many guises."

Many guises. Surely not the one Sarah was considering! Before she could pursue that outlandish thought, she realized they had caught up with the Mountheath sisters and their escorts.

"I declare, walking is my favorite form of exercise," Lucy was saying, while moving more and more slowly. "So healthy!"

Fanny nodded. "Indeed. We keep saying we must do more of it." Her voice was as breathless as her sister's.

Mr. Galloway was all concern. "Have we tired you? I fear I did not consider . . . that is, I walk so often—"

"Not being in possession of a carriage," Lord Peter whispered to Sarah. "His entire income appears to be spent on his wardrobe—which *is* always bang-up to the nines, to give him credit."

"Tired?" Lucy responded with a lightness that was marred by the small gasp following the word. "Not in the least. However, it does look like rain—indeed I feel a drop or two now."

Fanny glanced up at the now cloudy sky. "Oh, dear! And this is a new bonnet. We'd best head for home at once."

"No need, no need," Mr. Orrin declared. "We shall call for a hackney. I'd not have your esteemed mother deny us your company in future on grounds we are injurious to your health—or bonnets."

"That *would* be handsome of you, sir," Lucy said

with a simper. "I should hate to have my silk ribbons rain spotted."

"Consider it done, then," said Mr. Galloway with a bow. They all headed back to the Park gates, where the gentlemen were able to flag down a passing hackney cab. It was a small one, allowing for only two passengers, but the Mountheath sisters stepped up to it at once.

"Thank you ever so much, kind sirs," Lucy exclaimed, holding out her hand to be helped into the conveyance.

"But . . . Miss Killian—" Mr. Galloway began, but Lucy waved her other hand airily.

"Our dear cousin can make it back on foot, I am certain. She is wearing nothing that will be harmed by a sprinkle of rain."

Sarah hid a smile at what was clearly intended as an insult. "Quite true. I much prefer to walk, in any event. Pray have no concern on my account."

"And you can trust me to see her home safely," Lord Peter added, drawing a quick frown from Lucy.

Her concern for her ribbons apparently overcame any jealousy, however, for she said, "I thank you, my lord. Your willingness to discommode yourself for my comfort is most gallant indeed."

He bowed, hiding his face from the Misses Mountheath, but Sarah was able to discern the twitching of his lips. "At your service, as always," he murmured, a slight quaver in his voice.

Mr. Orrin paid the driver, who then whipped up the horse and headed back to Berkley Square. The remaining four stood where they were for a moment, before Mr. Galloway asked whether Sarah would require all of their escorts.

"No indeed, Mr. Galloway, though I thank you for the thought," she replied quickly. In fact, she was quite eager for more private conversation with Lord Peter. She still had a few details to fill in before she could decide whether her plan was too impossible to attempt.

"We will take our leave of you, then," said Mr. Orrin, inclining his head. "No doubt we will see you at the Wickburn ball tonight."

"No doubt," Sarah agreed, though after what Lady Mountheath had said earlier she considered it by no means a certainty. The two gentlemen headed off at a brisk walk that made her suspect they had something more important—or enjoyable—to do just then.

Lord Peter again held out his arm to her. "As I don't wish to exceed the allotted hour and incur Lady Mountheath's wrath, I suppose we should turn our steps toward Berkley Square. Unless you'd like me to hail another hackney?"

"That's not the least bit necessary, my lord," she replied. "It is barely raining at all, and I was being quite truthful when I said I prefer walking. It's the only form of transportation that was available to us in Cumberland."

He smiled down at her, making her stomach do an odd little flip. "I suspected as much. Tell me more about your life in Cumberland."

She fought a sudden tingle of alarm. But what harm could it do, really? He already knew she was an orphan, that her school was a charitable concern. Additional details would not reveal her prior life on the London streets.

"There is little to tell," she said, hoping he had not

marked her hesitation. "Frigid winters but pleasant summers, days spent in the classroom, evenings in study and prayer. Never quite enough to eat, though we did not starve."

"Not unlike my own boarding school, though lacking some of the comforts, from the sound of it," he commented. "Certainly, we never lacked for food—quite the opposite, as I recall."

"There was food enough in the kitchens. Miss . . . The headmistress simply had odd notions about the healthfulness of small portions. Luckily for us, the larder was not guarded at night," she said with a grin.

"Why, Miss Killian, I am shocked!" He laughed aloud. "I had always assumed girls were far better behaved at school than boys. Never tell me you yourself pillaged the pantries!"

"Of course I will tell you no such thing," she said primly, though she knew her smile betrayed her.

In fact, she had been the only one to make regular nocturnal forays to the kitchen, though the other girls had been glad enough to share the bounty. Perhaps she was more fitted for her outrageous scheme than she'd realized.

They had reached the corner of Berkley Square, but Lord Peter paused at the entrance to the mews, still chuckling. Glancing up, Sarah found him regarding her with amusement.

"You are quite the original, you know, Miss Killian. I can't recall ever enjoying a stroll so much. I do hope you know that if I can ever be of service to you, in any capacity whatsoever, you need only ask." The laughter had gone now—he was quite serious.

For a wild moment she was tempted to tell him

about her brother, about what he intended, and what she was considering to prevent him. "I . . . that is—" she stammered, trying to remember why that would be a mistake.

A light kindled behind his kind brown eyes and he leaned closer. "I do care, you know," he whispered.

She nodded helplessly, not sure if she feared he would kiss her or feared he would not. The moment seemed frozen in time, his lips hovering only inches from hers. She was afraid to move or speak, unwilling to break the spell that seemed cast over them both. Nervously, she licked her lips, just the barest moistening, and felt a tremor run through his arm, still under her hand.

"Miss Killian . . . Sarah," he said hoarsely, lowering his lips to hers for her first kiss.

It was a light kiss, a gentlemanly kiss, but something burned just below the surface that both thrilled and frightened her.

After what seemed the barest moment, he straightened, an alarm in his eyes that she was certain was echoed in her own.

"My profound apologies! I never meant . . . that is, I pray you will forgive me taking such a liberty, Miss Killian." His ears reddening, he glanced back toward the square. She did the same, and was relieved to see no one looking their way.

"Of course. That is . . . I hope you don't think . . . I mean—" What on earth *did* she mean?

He was smiling again, his color returning to normal. "I think you nothing but charming, and completely free of blame in the matter," he assured her gallantly. "Let it put you on your guard, however, for if someone like me can be tempted to steal a kiss, you can be sure the idea has occurred to many other gentlemen."

"Someone like you, my lord?" He was as handsome—and vigorous—as any gentleman of her acquaintance, even if he did favor brightly colored waistcoats.

He shrugged slightly. "I have a reputation of acting the conscience to my more, ah, dissipated friends. Most would tell you I am a thorough stick-in-the-mud. No fun at all."

She couldn't quite contain a delicate snort of amusement. "Then I fear your friends don't know you particularly well, my lord, for that is not at all how I perceive you."

"You have known me but a few days. Perhaps my more boring qualities will manifest on further acquaintance." His brown eyes were twinkling.

"Perhaps," she said, not bothering to conceal her skepticism. "I will let you know if they do."

"An honest woman is above rubies." He bowed deeply. "And now, I'd best return you to Lady Mountheath or we'll both have a peal rung over us."

Realizing that time was short, she again turned the subject. "You were telling me of the Saint before. Is it certain he has ceased his operations?"

"I am wounded to find you as fascinated by the rogue as most of the other ladies in Town. Mere mortals like myself stand little chance against his formidable reputation, I fear."

The look he slanted down at her made her heart flutter.

"But yes, I feel quite certain that he has . . . retired," he continued. "Previously, we could count on a report of some outrageous robbery every week or so, and now there's been none for some two months."

"Perhaps the sight of Lady Mountheath in her nightrail terrified him into a life of virtue," Sarah suggested.

He chuckled. "Would that it were so, but I fear that had little to do with it."

"What do you mean?" she asked, startled by what had almost appeared to be a flash of anger in his eyes.

"I'm sorry. It is not public knowledge, so I should not say."

She placed both hands on his arm, resolutely ignoring the thrill that went through her at the contact. "Please tell me."

He looked down at her, no trace of humor now on his face. "I have learned that the Saint's cessation of activity corresponded precisely with the capture of a notorious traitor. I believe that they were one and the same, and that the Saint was no hero at all. Quite the opposite, in fact."

"But—but what of his choice of victims? How—?"

"All a part of his false identity," he replied, staring past her with a coldness totally at odds with his normally genial face. "I'm sorry, Miss Killian, but I cannot bear to see you idolize such a man. Would that I could disabuse the rest of Society."

Sarah swallowed, chilled by the change in his manner. "Why can't you?" she couldn't help asking.

His smile was a mere mockery of the one he'd worn earlier. "They would never believe me, for one thing. For another, I do not know whether the investigation into the traitor's activities is complete. I would not wish to be the cause of even one of his accomplices escaping the gallows."

"I see," she said numbly, giving silent thanks that she had not yielded to her momentary temptation to tell him the truth about her brother. Surely, William could not have known—

"I did not mean to distress you," he said quickly. "I fear I have taken this rather . . . personally, because of certain events during the war. Come, let us speak of other things."

"Of course." It was more imperative than ever that she prevent William from becoming the Saint, she realized. And it appeared that the field was indeed open for her to implement her plan. Surely, a wicked plan. But if it was the only way to dissuade William from risk and folly . . .

Already they were nearing Mountheath House. "You have yet to give me any fashion advice," she pointed out before her silence could be marked.

"So I have. Whatever your cousins wear, choose something different. How is that?"

"As my wardrobe must be adapted from theirs, that may be difficult," she said, forcing a smile, "but I will endeavor to make as many changes as possible."

Just then, the front door of Mountheath House opened to reveal a bristling Lady Mountheath. "Miss Killian," she said in ominous tones, "I wish to speak with you. At once."

Sarah nodded, then turned back to Lord Peter. "Thank you for the walk, my lord. It was most . . . instructive."

"The pleasure was mine." He bowed deeply, first to her, then to Lady Mountheath. "Miss Killian, my lady, until tonight." With a touch of his finger to his hat brim, he turned and strolled jauntily away.

Sarah smiled after him for a long moment, before turning with an inward sigh toward the door, aware of the gathering rage on her benefactress's face. Wondering what she'd done this time—since surely Lady Mountheath could not know about her indiscretion in the mews—she headed up the stairs.

"Yes, my lady?"

Clearly unwilling for any passersby to have food for gossip, Lady Mountheath waited until the door was closed to round on Sarah. "How *dare* you walk home alone with Lord Peter? He has made his intentions toward Lucy quite clear, so do not think to go behind her back and steal his affections. Shameless. Shameless!"

"It was scarcely my idea for your daughters to ride ahead in a hackney, my lady," Sarah pointed out reasonably. "As I was not invited to join them, I had little choice in my manner of returning."

"Silence! I should have known that my kindness in allowing you into Society would be repaid by insolence. Considering your antecedants, I should have expected nothing else."

"I beg—" Sarah began indignantly, but Lady Mountheath held up a hand to silence her.

"Clearly I have been too indulgent, leading you to a mistaken belief that you are somehow on a level with my own girls. Alas, it is too late to make your regrets for tonight's ball. Camilla, the Duchess of Wickburn, is one of my dearest friends and I would not offend her for the world. But you will oblige me by refusing any—*any*—invitations to dance. You may sit with the dowagers and companions, as is more fitting."

"But—"

"No arguments! Now, go to your room and make whatever alterations are necessary to the gowns you will find there. I have arranged an interview for you tomorrow morning with Lady Winslow, who is in need of a governess. If she is satisfied, you will start at once."

So, Sarah thought as she headed upstairs, Lady Mountheath had taken immediate steps to get rid of the threat she posed. She should be pleased, she knew, but working as a governess would afford her little opportunity to move among the upper classes. How would she choose the Saint's targets? And how would she contact her brother, once the job was done?

She reached her room and examined the faded lilac ballgown and the outdated gray uniform Lady Mountheath had laid out for her interview tomorrow. She suspected it had belonged to whoever had taught the Mountheath girls, once upon a time.

Her first foray as Saint of Seven Dials would have to occur at tonight's ball, she realized in sudden panic. It might be her only chance for some time, and she *must* prevent William from taking on the role himself, particularly in light of what Lord Peter had said. Perhaps Lady Mountheath's ban on dancing would work to her advantage.

Pulling out her measuring tape, she tried to concentrate on the task at hand in order to keep worry at bay. But she wasn't certain whether it was the possibility of getting caught that had her insides in such a turmoil, or the knowledge that once she started work as a governess, she would almost certainly never see Lord Peter again.

Chapter 7

Peter entered the ballroom with a sense of anticipation. He'd always liked the jovial Duke of Wickburn, an old friend of his father's. Of course the Duke of Marland would be in attendance as well, but Peter had become inured to his father's criticism over the years. More important, Sarah would be here.

Since that unwise but thoroughly enjoyable kiss this afternoon, he'd been able to think of little else. From her reaction, he was fairly sure it had been Sarah's first, and he felt a totally inappropriate pleasure at knowing he'd been the one to give her that initial taste of romance.

For romantic that kiss had certainly been! Remembering its sweetness, its promise, he couldn't help feeling—

"I'm off to the card room," Harry said, breaking into his reverie.

Peter nodded absently. With an effort, he reminded himself that he still knew little about Sarah. He would try to remedy that, while doing his best to shield her from the Mountheaths' worst abuses. But first, he had to find her. The music had already begun, so he scanned the dance floor.

"Why, Lord Peter! I had begun to fear you would not attend." Lucy Mountheath, in a pink gown that emphasized the sallowness of her complexion, appeared without warning at his side.

"My apologies, Miss Mountheath," he replied, surreptitiously glancing past her in hopes of spotting Sarah. "At the last moment, I changed my mind about which cravat style I wished to wear." Sarah was nowhere in sight.

"Oh, I can certainly sympathize!" Lucy tittered. "This is the fourth gown I tried on tonight."

Peter stopped himself only just in time from telling her she should have gone for five. What was the matter with him?

"I still have several dances free," she informed him when he hesitated.

He managed a smile. "Then I trust you will do me the honor of partnering me for the next country dance." She was agreeing and simpering when he startled himself by adding, "I have not yet seen Miss Killian. Did she not attend?"

Lucy positively smirked. "No, she is here. I believe she is seated against the far wall, with the dowagers and companions."

"Indeed." Peter peered through the moving dancers, trying to spot Sarah among those seated on the far side of the ballroom. "If you will excuse me, Miss Mountheath? I promise to seek you out for our dance."

"So kind, my lord. If you should see Miss Killian, do remind her that she is not to dance. Mama was very clear on that point." Smiling sunnily, Lucy moved in the direction of Mr. Galloway—no doubt to inform him of her cousin's demotion to wall-flower.

Wasting no more thought on the vindictive Lucy, Peter skirted the dancers, making his way to the row of chairs ranged against the far wall. There he finally spotted Sarah, looking like a rose among weeds, seated between a whey-faced companion and a dowager who must be near eighty.

"I give you good evening, Miss Killian," Peter said, sweeping her a courtly bow. "May I persuade you to dance?"

As he'd expected, she shook her head, her cheeks pinkening most becomingly with her embarrass-ment. "I fear I cannot, my lord. Lady Mountheath has forbidden it."

He raised his brows in mock surprise. "Afraid you will cast all of the other ladies in the shade, I take it?"

As he'd hoped, that elicited a faint smile. "That was not the reason she gave, no."

"Then, presuming she has not also forbidden you from walking, perhaps you might enlighten me as to her reasons as we take a turn about the room?"

She hesitated for a moment, glancing about the ballroom, but then shrugged almost imperceptibly. "She did not specifically say I could not move about the room, though she *suggested* I remain here. I would be delighted to walk with you, my lord."

He took her hand and raised her to her feet, his heart accelerating at her nearness. Really, he must get his emotions—or at least his physical response to them—under better control.

His first object, he reminded himself, must be to help her—no, to determine whether she even wanted, or needed, his help. "You were going to tell me what prompted Lady Mountheath to put further restrictions upon you."

"She feels my chances of employment may be greater if I do not become too visible in Society." She did not meet his eye.

"Then it was nothing to do with my keeping you too long on our walk this afternoon? I thought she looked rather vexed when I returned you to her."

"She was a trifle put out," she admitted after a moment's hesitation. "But it takes very little to vex her, as I'm sure you have observed."

Peter frowned. "I cannot like seeing you at the mercy of so capricious a guardian, Miss Killian. Is there no one else who might be willing to lend you countenance? If I can help in any way, you have only to ask."

She smiled up at him warmly, and he was conscious of an intense desire to protect her, to keep her smiling at all costs. Dangerous ground, that. Very dangerous.

"That is very kind of you, my lord. However, I fear—"

"Lord Peter!" Lucy Mountheath's strident voice cut off whatever Sarah had been about to say, to Peter's frustration. "You promised to seek me out, yet here I have had to search for you. I have it on good authority that a country dance is next."

Peter turned, converting a grimace into a courtly smile. "My apologies, Miss Mountheath. As I had not your prior knowledge, I hope you will forgive me."

"Of course." Lucy tittered a moment, then turned on Sarah, her lip curling. "Did not Mama tell you to remain on the sidelines, cousin? What do you here?"

Though Peter noted with approval that Sarah's chin lifted and her eyes flashed, he spoke before she could get into more trouble by defending herself.

"It is my fault, Miss Mountheath. I quite bullied Miss Killian into walking with me. No doubt she felt it would occasion less notice to accede than to continue resisting."

Sarah sent him a speaking glance that said as clearly as words that she was quite capable of fighting her own battles, but Lucy Mountheath had already turned away with a sniff.

"We'll just see what Mama has to say about it. Come, Lord Peter, our dance is beginning."

Casting a look of apology over his shoulder, Peter allowed himself to be dragged to the dance floor, determined to dissuade Lucy from bearing tales to her mother before the conclusion of the dance. Somehow, protecting Miss Killian seemed as natural as breathing. In fact, dangerous or not, he realized it was fast becoming an obsession—no matter who she proved to be.

Though she had to admit she was coming to care far more for Lord Peter than was wise, Sarah watched him depart with more relief than regret. She had begun to fear she would have no chance at all this evening to put her plan into action.

On her own for the moment, she surveyed the

room and its occupants with a considering eye. Her first task, of course, must be to choose an appropriate target—a target in keeping with the Saint's modus operandi. It was a pity Lady Mountheath had already been robbed twice, as she was the epitome of the perfect victim. Perhaps someone Lady Mountheath considered a good friend?

Recalling her earlier comment about the Duchess of Wickburn, Sarah looked for her hostess. As it happened, she was at that moment deep in conversation with Lady Mountheath herself, and indeed seemed on intimate terms with her. Sarah recalled the woman's supercilious nod when she had been introduced to her upon arriving at the ball, drawing a clear distinction between Sarah and the Mountheath daughters. Yes, she would do nicely.

Her gaze shifted then to the Duke of Wickburn and she hesitated. He seemed a pleasant-enough man, and had greeted her quite kindly. She would therefore try to take something that the duchess would miss more than the duke would. Jewelry, perhaps.

Nodding and smiling at any acquaintances she passed, Sarah slowly made her way toward the duchess, pondering how she might accomplish her aim without getting caught. She was almost near enough to eavesdrop on the duchess's conversation with Lady Mountheath when she was accosted by Sir Lawrence Winslow.

"Miss Killian," he exclaimed. "I am astonished to see you at liberty. Might I persuade you to relinquish it for my sake?"

Sarah managed a smile. "I fear I cannot, sir. Lady Mountheath has requested I not dance tonight."

"Not dance!" he exclaimed in evident horror.

"Why, that is to deprive the entire company of the pleasure of seeing you on the floor—not to mention depriving *me* of a favorite partner. I will speak with her at once, to intervene on your behalf."

"No, you must not, sir. She will think I asked you to do so, which she will see as disobedience on my part." She had already dissuaded more than one gentleman from attempting that gallantry by similar arguments, but Sir Lawrence, who loved to dance, proved more stubborn.

"Fear not, Miss Killian. I will make it quite clear that the request comes from myself alone. We cannot have the brightest jewel in Town sitting upon the sidelines!" He headed determinedly in Lady Mountheath's direction while Sarah followed more slowly.

"Lady Mountheath," Sir Lawrence exclaimed upon reaching his object, heedless of her ongoing conversation with the duchess. "I wish to beg a boon from you."

Both ladies turned to regard him with rather affronted surprise. "Yes?"

Sarah expected him to retreat at Lady Mountheath's icy tone, but he was undeterred. "I am simply perishing to partner Miss Killian in the next dance, but she tells me you have forbidden it. Pray grant her a dispensation, for my sake." He cast a longing glance Sarah's way that she doubted would help her case.

Nor did it. "I'm sorry, Sir Lawrence, but allowing my ward to make a spectacle of herself is to hurt her chances for employment. I am doing her a kindness by preventing that, I assure you."

"Indeed," the duchess agreed with a frown in

Sarah's direction. "From what Lady Mountheath tells me, the girl needs her spirits *dampened*, not excited by young bucks such as yourself."

"But—" he began, only to be interrupted by the Duke of Wickburn, who joined the group just then.

"What seems to be the fuss? Ah, Miss Killian! Come join us."

Completely unable to refuse the summons of a duke, Sarah came forward. "Yes, your grace," she said, sinking into her deepest curtsey. What had Sir Lawrence gotten her into?

"Your grace," said Sir Lawrence with a bow, "I was merely trying to convince Lady Mountheath to allow her young cousin to stand up with me."

"And there is some problem with that?" asked the duke.

Lady Mountheath repeated her explanation, the duchess adding her agreements, but the duke waved a hand before they had finished.

"Tut tut! A pretty gel like this would be wasted as a governess. She'd do much better to marry, in my opinion. Let her dance, Lady Mountheath, let her socialize, and you'll have her off your hands in no time, mark my words. I'll look to see her at the embassy reception tomorrow night, as well."

"Of course, your grace," said Lady Mountheath stiffly, inclining her head. The duchess raised one supercilious eyebrow but did not dare to contradict her husband.

Sir Lawrence beamed. "Well, that's just famous. Thank you, your grace. Miss Killian, shall we?"

Sarah accompanied him to a set just forming, glad of an excuse to avoid Lady Mountheath's eye. She would pay for this later, she knew, but for now she might as well enjoy herself.

This proved more difficult than she expected, however. Though Sir Lawrence and the other gentlemen in the set chatted pleasantly, she found her mind straying to her plans for the evening. Would a "Saintly" theft still be possible, or must she abandon her scheme entirely?

At the conclusion of the dance, numerous gentlemen came forward to claim her for others. She consented to dance with those she had regretfully rebuffed earlier, but kept the waltzes and one or two other dances free. To preserve a chance of carrying out her plan, she told herself, unconsciously scanning the assembly for Lord Peter Northrup.

"Miss Killian?" Lord Ribbleton broke into her thoughts.

"Oh! Yes, my lord, of course," she said, taking his arm for the next dance. "I fear I am still easily distracted at such large gatherings."

He smiled down at her, a suggestive smile she did not entirely like. "Such an innocent," he said. "I admire that in a woman."

Sarah smiled back, tempted to tell him she was no such thing, but the start of the cotillion prevented such an indiscretion. Out of the corner of her eye, she identified Lord Peter in the next set, partnering Fanny Mountheath. Lucy and Mr. Galloway were the next couple along.

Fortunately, Lord Ribbleton required little from her in the way of conversation, freeing her to consider how she might slip away from the ballroom to make her way upstairs, where the duchess was apt to keep her jewelry. Unless it were in a safe somewhere, in which case it would be beyond her skills to obtain.

"Is something wrong, Miss Killian?" Lord Ribbleton asked as the dance brought them back together.

Belatedly realizing she'd been frowning, Sarah quickly smoothed her brow. "No, I was simply focusing on my steps. I've had little practice dancing in public," she added truthfully.

Mr. Pottinger partnered her for the next dance, a reel. This time Lord Peter was in the same set, opposite a very pretty lady she hadn't yet met. A pang of something that might just possibly be jealousy assailed her. Lord Peter glanced her way, and she quickly looked up at Mr. Pottinger and laughed, though he was in the middle of an involved and rather boring account of a cricket match. A surreptitious glance showed Lord Peter frowning. Good.

The music began, and the couples moved down the dance, changing partners as they went. When she found herself opposite Lord Peter, she tried for an indifferent air.

"I thought you were not allowed to dance tonight," he murmured as he bowed and took her arm for the turn.

"Lady Mountheath relented, at Sir Lawrence's urging," she replied, wishing she had the courage to ask who his partner was—and why he had asked her to dance.

"Quite the hero, Sir Lawrence, to beard the dragon," he said, bowing again as the dance forced them to move on down the line. Had she imagined an edge to his voice?

His pretty partner was beside her now, and she tried to catch some of her conversation with Mr. Orrin in hopes of learning her name. She was rewarded by hearing him call her Lady Beatrice as he made his second bow, before the dance moved her out of earshot.

They came back to their original partners to conclude the dance, promenading in turn up and down the line. It was all Sarah could do to maintain her carefree smile as she watched Lord Peter and *Lady* Beatrice sashay along. How could she have been so foolish to think he might care for her—her, with no title, no lineage, no fortune—when women like that were available?

The next dance was one she'd kept free, so she took the opportunity to go to the ladies' withdrawing room with the vague plan of looking for a back exit that might allow her access to the upper floors unobserved. Several other ladies were there, so she made a business of repinning the sash of her gown, waiting for the room to empty.

"Wherever did you find such a scrumptious shade of blue, Lady Beatrice?"

At the name, Sarah turned her head sharply to see Lady Beatrice speaking with two others.

"Papa ordered it specially from Paris," the beauty replied with a shake of curls a darker gold than Sarah's. "It is the very latest French glacé silk. Madame Fanchot was quite in alt about making it up into a gown for me."

The others tittered and sighed as Lady Beatrice went on to catalogue what her lace had cost in addition to the silk. Sarah thoughtfully regarded the sapphires and diamonds dripping from the young

lady's throat, wondering if she need venture upstairs after all. But how—?

"I've snagged my necklace on the lace, however,
and cannot seem to free it. I should hate to injure the
lace, after the trouble Papa had getting it from
Bruges."

Almost without thought, Sarah stepped forward.
"May I be of assistance?"

"Why, thank you, Miss—?"

"Killian. Miss Sarah Killian. Lady Mountheath's
ward."

"Lady Beatrice Bagford." The beauty inclined her
head. "Lucy Mountheath mentioned you, I believe.
You are looking for a position as a lady's maid, or
some such?"

It was an undeniable insult, but Sarah clung to her
smile, mindful of her goal. "Something like that. I'm
certain I can untangle the chain from your lace."

Lady Beatrice turned her back to Sarah to permit
her to try, while the other ladies, after a quizzical
glance and some whispering among themselves,
headed back to the ballroom. It took Sarah only a
second or two to free the necklace, but as she could
scarcely steal it now unnoticed, she continued to
fumble with the lace edging.

"I almost have it," she said, opening the clasp of
the necklace and snagging both ends of the chain on
the lace. That should hold long enough for Lady
Beatrice to return to the ballroom, but not much
longer than that. "There."

To her relief, Lady Beatrice did not reach behind
her to check. "Thank you, Miss Killian. I expect you
will find a position soon enough." She swept out of
the room with Sarah close behind.

The dance was still in progress, which allowed Sarah to follow Lady Beatrice to the refreshment table, keeping a discreet distance. When the beauty paused to curtsey to the Duke and Duchess of Wickburn, the sabotaged necklace slipped free. Lady Beatrice rose, the necklace on the floor at her feet, apparently unnoticed for the moment. Sarah moved forward more quickly.

"Your graces, I wished to thank you again for welcoming me to your home, and for your intervention on my behalf with Lady Mountheath," Sarah said, curtseying deeply as she spoke—on the exact spot where Lady Beatrice had curtsied.

"The pleasure is ours, Miss Killian," the duke replied, taking her hand to help her rise. With her other hand, Sarah scooped up the necklace, hiding it in the folds of her skirt.

"Of course," agreed the duchess sourly.

"Too kind," Sarah murmured, keeping her head lowered as the duke and duchess moved on, her heart hammering wildly in her chest. She found the slit in her skirt and dropped the necklace into one of the large pockets she'd tied about her waist against just such an opportunity as this. Then, feeling far more wicked than she'd expected to, she made her own way to the refreshment table.

As the evening progressed, Sarah was guiltily aware of the illicit weight against her left hip. More than once she nearly gave in to guilt, only preventing herself from returning the necklace by reminding herself of the danger William would face as the Saint of Seven Dials.

Her severest test came near midnight, when Lady Beatrice suddenly realized her necklace was gone.

The news filtered around the room as people began to search for it, reaching Sarah as she finished a dance with Lord Peter—their first of the evening.

"Sapphires, she said," Lady Jeller told them as they left the floor. "You haven't seen it by chance, have you?"

Lord Peter shook his head, but Sarah felt as though a hand had gripped her throat, cutting off her air. Did she look as guilty as she felt? Lady Jeller seemed not to notice anything odd, however.

"Do keep an eye open, won't you? Apparently the center sapphire alone cost Lord Sherbourne nearly one hundred pounds. He had the necklace specially made for her last birthday."

Sarah knew her grip on Lord Peter's arm had tightened, and he now looked at her curiously. She had to say something—anything.

"One hundred pounds for a single stone," she gasped, staggered by the enormity of what she'd done. "I . . . I had no idea—"

Oddly, Lord Peter's expression became sympathetic. "For someone who has lived as you have, I'm sure the excesses of the wealthy *are* rather shocking. And Lady Beatrice possesses many such baubles, as her father is so indulgent."

Her moment of temptation passed, Lord Peter's words assuring her that Lady Beatrice could well afford the loss of one "bauble" that might save her brother's life. The next challenge would be to blame the Saint for the theft, and then to get the jewels to William in a way he would attribute to the legendary thief.

"Penny for your thoughts?" Lord Peter said as the silence lengthened between them.

She mustn't forget how perceptive he was, nor underestimate him in any way, she reminded herself. "I, ah, was trying to recall whether I had promised the next dance to anyone." The strains of a waltz began just then. "No, clearly not." She answered her own question with a smile.

"If Sir Lawrence was able to persuade Lady Mountheath to let you dance, perhaps I can persuade her to allow you to waltz," Lord Peter suggested.

"You forget, my lord, that I do not know how," she reminded him. "Besides, she was quite reluctant to grant the first dispensation, so I dare not try for another so soon. She only relented because the Duke of Wickburn took Sir Lawrence's part."

Lord Peter guided her toward the edge of the ballroom. "I am relieved to learn that Sir Lawrence does not merit full heroic honors. The prospect of such competition was quite unnerving."

Though his meaning seemed clear, she glanced up at him in surprise. "Competition? For what?" Belatedly, she realized she might sound as though she were soliciting compliments, but it was too late to recall the question.

"For your attention, of course," he replied, his expression warm. "I find myself quite jealous of it—though I should not say so, I suppose."

She thought she understood why. "You need not fear I will form . . . unrealistic expectations, my lord," she said quickly.

"Why unrealistic? It is not as though I can claim any exalted stature."

Confused, she dropped her gaze. "But of course you can, my lord. Is not your father a duke? Your lineage would appear to be impeccable." *Unlike mine*, she added silently.

He responded as though she had spoken the words aloud. "Just as wealth does not denote a person's worth, neither does the accident of birth. I can scarcely claim credit for who my parents happen to be."

"But Society gives you that credit just the same," she pointed out. "Can you truly claim to see no difference between someone highborn and baseborn?" Though she knew it was a bold question, she held his eye, needing quite desperately to know his honest answer.

His smile was wry and self-aware. "No, I suppose I can't claim that, though I can *wish* to claim it. The distinctions of class have been impressed upon me from birth, making them impossible to ignore completely."

"And why should you wish to be so different from your peers?" she asked, not wanting him to feel she condemned his perfectly natural attitude. "I also cannot escape that consciousness, nor, I suspect, can anyone born and raised in England. Pray remember that class distinctions have served our country well for centuries, giving our people a secure sense of place within a necessary hierarchy."

"Was that part of a lecture from one of your teachers?" he asked, one eyebrow raised. "I must compliment you on your powers of retention, if so."

In fact, it had come from a lesson she herself had taught. "I remembered it because it rang true for me," she said. "Much as I might wish my own place on that ladder were . . . different, I refuse to condemn the system which created the ladder."

The respect in his eyes was gratifying, even if his agreement was rather depressing. "Nor do I condemn it. Without distinctions of class, we would have anarchy and chaos, I doubt not. But that does not mean a person cannot attempt to better himself—or herself—through honest means."

She suddenly, painfully recalled the jewels concealed inside her dress. Surely he didn't suspect—? But no, there was nothing of suspicion in his expression, merely an enjoyment of their debate and an eagerness to convince her of his viewpoint.

"No, of course it does not mean that," she agreed, somewhat distractedly. His voice, his nearness, had almost made her forget what she still had to accomplish tonight, but now she realized her time was running short.

"There! That is the signal for supper," he said as the waltz ended. "May I persuade you to accompany me so that we may continue this most stimulating discussion?"

Supper! Her time was even shorter than she'd realized. At the Plumfield ball, the Mountheaths had left soon after supper. "I would like that," she said, "but first I need to, ah, visit the necessary."

"Of course." His dark blue eyes sparkled with something that might have been amusement. Or . . . pleasure?

No matter. "I will return in a moment," she said, knowing it would likely be longer, if all went well.

She made her way back to the ladies' withdrawing room, and was relieved to find it deserted. She desperately needed this chance to think, to figure out her best course of action.

Earlier that evening, she had carefully created a

few "Saint" cards, cutting heavy paper into appropriately sized rectangles with her sewing scissors
and drawing a seven and a halo on each one with
black and gold ink she had borrowed from Lord
Mountheath's study. But how to use them now? She
could scarcely slip one down the back of Lady Beatrice's dress!

No, she would have to attempt her original plan.
Quickly, before anyone could enter and see her, she
explored the room. Yes, here was a back entrance,
doubtless for the use of the maids who emptied the
chamber pots. The narrow door opened onto a
dimly lit passage with a staircase. Slipping through
it, Sarah crept quietly up the stairs.

The family's chambers would likely be on the
floor above the ballroom, so at the top of the first
flight she tiptoed down another narrow passage to
listen at the door there. Silence. Stealthily, she
pushed the door open to find herself at one end of a
wide, well-lit hallway with doors on either side.

Which chamber would belong to the duchess?
Probably one of the front rooms, she decided, heading forward. But just as she reached for the handle of
the right-hand door, she heard steps behind her.
Someone was coming up the servants' staircase!

Quickly, her heart in her throat, she whisked
through the door, thanking heaven that it was not
locked, and closed it softly behind her. The steps in
the hallway came nearer, and she glanced wildly
about, looking for a hiding place in case the maid
came into this room.

It appeared she had guessed correctly, as the fur-
nishings she could see by the light of a small oil
lamp were both exquisite and feminine. Her glance

fell on the long draperies by the front window and almost without thought she scurried across the room to slip behind them, feeling as though she were ten years old again.

She had scarcely concealed herself before the door opened. There were sounds of footsteps, then a scrape and a crackle. Whoever it was must be lighting the fire in the grate, so that a cheery blaze would greet the duchess when she retired. More sounds indicated water being poured into a ewer, then some soft rustling. Sarah felt an ominous tickling in her nose, but dared not move. She held her breath, sternly willing herself not to sneeze.

Finally, after an agonizing eternity, she heard the door open and close again. An instant later, she sneezed. Horrified, she peeked from the draperies and found to her relief that the maid had indeed left. The bed was turned down, a lacy nightrail laid across the silken counterpane.

The added glow of the newly lit fire revealed the most opulent room she'd ever seen. Why, the bedstead alone must have cost hundreds of pounds, with all of its rich carving! She had no time for ogling, however.

If the duchess kept any jewelry in her chamber, it would likely be on or in her dressing table, Sarah decided. A quick search of that item revealed a pair of diamond earrings—small, but undoubtedly valuable. The truly expensive jewels would no doubt be in a safe, but after hearing what Lady Beatrice's necklace was worth, she didn't have the courage to take anything so valuable again—at least, not yet.

She checked the other drawers of the table and found a dozen gold guineas. *You can do this*, she told

herself. Quickly, before she could reconsider, she put
the earrings and guineas into the pocket with Lady
Beatrice's necklace. She then placed one of the cards
she'd made in the center of the dressing table.

After listening at the chamber door and hearing
nothing, Sarah quietly exited the room and retraced
her path, blessing her luck when she met no servants
along the way. Her breathing and heart rate began to
return to normal as she let herself back into the
ladies' withdrawing room and stepped around the
screen.

Only to find herself face to face with Lady Mountheath.

"So! You have found yet another way to embarrass me," she said accusingly.

Chapter 8

Peter was growing increasingly worried. Sarah had not appeared ill when she'd gone to the necessary, but after nearly half an hour he began to fear something terrible had befallen her. Still, it had probably been unwise to say anything about her absence to Lady Mountheath, though the woman *had* asked.

Unable to sit idly any longer, he excused himself to the other couples at the table and headed in the direction of the ladies' withdrawing room, though he had no idea what he would do when he reached it. He was spared that decision, however, when he saw Sarah emerging just behind a visibly angry Lady Mountheath.

"Miss Killian," he exclaimed, hurrying forward,

in hopes of averting further scolding. "I am delighted to see you are well."

Even as he spoke, however, he realized it was not so. Sarah was paper white and shaking, her eyes glistening with unshed tears. "Can I offer you any sort of assistance?" he asked with renewed concern.

Lady Mountheath responded before Sarah could—not that Sarah appeared equal to speech in any case. "Miss Killian is in need of a reminder about manners, which I feel more equipped to provide her than you are, my lord," she said coldly. "She had no business making an *assignation* to meet you for supper, then disappearing so that the whole world would learn of it. My poor Lucy is quite mortified, I assure you."

Unpleasant as Lady Mountheath could be, this instance went beyond the pale. "My lady, it seems clear to me that Miss Killian is unwell, which no doubt accounts for her briefly retiring from the company. And I can assure you there was no assignation. We were talking when the supper dance ended, so I invited her to join my table—that is all."

"As you had promised that dance to my daughter, I cannot so easily acquit Miss Killian—or you, my lord—of wrongdoing." Lady Mountheath's turban quivered with the intensity of her indignation.

"Promised—!" He had done no such thing, though he recalled Lucy Mountheath saying something about another—unspecified—dance later. He had been careful not to commit, however. "I fear your daughter may have been under a misapprehension, my lady," he said carefully, with another glance at Sarah. Her color was beginning to return, to his relief.

"Do you dare suggest my daughter would engage

in a falsehood about such a thing, my lord? I assure you, it is not in her nature."

He swallowed, realizing that Lady Mountheath's anger would be turned on Sarah later. He needed to defuse it somehow. "Of course not, my lady! I merely meant that Miss Lucy must have misunderstood our last conversation. I will of course apologize for giving her the impression I meant to dance the waltz with her. I am certain the fault is entirely mine."

Lady Mountheath's expression softened, but only marginally. "Yes, I think you had better do that. It pains me dreadfully to see her so distraught."

Again Peter glanced at Sarah, who was still looking apprehensive. "Suppose I take Miss Killian in to supper, then speak to Miss Mountheath while she fills a plate?" he suggested, determined to get Sarah away from this vindictive harpy.

"No, I think not," Lady Mountheath said, turning a gimlet eye on her ward. "I believe Miss Killian will be better served by going directly to our carriage and waiting there until we leave. It will keep her from getting into further trouble."

"Without supper?" Peter could not keep the outrage from his voice.

For the first time, Sarah spoke, though she did not quite meet his eye. "Thank you for your concern, my lord, but I find myself quite without appetite just now."

Though Peter did not believe it, he could scarcely contradict her. "If you are sure—"

"She is not your concern, my lord," Lady Mountheath informed him in no uncertain terms.

"Go find Lucy, do. I'll see Miss Killian escorted to our carriage."

"Very well, my lady." He tried again to catch Sarah's eye, to divine what was wrong and to provide her with some sort of reassurance, but she still avoided his gaze. To linger further would only anger Lady Mountheath again, so with one last glance over his shoulder, he returned to the supper room.

Clearly he had underestimated the abuse Sarah suffered at the hands of the Mountheaths. He must keep a closer eye on her. The moment he had proof of that abuse, he would confront Lady Mountheath and remove Sarah from her care—one way or another. It was his duty as a gentleman.

Sarah settled into the darkened interior of the Mountheath carriage with profound relief, despite her empty stomach.

She had been absolutely certain, when Lady Mountheath had confronted her in the ladies' withdrawing room, that her thefts had been discovered, that she would be hauled off to prison on the spot. Only when Lord Peter had inadvertently elicited an explanation for Lady Mountheath's wrath had she realized she was safe—from prison, at any rate.

In fact, she realized, she had succeeded beyond her wildest expectations tonight, and was now free of the house, free of the chance of being caught. Relief bubbled up into euphoria, but only for a moment.

The first step, the hardest step, was behind her. She still had to manage the next, getting the jewels to William without casting suspicion on either of them. The guineas she would keep against the possibility of Lady Mountheath turning her into the street, as she so often threatened to do.

She dared not venture into Seven Dials with the jewels on her. Her last visit had nearly ended in disaster because she had underestimated how conspicuous she would be. The inhabitants knew each other well enough that they would spot a stranger in their midst at once, however well she disguised herself.

She could send word to William to meet her, but that didn't solve the problem of convincing him that the Saint, not Sarah, had stolen the jewels. Considering how protective her little brother had been the other night, it was vital he not suspect the truth.

No, she must send the jewels to him by way of someone else, with a note saying they'd come from the Saint. By the time the Mountheaths returned to their carriage more than an hour later, she had what she felt sure would be a workable plan.

Sarah presented herself at Lady Winslow's house at precisely ten o'clock the next morning, armed with her credentials and references. She felt she looked every inch a governess in the high-necked gray gown, her hair scraped into a tight, unbecoming bun. As the door was opened by a starchy housekeeper, she hoped it would be enough. Given Lady Mountheath's continued animosity, any employment would be preferable to another day in that house.

"Lady Winslow awaits you in the drawing room," the housekeeper informed her, leading the way.

Lady Winslow rose with a smile as Sarah entered the room, taking in her appearance with shrewd gray eyes.

The smile dimmed slightly. "Miss Killian? Lady Mountheath informs me that you have been trained to perform the duties of governess?"

"Yes, my lady." Sarah kept her voice low and meek. "I am qualified to teach arithmetic, grammar, French, geography, history, drawing and music." She proffered the letter Miss Pritchard had reluctantly given her, detailing her marks as a student and experience as a teacher.

After reading it through, Lady Winslow nodded. "This appears acceptable. Lady Mountheath tells me this will be your first post as governess and that therefore you will be willing to work for six pounds per annum."

Sarah blinked, as this was but half the usual wage for a governess, though almost twice what she'd been paid at Miss Pritchard's. Nor had she agreed to any such thing. "My . . . my lady?" she said uncertainly, wondering if she were expected to bargain for her wages.

Lady Winslow raised an eyebrow, but at that moment a bustle was heard in the hall, and a moment later Sir Lawrence advanced into the room. Alarmed, Sarah was careful not to meet his eye.

"Give you good morning, Mother, but I see that you are occupied. I'll just—Miss Killian?" He stared at Sarah in disbelief. "What do you here, in that getup? Never say *you're* to be Claudia's new governess? Is that the employment you mentioned last night? How perfectly famous!"

Sarah could hardly refuse to look at him now, though she tried to convey with her expression that he was doing her cause no good. "It's nice to see you again, Sir Lawrence," she said coolly.

Undeterred, he walked over and seized one of her hands. "It will be delightful having you here," he rambled on, while Sarah glanced nervously at Lady Winslow's gathering frown. "When you're not occupied teaching Claudia, I can show you the sights. Won't that be—"

His mother finally cut him off. "Lawrence! You will please leave us alone. I have not yet hired Miss Killian."

"Oh! Oh, certainly. A thousand apologies." Then, turning back to Sarah, he said in a loud whisper, "We'll talk later."

Lady Winslow waited until his boots were heard ascending the stairs, then turned back to Sarah. "Lady Mountheath did not mention that you had been in company—or that you had met my son."

"She was, ah, kind enough to allow me to accompany her daughters to a few of the entertainments they have attended since my arrival in Town," Sarah said carefully. "I believe she felt exposure to the highest strata of Society would give me experience valuable in a governess."

She knew Lady Mountheath had considered no such benefit, but hoped the explanation might allay Lady Winslow's obvious concern. There was no knowing when another chance at employment might present itself, and she had no desire to keep stealing.

"I see," said Lady Winslow after a pause. "Commendable of her, no doubt, but I fear I do not agree. In my experience, tasting a higher society than a person's own sphere tends to make that person discontented with her lot. I'd as soon not employ a governess for my daughter who is continually on the lookout to better her position—perhaps inappropriately."

Sarah's cheeks burned at the implication, but she bit back the retort that sprang to her lips. "I assure you, my lady, that should you engage me to teach your daughter, I would have only her interests at heart." Even as she said it, she knew it was not true. Her brother's interests must come first with her, always.

Though Lady Winslow's mouth firmed to a prim line, her eyes held what appeared to be genuine sympathy. "I'm sorry, my dear. Knowing what I do of the Mountheaths, I have no doubt you are eager for a position, but I must think of my daughter first—and my son. I believe you would be better suited elsewhere." She rose, signaling the end of the interview.

Pride prevented Sarah from making another attempt to change Lady Winslow's mind. Pride, and the reluctant realization that she was probably right.

"Thank you, my lady, for agreeing to see me," she said, rising. "I hope you will find someone perfectly suited to both your daughter and your household."

"And thank you for understanding, Miss Killian. Please believe that I wish you all the best."

Sarah did believe her, but it did her little good. Lady Mountheath would surely blame her for failing to secure the position, using it as an excuse to be even nastier to her.

On leaving the Winslow house, Sarah realized she had at least a half hour before she would be expected back—just enough time to implement her plan for getting last night's valuables to William. She'd brought them along in hopes that such an opportunity might occur.

Holding tightly to her plain leather reticule with its precious contents, she turned left instead of right, heading for the intersection where she'd first met the young crossing sweeper, Paddy, who had directed her to Lord Peter's house.

To her relief, the lad was again there. As she watched, he swept the dust and debris from before an elegantly dressed couple, then doffed his cap as they rewarded him with a penny. She waited until he was alone, then cautiously approached him.

"Paddy?" she said. "Do you remember me?"

A wide grin split the boy's face. "Oh, aye, miss! I ain't like to forget a face like yours. Did you find your friend, that Flute fellow?"

"I did, thanks to you. I wished to reward you, as I promised—and to ask another favor of you."

The lad looked down at his battered shoes, his ears reddening. "Ain't no need for no reward, miss. I be glad to do it, and anythin' else you might need."

"You're a generous lad, Paddy," Sarah told him. "But I insist, particularly since this favor is a bit more involved."

He glanced up eagerly. "I'll do it, miss. Is it dangerous, like?"

"Not dangerous," she said, hiding a smile, "but very important. I need you to deliver something to my friend Flute, through Renny, but it's vital that you not tell him where it came from."

"Aye, miss, that's easy enough." He nodded, his eyes shining. "I see Renny regular-like anyway. Not a bit o' trouble to drop 'round and give him—what is it I'm to give him?"

Sarah pulled the small packet from her reticule—the jewels, securely wrapped in brown paper, a carefully worded letter to Flute tucked inside. "Just this little package. It's—something he needs."

He put it into his pocket, nodding again. "I'll take it to Renny now. And mum's the word on where I got it."

"You needn't leave your job here at once, as long as you can get it to him sometime today," she said. "Oh, and here's the reward I promised." Reaching back into her reticule, she extracted one of the gold guineas she'd taken from the Duchess of Wickburn's chamber last night.

Paddy's eyes widened. "'Cor, miss, you don't mean to give me all that, do you?"

In truth, she had little choice, as these were the only coins she possessed, but she hoped the amount would ensure that he would do as she asked rather than open the package himself.

"You've done, and are doing me, a great service, Paddy," she said, "and I may need your help again in the future. I'm also hoping this will remind you how important it is that you keep my secret, no matter how curious Renny might be."

He clutched the guinea tightly, as though fearing it might vanish, and looked up at her adoringly. "Anything you need, miss, ever, you just ask," he said. "Paddy'll be here to do your bidding."

"Thank you, Paddy. And bless you." Then, feeling she'd done all she could for the moment, she reluctantly turned her steps toward Berkley Square.

Lady Mountheath took Sarah's news quite as

poorly as expected. "I doubt not you intentionally botched the interview," she exclaimed angrily, her daughters looking on in frowning agreement. "Put on airs, did you? Or made unreasonable demands as to salary?"

"I assure you I did not, my lady. It was learning that I had been in company that appeared to decide Lady Winslow against employing me—as you predicted," Sarah confessed, hoping satisfaction at being right might mute Lady Mountheath's anger.

"And how, pray tell, did she learn of that? For I know she attended none of the entertainments we did. She rarely goes out. I see how it is, missie—you do not wish to leave your easy existence here for honest work."

Though she knew it would do no good, Sarah felt obliged to defend herself. "I assure you, I told her nothing about it, for I am indeed quite eager to obtain a position." *Any position, if it will get me away from you*, she added silently. "It was her son, Sir Lawrence, who brought it to her notice."

Lady Mountheath snorted. "Clearly I have been far too indulgent from the first, allowing you to meet so many of your betters. I should have guessed that your forwardness would damage your chances of respectable employment."

Sarah stared. "My forwardness?"

"Not another word, miss. You will go to your room at once, and remain there until we leave for the embassy reception this evening—the *last* event you will attend with us. Meanwhile, I'll see that Grimble finds plenty to keep you busy."

Biting back a retort, Sarah took a step toward the staircase.

"No, use the back stairs. I am expecting callers at any moment, and they mustn't see you dressed like that."

In truth, Sarah was more amused than irritated by Lady Mountheath's hypocrisy, her spirits still buoyed by the certainty that William would soon be abandoning his risky plan. As she mounted the stairs, however, her stomach growled. She would wait a bit, then creep down to the kitchen for something to eat—just as she used to do at school.

Peter prepared to call at the Mountheath house with mingled anticipation and dread. He had successfully smoothed Lucy Mountheath's ruffled feathers last night, but at what he feared was a terrible cost. She was more convinced than ever that he meant to pay his addresses to her, despite his diplomatic attempts to persuade her otherwise.

However, reluctance to face the simpering Miss Mountheath could not overshadow his eagerness to see Sarah again, and to assure himself that she suffered no lingering ill effects from whatever had ailed her last night.

"No, never mind the mathematical," he said distractedly to Holmes, who was working Peter's cravat into an intricate arrangement. "It takes too long. Just tie it up any old way."

Though clearly startled, his valet nodded. "As you say, my lord." Deftly, he knotted the neckcloth into a simpler—but still elegant—design. "Will that do?"

Peter did not even glance into the pier glass. "It's fine. I'll return before dinnertime."

Walking the short distance to Berkley Square, Peter wondered at the change in himself. Not since returning to England after the fall of Paris had he neglected any detail of dress. Now such frippery seemed, well, frivolous.

"You are in good time today, my lord." Lady Mountheath greeted him complaisantly when he was announced. "In fact, you are the first caller to arrive. Come, sit by Lucy, do."

Lucy Mountheath smirked up at him with a complaisance matching her mother's. "Good day, my lord. I knew you would not disappoint me again." This was said with a significant look at her sister, who tittered obediently. Sarah was not in evidence.

"I hope I find all of you well today," Peter said with a bow before seating himself in the indicated chair. "Miss Killian's indisposition was not contagious?"

"Indisposition?" Fanny echoed.

Lady Mountheath overrode her. "No, it was merely something she ate," she said, in defiance of the fact she'd sent Sarah out to the carriage before supper last night. "I recommended she remain in her room today, to avoid the possibility of a relapse."

How convenient, thought Peter sourly, disappointment settling like a stone in his stomach. "Then she will not be attending the embassy reception tonight?"

"She will be there," his hostess replied with a frown that told him he was showing far too much interest in her ward. "The Duke of Wickburn particularly requested her presence. He seems to feel I would be better served to marry her off than find her employment—assuming anyone will have someone of her background."

Peter burned to ask about that background, but he didn't dare risk alienating the Mountheath ladies by more questions about Sarah—not yet. "It would be a more . . . permanent solution, I suppose," he agreed with careful blandness.

Clearly weary of talk about her cousin, Lucy Mountheath claimed his attention then with a rendition of how she and Fanny had mortified Miss Peterson last night by revealing her father's dabbling in trade the year before.

"She had no suspicion of what we were going to say," she said with a spiteful laugh. "Mr. Galloway had been paying her an excessive amount of attention until he learned where her fortune originated. But then she seemed to lose her charm for him—did she not, Fanny?"

Peter let the sisters' chatter flow over him, paying only enough attention to nod in appropriate places. He was finding them more distasteful than ever, but couldn't bring himself to leave while Sarah was imprisoned upstairs. Surely there must be some way he could help her.

Other callers were announced, allowing him to withdraw further from the conversation. His attention was caught, however, by Mr. Pottinger's inquiry after Sarah. Though he received the same response Peter had, he was not so willing to drop the subject.

"Might I send word up to her, my lady? She must be having a dreary time of it, stuck in her room all day. Perhaps I could send a few books over this afternoon, to help her while away the time."

"You are too kind, Mr. Pottinger," Lady Mountheath said coldly. "But I assure you that Miss Killian has plenty to occupy her. She has been accustomed to work, you see, so I have made certain she is given some task to do each day."

Mr. Pottinger's courage was not equal to Lady Mountheath's quelling glance. "I . . . I see. That is, er, thoughtful of you, my lady."

Peter listened in growing indignation, his suspicions again confirmed. "Surely you are careful not to weary her, my lady, when she is already feeling unwell?" he could not help asking.

Lady Mountheath's lips thinned. "Of course. Her health is in no danger, I assure you."

Fearing that if he remained longer he might be driven to outright rudeness, Peter rose. "I see I have exceeded my quarter hour. I give you good day my lady, Miss Mountheath, Miss Fanny."

He bowed and retreated from the parlor with a vague plan of asking the butler to take a message up to Sarah, but the hall below was empty at the moment. He cast a glance toward the back of the house, then blinked. Sarah herself was peering through the servants' door at the far end of the hall.

"Miss Killian?" he whispered.

She blinked, just as he had, then put a finger to her lips. He started toward her, then paused to listen at the panels of a door midway down the hall.

"Quickly—in here," he whispered, opening the door. The room proved to be a library, though thin of books, and deserted.

"I don't dare stay more than a moment," she said softly as they retreated into the room. "Lady Mountheath thinks me locked in my room in the attics."

"Then she does lock you in your room?" He felt

the stirrings of the strongest anger he'd felt in some time.

She shrugged, a smile playing about her lips. "I have the means to escape when necessary." Reaching inside her drab gray gown, she pulled out a key. "I pilfered this from another room my second day here."

"Very resourceful," he said with a quiet chuckle. "But why does she wish to keep you prisoner? Why today?"

Now Sarah sighed, a sound that struck him, most inappropriately, as erotic. "Lady Mountheath has decided that she erred in allowing me into company in the first place, and vows not to repeat her error after tonight."

"But why?" he asked. "Surely not for the reason she gave last night, that it would hurt your chances of employment?"

"In fact, it appears she was quite right. Lady Winslow refused me a position upon learning I had been out in Society. As you may imagine, Lady Mountheath is quite eager to dispense with her charity on my behalf—almost as eager as I am for her to do so." She smiled as she spoke, but Peter was able to detect the anxiety beneath.

"I am certain other options will present themselves," he said carefully, powerfully tempted to offer her a permanent solution.

"No doubt," she agreed lightly. "Though the option Lady Winslow feared is not one I could ever accept."

At his questioning look, she continued, "Sir Lawrence seemed far too pleased at the prospect of my teaching his sister for his mother's peace of mind."

Peter was startled by the red rage that suddenly threatened to obscure his very sight—a rage he hadn't felt since the battlefield. "Did Sir Lawrence make you an improper offer?" he grated through his teeth, striving to bring the anger he'd thought never to feel again under control.

She glanced up at him in surprise. "No, of course not. But I believe it is what his mother feared—though no doubt she would disapprove of a proper offer even more strongly." This was said with a wry self-awareness that nearly undid him in a completely different way.

"Please, Miss Killian, do not underestimate yourself, even in jest," he said earnestly. "You are worthy of a far more exalted position than governess—or even Sir Lawrence's wife."

She regarded him quizzically. "How can you say so, my lord? You know nothing of my antecedants."

"I consider myself an excellent judge of character," he said, ignoring the fact that she was right. "Will you tell me about your parents?" The more he knew, the better able he would be to help her. "How old were you when they died?"

For a long moment he thought she would not answer, but then she said, "My father's name was Kenneth Killian, originally from Ireland. My mother's name was Mary—Mary Severn. According to Lady Mountheath, my father was her tutor, and she eloped with him, after which her father cast her off. I was but nine when they died, so they never told me such details."

"Understandable," he said, filing away the name Severn. Orphaned at nine, unacknowledged by her mother's family—how had she lived? What sorts of hardships had she endured? His heart ached to imagine, but he still trod cautiously.

"And you went to school, what—three years later? How did you live in the interim?"

When she did not answer, he glanced down to find her color again high. "I, ah . . . You remember Mrs. Hounslow, my lord, that first time we met, on the street? She is a most charitable woman, a member of the Bettering Society, and she helped us—me—enormously."

"I see." Perhaps he would have a talk with this Mrs. Hounslow. She might be able to fill in a few blanks about Sarah's background—and Sarah's mysterious brother. "So she took you in, then arranged for your schooling?"

Sarah nodded, though he noticed she did not meet his eye. Recalling their conversation at the Plumfield ball—the one about her fictitious "friend," Peter thought he understood why. She had known of Mr. Twitchell's gang of thieves, perhaps even been connected with them in some way. He'd meant it when he'd said a child of that age could not be held accountable, but clearly she saw things differently.

"And what is your relationship to the Mountheaths?" he asked then, ready to fit the last piece into the puzzle.

Again she hesitated, then gave him a wry smile. "Lady Mountheath has asked me not to say, but I don't much care now. My mother was her cousin—the black sheep of the family, of course."

"And so she mistreats you, resenting her enforced

charity." The anger began to stir again. "Are you quite well today? Did you ever get anything to eat last night?"

She shook her head, though she was still smiling. "I can't claim to like the Mountheaths, but this is the grandest place I've ever lived, and it's not as though they beat me. As for food, that is why I crept downstairs. The kitchens, as at school, are well stocked and unguarded. But please, my lord, you should go. It would not do for us to be found here."

Peter admired her courage under adversity more than ever, but only said, "Very well. I will look to see you tonight at the embassy reception. Goodbye, my—" He turned away before he could say more than was wise and took a step toward the door.

Then, just as quickly, he turned back and closed the distance between them. Without a word, he took her in his arms and kissed her, quite thoroughly. She melted against him for a moment, returning his kiss with sudden passion of her own, but then she stiffened. He released her at once, of course, though he could not—quite—regret his action.

"Footsteps," she hissed, and she was right. A measured tread was heard outside the library, and then up the stairs. Another visitor must be arriving.

Peter stood motionless, his hand still on her shoulder, willing to acquiescence the desire that threatened to overset his common sense. "My apologies again," he murmured as the footsteps receded. "Clearly it is not safe for me to be alone with you."

Though she blushed charmingly, her expression was by no means condemning. "So it would seem, my lord. And this after you already put me on my guard. I clearly did not take your warning to heart as I ought."

"Let this be a sterner lesson to you, then," he said with mock seriousness. "Never relax your guard with a gentleman—any gentleman. We're a feckless lot, and not to be trusted."

"So I perceive." A smile twitched the corners of her mouth. "And now, my lord, you really must go."

Chapter 9

Sarah smiled to herself as she listened at the library door until the front door opened and closed. For the first time since her parents had died, she felt cared for, protected. Lord Peter was aptly named, she reflected, for he was surely her own rock, the one she could turn to if she found herself in real trouble.

Cautiously, she emerged from the library and floated toward the servants' stairs again, her thoughts happily occupied. Since that first quick kiss on the street yesterday, Lord Peter had dominated her thoughts—and her dreams last night—even though she had tried to tell herself the kiss meant nothing.

Now, however, she knew it had been a mere taste of the real thing. What she—they?—had experienced just now had been something more, something profound. It had seemed to promise greater delights to come. She both longed for and dreaded her dreams tonight, knowing that her imagination would tantalize her with wicked images of what those delights might be.

Humming softly to herself, she pushed open the servants' door and nearly bumped into Lord Mountheath, who waited there, a broad smile on his thick lips.

"Well, well, Miss Killian. I see you are feeling much more the thing. Let me congratulate you on your recovery."

Before she knew what he was about, he seized her by the shoulders and planted a wet kiss on her mouth. She shrank away from him, but he followed her until he had her trapped against the wall, one arm on either side of her.

"Come, now, don't be so shy. I can do you a great deal of good, you know, if you will only be nice to me." He brought his face close to hers again.

Frantically, Sarah shook her head, pushing against his chest with both hands. "Please do not, my lord!"

"No? Why not? You may find it more pleasurable than you imagine," he whispered.

"I . . . I shall scream," she warned him, both angered and sickened that the lovely memory of Lord Peter's kiss was now sullied by the disgusting sequel of Lord Mountheath's.

To her surprise, he chuckled. "If you do, my dear, I will tell my wife that you have been entertaining gentlemen callers in the library and then tried to entice me—and that you only screamed when I refused to match whatever sum young Northrup offered you. Who do you suppose she will believe?"

Sarah stared at him, her heart hammering with fright as she realized he was right. She had not thought him so vile as this. His expression, however, was not angry, but merely lustful—and weak. She opened her mouth to plead with him again, when footsteps sounded on the kitchen stairs.

Abruptly, he straightened, shot her a warning glance, then disappeared through the door to the front hall without another word. Sarah took a deep breath and continued to the kitchen, mustering a shaky smile when she passed the scullery maid who had unwittingly rescued her.

Luxurious though it might be, this house was no longer a safe haven. She *must* leave it soon—one way or another.

Peter walked briskly, resisting the urge to go back and make sure that his tryst with Sarah had not been discovered, that she would suffer no additional punishment because of the brief kiss they had just shared.

Brief, but not insignificant, he thought, turning his face up to the thin midday sunshine. Far from it, in fact. The first time he'd kissed Sarah it had been an impulse, a weakness. This time it had been a decision and a question—one she had answered, though he wasn't certain she realized it.

He knew now that she felt something for him, that the bond between them was real. He also knew that he could not ignore it, or convince himself that he only wished to help her out of some high-minded sense of duty. No, unwise as it might be, he was well on his way to being head over heels in love with Sarah.

Harry was waiting for him when he returned to Grosvenor Street. "Glad you're back, Pete!" he exclaimed before Peter could so much as take off his hat. "This came while you were out, and you'll want to deal with it at once." He held out a small, sealed note.

Brought back to earth against his will, Peter broke the seal and scanned it. Nothing terribly urgent, actually—just a note from his father's man of business saying his quarterly allowance was available at his convenience.

"You know, I find myself a bit short of funds at the moment," Harry said with studied casualness. "Wondered if you might see your way clear to a small loan, just until my Army check comes, don't you know."

With a piercing glance at his friend, Peter turned the note over and checked the seal he'd just broken. "You perfected certain skills far too well in Vienna, I perceive. Didn't think you'd use them to read the correspondence of friends, however."

"Nor do I," said Harry, clearly affronted. "Knew your quarterly was due, that's all, and thought that might be notice of it. Seen the duke's footmen deliver 'em before, you know."

"Sorry, Harry. I should have known better." Sarah must be unsettling his wits. He knew full well that for all his faults, Harry was fiercely loyal to his friends, and honorable where it counted.

"Then you'll float me that loan? Dear Pater has cut off my funds—for my own good, of course," he concluded in his father's sententious voice.

"Really, though, Harry, he's right. You really must

learn to live within your means. A major's half-pay isn't much, but as you're paying precious little rent for those lodgings of yours, you should be able to survive, and even save a bit." He knew he sounded pedantic, but he also meant every word. He was worried about his friend.

Not that Harry appreciated it. "Fine one you are to talk, with your colonel's half-pay *and* your quarterly allowance. Not to mention that tidy bonus you invested. Are you sure there's nothing left of the bit I gave you of mine to invest?"

Peter shook his head, quelling a pang of guilt as he did so. "You asked for it back six months after you gave it to me, remember? Pity, for I'd have likely doubled it for you by now."

"Yes, well, I never expected to live long enough to need it," Harry said with a grin. "It'd be a real tragedy to die with money in the bank, after all."

"A worse tragedy to live in poverty and die alone, I should think. Well, I'm off. I'll advance you five pounds when I return. You'll pay it back when you get your check?"

"Of course!" Harry's shocked expression fooled Peter not at all. "How can you ask?"

It was but a moment's walk to the Duke of Marland's house on Grosvenor Square, where Peter was shown into Mr. Fairley's office at once. "Your quarterly," said the duke's man of business, pushing an envelope across his desk as Peter seated himself. "And now I suppose you want those figures you requested last quarter?"

Peter nodded. "My father knows nothing of this?"

Mr. Fairley primmed his thin, wrinkled lips. "My

first loyalty is to the duke, but as your private business interests in no way concern his, you need not fear I will betray your confidence, even should he ask. Which he has not."

"I apologize. Where do I stand as of this month?"

Now Mr. Fairley's lips formed something a generous person might call a smile. "Quite nicely, my lord. Quite nicely indeed. See for yourself." He passed a ledger sheet across the desk.

Peter scanned it, then gave a low whistle when he reached the figure at the bottom. He'd known his investments were doing well, but hadn't realized just how well. "At this rate, I'll be worth half as much as my father in another two or three years."

"Indeed. Your suggestions have performed remarkably well. Still, you should consider putting a portion into land, which is far safer."

"I'll give it some thought." Peter handed the ledger sheet back. "Now, what of Mr. Thatcher's account?"

"I have it here as well." Mr. Fairley handed Peter another sheet, detailing the progress of the investments he'd made on Harry's behalf. Though the total didn't come close to Peter's own, as he'd been forced to give the principal back to Harry only six months after investing, it was still a tidy sum.

Peter nodded, satisfied, then counted out half of the allowance he'd just been given. "Thank you, Mr. Fairley. Please add this to my own investments, as well as five pounds from Mr. Thatcher's account." Harry need not know he was borrowing from himself rather than Peter—not yet.

Walking back to Marcus's house, Peter wondered

whether he was helping or hurting his friend by keeping Harry's small fortune a secret. If Harry knew, Peter had no doubt he'd gamble and drink it all away in a month's time. But was it really Peter's place to guard it until the day Harry developed a sense of responsibility? Suppose that day never came?

He'd give it a while longer, he decided. Harry couldn't go on as he was indefinitely.

As for Peter's own fortune, he could no longer call it a small one. He'd known those West Indies shipping concerns would yield good returns, but they had exceeded his wildest expectations.

More good news awaited him on his return.

"My inquiries have finally borne fruit," Holmes informed him the moment he reached his chamber. "I would have told you sooner, but you went out again too quickly."

"Indeed! Did those inquiries lead you to a Mary Severn?" Peter asked.

Holmes bowed. "As usual, you are ahead of me, my lord. A Kenneth Killian wed a Miss Mary Severn in '95. It was an elopement, which the bride's father refused to recognize."

"Thus explaining why he never sent the information to *Debrett's*," Peter concluded. "And this father, he is the connection to the Mountheaths?"

"He was indeed, my lord. Baron Wragby of Littleport, Cambridgeshire, recently deceased, brother to Lady Mountheath's mother, who was born Agnes Severn."

Now this was news! "A baron? Are you certain?"

"Quite certain, my lord. I was able to discover little else about him, however, for he was reclusive and ill-natured even before he fell sick, judging by one or two written references."

"Thank you, Holmes. That is extremely useful information."

The valet bowed again and left him, but Peter scarcely noticed, for this revelation had spurred ideas thick and fast. Sarah was indeed a member of his class, granddaughter to a peer, no matter who her father was—though from what she had said earlier, he was not certain she realized that.

In fact, over the past hour, the obstacles separating them seemed to have magically melted away. Peter had no need to consider fortune in a wife. He could rescue her from the Mountheaths, and from a future life of drudgery as a governess. She could live like a duchess—as she deserved.

The pleasant fantasy wavered. To do that, he would have to reveal his fortune, and to more than just Sarah. He would have to pick his way carefully if he was to avoid wounding Sarah's pride and alienating his friends. Somehow, though, he was determined to make that fantasy a reality.

In fact, if the opportunity presented itself, he might well make her an offer this very night.

Flute unwrapped the heavy parcel and stared at the glittering booty within, giving out a low whistle. "Who did you say gave you this, Renny?" he asked the lad who had delivered it to his lodgings in Seven Dials.

"Paddy, a friend o' mine what works as a crossing sweeper. He wouldn't tell me who give it to 'im, though," said Renny. "Just said it was for you, and asked me to bring it. Do you suppose—?"

"Wait, there's a note." Flute pulled a piece of paper from beneath the jewels. "These should bring enough money to help the Heinrichs, as well as others in need," he read aloud. "More will follow as I have opportunity. It's signed with the Saint's symbol, the seven and halo. I don't recognize the hand."

Renny craned his neck to look at the note. "Then you reckon one o' their lordships sent it? Or do you think someone else has took over as Saint?"

"One or t'other," said Flute, frowning. He hadn't told Renny his plans in that direction—hadn't told anyone except Sarah. Had she somehow put some new gent up to the job to keep him from trying it? He'd have to ask her.

Though he couldn't help feeling disappointed, he was a tiny bit relieved as well. He hadn't told Sarah, of course, but one or two of the Runners now knew him by sight. It made his plan to play the Saint much riskier than he'd let on to her—not that it would have stopped him.

"These look to be good quality. I'll get 'em fenced and see what it comes to," he said. "Feels good to be working for a Saint again, whoever he is."

"Aye, it does that," agreed Renny. "I'll spread the word he's back in business. By tonight, we'll have a whole list o' folks what need his help, I'm thinking."

Flute nodded. "I'll ask around, sift the layabouts from the deserving ones. Then I'll give you the names and you can pass them on to Paddy. You can tell him to see the Saint gets them."

"Good plan. I'm off, then." Renny touched a finger to his head, a show of respect that startled Flute.

Once he was gone, Flute had to grin. So much for Ickle's attempts to lure his lads away! The thief-master, long a rival of Twitchell's, promised the boys a living that Flute hadn't been able to provide, except for those few for whom he'd found honest work. He'd promised Lord Hardwyck, the first Saint, that he wouldn't let the lads go back to thievery, but it had become more and more difficult to convince them as their bellies went empty.

He glanced down at the gems again. Unless he missed his guess, this lot would bring enough to feed all of them for a good long time, even allowing for those families with pressing needs. "Take that, Ickle," he said aloud.

Stuffing the jewels in his pocket, he headed out to convert them into much-needed cash.

Sarah tugged at her gown, wishing again that she'd had enough tulle to finish out the ruffles. It was the same dress she'd worn her first night in Town, to Lady Driscoll's ridotto, but she had sewn on new sleeves in hopes of disguising it somewhat.

A tap came at her door and she shrugged. This would have to do. If Lady Mountheath was embarrassed, she had only herself to blame. Picking up the rather frayed shawl Fanny had given her, she opened the door.

"Is it time for me to go down?" she asked the maid waiting there—the same scullery maid who had interrupted Lord Mountheath this afternoon.

"Not quite, miss. But there's someone at the kitchen door wants to speak with you." The girl cast a furtive look behind her.

Sarah's heart leaped. It had to be William! "Thank you, Gretchen. I'll come at once."

As she'd guessed, her brother awaited her in the kitchen garden. "What are you doing here?" she whispered as soon as the door closed behind her.

Flute's eyes widened. "Cor! But you clean up nice, Sarah. A real lady, you look."

"I told you not to visit me here," she reminded him. "What if that maid tells Lady Mountheath?"

"She won't," he said with a grin. "I gave her a shilling to keep it quiet. Anyway, I've got good news."

Though Sarah had a pretty good idea what that news would be, she pretended ignorance. "News?"

Flute lowered his voice to match her whisper. "The Saint o' Seven Dials. He's back. I think."

"You think?" she echoed, not sure whether to act delighted or confused.

"A friend o' mine brought me summat to fence, summat he got from a friend o' his. The note inside said it came from the Saint, but he never sent me anything that way before."

"Still, that's good, isn't it?" Sarah asked. "It means you won't have to . . . do what you said."

Flute regarded her shrewdly. "You didn't put some swell up to it, did you, Sarah, get him to send me stuff?"

"Of course not!" she responded, quite honestly. "I don't know anyone in London that well yet." She thrust away a sudden vision of Lord Peter's face.

"Aye, well, I knew you'd want to know, worried as you were t'other night."

Though his concern for her came a bit late, considering his disappearance from school seven years ago, Sarah was touched. "Thank you for telling me. I'll sleep better knowing you'll stay safe."

Flute shrugged. "I just hope it's not a one-shot deal. I've already got a dozen names of folks what need help, what with the Saint being gone so long. I'll be sending them on to him tomorrow. Anyways, I'd best not keep you."

"No, I need to get back before I'm missed. But thank you for telling me, William!" Sarah gave him a quick hug, ignoring his frown at the name, as well as her own sudden panic.

It appeared her career as Saint of Seven Dials had only just begun.

From her place near a potted palm, Sarah watched the shifting crowd at the embassy reception. Lady Mountheath had warned her not to stray from this spot, and for once she was happy to obey. Truth to tell, she was more than a bit intimidated by the importance of so many of tonight's guests: foreign ambassadors and princes, more than one royal duke and, she had overheard, the Prince Regent himself. She felt more insignificant than ever by comparison.

Then Lord Peter was announced, and every other thought fled. Would he even see her here? Yes, he was already coming this way. Determinedly, she willed her color to remain normal, her heart rate to slow to its usual pace.

"Good evening, Miss Killian," he said with a bow. "I take it you are completely recovered?"

"Of course. As I said," she began, then realized there were several people within earshot. "As I said last night," she continued, "I was only slightly indisposed."

His eyes approved her discretion and she suddenly felt warmed right down to her toes. "I am glad to hear it," he said. "Come. There is someone I would like you to meet."

She hesitated, mindful of her instructions, but he added, "You need not worry. I have an argument ready, should Lady Mountheath object—not that I believe she will dare to do so."

"How is it you always seem to know what I am thinking?" she asked, taking his arm. "I confess it is rather unnerving at times." Indeed, it was a wonder that she was able to keep any secrets at all from this man.

"Did I not tell you I am considered an excellent judge of character? Part of that is discovering and remembering all I can about someone, while another part is simple observation—discerning from expression and gesture what people mean but do not say."

"A formidable gift indeed," she said with assumed lightness, not daring to meet his eye for fear of what he might read there. He now knew about her parents, and much about her early life. Did he know how she had come to feel about him? But then she had to smile. If her eyes had not told him, assuredly her lips must have, this afternoon in the library.

Unfortunately, she was not similarly talented at divining others' thoughts and was therefore unsure whether that kiss had meant as much to him as it had to her. Suddenly embarrassed, she tried to think of something else, only to have his next words undo her efforts.

"I trust you suffered no repercussions from my, ah, visit earlier today?"

An unpleasant vision of Lord Mountheath's leering face intruded, but she shook her head and changed the subject. "I meant to thank you for your kindness last night. It was good of you to be so concerned for my welfare."

His eyes held hers for a long, breathless moment. "It is my earnest desire to be of service to you whenever necessary, Miss Killian. I hope you realize that by now. Ah! Here we are."

Before she could decipher her feelings, Sarah found herself facing three men, all of whom exuded an air of authority. Knowing instinctively that their stations must warrant it, she sank into her deepest curtsey before Lord Peter could make introductions—and was glad of it when he did so an instant later.

"Gentlemen, I would like to present to you Miss Sarah Killian, lately of Cumberland, cousin and ward of Lady Mountheath. Miss Killian, my father, the Duke of Marland, my brother, Lord Bagstead, and His Royal Highness, the Prince of Wales."

Sarah felt her breath coming in short gasps. The Prince Regent? What should she do? What should she say? Thankfully, her schooling came to her rescue. Forcing her trembling legs to bear her weight, she extended a hand and the prince himself drew her to her feet.

"Your Royal Highness," she murmured, keeping her head respectfully bowed. Then, to the duke and his eldest son: "Your Grace. My lord."

"How exceedingly charming," the Prince Regent declared in a voice loud enough for everyone nearby to hear. "Lord Peter, you are as discriminating as al-

ways, to have discovered such a diamond in so unlikely a mine. Do you not agree, Marland?"

Though the duke looked so sour and austere that
Sarah wondered how he could have sired a man as
kind and cheerful as Lord Peter, he directed a thin-
lipped smile her way. "Indeed, Your Highness."

Lord Bagstead, as austere as his father, also managed a nod. "Yes, quite lovely," he said, then immediately turned back to the Prince Regent. "But pray,
Your Highness, do continue with your story. It was
most fascinating."

Sarah glanced questioningly at Lord Peter, wondering if they should now retreat, but he laid a reassuring hand on her arm. Trying to ignore the thrill
that contact sent through her body, Sarah concen-
trated on His Highness's words.

"—pity I was not at the Wickburn do last night, really. I've no doubt that if I were there, I'd have spotted the cheeky scoundrel at once. No footman
disguise would have fooled *me*."

"Of course not, Your Highness," Lord Bagstead
agreed. "I've no doubt you'd have caught the fellow
for us."

Sarah felt an odd prickling up the back of her
neck. Surely they could not mean—?

The Duke of Marland answered her unspoken
question. "I have heard, however, that the authorities suspect it may not have been the Saint at all, but
someone aping his style. Certainly, though, it was
like his impudence. The effrontery of robbing a
ducal household!"

The Prince Regent nodded. "I'd love to see the fellow caught, though I'm not certain it wouldn't be

more politic to knight him than to clap him in prison, given the stature he has attained with the common folk. Whether last night's theft was his work or not, I daresay we've not seen the last of the Saint of Seven Dials."

Chapter 10

Though startled by this news, Peter joined in the murmurs of agreement with the Prince Regent's words. If his deduction about the Black Bishop was correct, last night's thefts couldn't possibly have been the work of the real Saint. One of his accomplices, perhaps?

"It almost seems the fellow is able to become invisible at will," he said, since voicing his suspicion was out of the question. "Why, I was telling Miss Killian just the other day—" He glanced at Sarah, only to find her as pale as she had been last night before Lady Mountheath had sent her to the carriage. "Miss Killian?" The Saint, even the regent, were forgotten in his sudden concern for her.

"Pray continue," she said, rather breathlessly, he

167

thought. "As I told Lord Peter, I find stories of the Saint fascinating."

The Prince Regent chuckled. "All of the ladies do. I'd have most of them, along with the common folk, clamoring for my head if I had him executed or deported, I fear. Perhaps it's as well he's not been arrested, though I confess to a large degree of curiosity myself as to his identity."

"Should he turn out to be ill favored, no doubt the ladies would lose interest and you would be free to act as you see fit, Your Highness," the Duke of Marland said. "I, for one, should like to see this self-styled Robin Hood permanently removed."

Peter noticed that Sarah was still pale, her eyes unfocused. "If you will excuse me, Your Highness, Your Grace, I should return Miss Killian to her guardians." He bowed, supported her as she curtsied, then led her away.

"Are you certain you are not ill again?" he asked in an undertone as they slowly headed back across the crowded room. "You look much as you did last night."

She smiled up at him weakly. "It must be the heat and the press of people. I am not yet accustomed to such crowding."

"Of course. I will return you to your out-of-the-way corner." Had he been mistaken, then? Perhaps Lady Mountheath had not been to blame for her distress last night after all.

Just as they reached the potted palm, the crowd shifted and Lady Mountheath herself confronted them.

"Miss Killian! Did I not *explicitly* say you were not

to stray from this spot? And you, Lord Peter, seem in danger of becoming as rakish as your friend Mr. Thatcher. Twice in two evenings you have persuaded Miss Killian to disobedience while toying with my daughter's affections."

Peter bowed, suppressing an almost irresistible urge to tell this harridan what he thought of her. He could not do so yet, however. Not until he had Sarah secure.

"A thousand pardons, my lady, but His Royal Highness wished to make Miss Killian's acquaintance. I could scarcely refuse to oblige him."

To his amusement, this information deflated Lady Mountheath's indignation like a pricked bubble. "Oh! Oh, I see. Why did you not tell me you had been introduced to His Highness, Miss Killian?"

Sarah still seemed subdued, so Peter responded for her. "I'm sure she would have at first opportunity, my lady. It seems the Duke of Wickburn may have given you good advice last night."

Lady Mountheath darted a suspicious glance at him, then at Sarah. "Perhaps so. I had wished her to remain here against the necessity of finding her when we are ready to leave, but—"

"But that will not be an issue for some time," Lord Mountheath said, joining them just then, "as no one may leave until the Prince Regent and his brothers have gone."

Lord Mountheath's indiscretions were well known, and Peter did not at all care for the look he gave Sarah as he spoke. Was that why her eyes were still downcast? He fought down a sudden, ridiculous urge to challenge the older man.

"Ah . . . yes." Lady Mountheath agreed reluctantly. "Exactly. I suppose you may as well introduce Miss Killian to other eligible gentlemen, Lord Peter. If His Royal Highness has recognized her, no doubt *some* will be willing to overlook her shortcomings."

"Undoubtedly." He didn't trust his voice for anything longer.

"Mind you don't let this go to your head, miss," the harpy said in parting.

Sarah made a small sound that might have been an attempt at a laugh. "No fear of that," she said as the Mountheaths moved away.

Relieved to see that her sense of humor was returning along with her color, Peter grinned down at her. "Shall I take you about to meet those undiscriminating eligible gentlemen?"

"I suppose it would be preferable to lurking here." Her answering smile seemed only partially forced. "Perhaps if I polish up my wiles I might snare an unwary earl."

Peter chuckled, as she was clearly jesting, but her words still caused an unpleasant twisting of his heart. He had no doubt whatsoever that if Sarah put her mind to it, she could "snare" any man she set her sights upon. That she must realize such a course would be her easiest way out from under Lady Mountheath's thumb disturbed him more than he cared to admit.

"So! What are your requirements, Miss Killian?" he asked lightly. "More wealth than brains, to begin, I suppose."

Her blue eyes twinkled up at him, making his vitals tighten. "Of course! The richer—and stupider—the better. And someone of at least eighty would be best, so that he might leave me a wealthy widow in short order. Have you anyone to suggest?"

Reassured by her absurdity, Peter pointed across the room. "There's Lord Gorefax. He is approaching ninety, and he's certainly rich enough. He dotes on the Dowager Lady Glinnon, but as she is past eighty herself, I've no doubt you can steal him away from her. His mind is not what it used to be."

"He sounds perfect. I'm not certain I could bear to undercut poor Lady Glinnon, however. Who else have you to suggest?"

Myself. Peter realized he'd nearly said it aloud. How would she respond if he did? The temptation to find out was strong, but this was hardly the time or place for a declaration.

"Lord Ribbleton is not so old, but he's undoubtedly richer, and not nearly so bright as Lord Glinnon was in his prime. He should stupify nicely as he ages. And he's a marquess."

Sarah turned to look at Ribbleton, giving Peter an opportunity to admire the purity of her profile—and to question his own judgment. Had *his* head been turned by mere beauty?

"But he cannot be much above forty," she objected. "I'd not have control of his fortune for decades, perhaps. If I settle for a man so young, he must at least be exceedingly handsome, to make the wait less tedious."

No, there was definitely more to her than beauty! Peter laughed. "What exacting standards you do have, Miss Killian. It's a pity His Royal Highness is already married, and with at least one mistress as well. But perhaps he is not handsome enough for you, either."

She laughed with him, but her color rose and he realized it had been clumsy of him to mention Prinny's mistresses. Surely she didn't think he was suggesting—?

"Is it not a charming coincidence that the Saint of Seven Dials may have struck at the very ball we attended last night, on the heels of our conversation about him?" he asked, in his desperation to change the subject.

To his surprise, she pinkened further. "Charming indeed. Now he will doubtless be on everyone's lips and I will learn as much of the Saint as I could ever have hoped." Her smile seemed strained. "But if, as you say, he was arrested as a traitor, it can't really have been the Saint, can it?"

"I don't see how. My father did say the authorities doubt it was the actual Saint, and he has a formidable information network. Often he seems to know things almost before they happen." Though this had often irritated him in the past, now Peter took comfort from it. Otherwise, he'd have to believe that the Black Bishop had escaped—or that his surmise had been completely wrong.

"Still, it had to be someone," he continued aloud. "Shall we try to guess who the thief might be? Let's go over last night's guest list." He was determined to divert Sarah's mind from the subject of mistresses.

Did he imagine the alarm in the look she shot him? But if she guessed his purpose, her words did not betray it. "There were dozens of active young men present, as I recall. Any of them might have stolen—whatever was stolen."

"Dozens indeed, and you danced with many of them." Peter was pleased with his control, which allowed no edge whatsoever to creep into his voice. "Did any of them act suspiciously?"

Her complexion had returned to its normal hue. It appeared his distraction was working. "Hmm. Mr. Orrin repeated the same compliment three times, but I attributed that to a mere lack of imagination."

"As the Saint—or this pretender—clearly does not lack imagination, that would seem to clear rather than accuse Mr. Orrin."

She laughed, her earlier discomfiture apparently forgotten, much to Peter's relief. Just then, however, they were interrupted by one of their earlier figures of fun, Lord Ribbleton.

"How delightful to see you here, Miss Killian," he said with a bow. Straightening, he gave Peter a look that was clearly intended to dismiss him.

Peter ignored the hint, saying, "Lady Mountheath suggested I introduce Miss Killian to some of the luminaries here tonight." Something about Ribbleton had always set his teeth on edge.

"I fancy I am better acquainted with most of them than you are, Lord Peter," he said condescendingly. "I would be honored to take over your office." He extended an arm to Sarah, who glanced from him to Peter and back.

"Rather unsporting of you to force the lady to make a choice, Ribbleton," Peter pointed out. "Now she must choose between slighting someone of superior consequence by refusing, or abandoning her original escort."

Sarah's brows rose. "I will thank both of you to cease speaking of me as though I am not present. Lord Peter, I have monopolized too much of your time already, I fear." Releasing his arm, she took

Lord Ribbleton's. "Who do you feel it is important I should meet, my lord?"

Stunned, Peter watched as she walked away in company with the marquess. Had he offended her after all? Or—insidious thought—was there a modicum of truth to her earlier banter about snaring a wealthy husband? Frowning, he turned away, only to be accosted by Lucy Mountheath.

"Lord Peter! You must tell me what His Royal Highness had to say about this latest robbery by the Saint of Seven Dials. I declare, I shall not feel safe even in such an assembly as this without a strong gentleman by my side."

Stifling a sigh, Peter forced a smile and began to relate the latest news about the legendary—but doubtless counterfeit—thief.

Had she done the right thing? Sarah wondered as Lord Ribbleton droned on about how highly he was regarded by various important personages. Her defection had clearly startled Lord Peter, but his talk about last night's theft had been making her exceedingly nervous and she had seized Lord Ribbleton's offer as an opportunity to escape his too-perceptive scrutiny.

As well, there was the added embarrassment of Lord Peter's mention of mistresses, which he had too-obviously regretted. Despite his assurances of her "worthiness," she wondered if that might have been his gentle way of telling her that such a role was the best to which she could reasonably aspire.

The idea stung quite sharply.

She had another problem, as well. If the authorities doubted that the Saint had committed last night's theft, surely William must as well—in fact, he'd hinted at just that, earlier. Should she attempt another robbery here, tonight, however risky it might be, to convince them all that the Saint had indeed returned?

"Have you been introduced to anyone here tonight, or did Northrup keep you to himself?" Lord Ribbleton's question was a welcome interruption of such uncomfortable thoughts.

Still, Sarah did not care for the dismissive way he spoke of Lord Peter. "Indeed, he introduced me to his father, the Duke of Marland, as well as his eldest brother, Lord Bagstead. Oh, and His Royal Highness, the Prince Regent."

She had the satisfaction of seeing Lord Ribbleton's eyes widen slightly, marring his habitually bored expression—though only for a moment.

"I see," he drawled after a brief hesitation. "A good start, I suppose. I presume you have not yet met the Princess Esterhazy, wife to the Austrian ambassador?"

Sarah was forced to shake her head.

He smiled. "An important connection, as she is one of the patronesses of Almack's. I will undertake to introduce you to her, and to the Countess Lieven, another patroness, and wife of the Russian ambassador."

Though Almack's did not hold its vaunted subscription balls this time of year, Sarah had heard enough mention of it to realize the importance of acceptance there to anyone with serious social aspirations. Lady Mountheath spoke of it frequently.

Her anxiety returned as Lord Ribbleton led her across to where the two ladies mentioned stood conversing. She felt nearly as unequal to meet them as she had to meeting the Prince Regent. "Are you certain . . ." she murmured as they drew close, but he ignored her.

"Princess, Countess, may I present Miss Killian, ward of Lord and Lady Mountheath. Miss Killian, the Princess Esterhazy and the Countess Lieven."

Sarah sank into yet another deep curtsey—she was becoming quite practiced at it tonight—then rose to greet the two ladies with appropriately downcast eyes.

"Charming," said the plump, pretty princess. "Quite charming."

"I must scold Lady Mountheath for failing to bring you to our attention," agreed the countess, a thin, exotic-looking woman.

"I am honored, Your Highness, my lady," said Sarah demurely, wondering what price the countess's diamonds might fetch on the street.

Though the princess smiled kindly, the countess seemed disinclined for further talk, so with another bow, Lord Ribbleton led Sarah away—before she could concoct any sort of plan to obtain those diamonds. She would simply have to keep her eyes open for any other opportunities that might present themselves for the balance of the evening.

"Lady Jersey seems not to be in attendance," Lord Ribbleton said as they retreated, "but I see Lady Castlereagh over there, with the Foreign Office crowd. She is yet another patroness and a valuable person to know."

Though this was only her fourth foray into high Society, Sarah found herself developing a distaste for its artificiality. "Is there anyone . . . *nice* . . . to whom you might introduce me?"

Lord Ribbleton lifted a quizzing glass to regard her, eyebrows raised. "Nice? As in pleasant? What has that to do with anything?"

Sarah smiled and gave a half shrug, glancing away from him. "Nothing, I suppose." Except that the Saint would not target such a person—assuming any existed.

Almost without her volition, her eye sought out Lord Peter. Lucy Mountheath clutched his arm, chattering away determinedly. Though he was almost certainly bored, he hid it admirably, smiling and nodding as she droned on and on.

Society might not place much value on kindness, but Sarah could not imagine caring for a man who lacked that trait. It ranked higher than wealth or a title, in her estimation—and seemed far less common a commodity.

Lord Ribbleton followed her gaze. "Miss Killian, I feel obliged to put you on your guard."

She glanced up at him questioningly.

"I fear Lord Peter may be raising false, ah, expectations in your pretty breast."

Though she felt herself flushing with embarrassment that her feelings should be so transparent, Sarah attempted nonchalance. "Whatever do you mean, my lord?"

He smiled down at her indulgently. "You would not be the first to mistake Northrup's general affability for romantic interest. However, as a fourth son, he has no need to marry. And even if he wished to, unless he has recently come into a deal of money, he would need to look for a woman of means."

Which Sarah plainly was not. Though her cheeks still burned, she looked up at Lord Ribbleton defiantly. "I assure you, my lord, that I have formed no expectations whatsoever with regard to Lord Peter—or anyone else."

"Yes, Lady Mountheath told my mother that you are looking for a governess position?"

Sarah nodded.

"I confess, I can't imagine any woman of sense hiring you, Miss Killian. Beautiful as you are, however, it is possible you'll find a man of means willing to wed you. If not, there are other options, far more lucrative than governessing." His smile now reminded her uncomfortably of Lord Mountheath's.

Sarah felt a cold weight in the pit of her stomach at this unmistakable affirmation of what Lord Peter had merely implied. "I am interested only in honest employment, my lord," she said stiffly.

"Of course, Miss Killian, of course. And I do wish you all luck in finding it."

Humiliated, Sarah would have preferred to leave the party that instant, but Lord Ribbleton continued to escort her about the room as though they had discussed nothing of more emotional import than the weather. She could scarcely make a scene, so she smiled and nodded as he made her known to any person who might benefit her socially.

As they moved from one supercilious group to another, Sarah couldn't help taking note of dangling jewels and other ostentatious displays of wealth. At the same time, her conviction grew that there must be more to life than this.

For years she had fantasized about what it would be like to move in such circles, to afford such baubles, but now that she was here, she realized that these people, for all their wealth, seemed no more happy than the urchins of the street—less so, in many cases.

Nor would most of them suffer unduly by the removal of a modicum of that wealth.

Finally, unable to bear another moment in Lord Ribbleton's stuffy, hypocritical company, she made use of the same excuse that had served the night before and retired to the ladies' withdrawing room. It was crowded, offering no chance to slip through a back door, nor did an opportunity such as Lady Beatrice had presented last night occur.

Sarah dawdled for a few minutes, then emerged to scan the hallway leading back to the large assembly room. Several doors opened off it, most of them open. Slowly, she meandered along, glancing into the rooms she passed.

A few gentlemen were playing cards in one anteroom. From another, with door half closed, a cloud of smoke told of the cigar smoking within. The next room along appeared to be a study—and it was empty. She paused. Two women hurried past her, talking together animatedly, then vanished into the ladies' room. Alone in the hall for a brief moment, Sarah slipped into the study.

The room was small, furnished only by a desk, two bookshelves and a few chairs. Her back to the door so that no chance passerby could see what she was doing, she examined the desk, still unsure of what she meant to do. At first glance, the drawers and cubbyholes yielded nothing beyond paper, pens and ink.

Searching further, she found a ten-pound note

tucked into the back of a drawer. Almost without thinking, she slipped it into her pocket and put one of her Saint cards in its place. Not much, but it was something.

Heading back toward the assembly, she realized that she had finally abandoned her foolish dreams of a fairy-tale marriage. Instead, she would control her own destiny—and safeguard William's—by fully assuming the role of the Saint of Seven Dials.

From the opposite side of the room, Peter frowned, watching as Sarah emerged from the alcove leading to the various anterooms. She'd been gone so long, he had begun to worry as he had last night. Perhaps she had some health problem she was reluctant to discuss? That might explain her furtive expression, he supposed.

But then, as he watched, Lord Mountheath approached Sarah and spoke to her. She shook her head, and he put a hand on her arm in what seemed to Peter a far too intimate manner—a perception reinforced when Sarah flinched away.

He started across the room, determined to come to Sarah's aid should she need it, but just then the Mountheath sisters joined their father, who quickly took a step away from Sarah. The sisters appeared to scold Sarah, who listened in silence, and then all three Mountheaths moved away, leaving Sarah alone again.

She glanced after the trio with a grimace, then made her way along the perimeter of the large room. It almost appeared as though she were looking for something—or someone.

A feminine voice interrupted his observations.

"You seem quite lost in thought, Lord Peter." He turned to find Miss Cheevers regarding him flirtatiously.

"Merely gathering my resources before launching myself back into the fray," he replied.

She took his arm. "Come, then—we'll brave the crowd together."

Though he'd have preferred to continue watching Sarah, he could scarcely refuse without appearing rude. "Very well. Would you care for something from the refreshment table?" Sarah had been headed in that general direction.

"Indeed, I am quite parched, it is so hot in here. I can't help thinking the guest list should have been more exclusive. There are some here with only the most tenuous of ties to the diplomatic circles." She made a moue of distaste at a passing couple Peter knew to be distant connections of Lord Castlereagh's.

On reaching the refreshment table, where footmen ladled out punch and poured glasses of champagne to accompany the delicate biscuits laid out on crystal platters, Peter caught sight of Sarah again. She had been accosted by Sir Cyril Weathers, who was chattering most animatedly—and, Peter suspected, drunkenly.

Indeed, as he watched, Sarah seemed to stifle a yawn, though she still smiled up at Sir Cyril. Then, turning slightly, her eyes met Peter's across the table. He felt an almost physical connection with her, as though a cable stretched between them. He smiled and her color deepened slightly.

"I believe I should like a glass of that punch," Miss Cheevers said then, gripping his arm more tightly. "If you wouldn't mind?"

Reluctantly withdrawing his gaze from Sarah's, Peter nodded. "Of course." He procured two glasses, extricating his arm in the process. As they both sipped, he glanced back toward Sarah, to see that she had moved away from Sir Cyril to stand near the cart holding the extra crystal and silver.

A black-clad gentleman then blocked his view. "Well met, Northrup. What is that blackguard Thatcher up to this evening?"

"Ah, Lord Edgemont. How good to see you. I'm afraid I've no idea what Harry is doing tonight. You know Miss Cheevers, do you not?"

Lord Edgemont bowed over Miss Cheevers's hand and she simpered up at him, quite willing to transfer her attention to a man of greater consequence. After seeing them engaged in conversation, Peter excused himself.

Sarah was still near the silver cart, now standing in the doorway just behind it. He saw Lord Mountheath a short distance away, which might account for her attempt to remain inconspicuous. Peter rounded the table to head in her direction, but though he tried to avoid eye contact with those he passed, twice he was briefly detained by greetings.

Finally he approached Sarah, who appeared not to see him. Instead, she was looking off to her left, the direction Lord Mountheath had gone, and was backing slowly through the doorway behind her. He stepped forward to offer her another way of escape but before he could reach the door, she disappeared through it.

Peter glanced around, but no one seemed to have noticed Sarah's unorthodox maneuver. He waited a few moments to be certain he would not be observed either, then followed her into what proved to be a narrow butler's pantry. A long sideboard ran the length of the room, with cupboards above it and drawers below.

The pantry was empty except for Sarah, who stood at the far end, her back to the door. She appeared to be fumbling for something inside her dress. A handkerchief? Was she crying?

"Miss Killian? Sarah?" he said softly.

Sarah whirled at the sound of his voice, snatching her hand from her pocket to cover her mouth, her heart in her throat. With her hip, she silently pressed the silverware drawer closed. "What . . . what are you doing here?"

"I'd meant to ask you that, but I didn't mean to startle you." His eyes held no trace of suspicion—only concern.

Desperately, she sought a plausible excuse, then fell back on the one she'd used before. "I . . . I was just . . . It was the crowd again. I wanted to be alone for a moment." Maybe he would leave long enough to allow her to wrap a muffling cloth around the dozen silver spoons she'd just taken.

Instead, he stepped to her side, putting a comforting hand on her arm. "I saw Lord Mountheath speaking to you earlier. Is he threatening you in some way?"

Sarah averted her gaze, afraid of what he might read there. "Not . . . precisely, though I hope they did not see you follow me in here. Lady Mountheath has made it clear that she would love an excuse to evict me from her house."

"Please believe that I will not allow you to suffer in any way, particularly on my account. In fact—"

But before he could continue, a pair of footmen carrying trays of biscuits and glasses came through the door from the kitchens. They halted, clearly startled. Sarah thanked heaven they hadn't arrived two minutes earlier, as she'd been plundering the drawer. She'd taken a greater risk than she'd realized.

"Carry on, men," Lord Peter said briskly. "The lady merely nipped in here to retie a ribbon. If you're finished, Miss Killian, let us rejoin the party."

Sarah took his cue. "Yes, it is fixed now." Taking his extended arm, she accompanied him from the pantry, walking carefully to prevent the purloined spoons from clinking in her pocket. Once they were back in the main room, the volume of conversation was enough to cover any such betrayal.

"Now, perhaps you can tell me—" Peter began, when the young lady he had been speaking with earlier accosted them.

"Lord Peter, wherever have you been? Oh, is this the Mountheaths' ward, of whom everyone is speaking?" She examined Sarah with an openly critical eye.

Though grateful for her interruption, Sarah's smile was stiff. She'd noticed how this lady had been hanging on Lord Peter's arm earlier. Clearly, she had designs on him. Futile designs, if Lord Ribbleton was to be believed. Sarah's stomach twisted again at the memory of that gentleman's words, the death knell of hopes she'd barely known she'd nursed.

"Miss Cheevers, have you not met Miss Killian?" Lord Peter asked now. When she shook her head, he quickly completed the introduction. A few others joined their circle then, making private conversation even less a possibility. Good.

Smiling at a comment Lord Edgemont had just made, Sarah kept despair and humiliation at bay by considering what she'd done so far this evening. Ten pounds and a few silver spoons were hardly worthy of the Saint, though the cards she'd left would surely be noticed. She needed more.

Pretending to listen attentively to the ongoing discussion about the orange ostrich plumes on Lady Plumfield's new bonnet, she considered her options. Sir Cyril joined them then, clearly the worse for drink, jostling Lord Edgemont who in turn bumped Miss Cheevers into Sarah, causing Miss Cheevers's reticule to slide down her wrist to touch Sarah's hand.

Almost without thought, Sarah found the opening of the reticule, reached in and extracted several heavy coins which she just as smoothly deposited into her pocket. Sir Cyril was apologizing profusely while the others laughed and chided him for overindulging. Laughing along with the group, Sarah pulled another card from her pocket and slipped it into Miss Cheevers's reticule just before the other woman moved away.

Though she carefully kept her attention on those speaking, Sarah silently marveled at what she'd just done. Lord Edgemont made another deprecating comment about Sir Cyril and she grinned, though more in relief and satisfaction at her own prowess than at Lord Edgemont's indifferent attempt at humor.

Who would have guessed that her skills as a pickpocket, unused for eight years, would still be so sharp? William—and the authorities—should be thoroughly convinced after this.

Still smiling, she glanced Lord Peter's way, only to find him staring at her in shock and disbelief.

Chapter 11

Peter watched the color drain from Sarah's face. For a moment he tried to convince himself he had imagined what he'd seen, it had happened so quickly, but her expression now proved otherwise. In fact, she looked as though she might faint.

Even as he took a step toward her, however, she rallied with an obvious effort. Holding his gaze, she sent him a silent plea. For a long moment, he hesitated. Was it possible that Sarah was actually a common thief who had insinuated her way into the Mountheath household with a false name and story of kinship?

But then he recalled her courage, her humor, the innocence of her lips beneath his. Besides, Holmes's research had verified her story. His eyes still locked with hers, he gave a slight nod, reassuring her, and saw some of the tension leave her body. He then pulled his gaze away before their silent exchange could be noted by the others in the group.

"—only to discover he'd been wearing it all the time," Lord Edgemont concluded, to a general laugh. Peter managed to laugh with the rest, though it took some effort.

"Miss Killian, would you care for a glass of punch?" he asked, ignoring Miss Cheevers's indignant frown. It was imperative that he get Sarah alone long enough to demand an explanation for what he'd seen. Surely she would have one. Perhaps her brother desperately needed money to survive. It was likely the Mountheaths had not given her so much as a shilling. Or, could it be Lord Mountheath who—

"I . . . I'm not thirsty, my lord," she replied, not quite meeting his eye. "Perhaps later."

Frustrated, Peter gave a curt nod. So, she did not wish to explain? His doubts flooded back. She had pilfered Miss Cheevers's reticule like a seasoned cutpurse. That certainly was not something she had learned at Miss Pritchard's Seminary.

Lady Mountheath's voice broke into his thoughts. "There you are, Miss Killian. I have been looking for you this quarter hour past."

Sarah greeted her with something that looked suspiciously like relief, taking two quick steps toward her—and away from Peter. "My lady?"

"I did say I wished you to be ready to leave at a moment's notice, did I not? His Royal Highness has gone, as has the Duke of Kent."

"I am quite ready to leave," she assured Lady Mountheath. She smiled a vague goodbye to the group but they scarcely noticed, already involved in listening to another funny story.

"You are going, then?" Peter asked, turning from the others. "I'd hoped—"

Still Sarah did not meet his eye. "Yes, the Mountheaths prefer not to keep late hours. I'm sure I will see you again some time or other, my lord. Shall we go, my lady?"

Sarah followed Lady Mountheath toward the front of the house with a sense of profound relief— even though it meant being shut up with the family for the drive to Berkley Square. As last night, she was acutely conscious of the illicit booty weighing down her pocket. She would have to be exceedingly careful in the carriage.

"Why do you hold your side like that?" Fanny asked as Sarah preceded her into the conveyance. "If you have an upset stomach, pray do not sit next to me."

Sarah did not answer, but seated herself on the opposite side of the carriage, only removing her muffling hand from the silver and gold in her pocket once she was settled.

Lady Mountheath launched into a lecture before the coachman could whip up the horses. "I noticed that you spent nearly an hour in Lord Ribbleton's company tonight, Miss Killian. I hope you are not forming designs upon him now. He is far above your touch, I assure you."

"At least for any sort of *respectable* liaison," Lucy agreed with a malicious smile. Fanny put a hand to her mouth and tittered.

Their mother sent them a quelling glance, then turned an outraged eye on Sarah. "Is that now your intent? I should have known. Make no mistake, I'll not house a lightskirt under my roof. One whiff of scandal and you will be out on the street, missie!"

Sarah was glad the interior of the coach was dark enough to hide the blush she felt staining her cheeks as she recalled Lord Ribbleton's words—and Lord Peter's. Was all of Society making similar assumptions? "I assure you, my lady—"

Lord Mountheath came to her defense before she could finish. "Now, now, m'dear. No need to be so suspicious. I'm sure our dear Miss Killian only wishes to better herself. Nothing wrong with that." He smiled reassuringly at Sarah, which reassured her not at all. He, at least, clearly shared Lord Ribbleton's view.

Lady Mountheath harrumphed. "I trust, my lord, that you would not wish your daughters associating with a woman who would try to better herself through wickedly immoral means."

"I'm not—" Sarah began again, and again Lord Mountheath cut her off.

"Pish, tush. Seen no such evidence yet." He sounded almost disappointed.

Sarah realized any further defense would do her no good, so stared out the window for the remainder of the drive while the Mountheaths argued about her. Besides, she thought as she climbed down from the carriage in Berkley Square, could she honestly claim she was not attempting to better herself through "wickedly immoral means?" Stealing went against the Ten Commandments as well.

Not that she was stealing for herself, of course.

She was doing it for William—to prevent his taking untenable risks. And now she needed to deliver her latest haul, such as it was.

Little Paddy would not be at his post so late, of course. She could take it directly to Renny herself, but she trembled at the idea of another encounter with Lord Peter before she'd had time to concoct a plausible explanation for what he'd seen.

On reaching her room, she was finally able to examine her takings—with disappointing results. Ten pounds, five silver spoons and a handful of coins, not all of which were even gold. Hardly a haul worthy of the Saint of Seven Dials.

If she was to convince William—and the authorities—that the Saint had returned, she would have to send him more than this.

Peter returned from the embassy reception in the foulest mood he'd experienced for a very long time. He'd botched everything he'd said or done tonight, from inadvertently insulting Sarah to not protecting her from Lord Mountheath to failing to discover her motive for stealing. If he'd managed to make his intentions known sooner . . . But perhaps it was as well he had not.

A footman was hovering, waiting for his hat and cloak. Peter undid the fastening at his throat, then abruptly refastened it. "I'm going back out, George. Should Mr. Thatcher stop by before I return, tell him I'm at the club."

He felt far too unsettled for sleep, and a brisk walk in the evening air might help him to think through his problem.

Passing Berkley Square ten minutes later, he

paused—but of course it was far too late to stop at the Mountheath house. The family—and Sarah—would all be abed by now. And tomorrow was Sunday. Muttering under his breath, his emotions in turmoil, he continued on to St. James Street and the Guards' Club.

There he found a fair crowd, including Harry, who greeted him with obvious surprise. "Ain't it past your bedtime, Pete? Only us dissipated types are about this time of night, you know."

Peter forced a chuckle. "I'm not quite in my dotage yet, though I may act it at times. What's the play?" He'd half-formed the intent of sharing his dilemma with Harry, but now decided against it. While he wouldn't hesitate to put his own life in Harry's hands—had done so on more than one occasion, in fact—Sarah's was another matter.

But how in hell was he to protect her if she kept secrets from him?

"Caperton just bested Thomas at a bangup game of piquet. Took him for more than a monkey—half the room was watching by the end. I believe Phillips is trying to get up a group for vingt-et-un over there." Harry pointed.

Perhaps losing a few hundred pounds would do him good tonight, Peter thought, heading toward the indicated table. Certainly he deserved it, after the way he'd failed Sarah.

Sir Barney Phillips, a young man who fancied himself a sophisticated wit and an arbiter of fashion, looked up as he approached. "Northrup! Never say you're wanting to play? Bit rich for your blood—hundred pound minimum."

"Deal me in," Peter snapped, seating himself.

"If you're sure you're good for it. Can't have much left after whatever you spent on that appalling yellow waistcoat." Sir Barney glanced about the table to invite a chuckle.

Peter leveled a quelling glare at the insufferable stripling. "I said, deal me in."

But Sir Barney had the attention of the crowd and was loathe to give it up. "An appropriate color for you, Northrup. Yellow."

A sudden hush fell, but Sir Barney seemed not to notice. "Heard about that retreat you led at Toulouse—or was it a rout? Never could understand why Wellington called you a hero. No wonder you never talk about your time in the war."

There were a few indignant murmurs, and one whispered warning to Sir Barney to watch what he was about, but he only sniggered.

"Northrup won't do anything," he said. "Never does, no matter how he's insulted. Were you this way on the peninsula, Northrup?"

"You're mighty cocky, Phillips, for a man who used that scratch you received in your first battle as an excuse to go home," Harry commented loudly, drawing a laugh from those within earshot.

Sir Barney flicked him a look of dislike, then turned back to Peter, who had remained silent, knowing Phillips's venom was rooted in jealousy and insecurity. Normally he let the fellow's jibes roll off his back, but tonight he found himself itching to plant him a facer.

"I see you have a champion," Phillips said, leaning forward. "I guess you need one, soft as you've turned since the war. Shame you can't do better than a drunken cripple."

Without warning, Peter lunged, his chair toppling with a crash. Catching Phillips by the throat with one hand, he clouted the side of his head with the other, then released him so that he crashed to the ground. When he tried to rise, cursing, Peter planted a gleaming boot on his chest, pinning him down.

"If you don't care to lose substantially more than a limb, I advise you to remain where you are—and silent," he said coldly.

Sir Barney glared up at him, but must have seen something in Peter's expression that penetrated to his senses, for he abruptly paled and stopped struggling.

"Wise decision," Peter said, to a general murmur of approval and a few chuckles. Turning to Harry, he said, "I find I've lost my enthusiasm for a game. Care to have a last drink at home?"

Harry was staring at him in disbelief, but managed a nod. Not until they were on the street did he speak. "Can't say I like you fighting my battles for me, but damn, it was good to see that you still have it in you, Pete. A bit like old times, that was."

Peter stopped mentally berating himself for his lack of control and grinned. "It was, wasn't it? Still, I'm sorry, old chap. Should have let you take him down yourself, but, well, I needed that."

"Thought so. You've been on edge for days, and I could tell the moment you came in you were close to the boiling point. Miss Killian again?"

But Peter still wasn't ready to tell Harry about his suspicions—or his feelings. "Among other things. But I believe I know what to do about it."

An offer of marriage would give Sarah a viable alternative to stealing, whatever her motives. He would speak with her tomorrow, one way or another, Sabbath or not. If conventional means would not serve, unconventional means would have to do.

Shortly after the Mountheath family returned from church the next day, while they were taking a light luncheon in the parlor, Lord Peter was announced. Lady Mountheath sent an irritated glance Sarah's way, no doubt because there was no opportunity to send her from the room before he entered.

"I apologize for the intrusion," he said, bowing, "but I wished to pay my respects, and to invite Miss Killian for a brief walk, as the weather is so fine."

He sought Sarah's gaze and held it, his expression intense, significant. She flushed and looked away, fearing she knew precisely why he wished to speak with her privately.

"Certainly not!" Lady Mountheath exclaimed, her daughters echoing her shocked expression. "That would be most unseemly, my lord, particularly on the Sabbath." She then leveled a glare at Sarah. "Did you suggest this to him, miss? I suppose I should not be surprised. It is all of a piece with your loose behavior."

"She did no such thing, my lady," Lord Peter protested before Sarah could speak. "I merely wished to continue a conversation we began last night, that is all. Miss Killian's behavior has been exemplary."

Sarah wondered that he could say such a thing, after what he had seen her do last night, but she was grateful for it nonetheless.

Lady Mountheath, however, seemed far from convinced. "I should not call flirting with gentlemen far above her station 'exemplary,'" she said. "Indeed, it would not surprise me to learn she has made assignations with other gentlemen besides yourself, my lord. Pray do not allow her innocent mien to deceive you."

Unprepared for such a direct attack before a visitor—particularly one whose opinion she valued so highly—Sarah could only stare in stunned silence while the Mountheath sisters tittered together at her discomfiture.

Lord Peter seemed similarly taken aback, but he only said stiffly, "I cannot agree with your assessment, my lady. If you will not allow her to walk out with me, however, I had best take my leave."

Lucy Mountheath sobered abruptly. "But my lord, I thought—"

"I'm sorry, Miss Mountheath, but I have a pressing engagement." Sarah thought the lines about his mouth might possibly be caused by anger—on her behalf? "Your servant, ladies." With a stiff, mechanical bow, he was gone.

Though his parting look told Sarah he would not rest until he had confronted her with what she'd done last night, she watched him go with more disappointment than relief. Much as she wished she could bare her heart, though, she knew it would not be fair to force such a choice upon him. No, far better he remain ignorant, even if it meant permanent estrangement from him.

This melancholy line of thought was interrupted by Lady Mountheath ordering her to her room with a strict admonition to stay there for the remainder of the day. As this suited Sarah quite well, she went without complaint.

After a third person glanced warily his way, Peter realized that he was muttering angrily to himself as he walked. He turned his recriminations inward, but could not stop them. What a useless blockhead he was!

He hadn't expected to be allowed to speak privately with Sarah, but he should never have left before giving Lady Mountheath the set-down she deserved for her vile aspersions on Sarah's character. "Loose ways," indeed!

It did no good to tell himself that defending her might have rebounded on Sarah's head. He had been cowardly to leave rather than speak—afraid that he would lose control entirely. He *would* master his anger in such circumstances. He must, if he were to help Sarah escape her situation.

Harry was just finishing the breakfast to which he'd invited himself when Peter returned to the house on Grosvenor Street. "You're about early," Harry remarked, then sharpened his gaze. "What has you in a lather already?"

"It's not early. It's nearly one o'clock," Peter snapped. "Most people have been up for hours already."

But Harry only grinned. "Don't take it out on me, whatever it is. Miss Killian still leading you a merry chase, is she?"

Peter glared at his friend, in no mood for his banter. "Miss Killian is none of your concern. But if you hear anyone slinging her name about, tell me at once so I can call the blackguard out."

"Lining up duels now, are you? What, has she done something to tarnish her reputation? Or is it something you've done? No wonder you were on edge last night."

"Don't make me erase that smirk from your face, Harry," Peter warned. He'd tried to forget his violence at the club the night before, a reminder of the risk he ran if he followed his chosen course. "It's that damned Lady Mountheath, making insinuations. Foul-mouthed fishwife! I should have—" Peter made a convulsive motion of his arm.

Harry's eyes widened. "Glad to see you've got over your tendency to overreact. Clearly the harpy needs to be exterminated. Should I see to it, by way of repayment for your championing me last night?"

The absurdity of the suggestion brought Peter up short. "You're right. It seems I can't safely form an attachment. My reason goes right out the window."

"Attachments are overrated." Harry shrugged. "Tumble the girl and the madness will pass. Best way to get a wench out of your system, I've found."

"How dare you—?" But then Peter realized Harry was still baiting him. "It's not that easy, at least for me. Not that I would . . . or she would—Damn it, Harry, don't start me thinking along those lines!" But he'd already been thinking along those lines for some time, without Harry's help.

"Figure a way to get her away from the Mountheaths, then," Harry suggested. "If she's not being put upon, you won't feel a need to spring to her defense. There must be others willing to take her in."

Most of them male, thought Peter sourly. Then he

remembered Mrs. Hounslow. "I need to go out again for a bit. Try to stay out of trouble."

Peter had the carriage brought around, and a few minutes later he was on his way to Gracechurch Street. Once there, he made an inquiry or two and was soon directed to Mrs. Hounslow's small house. His knock was answered by the same maidservant he had tended a week ago.

"Good afternoon, Maggie," he said, sweeping her a bow. "How is your ankle?"

Though she must have been near sixty, Maggie blushed. "It's fine, sir, thank you for asking. But how—?"

"I was hoping I might speak with your mistress. Would you tell her that Lord Peter Northrup has come to call?"

The maid's eyes widened. "Lord—Yes, yes, I'll tell her. Do come in, my lord." Leaving him to enter the house on his own, she scurried off.

A moment later, Mrs. Hounslow entered the tiny hall. "Come into the parlor, do, Lord Peter. I am delighted to have this opportunity to express my gratitude again for your kindness on Monday. Dare I hope that you have seen Miss Killian, the young woman who was with me, in company since then?"

Peter blinked, but followed the still-chattering woman into a small, neat parlor and took the seat she indicated. Maggie bustled back in with a tea tray, curtsied, then backed out of the room, her eyes wide.

"It is Miss Killian about whom I have come to speak with you, Mrs. Hounslow," he said when she finally paused for breath. "I fear her situation with the Mountheaths is far from ideal."

Mrs. Hounslow clicked her tongue. "Truly, I

thought after that wickedly accurate portrayal in the *Political Register* last month, Lady Mountheath would leap at a chance to appear philanthropic. But perhaps it is simply not in her nature. What, my lord, do you mean by 'far from ideal?'"

"It is clear that the Mountheaths spend nothing on her clothing, forcing her to wear castoffs. I suspect Lady Mountheath keeps her in her room much of the time, and on at least one occasion she has been denied supper. In addition, Lady Mountheath speaks . . . rudely of her." The list of grievances that had roused him to such indignation on Sarah's behalf sounded rather petty when spoken aloud.

"I see." Mrs. Hounslow's expression might have been called calculating in a face less kindly than hers. "Then you have spent a deal of time in Miss Killian's company, my lord?"

Peter shifted in his chair. "Not a great deal of time, no, but I have an observant nature. Is there no one else who might be induced to take her in?"

Mrs. Hounslow shook her head. "With the decease of her grandfather, the Mountheaths are her nearest relations—which is why I brought her to them. I'd have had her with me, but I've no room. Nor can I offer her the opportunities the Mountheaths can."

"What of when she was first orphaned?" he asked then. "Didn't she live here before she went away to school?"

"Alas, no," the kind lady replied. "The poor dear escaped from a workhouse and was living on the streets when I discovered her. I shudder to think what would have become of her, had I not convinced her grandfather to send her to school."

So that was when Sarah must have learned to pick pockets—while fending for herself as a mere child. Again, his heart twisted to think of what she must have endured, at the mercy of the London streets and predators like that thief-master she had once mentioned.

"I'm very glad you found her," he said as he stood to take his leave. "Thank you for your time, Mrs. Hounslow. Shall I give your regards to Miss Killian when I see her next?"

"Please do, my dear boy." She took his hand with a grandmotherly smile. "And thank you for keeping an eye on her. I hope you will continue to do so, as you are in a much better position to protect her than I am. She is quite alone in the world—poor, sweet dear."

Though chagrined that she had read him so well, Peter nodded. "You may trust me to do so, madam." In fact, he intended to keep a far closer eye on Sarah than he'd done thus far.

This had been one of the longest Sundays Sarah could remember, and it was by no means over yet. As Lady Mountheath had commanded, she had spent the afternoon and evening in her room, her solitude enlivened first by more mending and then by an assortment of brasses she was required to polish.

Now she picked at her dinner, a plate of cold chicken, regretting not at all her banishment from the dining room. The continuous jibes from the Mountheath ladies and the unctuous courtesies of Lord Mountheath tended to steal her appetite, quite apart from her need to think and plan alone.

The family would be staying home tonight, but

she had hopes that they might retire early. Pushing away her plate, she penned the letter she meant to enclose with her next parcel for William. Now she had only to wait for the household to retire, and she would be ready for her next foray as Saint of Seven Dials.

Wishing in vain for a novel, she passed the time concocting various housebreaking plans and the excuses she would use should she be caught. Finally, she stretched out on her bed for a nap. She would need to be alert and well-rested for the night ahead.

Sarah jerked awake with a start. How long had she slept? Her room boasted no clock, so she stepped softly to her door to discover it had already been locked for the night. The family must be abed, then. Donning the same cloak and shawl she'd worn for her foray to Seven Dials, she unlocked the door and peered into the hallway, to find it dark and silent.

Creeping into the hallway, she made her way out of the house just as she'd done twice before. Her plan was to find an unlocked door or window nearby, slip inside, and find a few things to sweeten the package she meant to send to William. She assuaged her conscience by telling herself that nearly every wealthy person she had met thus far merited the Saint's attention.

She would stay well away from Lord Peter's residence, of course.

Once out the garden gate, she stuck to the mews, sizing up each great house as she passed it. Some still had lamps blazing, attesting to ongoing social events. Though doors would doubtless be unlocked, she didn't quite have the brazenness necessary to enter one of those. Instead, she focused on the dark houses, where the inhabitants were either abed or away.

She was about to slip into the back garden of one such house, only three doors down from the Mountheaths', when a soft whistling alerted her to a stable lad who was filling buckets with grain in a building behind her. Trying to appear as though she were on some sort of errand—though what that might be at such an hour she couldn't have said—she continued on her way.

The next house was dark as well, and this time she carefully glanced around before proceeding. For a moment she thought she saw a shadow in the direction she'd just come. It slipped aside before she could focus on it, however, and she convinced herself it was likely a cat, magnified by the fog—or perhaps some other person on secretive business that had nothing to do with her.

Silently, she unlatched the gate and made her way to the back of the house to try the doors and ground-floor windows. All, unfortunately, were locked. Disappointed, she tried her purloined key in the back door, but it was far too small, nor did she have any particular lock-picking skills. She'd have to try elsewhere.

Slipping back into the mews, she continued along the remainder of that side of Berkley Square. The next house was lit. The one after that, the last one backing onto the mews, appeared dark, but halfway across the garden she saw firelight and movement from the kitchen windows. Increasingly frustrated, she retreated again. Surely there must be an easy target somewhere nearby?

She emerged onto Mount Street, which was distressingly well lit by streetlamps despite the fog, and which further boasted a watchman making his rounds only a short distance away. Sarah lurked in the shadows until the watchman's back was turned, then used the clatter of a passing carriage to disguise any sound she might make hurrying across the street.

An alley led to the mews between Mount and Grosvenor Streets, where she continued her quest for an easy mark. The second house along the mews was dark, and again she crept across its back garden to discover whether she might be able to gain entrance.

The kitchen door was locked, as was the garden door from the ground floor. She was just turning away with another stab of disappointment when she noticed a ground-floor window that was open an inch or two. Finally! The casement was stiff, which perhaps explained why it had been left open. Five minutes of tugging yielded results, however, and at last she was able to clamber through the opening with an inch or two to spare.

Once inside, she stood motionless until her eyes adjusted somewhat to the darkness, the window behind her letting in only the merest glimmer of light from Mount Street. The room appeared to be a library or study with a desk, a couple of large chairs, and shelves lining at least one wall.

Cautiously, fearful of knocking over something in the dark, she moved to the desk. Though she opened drawer after drawer, she found nothing but pens, ink and writing paper. Perhaps the owners of the house were away from Town and had taken everything of value with them. Stifling a sigh, she crossed to the door and slowly pushed it open, cringing when the hinges uttered a faint squeal.

She froze, but when several fearful heartbeats later there was still no other sound, she stepped into the hall. Assuming this house was laid out like most others she'd seen, this floor would contain the dining room, while upstairs would be a parlor or two, along with the bedrooms.

She had no real assurance that the house was truly empty—indeed, the open window argued against it—so she crossed to the dining-room door rather than risk the stairs. Inside she found the usual table and sideboard, gleaming faintly in the dim light from the tall windows.

Sarah smiled. Here, finally, was her reward for the frightening hour she'd just spent. The table was set for the next day's meal, with silver and crystal for six. In addition, the sideboard held several silver serving pieces. Unfolding one of the heavy linen serviettes, she rolled as many pieces of silver as would fit into it, ensuring that they would not clink together.

She did the same with the other five serviettes, then placed one of her Saint cards on the sideboard before carrying her bundle back to the library. There she pulled out the oilcloth and twine she'd pilfered from the Mountheath pantries, and wrapped the whole lot into a tight parcel, her note to William inside. Perfect!

Breathing a sigh of relief that this stage of her evening's adventure was over, she went to the window and dropped her parcel through, then climbed after it herself. As she did so, however, her skirts snagged on the sill inside, catching her halfway through, her legs dangling outside while her head was still in the library. What a mercy she was alone, she thought, for she surely looked quite ridiculous.

Torn between panic and an hysterical urge to laugh, she pulled herself partly back through the window so that she could uncatch her skirts, then finally made her way awkwardly to the ground. She stooped to retrieve her parcel, then froze. A watchman, either the same she'd seen before or another, was sauntering down the mews, his lantern swinging as he called out the time—half past one—and the state of the weather.

Vainly she recalled how little she and the other street children had feared the Watch, how inept the old "charleys" seemed to be. She had far more at stake now, and to be caught would be disastrous. A vivid vision arose of Lady Mountheath answering the door in her nightcap to be confronted by Sarah in the grip of the watchman—and then ordering that she be clapped in prison.

Crouched in the shadows, she bit her lip as he paused at the very garden gate through which she had come and peered in her direction, his lantern now held high, a luminous sphere in the fog. "Hoy! Who goes there?" he called out.

Knowing no other recourse, Sarah stayed still as a mouse, closed her eyes tightly, and prayed.

"You there! Watchman!" The shout roused her from her huddling terror. "One of your fellows needs assistance on Berkley Square."

"Eh? What?"

The other man repeated his news. "A group of

young ruffians," he added. "Two of you should be enough to disperse them."

The watchman thanked the unseen man in the quavering tones of the elderly, then shuffled back the way he'd come. Sarah remained frozen, hoping the newcomer would not notice her, trying to convince herself she'd only imagined she recognized his voice.

But then, unmistakably, she heard Lord Peter say, "You may come out now, Miss Killian. He's gone."

Chapter 12

Peter would have laughed at the expression on Sarah's face as she came toward him if not for the knot of disappointment and worry in the pit of his stomach. Up until the moment she'd gone through that window twenty minutes earlier, he'd tried to convince himself that she had some honest reason for creeping around back gardens in the dead of night.

Not that he'd really believed it.

"What . . . what are you doing here?" she asked, stopping just the other side of the gate.

"Trying to keep you out of trouble," he said, "though with indifferent success, it seems. Now, suppose you tell me exactly what is going on."

Sarah bit her lip, staring down at the bulky bundle she held for so long that it seemed she would not answer. Then, with a little shrug, she met his eyes squarely. "Trust me, my lord, you would be far better off not knowing."

"I'll decide what is best for myself, I believe. But come. This is no place to talk." He held the gate open for her just as though they were at some polite gathering rather than skulking behind a house that did not belong to either of them.

After another, briefer hesitation, she passed through the gate to stand at his side. "Where do you wish to go?"

He considered, but there was really only one answer, improper as it seemed. "My house. It's just around the corner."

"I know," she said softly. "But—"

"No one will see us enter, and I'll take care no one sees us leave. Can you think of anyplace safer?"

She shook her head.

"Nor can I. Here, let me carry that for you." He reached for her bundle. Not surprisingly, she clung to it.

"It's . . . it's not heavy. Besides—"

"It's only fitting that you carry the burden of your sins yourself?" he asked.

She opened her mouth, closed it, and finally nodded again. "Something like that."

Sarah balanced the parcel against one hip and Peter tucked her other hand into the crook of his arm. Why he persisted in behaving as though she were merely a lady on an unorthodox outing, he didn't know. Was he still trying to delude himself?

They crossed Grosvenor Street and a few moments later reached Marcus's house. A glance up and down the street showed no one within sight. "I told the footmen not to wait up," Peter explained as he unlocked the front door himself.

Sarah preceded him into the hallway, and he then showed her into the library, which somehow seemed the best setting for an inquisition. She took the seat he indicated while he stirred the embers on the hearth back into flame. Then, seating himself opposite her, he simply said, "Well?"

"I don't suppose you would believe me if I said I was merely retrieving a ... er, cloak that Lady Mountheath accidentally left at that house?"

Peter shook his head, sternly suppressing a most inappropriate urge to smile. "I would not. Particularly since I heard earlier this evening that Miss Cheevers discovered one of the Saint's calling cards in her reticule last night, upon her return home. May I assume that the Llewellyns will find one as well?"

"Yes," she admitted after another long hesitation. "But I'm ... I'm not actually the Saint of Seven Dials, you know."

"No, I don't see how you can be. The authorities, however, now seem convinced that their earlier guess was wrong and that the Saint is indeed back in business."

To his surprise, Sarah actually smiled. "They do? Good."

He regarded her questioningly and her expression changed, became more guarded.

"I mean, as long as they are looking for the real Saint, they are unlikely to suspect me," she explained, a little too glibly. He was certain this was not the real reason for her relief.

"You must remember, however, what I told you. Though it appears the Runners do not know of the link between the Saint and the traitor, you can be assured that certain men in government do. Believe me, Sarah, you do not want your name brought into that."

She swallowed visibly. "No, of course not. But surely there is little risk of that. I can prove that I was not in London at the time of the previous thefts, or during the traitor's activities."

"True. But now, I'd very much like to know why you are stealing in the first place. Is someone demanding money of you?"

She appeared to think for a moment, then shook her head. "I am merely trying to lay a bit by, against the inevitable day when Lady Mountheath finally turns me out."

"Ah. Then it's nothing to do with your, ah, friend's brother, the boy you were looking for earlier?"

Her blue eyes went wide and worried. "What do you—? No, no, of course not."

Peter merely looked at her, for her reaction had answered his question clearly enough. She seemed to realize it.

"I told you that after I was orphaned, I lived in London," she continued after a moment. "It happens that I still have a few friends from that time—friends who are in need."

"So the story you told me of your friend's brother was entirely fictitious? That lad, Flute, was really one of these 'friends' you were attempting to locate?"

Again alarm flared in her eyes, but she nodded, slowly. "One of them, yes. He's just a boy, of course," she added. "He knows nothing of what I've done."

"I see." She seemed quite anxious to protect these "friends." "Surely there must have been a safer way for you to acquire money besides stealing?" he asked then.

The look she gave him was far too cynical for her young face. "I have tried to get employment, if you recall. I intend to keep trying, but everyone tells me I have little chance of success. It may be difficult for a man to understand, but a young woman alone in the world has few options—and even fewer respectable ones."

He blinked, surprised to realize that not only was she right, but he'd never really thought about it before. Where a boy or young man might put his muscles to work if his brain would not serve, a female had few choices. Sarah was too young to be employed as a companion and too pretty to easily get a position as governess—and those comprised the extent of respectable positions for an educated woman. That, and—

"There is always marriage." The words seemed to escape without his volition.

"So the Duke of Wickburn suggested to Lady Mountheath," she replied. Though she continued to meet his eyes, her color deepened slightly. "But given my . . . situation, that seems more dishonest than stealing. Am I to persuade some man to take a pig in the poke simply to escape the Mountheaths' tender care?"

"You are no 'pig in the poke,' Sarah, but an intelligent and exceptionally beautiful young lady," Peter said, leaning forward to take her hand in his. "And I know of one man, at least, who would need no persuasion at all."

She stared, the rosy hue abruptly leaving her cheeks. "Is that an offer of marriage, my lord?"

"Not very eloquent, eh? But I would be greatly honored if you would become my wife, Miss Killian. I—"

But she was already shaking her head. "I know, both from my own experience and from what others have said about you, that you are exceedingly kind and often rescue those in trouble. While I am most grateful for your gallant offer, I fear I could never— that is—" She choked on something suspiciously like a sob.

To his dismay, he saw tears shimmering in her lovely blue eyes. At once he was beside her, his arms enfolding her, desperate to ease her pain. "Please believe me, Sarah, that I do not offer out of pity, but because I truly believe we could be happy together. Do you not believe so as well?"

She managed a watery smile. "I can scarcely deny I'd be far happier as your wife than as Lady Mountheath's ward—as you must know. But I could not live with myself if I allowed you to make such a sacrifice on my behalf."

"Sacrifice!"

Even now, it seemed, she was unwilling to put her own interests ahead of his. "Does this seem like sacrifice to you?" Peter covered her lips with his and began to show her in the most direct way possible just what she meant to him.

After a stunned moment, Sarah melted into the kiss, feeling for an instant that she'd found heaven. For a few blissful seconds she felt loved, cherished, protected—but then grim reality intruded, even as Lord Peter's lips thrilled her senses.

He desired her, yes, but she already knew that. Desire alone could never sustain the sort of union he proposed, unequal in every way. He had social position, a noble lineage, and enough money, at least, to live comfortably. She had nothing—nothing but the beauty she had almost come to regard as a curse.

And now it threatened to curse Lord Peter as well—the only person other than Mrs. Hounslow who had ever been kind to her. She could think of only one way to repay him, to prevent him from ruining his life for her sake.

Tilting her head back, she allowed him to rain kisses on her throat as she undid the top buttons of her dowdy gray gown. With a throaty growl, he followed her fingers with his lips, trailing fire down her chest, to the cleft between her breasts.

Quickly, her heart pounding, she undid the rest of her bodice, baring herself to the waist except for her sheer chemise. Perhaps this would be no sacrifice after all! With shaking fingers, she untied the strings at the top of the chemise.

His hands roved over her bare shoulders, her upper back, while his lips caressed the upper swells of her breasts. Sarah felt her breath coming in quick gasps, ready and more than ready for whatever might follow.

Then, suddenly, he stilled. "What . . . what are you—what are we doing? There will be time enough for this once we are wed. I'll procure a special license tomorrow, and then—"

Smiling, Sarah shook her head. "There is no need. Don't you see? You need not marry me. I am willing to give myself to you with no strings attached."

Instead of the delighted surprise she expected, he looked shocked. Pulling away from her, he said, "I'm not sure I understand. You are offering . . .

what? A night of pleasure in payment for my help tonight—and my silence?"

Put like that, it sounded sordid, even mercenary. She put out a hand, hoping to somehow recapture the passion that had been growing between them only moments ago. "No! I simply want—" *You*, she nearly said aloud "—to make you happy," she continued. "You have been so kind to me, even knowing—"

"What will make me happy is to know that you are safe. I'm not certain you realize the danger you are in, Sarah. We cannot know that no one else saw you stealing from Miss Cheevers's reticule last night. Now that the alarm has been raised, rewards will be posted again for the capture of the Saint. As your husband, I can protect you."

The concern in his eyes melted Sarah's heart. To be Lord Peter's wife would be the fulfillment of every fairy-tale fantasy she had ever entertained. But at what price?

Sadly, she shook her head again. "You cannot have thought this through, my lord. What would your family say, were you to marry someone like me?"

"Do you think I care—" he began, but she silenced him with a finger to his lips.

"Apart from my lack of family or fortune," she continued, "there is the very risk you mention. Should I be suspect as the Saint of Seven Dials, that suspicion might well reflect upon you as well. That would be a fine way to repay your generosity to me, would it not?"

He scowled at her. "Don't you see that I care nothing for that?" he demanded.

"But I do," she said quietly. "I would not be able to

abide myself if I brought any sort of harm to you—
or to your name."

For a moment he stared at her, an arrested expression in his eyes, then he seemed to relax slightly. "Will you at least promise not to steal again?"

She thought for a moment. If the pursuit was really as hot as he said, she wasn't sure she dared attempt another robbery. Besides, if she refused, he would undoubtedly resume his insistence that she marry him, whatever price he might eventually have to pay. She wasn't sure she could hold out against him much longer. Her unselfishness had its limits.

"I promise. In fact, here are my remaining Saint cards, as surety." She pulled the last five cards from her pocket and handed them to him. "Please, though, let me dispose of this last package as I see fit."

Taking the cards from her, he nodded. "I'll see you home," he said.

Home. To think, had she chosen, her home might have been with him instead of the odious Mountheaths! Had she been unconscionably stupid to refuse his offer? Lady Mountheath and others of her ilk would certainly say so.

At one time she'd thought she would do anything short of sacrificing her virtue to take care of her brother. Tonight had shown her how wrong she was. She had been ready to give her virtue away, even without material advantage—but the one thing she would not do was allow this kind man—this man she had grown to love—to give up everything for her sake, or even William's.

Taking his arm, she reluctantly let her brief, beautiful fantasy dissipate into nothingness, resolved to take what satisfaction she could from knowing she had done the right thing.

Peter glanced down at the amazing girl by his side as they made their way along the mews behind Berkley Square. What a gallant spirit she had! Even now, with the authorities practically on her heels and no real prospects, she sought to protect others before herself.

Whether or not young Flute was her brother, Peter couldn't help admiring the determined way she had insisted he was not involved in her crimes. She must be stealing to provide for him, and perhaps others, but not for herself. Understandable, he supposed, that she would be so protective of youngsters living on the streets, as she had once lived herself.

But she was also trying to protect him, Peter. He was amused, but even more, he was humbled. Surely, he had done nothing to deserve such selfless sacrifice on Sarah's part? Nor, of course, could he allow it. Not when it was in his power to save her from her generous folly.

"Here we are," he murmured as they reached the Mountheaths' back gate. "Again. Really, we seem almost to be making a habit of this."

She dimpled up at him in the darkness. "You are very kind to me, my lord. Thank you."

A lance of desire went through him but he restrained it. By this time tomorrow, he would have her agreement to marry him. "Surely you know me well enough now to call me Peter? You have been 'Sarah' in my thoughts for several days now."

"Peter, then," she whispered—a seductive sound.

"Good night, Sarah." It seemed the most natural

thing in the world to take her in his arms for a farewell kiss, nor did she hesitate this time in returning it.

He released her before he could lose himself in her sweetness. For that, he was willing to wait—though not very long. As before, he watched her into the house, a smile curving his lips. Then he turned his steps toward home. Tomorrow promised to be a big day. And the day after, the biggest of his life.

Despite her conflicted emotions, Sarah slept well—too well. Though she'd intended to rise early and slip away to deliver her package of purloined goods to Paddy before the family was astir, she was roused by Fanny's maid, Libby, touching her shoulder.

"Her ladyship wants that you should help me refurbish Miss Fanny's bonnets this morning before the ladies go out shopping," Libby told her, setting coffee and a bun on Sarah's dressing table. "I thought we should start directly, once you've had a bite. I'll wait in the servants' hall with the bonnets and trimmings."

"Thank you, Libby."

Sarah wiped the sleep from her eyes and took a fortifying sip of the lukewarm coffee, cursing her sluggishness. At least retrimming bonnets would be less odious than polishing brasses, and she had both her bittersweet memories of last night and planning for her necessary escape to keep her thoughts occupied.

Guessing that she would not be allowed into the parlor at all today lest she practice her evil wiles on any male visitors, Sarah dressed in one of her old gowns. Then, picking up her sewing things, she headed down the servants' stairs.

As before when she'd been belowstairs, the servants seemed not to know how to act toward her. She couldn't blame them. Lady Mountheath's inconsistency made Sarah neither fish nor fowl. So, though they didn't include her in their conversations, they seemed willing enough to talk in front of her.

"Fair landed on his feet, young Woodruff has," Mrs. Mann, the head cook's assistant was saying. "Sully was sayin' how he's lordin' it over Hardwyck Hall. Fancy, a stripling like him playing at bein' a butler!"

"Aye, I'll bet Miss Fanny'd never have had her ladyship turn him off if she'd known how well he'd end up," said one of the footmen with a chuckle. "Wish it'd been me she blamed instead, when she broke her fan. Think you Lord Hardwyck is still hirin' on staff?"

Libby, sewing next to Sarah, gasped aloud. "Hush now, Thomas! If word gets back to her ladyship you're talkin' like that, you'll find yourself in the street right enough." A sullen murmur of agreement followed this statement.

Clearly, Sarah reflected, being of lower class didn't guarantee happiness any more than did exalted status. It all depended on one's outlook, and one's situation relative to one's peers. But who *were* her own peers now? She wasn't sure she knew.

Had she accepted Lord Peter's offer . . . but no. She mustn't think along those lines, for that way lay regret and unhappiness. He had at least saved her from her momentary weakness, during which she'd come close to fulfilling Lady Mountheath's dire prophecies about her prospects. There was still the respectable alternative of governessing.

Why that thought should depress her so, she wasn't certain.

When she had been sewing for nearly two hours and was finishing the last bonnet, a footman approached her. "Miss Killian?" His tentative expression underscored her uncertain status.

"Yes, Casper?" She smiled kindly at the young man, feeling a need to do all in her power to cheer this cheerless lot.

"There's a gentleman upstairs askin' for you, miss," he said softly. "For you specially. Her ladyship is putting 'im off, but he seems mighty determined. I . . . I thought you should know."

Sarah's heart began to pound. It must be Peter, but why should he be so insistent today? She had refused him in no uncertain terms last night. Had he discovered something else about the authorities' pursuit of the Saint?

"Thank you, Casper." A quick glance showed that none of the other servants seemed to have overheard them. "If you can, tell him I'll be up directly."

Casper nodded, tugging his forelock, then left. Sarah finished attaching the sprig of artificial flowers she'd been working on, laid the bonnet aside and stood.

"I'll be back in a few minutes, Libby," she said to the maid's questioning look. "I've, ah, forgotten something upstairs."

She wished now she'd worn something more attractive, but there was no time to go up to her room and change. Smoothing her hair with her fingers, her nerves humming with anticipation, she made her way up the back stairs to the first floor, then tip-toed to the parlor door.

"Should Miss Killian not have received my message by now, my lady?" Peter was saying.

"No doubt," Lady Mountheath replied. "Likely she is composing a reply, saying that she does not feel equal to coming downstairs—just as I've been telling you."

Smiling, Sarah entered the room. "How good of you to inquire after me, Lord Peter. I am feeling much more the thing now, my lady, but I thank you for your concern."

Flushing, Lady Mountheath opened her mouth then shut it again, apparently realizing that to order Sarah from the room would be to contradict whatever tale she had concocted to account for her absence.

"I'm delighted to see you so well, Miss Killian," said Peter, springing to his feet. "And what a fetching gown that is."

Sarah glanced down at her old gray homespun, then back up, to see his eyes dancing. She nearly laughed aloud, but caught herself in time.

"You are too kind, my lord," she said with only the smallest tremor to her voice. She dropped a small curtsey and he took her hand as she rose.

"Not at all. It is perfectly proper to compliment the woman I hope to make my wife."

A stunned silence greeted his words. The Mountheath ladies all gaped, while Sarah herself felt the color drain from her face. How could he do this, after she had unequivocally refused last night to marry him?

"I . . . I beg your pardon, my lord?" she finally

managed to gasp, risking a quick glance at Lady Mountheath, who was opening and closing her mouth, not unlike a codfish.

He kept his hold on her hand, the warmth of his fingers penetrating his glove. "I am asking you to marry me, Miss Killian." Though he still smiled, there was a determination behind his twinkling brown eyes that told her he knew exactly what he was doing.

Helplessly, Sarah began to shake her head. "I told you—that is, I cannot—"

"Of course she cannot," Lady Mountheath exclaimed, abruptly finding her voice. "She knows full well that you have been courting *my Lucy*, Lord Peter. What sort of perfidy is this?"

He turned, his expression unruffled. "With all due apology, my lady, I have been doing no such thing. Can either of you cite anything I have actually said that implied I had intentions toward Miss Mountheath?"

Both appeared to be cudgeling their memories, but after a moment Lucy retreated to a pout. Sarah was relieved to note that it appeared her pride was more wounded than her heart. Lady Mountheath was not willing to give up so easily, however.

"You have called frequently, my lord, and have danced with my daughter on more than one occasion."

"I have danced with both of your daughters, my lady, but only because they rather brazenly put themselves in my way."

At this, Fanny, who had been grinning maliciously at her sister's discomfiture, abruptly sobered.

"My object in calling has been to see Miss Killian,"

he continued, "as I think you have suspected for some time. You have made it quite plain that it is burdensome to keep her under your roof. I should think you would be happy to be relieved of your responsibility for her."

By now Sarah had managed to gather her wits, determined that she would not be bullied into a course she knew to be wrong—or, at least, not in Peter's best interests. "You forget, my lord, that I have not consented to marry you," she said. "Nor do I intend to do so."

Lady Mountheath gave a snort that might have denoted satisfaction, but Peter seemed undeterred. "A word alone, if you please, Miss Killian. If we may, my lady?" This last was directed to Lady Mountheath, who stiffly inclined her head.

"Come, girls," she grated to her daughters, who followed her from the room with obvious reluctance. She left the parlor door pointedly ajar.

The moment they were gone, Sarah hissed, "How dare you try to force my hand like this? I thought I had made my feelings perfectly clear."

To her surprise, he smiled. "I flatter myself that your feelings are far from indifferent to me, despite your stubborn determination to refuse my hand. Am I wrong?"

She could not deny it, so she merely glared. "My reasons—"

"Your reasons do you credit, but I fancy I know a bit more of the world than you do. You will simply have to trust my judgment in this."

"Will I, indeed?" she asked, both startled and angry at his high-handedness. "And why is that?"

He shot a quick glance at the parlor door, and if

anything his smile broadened. "Because, Miss Killian, after spending much of last night alone with me at my house, you really have no other choice."

Sarah opened her mouth to inform him that she most certainly did have a choice, when the parlor door was flung wide to reveal a scarlet-faced Lady Mountheath.

"You young hussy!" she exclaimed, her ample frame quivering with outrage. "Is this true? You deceitfully crept out of the house last night to keep an assignation with . . . I am not certain I can now term you a gentleman, Lord Peter. I am shocked. Shocked!"

While Sarah looked on in horror, he bowed his head as though in penitence, though she could see the corners of his mouth twitching. "I fear it is true, my lady. Our passions overcame our reason, though of course I take full blame. Had I known Miss Killian had no intention of accepting my hand, I would never have been so indiscreet."

"Indiscreet?" Lady Mountheath echoed suspiciously.

He shrugged. "If I could be certain that no one saw her enter or leave my house, then I suppose we could agree to pretend that nothing happened. As it is, however . . ." His voice trailed off, his hands spread wide as though open to suggestions.

"Do you mean you were *seen*?" Lady Mountheath's horror now appeared to exceed Sarah's. "But the scandal . . . It is well known she is my ward—" She rounded on Sarah, waving a finger in her face. "You will marry Lord Peter without delay, miss. Without delay! Or you will find yourself with no roof over your head this very night."

Before Sarah could respond, she turned back to

Peter. "I assume you can make the arrangements, my lord? Time is of the essence."

Maddeningly, he smiled again and patted his breast pocket. "Indeed I can, my lady. It happens that I have procured a special license this very morning, which only requires your signature. Assuming you will provide it, we can be married by noon tomorrow."

Chapter 13

Before Sarah could summon her voice to protest this peremptory ordering of her future—of the rest of her life!—Lady Mountheath and Lord Peter had launched into a discussion of announcements and the time and place for the ceremony.

"I dropped off an announcement to the papers on my way here," he was saying. "We will be married from my father's house, at half past ten tomorrow morning. I trust that will be convenient for your family, my lady?"

"My—Goodness, I must inform them at once! A wedding at Marland House! Lucy and Fanny must choose their ensembles. Miss Killian, would you—? Oh. No, I suppose not. If you will excuse me?" Still muttering to herself, she bustled off.

Sarah thought that Peter turned back to her rather

reluctantly, his brows raised in a boyish expression of apologetic appeal that nearly melted her heart again. Nearly.

"You . . . you orchestrated this whole thing," she sputtered. "You know perfectly well we were not seen last night. And you knew that Lady Mountheath was listening outside the door!"

"Guilty on all counts," he confessed, though his look of contrition was marred by his dancing eyes. "I could think of no other way to overcome your noble if misguided insistence on sacrificing yourself for my sake. Trust me, Sarah, it is better this way."

She wanted to. Oh! how she wanted to. But—"You said we are to be married at your father's house? Does that mean you have already informed him of this? How did he respond?"

Now he looked rather sheepish. "Truth to tell, I haven't yet been to see him. I, er, wanted to be secure of you first, you see. He is wont to question the judgment of others. I didn't wish to give him a chance to gloat, should you have refused me."

"But I did refuse you," she pointed out.

"Only because you wanted to protect me. Now, however, my reputation will be in far worse shape if I do not marry you than if I do. Lady Mountheath will see to that," he concluded cheerfully.

Appalled, Sarah realized he was right. If she persisted in her refusal, not only would her 'benefactress' pitch her into the street, she would certainly do everything in her power to blacken Lord Peter's name along with Sarah's.

"It would appear I have no choice," she finally admitted. "Of course I cannot allow the world to censure you on my account. Nor do I much fancy living on the streets. I'll not forget that you forced my hand, however." It was surprising how angry she felt about something that should have filled her with joy.

Peter sobered. "No, I suppose not. But I do hope you will find it in your heart to forgive me eventually."

Sarah felt her heart softening already, but resisted the feeling. "Perhaps, given enough time. *Some* things cannot be rushed," she said, then immediately regretted her acid tone.

He appeared—or pretended—not to notice, however. "With so much at stake, I dared not tarry. Nor should I tarry now. I have still to visit my father, and make arrangements with the clergyman for tomorrow, among other things."

Sarah's earlier fears suddenly revived. "Suppose he refuses to accept our marriage, or to allow it to take place in his house?"

"Then we will hold it elsewhere," Peter said lightly, leaning down to give her a swift kiss before picking up his hat. "I am not dependent upon his approval. As he has met you, however, I have no doubt he will be delighted. You need not fear on that head."

"Absolutely not," declared the Duke of Marland with a scowl. "I forbid it."

Peter stifled a sigh. He'd known his father would take some persuading, but he hadn't expected such vehement opposition. "I thought you and Mother were anxious for me to marry," he said reasonably.

The duke's scowl deepened. "To marry a woman befitting your station and lineage, yes. This Miss Killian may be beautiful, but she is scarcely worthy of a Northrup."

"She is more than worthy," Peter snapped, his own anger stirring at this echo of Sarah's own words about herself. "I have come to know her quite well over the past week or so."

"A week—what is that? Not three months ago Marcus was forced by scandal to marry that American he'd only just met, and now you do the same thing. I had thought your judgment superior to his, but it appears I was wrong. You did not even learn from his mistake."

With an effort, Peter kept his voice level. "Marcus and Quinn are deliriously happy, so I would scarcely call their marriage a mistake. Nor will I remain while you slander my future wife."

The duke raised one thin, graying brow. "The truth is scarcely slander. My inquiries show that Miss Killian's father was a penniless Irish tutor, her mother the cast-off daughter of a minor baron. That in no way puts her on an equal social footing with you."

Peter was startled to discover the duke already knew about Sarah's grandfather's title, which Peter himself had planned to use as persuasion. Trust his father's network of informants to ferret out the truth, and only two days after first meeting Sarah. He was careful not to let his surprise show, however.

"You speak as though I am marrying a scullery maid. Miss Killian's lineage may not equal mine, but it is respectable enough. As her parents are both dead, you need not fear they will be a source of embarrassment to you."

Though the duke snorted, he did not argue the point.

"I merely wished to inform you, as a courtesy, so that you would not learn of my plans from the afternoon papers," Peter continued. "As it appears I must find another venue for my nuptials tomorrow, I will take my leave of you." He turned to go.

His father's voice stopped him. "No, no, you must be married here. Whether I approve or not, the girl will be a Northrup, so the family must be seen to validate her. Whatever our differences, I'll not have them become a source of common gossip."

"As you wish." Peter concealed a smile. His father's pride made him a rival of Lady Mountheath in his determination to avoid public scandal. "I will ask the Mountheaths to have her here at a quarter past ten tomorrow."

"Very well. I only hope Anthony does not take it into his head to marry some chance-met girl next week. I'm not certain my constitution could take it." With that, the duke waved him away.

"You understand, then?" Sarah asked Paddy, who already clutched the package she'd given him.

Not until evening had she been able to slip away, for Lady Mountheath had insisted Sarah accompany her and her daughters on their shopping expedition, after which she'd been subjected to a lengthy lecture on the gratitude she owed the family—a gratitude Lady Mountheath hoped she would express to all.

"Aye, miss. This goes the same way as the last, and if I needs to get word to you about anythin' you'll be at Renny's house." Paddy grinned widely.

"I knowed you'd find a rich nob to take care o' ye, miss!"

"Lord Peter is *marrying* me, Paddy," Sarah said, wondering again at the miracle as she spoke the words. The boy's awestruck expression showed she'd been right that he'd misinterpreted her news. How many others might make the same assumption?

"Cor! Can't say I blame 'im, though. If'n I was older, I'd want to marry you myself," he said with a grin and a wink. "Oh, I almost forgot." He dug into his pocket and pulled out a grimy slip of paper. "Renny give me this to pass along, should I see you again."

Sarah smoothed the sheet and scanned it. "It's a list of names," she said. "But who are they?"

Paddy shrugged. "He said 'the bloke what sent the package' would know. I didn't tell him it weren't no bloke, o' course." He grinned again.

Some of the names, she noticed, had notations next to them. *Simpkins: rent. Kramer: surgeon.* These must be the families William had mentioned as needing the Saint's help. She sighed, for she knew she would not be in a position to send anything more.

"Thank you, Paddy. And now I must hurry back, before I am missed."

"Don't forget Paddy once you're a fine lady, miss."

"I won't," she promised, though she doubted she'd be able to help him any more than she could those others on the paper William had sent.

Walking briskly back to Berkley Square, she

glanced at the list again. Even if Peter were a rich man, she would not ask him to donate any money. He had done so much for her already. She wasn't even bringing a dowry to this marriage, which made her little more than a charity case.

Though having the power of choice taken away still stung, Sarah knew Peter had done this to protect her, and she loved him all the more for it. After all, she herself had built much of her life around her determination to protect her brother.

Thoughts of William brought up yet another dilemma. Just last night, she had told Peter that Flute was but a friend. How to admit to him that she had lied—again? Someday he would have to know, particularly if Sarah hoped to get William off the streets.

But not now. Not while the idea of the Saint of Seven Dials was yet fresh in Peter's thoughts. Remembering his face when he'd spoken of the original Saint's treason, she doubted that whatever he might feel for her was strong enough to overcome his desire to see the Saint's accomplices brought to justice.

No, her relationship to Flute would have to remain a secret for a while longer.

"Fanny! Take that spray of white roses from your hair and have your maid work it into Sarah's instead," Lady Mountheath commanded. "It will go perfectly with her white satin gown."

"*My* white satin gown," Fanny grumbled, reluctantly unpinning the silk flowers from her wispy chignon.

Sarah sat bemused amid the flurry of preparation for her wedding, which was to take place in less than an hour's time. So anxious was Lady Mountheath that the Duke of Marland find no fault with her care that she was taking great pains with Sarah's appearance—to her daughters' evident disgust.

"It seems wrong, Mama, to *reward* Miss Killian for stealing Lord Peter away from me," Lucy said petulantly as she directed the crimping of her own curls.

"Were you truly attached to him, then?" Sarah had to ask. "I never meant—"

"Attached? What has that to do with it?" Lucy replied, clearly affronted that Sarah had dared to address her. "Of course I was not *attached* to him—he is neither so handsome nor so charming as Mr. Galloway. But he *was* my most eligible suitor, and you had no right to seduce him away from me."

Sarah gasped. "I did not—!"

"Girls, girls," Lady Mountheath admonished, for once not taking sides. "We have no time for bickering just now. We are expected at Marland House in half an hour. Fanny, where is your blue bonnet, the one that matches your gown?"

Twenty minutes later they all bundled themselves into the carriage for the short drive to Grosvenor Square. Even the Mountheath daughters now seemed excited at the prospect of a wedding in such exalted surroundings. Only Lord Mountheath looked discontented, and Sarah could not bring herself to regret that.

Indeed, she was not sure what she felt. Everything had happened so quickly, her emotions had not yet caught up to the reality of her situation—which would change yet again once the ceremony concluded. It was as though she were caught in a current, being swept along, helpless, to a place she could not yet see.

On reaching the Marland mansion a few minutes later, they were ushered up wide marble stairs, through an enormous pair of double doors and into a wide entry hall. Numerous liveried footmen flanked the passage they traversed behind an imposing butler, until they finally reached the chapel at the rear of the house.

Sarah fought against a sense of unreality, overwhelmed by the magnificence of her surroundings. She had been in other fine houses since coming to London, but this was different. This one belonged to her future family, impossible as that seemed.

That future family was waiting in the chapel, and a glance showed that most of them appeared no more eager to be there than Sarah had expected. The Duke of Marland she recognized, and Lord Bagstead. The women with them must be their wives.

Another gentleman she assumed to be another of Peter's brothers—did he not say he had four? This unknown brother and his wife, at least, looked less disapproving than the others. That was comforting, as was the grin Mr. Thatcher sent her way when she caught his eye.

And there, at the far end of the room, stood Peter himself, heart-stoppingly handsome in subdued black and cream. Her eyes met his across the length of the chapel, and he smiled reassuringly. Unexpected warmth flooded her at that smile, and for a moment she was able to believe that everything would be all right.

"Oh, my dear, I am not late, am I?" came a hurried whisper from behind her. Turning, she saw tiny Mrs. Hounslow, her hands fluttering with excitement.

Sarah gave her a quick hug. "Thank you so much for coming."

"Goodness, I would not have missed this for the world. Especially after Lord Peter—that is—"

A word from the clergyman signaling the start of the service compelled her to silence, and any curiosity over what Mrs. Hounslow had been about to say fled Sarah's mind. Again her gaze sought Peter's, and again she felt that comforting warmth flow through her.

Then, she was moving down the center aisle toward him, to change her circumstances forever.

Though a week earlier Peter would have sworn he never intended to marry, he now found himself repeating his wedding vows steadily, with no reluctance whatsoever. How had Sarah come to mean so much to him in so short a time? It seemed natural, even inevitable, that she should be his wife.

She was as beautiful as he'd ever seen her, in a white satin gown that actually appeared to be new. That in itself was a relief, as there'd been no time for him to have anything made up for her. He had Lady Mountheath's pride to thank, no doubt.

Sarah stumbled over her own vows once or twice, but he hoped that stemmed from nervousness rather than reluctance. When the clergyman at last pronounced them husband and wife, his sense of exultation offered proof that he'd done the right thing.

He hoped Sarah would come to believe that as well.

"Never thought you the impulsive sort, Pete, but you generally know what you're doing," said Harry, the first to come forward. "I suppose congratulations are in order, though I trust you'll shoot me if I ever show signs of the same madness."

Peter had to laugh. "It's a sublime madness, Harry. You'll enjoy it well enough when your turn comes."

Harry recoiled in mock horror. "No need to speak of it as a certainty, old chap! Unlucky, that, I'm sure of it."

He then made way for the other guests, who offered their congratulations with varying degrees of sincerity. As there had not been time before the ceremony, Peter now introduced Sarah to his brother Edward and his wife, as well as to his mother and Robert's wife, Lady Bagstead. Sarah, he noticed, was looking rather dazed.

"You've now met most of my family," Peter told her, drawing her a little apart. "I was unable to get word to two of my brothers in time for the ceremony, however. Marcus is visiting an estate he just purchased with his wife, Quinn, and Anthony is in the Shires, hunting, as he generally is at this time of year."

"I see," she said vaguely, clearly overwhelmed—not that he blamed her. His family did tend to be a bit overwhelming, he supposed.

"Marcus married only last August. You'll like him, and Quinn, I think. She is American and quite personable."

"I, ah, look forward to meeting her." She still seemed ill at ease.

"If it is any comfort to you, their wedding was

nearly as hurried as ours, and under somewhat similar circumstances."

She raised startled brows.

"A threat of scandal," he clarified. "Threatened, ironically, by your own Lady Mountheath. She is becoming quite the family matchmaker."

Sarah gave a small snort of what might have been laughter and glanced over at the Mountheaths, who looked as though they felt nearly as out of place as she did.

"Anthony—well, Anthony can be quite the charmer," Peter continued, trying to keep her mind from her fears. "Perhaps I'm as glad you haven't had a chance to meet him yet. At any rate, he's not at all stuffy—not like Robert there." He nodded toward his eldest brother.

Mrs. Hounslow came up to them just then. "Lady Peter Northrup!" she exclaimed. "How fine it sounds! I knew you were destined for a better life than that of a governess, my dear."

Sarah smiled, her first genuine smile since entering the chapel, though she blushed a deep and charming pink and glanced at Peter in obvious embarrassment. "I . . . er, thank you, Mrs. Hounslow."

"You will take good care of her, won't you, my lord?" The diminutive woman pinned him with a steely look at odds with her affable appearance.

"You may depend upon it, madam," Peter replied with a deep bow. Apparently satisfied, she nodded and moved away.

"What . . . what will I be expected to do next?" Sarah asked then, clearly not completely reassured by the exchange.

Peter placed a hand on her shoulder, startled to discover she was trembling. "Nothing you do not wish to," he assured her. "Come, now, Sarah, surely this can not be as terrifying as other things you've done since coming to London?"

He dared not speak plainer in company, but her glance showed quick comprehension.

"One would think so. However, the past week seems to have been an ever-escalating series of trials, each more fearsome than the last." Her look implied that the next might be worse yet.

He smiled down at her, determined to calm her fears, trying to infuse more confidence than he felt into his expression. "Your trials are at an end now, Sarah. You may trust me to make certain of that."

"I hope so," she said, but her smile was doubtful.

By the time she and Peter returned to the house on Grosvenor Street, Sarah was exhausted, even though it was barely two. The duchess—her mother-in-law!—had insisted on serving an elaborate wedding breakfast, though few seemed inclined to partake. Only Mr. Thatcher and Mrs. Hounslow had evinced much appetite.

The Mountheaths had outstayed their welcome, in Sarah's estimation, for it was clear that none of the duke's household held them in much regard. That, at least, spoke well of the discernment of her new family. It had been a profound relief to see Lord and Lady Mountheath depart, along with their daughters, and to realize she would never again be answerable to any of them.

Now, however, she had new fears to face.

"Here we are," Peter announced cheerfully as the

front door swung open at their approach. To Sarah's amazement, a double row of servants was ranged along the hall within to receive them.

Peter grinned at her surprise, then turned to the staff. "Everyone, please welcome Lady Peter Northrup, your mistress until Lord and Lady Marcus return."

Each male bowed and each female curtsied. As Sarah induced her feet to move again, each one stepped forward.

"Congratulations and welcome, my lady," said the first woman on the right, who boasted a large ring of keys at her waist. "I'm Mrs. Walsh, the housekeeper, and I'm completely at your service. Just you let me know what I can do to make you comfortable here."

Totally unused to such deference, Sarah could only smile and murmur her thanks.

"George, head footman, my lady," said the young man opposite the housekeeper. "I serve here in the stead of a butler."

So it went along the line, until she'd met every member of the staff, down to the redheaded scullery maid, Polly. Only Mrs. MacKay, the cook, was familiar to her. She wondered if she would ever learn all of their names—or if she would be here long enough for it to be necessary.

"This house is your brother's?" she asked as Peter finally led her into the parlor, a more formal room than the library they'd occupied the night before last.

He gave orders for tea to be brought, then sat at one end of a small, elegant sofa, indicating that she should join him.

"My father's, technically. It's been in the family for generations," he said as she tentatively seated herself at the opposite end. "Until his marriage, Anthony and I shared it with Marcus, but we cleared out so he and Quinn could use it as their home. I hadn't arranged for permanent lodgings yet, so Marcus offered me the use of it while he's away."

Sarah nodded, then tried again to frame her true question. He answered it before she could.

"You're wondering, I imagine, where we will live once Marcus returns—which he may do at any time."

"Well . . . yes. Do not feel that I require anything grand, however," she added in a rush. "Quite the opposite, in fact. Never having been accustomed to luxury, I would doubtless find it difficult to get used to."

To her surprise, he was grinning. "Afraid you might pauper me? I'm wounded. Next you'll be offering to take in mending to help make ends meet."

In fact, she had considered just that, but had feared to offend his pride. "I don't wish to be a burden, that is all."

His expression grew serious and he held her gaze with his own. "Sarah, you are no burden. Please believe that. You can never be a burden to me. I married you because I wanted to, and for no other reason."

She regarded him uncertainly. "I thought you did it to protect me—from my own folly."

"Well, yes." He was grinning again. "But only because I *wanted* to. Your folly simply gave me the perfect excuse to do something I already wished to do—almost since meeting you, in fact."

"Oh, come. You'll not convince me you had marriage in mind when you helped poor Maggie on the street. Nor when you saw me again at the Driscolls' rout, wearing Fanny Mountheath's castoffs. As I recall, you tried to push me off on Mr. Thatcher."

He shrugged. "Yes, well, I'd convinced myself that his need was greater than mine. But by the end of the evening, I assure you that I found myself resenting every word he spoke to you."

"I appreciate what you are trying to do, but it is not necessary. I am truly grateful for your—" She almost said "sacrifice," but knew that he would protest the word. "—your generosity in rescuing me from an unpleasant situation. You needn't try to convince me that your reasons were romantic rather than chivalrous."

"Then you are content to find yourself in a marriage of convenience?" he asked, his expression suddenly guarded. "To make no demands of affection upon me, and to expect none in return?"

It wasn't what she preferred at all, but she could hardly say so. "Yes."

"I see. But suppose I want something more?"

Her breath caught. He'd made it clear he desired her when she was last here, and she'd known marriage would likely entail a sating of that desire. Indeed, anticipation of exactly that had dominated her thoughts for the past few hours.

"I was willing to give myself to you without marriage," she reminded him shyly. "You must know I will not deny you now."

"Now that you owe me an even greater debt, you mean?"

She nodded, though she meant much more than that. Now that he'd brought the physical aspect of marriage into the open, she could not deny the stirrings of desire that had so startled her before. Would he—?

"Consider your debt canceled. You owe me nothing."

"But—"

His smile now seemed almost sad. "Don't you see? I could never take you that way, with you under an obligation to me. What sort of hero would that make me? No, when you come to me of your own volition, because you desire me as much as I you, then—and only then—will we pursue that aspect of marriage."

Sarah bit her lip, wondering how to convey to him that she did indeed desire him, did indeed wish to explore what he mentioned so obliquely, to discover what delights the marriage bed might hold. Her eyes caressed the firm line of his jaw, the endearing curl at his temple, her pulse quickening at the thought.

Abruptly, he stood. "I will have Mrs. Walsh show you to your chamber so that you can settle yourself. Meanwhile, I will make inquiries about a more permanent residence, against my brother's return."

He bent over her hand with perfect courtesy, his smile holding nothing but goodwill, though he did not meet her eyes. Then he was gone, the very picture of politeness. Sarah felt like throwing something.

Frustrated desire was a new sensation, and she found she didn't care for it at all. Surely there was some way to tell him that she did indeed want him as he wanted her . . . assuming he really did want her? Could he have said that simply to flatter her rather bruised vanity?

Before she could pursue that unpalatable idea, Mrs. Walsh bustled into the parlor.

"Lord Peter says I'm to show you your chamber, where you can make yourself comfortable," the housekeeper said. Her expression held a trace of disapproval, but whether for Peter's order or Sarah's presence, Sarah couldn't tell.

"I'd . . . like to see my room, yes," she said, rising.

Motioning to a hovering maid to remove the untouched tea tray, Mrs. Walsh conducted Sarah out of the parlor and up the stairs to the next floor, where she opened a door on the right.

"This will be your chamber, my lady." Sarah couldn't suppress a small start each time she heard her new title. "I hope you will find it to your liking."

Sarah paused in the doorway, blinking at the feminine pink-and-yellow decor. Crisp primrose curtains hung at the windows and around the four-poster bed, complementing the rose-pink counterpane and upholstery. Her own small trunk stood at the foot of the bed. Had this been managed in only a day, or had this room belonged to another woman before her?

"Whose are the other rooms?" she asked, oddly reluctant to commit herself to this luxurious new abode.

"The next one along is Lord Peter's, the same one he's used for years," said the housekeeper, pointing. "Lord and Lady Marcus have the rooms across the hall. Your chamber has sat empty for some time, used for storage and such, but we've done our best to clear it out and refurbish it. You've only to let me know if anything is not to your liking, of course, my lady."

"It's lovely," Sarah told her, finally entering the room. This had been done just for her? What a lot of work it must have been for the staff—and no small expense for Peter, she thought guiltily.

The maid followed her inside, setting the tea tray on a low table near a comfortable-looking armchair by the window. A cheerful fire crackled in the grate, and not a trace of dust could be seen anywhere. Despite her uncertainty, Sarah felt her spirits rising in such warm, bright surroundings.

"Lord Peter says you've no lady's maid as yet, but if you'll just ring, I'll send up one of the girls to help you with anything you need. I've already sent word to one of the employment agencies to fill the position as quickly as possible."

Sarah blinked at the housekeeper, unable to wrap her mind around the thought of having her very own lady's maid. "Thank you," she said inadequately, gratitude again welling up at her dramatic change in circumstances.

"We'll leave you to settle in, then." With another kind smile, Mrs. Walsh left her, the maidservant in tow, and closed the door behind them.

Sarah moved slowly around the room, delighting in every detail, from the charming clock on the polished mantelpiece to the dainty lamp on the bedside table. All hers, at least for the moment. The sense of unreality that had held her in its grip all day intensified in the face of such luxury and comfort.

Suddenly, she remembered the fantasy she had

entertained her first day in London, of some handsome gentleman—it had been Lord Peter in her thoughts even then—falling in love with her, marrying her and solving all of her problems.

It appeared her dreams had come true—except for one or two little details.

She had yet to tell Peter about William, or William about her marriage. And though she had fallen quite thoroughly in love with Peter, not once, in all of his protestations about truly wanting to marry her, had he said a word about loving her.

Kneeling by the bed to give thanks for every material thing she had ever wished for and more, Sarah began to cry.

Chapter 14

〜〜〜〜〜

"**N**o, I want something grander than this," Peter said, gazing about the entry hall of yet another town house. "It needn't be over-large, but I require more in the way of elegant touches—marble floors, generous windows, a broader staircase. What else have you to show me?"

The agent bowed, though his irritation was evident. "If your lordship could give me a clearer idea of the amount you are willing—"

"I told you not to worry about that." Peter was growing irritated himself at the agent's obsession with money. Clearly the man had his own idea of what Peter could afford. "If you can show me what I want, I'll pay for it."

"Right, then. Perhaps you'll like this next house." From the agent's smug expression, it was clear he meant to show Peter something much more expensive, and that he was looking forward to seeing Peter back down. Peter only hoped it would finally be what he was looking for.

It was.

Situated on Curzon Street, the house was double-fronted with one of the most beautiful staircases Peter had seen, its golden oak perfectly complementing the amber-veined marble of the entry hall. Along with four nicely-sized bedrooms, the house boasted a parlor and dining room of perfect proportions, each sporting an Adams fireplace.

"This building was originally built for the Prince and Princess of Tirol, with an eye to a setting worthy of royalty," the agent told him. "Given its prime location and exquisite styling, the owners are of course asking more than one might—"

"How much?" Peter asked, already envisioning Sarah in the house, looking like a queen amid its elegance.

The agent named a sum he clearly expected would shock his client.

"I'll take it," Peter said firmly. "Have the contracts drawn up at once."

The man stared for a moment, then began to bow and scrape, suddenly far more obsequious than he'd been thus far. "Yes, my lord. Of course, my lord. If there's anything I can—"

"In fact, there is. I'd prefer to keep the details between myself and the owners. Hold your tongue and there'll be a bonus in it for you."

While the agent babbled his assent, Peter decided that his next task must be Sarah's wardrobe. But much as he would have liked to surprise her with an array of new gowns, that project would need her input, as her measurements would need to be taken. Some things, however, he could purchase on his own.

If he must reveal the secret of his wealth, he wanted to do so by wrapping Sarah in the riches she'd been denied all her life. He was quite looking forward to it, for she seemed to believe he had only enough to scrape by. He would disabuse her of that idea with a flourish—tomorrow.

Then he would bring her to their beautiful new home and surround her with jewels, furs, carriages— all the trappings of the wealth she'd never had. That should finally convince her that she was indeed worthy of the best that life could offer.

In time, she might even develop some fraction of the feeling toward him that he already felt toward her.

Sarah's tears were short lived but not without benefit. After a ten-minute cry, no doubt the product of wedding-day nerves, she felt calmer and more able to properly count her blessings.

So what if Peter did not love her? She could hardly expect it after a mere week's acquaintance. Love at first sight was romantic enough in novels, but she rather doubted it occurred with any sort of regularity in the real world. Two days prior, she'd had no prospects, no future, and now—

In truth, she wasn't quite sure *what* she had now, but it was far better than anything she'd had before. She owed Peter so much. And while she had no dowry—indeed, nothing material to contribute to this marriage—she could do everything in her power to make him happy, beginning the moment he returned.

Smiling, she opened her trunk, but quickly realized that nothing within was as pretty as the dress she now wore. She therefore turned her attention to the looking glass, pinning up a stray curl and dabbing all traces of tears from her cheeks. Satisfied that she again looked her best, she headed downstairs, determined to somehow make herself useful until Peter returned.

"No, my lady," replied a puzzled Mrs. Walsh a few minutes later. "There's no mending to be done. What I don't have time to do myself, Millie manages. She's quite good with a needle. Is there something you need mended, then?"

Sarah shook her head, suddenly realizing how odd it would sound for her to offer to help with any of the more menial tasks about the house. "Perhaps Mrs. MacKay needs advice on the dinner menu?" she suggested. "What does Lord Peter favor?"

The housekeeper smiled. "She's having a grand time putting together all of his favorites, along with what he specially said *you* might like, my lady. Let her have her surprise, do."

"Of course." Clearly the staff was used to running the household perfectly well without her assistance—or interference. Wandering into the parlor, she decided to improve her musical skills by practicing on the spinet piano she found there. Only a few pieces of sheet music were available, none of which she knew, so her progress was slow.

"A charming prelude to dinner," came Peter's

voice from the doorway as she finished a rather la-bored rendition of a prelude more than an hour later.

Instantly, her heart increased its pace and she could feel the color rushing to her cheeks. "Oh! I . . . I did not hear you come in, my lord. I fear I am not yet able to play at tempo, but as I grow more familiar with these pieces—"

"If you have favorites, I will see that you get them, of course, but I thought your performance quite pleasing," he said, coming forward with a smile.

She glanced down in confusion, her bold plan to greet him with a kiss forgotten.

"I must apologize for my lengthy absence on our wedding day," he continued. "I'd thought to con-clude my business more quickly."

Surprised, she looked up. "Did you find a . . . place for us to live already, then?" She'd almost said "house," but did not want him to think she would be disappointed with something much smaller. A one-room flat would make her happy, so long as she shared it with him.

"I did indeed, but it will be a day or two before I can show it to you." He seemed not at all abashed, leading her to believe it could not be too mean a place, whatever it was. "Perhaps over dinner you can give me an idea of your tastes that I might have it decorated with them in mind."

"Goodness, there is no need—that is, I am quite willing to do my share of work in whatever refur-bishing is necessary." In fact, the prospect of deco-rating a set of rooms of her very own appealed to her greatly.

His gaze was warm, kindling an answering warmth within her. "I'm sure you are, and I promise to leave many of the details for you to direct your-self. But now, about dinner. I see you are yet in your wedding dress. Did you wish to change?"

Again she felt the color creeping up her neck. "I did consider it, but I fear this is the finest thing I have—and the only thing you won't already have seen on either Fanny or Lucy Mountheath."

A curious expression flitted across his face, but then he grinned. "Not counting the charming gray thing you wear for housebreaking, I suppose?"

Alarmed, she glanced toward the parlor door. "That was my school uniform. Scarcely appropriate for dinner, I think."

"I don't know—I've developed rather a fondness for it. But if you're determined, we may as well go in to dinner at once." He extended an arm to escort her to the dining room. "I have it on good authority that Mrs. MacKay has outdone herself tonight."

Indeed she had, judging by the array of dishes that were soon presented: two fragrant soups, sumptuously prepared fish, meat and poultry, veg-etables that must have been difficult to procure so late in the year, and an assortment of breads.

"You look as though you've never seen so much food in your life," Peter commented as Sarah won-deringly gazed around the table. "I know the Plum-field's buffet exceeded this." In spite of his teasing tone, his eyes were kind.

"Yes, but that was a grand ball. This is for only the two of us. I'll never be able to do it justice, I fear." She picked up her spoon and dipped it into her soup, determined to make her best effort, how-ever.

Peter followed suit. "All Mrs. MacKay—or I—

require is that you enjoy whatever you do eat. I fancy you've experienced few feasts in your life."

"None at all, that I can remember," she admitted, then tasted the soup. "Oh! This is delicious."

They ate in silence for a few minutes, Sarah thoroughly enjoying every bite. Mrs. MacKay was definitely a better cook than the Mountheaths', and there was of course no comparison to the fare served the students and staff at Miss Pritchard's.

She was well into a plate of curried chicken when she glanced up to find Peter's eyes intent upon her. Suddenly self-conscious, she set down her fork.

"No, don't stop," he said. "I quite enjoy watching you enjoy yourself. Your relish for new experiences is most refreshing."

Sarah wished she could stop the blush she felt rising as his words conjured an image of other experiences she was eager to taste. She quickly lowered her eyes for fear he would read her thoughts, as he so often seemed able to do.

"Until this week past, I have led a rather circumscribed existence," she said to her plate. "Nearly every experience since my coming to Town has been a new one."

"Yet you do not tire of novelty?"

Could he mean what she thought he did, or was she simply obsessed with a single idea? "Not yet." Summoning her earlier resolve, she dared a shy smile at him.

His brows rose. "Then perhaps we can find other novelties to . . . amuse you."

There was no mistaking the heat in his eyes, but though she felt her color deepening further, she did not look away. "I should like that, I think." She tried for a seductive tone but her voice came out high and breathless.

Still, he seemed to take her meaning, judging by the intensity of his gaze. "Would you? There is much I can show you, if you are certain you are willing."

She swallowed, the repast before her quite forgotten. "Most willing, my lord."

Belatedly, she realized that the use of the title had been a mistake, for he blinked and perceptibly withdrew. "You promised to call me Peter," he reminded her. "And I promised to ask about your preferences in decorating over dinner."

He signaled for the footman to clear away the dishes, then asked, "What colors do you favor? What styles? Normally I pride myself on being able to guess such things from the fashions a person chooses, but as yours have been chosen for you thus far, they are no true indicator."

Sarah tried to stifle her disappointment at the change of topic, reminding herself that she had time—all her life, in fact—to convince him of her desire. "I like cheerful colors," she said, thinking of her room upstairs. "And simple styles, I should say. At any rate, I dislike excessive ornamentation."

"Such as the Mountheaths seem to favor?"

"If you take the Mountheath house as a model and go in the exact opposite direction, you cannot go far wrong," she agreed, echoing the advice he'd once given her on dress.

He chuckled. "I am relieved to discover our tastes are similar. That will make sharing a home far more pleasant."

And suddenly they were back on dangerous

ground. She seized the opportunity. "I imagine it
will be very pleasant indeed."

Again he took her meaning at once. "I hope so,
Sarah. I want to make everything pleasant for you—
everything within my power."

She was about to assure him that she wanted to do
the same for him when the footman returned with
an assortment of fruit, puddings and sweetmeats.
Rather than speak plainly in the servant's presence,
she merely said, "Thank you," trying to put all she
felt into her voice and expression.

Though the sweet course was as delicious as
everything else had been, Sarah's attention was
more on the man opposite her than any exotic pud-
ding. He watched her eat as she watched him. Were
his thoughts similarly preoccupied? She hoped so.

"Shall we retire to the parlor?" he asked a few
minutes later, when their spoons had slowed.

"I rather like the library," she said, remembering
the passion that had flared between them two nights
earlier. Perhaps in the same setting her courage
would be stronger.

One corner of his mobile mouth quirked up. "Very
well. The library, then." He escorted her across the
hall and, as he'd done the other night, poked the fire
to crackling life before seating himself in the same
chair as before.

"Now, can you tell me more about your tastes?
About yourself?" he asked.

Her heart pounded as she gathered her courage.
"You seem to know me nearly as well as I do." She
thought briefly of William, but this was not the time
to mention her brother. "As for my tastes, I find . . .

you . . . very much to my taste." She held her breath for his response.

"Then that is something else we have in common," he said softly, "for I assure you that you are very much to my taste as well, Sarah."

She leaned forward to take his hands in hers, startled by her own boldness. "Show me, then," she whispered.

Surprise flickered in his eyes, but it was quickly swallowed by desire. Clasping her hands, he pulled her to him until she was seated across his lap. "Are you sure?" he murmured.

Sarah nodded, though in truth a tendril of fear, fear of the unknown, snaked through her. Determined that he not sense it, she closed her eyes, tilting her face for his kiss.

For a long moment, Peter struggled with himself, desire demanding that he take what Sarah offered even as his rational mind doubted her motives. He lowered his mouth to hers, for to refuse the kiss she offered would wound her, whatever her motive. He could always stop at a kiss. . . .

Her lips melted against his and reason left him. She felt so soft, so right. His wife. Deepening the kiss, he caressed the nape of her neck, her back and arms, firm and warm beneath sensuous white silk. She clutched at his shoulders, twined her fingers in his hair, pulled him closer.

Dimly conscious of the unlocked library door, he murmured against her lips, "Let's go upstairs." She nodded, still pressed against him.

Even knowing greater delights lay ahead, it took an effort to separate from her long enough to stand.

She looked as dazed as he felt. This evidence of her innocence—and desire—broke down the last vestiges of his resistance.

Taking her by the hand, he led her from the room, heedless of any watching servants in the hall. Sarah was his wife and this was their wedding night. To take her completely would be as natural as breathing, and no cause for scandal.

She clung to him as they climbed the stairs. Peter felt as though he ought to say something, but he feared to break the fragile bond between them. In silence, therefore, they achieved the landing above and in silence he led her to his chamber.

Holmes was within, and Peter felt Sarah stiffen at his side. A glance was sufficient to dismiss the man, however, and a moment later they were again alone, the door closed and locked behind them. The delay, however, had allowed a modicum of reason to return.

"You're sure, Sarah?" he asked again, delving into her eyes to read the truth. "I meant what I said earlier today."

Her eyes met his without guile or hesitation. "I'm sure." The tiny quaver in her voice might be attributable to nerves, completely understandable. He set about soothing them.

"Come to me, then," he said, folding her in his arms again. "Let's get to know each other—completely."

A quick, indrawn breath, and then her lips were against his again, her arms around his neck. Before, she had unbuttoned her gown for him, but her wedding gown fastened down the back, out of her reach.

Deftly, he undid the tiny, flat hooks, muttering something about not wishing to wrinkle her dress.

He felt her lips curve against his in a smile. "That's very thoughtful of you," she murmured. "I will try not to damage your cravat, either." Already she was fumbling with the intricate folds of his neckcloth.

He chuckled, deep in his throat, as he undid her last hook. "No, we want to keep you in Holmes's good graces," he said, helping her to untie his cravat before easing her gown over her shoulders to reveal perfect, creamy skin nearly as white as the satin. Her thin chemise barely skimmed the top of her full breasts.

While she worked at his buttons, he untied the ribbon holding her undergarment closed. The chemise fell open to display the shadowed cleft between her breasts but clung to her nipples, concealing them, tantalizing him.

Leaning forward, he trailed kisses from her throat to that cleft, pushing the chemise lower with his chin until it joined her gown about her waist and elbows, leaving her upper body bare. He paused, devouring her with his eyes. "You are so beautiful," he whispered.

She made a small motion that he first interpreted as an effort to cover herself, but before he could convince himself to help her, she said, "You have me at a disadvantage—I cannot reach the rest of your buttons now."

He laughed in his relief. "No matter." Quickly, he divested himself of his coat, waistcoat and shirt so that he also was bared to the waist. The surprised delight in her eyes as she surveyed him inflamed him more than he'd have thought possible. Never had a woman affected him so intensely.

"You approve?" he asked, though her expression had already answered him.

She nodded, her eyes still wide. "I've never seen a man's body before, but surely yours must be among the finest—a body to inspire sculptors and artists."

Peter blinked, as embarrassed by her frank appreciation as he was gratified. "I should say these two beautiful bodies belong together then," he said teasingly.

Smiling, she came to him, pressing the soft fullness of her breasts against his chest. "Like this?" she asked.

"It's a good start."

At the flicker of uncertainty in her eyes, he smiled tenderly down at her. "Don't be afraid."

"I'm not. I don't believe I could ever be afraid of you."

She couldn't know how much that meant to him, how her words healed wounds he hadn't realized he was still nursing after more than two years. He kissed her again, deeply, before gently stripping off her gown and chemise. He could feel her fingers trembling as they determinedly fumbled with the buttons of his breeches until all were undone.

He led her to the bed a few steps away and seated her on the edge so that he could remove her slippers. Untying her garters just above her knees, he rolled down her stockings, kissing her knees and calves as he went. When she was completely unclothed, she tugged at him, guiding him to sit on the bed so that she could do the same with his shoes and breeches. He swallowed, hard, as her lips touched the sensitive skin of his thigh, her hair falling forward to brush his straining erection.

The moment he was as naked as she, he pulled her onto the bed beside him to again kiss her thoroughly, his hands exploring the curve of her waist, the flare of her hips. Her hands skimmed over his body as well, turning him to fire wherever she touched. He knew he was nearing a breaking point, but he was determined to be gentle even if it killed him—which at the moment he considered a distinct possibility.

Slowly, he reclined beside her until they were touching from knee to shoulder. "You must let me know if I hurt you," he whispered. "I will try very hard not to, but—"

"I'm not afraid," she repeated, her eyes wide and trusting, humbling him, igniting him. How could she ever have believed she was not worthy of him? It was he who could never be worthy of such trust, such loveliness, such generosity. Not after—

He closed his eyes against old memories, letting the present blot out the past.

Sarah was more amazed every moment by the intensity of her feelings, her desire for this man she had known such a short time. What was he doing to her? At first she had simply been determined to see this through, no matter how her feelings might change—for she had heard fearful whisperings at school about what men did to women. But now she felt that the most terrible thing he could possibly do would be to stop caressing her.

His length pressed against hers, he kissed her again, each kiss more exciting than the last, while he stroked her back, her hips, her breasts. Instinctively, she arched toward him, wanting to intensify the contact, wanting more . . . of everything.

He seemed to understand, for his hands increased their pace, his body pushing closer, the part of him that had so startled her with its size pressing against the very spot that seemed to cry out for his touch. His mouth still fastened to hers, he rolled her from her side to her back, supporting himself on his arms as he kissed his way down her throat and chest until he took the tip of one breast into his mouth.

The sensation was exquisite, making her whimper, but she still wanted more. He gave it to her, sliding a hand between their bodies to touch the place that needed him most. She gasped again at the shock of pleasure his stroking finger sent through her. Squirming, she parted her thighs to allow him better access, pressing upward with her hips, demanding she knew not what.

Still sucking her breast, he stroked again, then again, then slipped a finger inside her. She felt herself clenching around it and then heard him groan. Now he moved his whole body, his manhood stroking her as his finger had done, his mouth releasing her breast to claim her lips again.

Sarah knew she was groaning too—or perhaps growling—but she didn't care. Arching higher, spreading her thighs farther, she invited him in. Slowly, slowly, he accepted her invitation. She stretched to accommodate him, the stretching a new and exciting sensation, until he filled her completely. Then, rhythmically, he began to move within her.

She could feel him trembling, knew he was reaching a crisis of some sort, but then he again slipped a hand between her legs to drive her to a crisis of her own, a crisis of such intense pleasure she was not sure she would survive it. As he drove into her again and again, stroking her cleft in rhythm with his thrusts, she climbed higher and higher until her world exploded in a mad rush of bliss. Dimly, she heard him cry out even as she did, her name on his lips as his was on hers.

He paused, his breath rasping in her ear, then began to move again, slowly. She was so sensitive now that she twitched beneath him, and then, without warning, she rushed up over the crest again, convulsing about him, her pleasure as intense as before.

She felt him relax above her, though still supporting much of his weight on his elbows. A sweet languor swept through her, the aftermath of the most incredible experience of her life.

"That was amazing," she breathed. "I never thought—never realized—"

Peter kissed her, then shifted onto his side, smiling into her eyes. "Neither did I."

Sarah frowned, puzzled. "But surely you knew—? I mean, this can't have been—"

Tenderly, so tenderly her heart melted, he kissed her again. "I've lain with women before, yes, but never like this. You are something special, Sarah. This, what we shared, was something special."

She could not doubt the sincerity in his eyes. "I'm glad. As this is all I can offer you, I so wanted it to be . . . special for you."

Leaning away from her, he frowned. "Is that why—? I told you I did not want this out of gratitude or obligation, Sarah."

"No!" she said quickly, placing a finger against his lips before he could say anything they both might regret. "I'm grateful to you, yes, but I ... I truly did want this. Though I'd have wanted it even more had I known how enjoyable it would be." She felt herself blushing again.

His frown dissolved and he kissed her finger, then her lips. "Never believe this is all you can give me, Sarah. As pleasurable as is the physical side of marriage, I find even more satisfaction in knowing you are safe under my protection. You delight me—in many, many ways."

Sarah tried to ignore the little bubble of disappointment produced by his words—or, rather, by the words he had not said. He had never claimed to love her, nor could she expect it, even after what they had just shared together. If peace of mind was what he most craved from her, then she would make certain she provided that—as well as anything else he might want.

Though she dared not speak of love, she nestled against him and said, "You are a good, kind man, Peter. I am the luckiest woman alive to have you as my husband."

Sarah awoke from the deepest, most comfortable sleep she could remember to see Peter, in a deep blue dressing gown, reentering the bedchamber with a tray from which emanated the mouth-watering fragrances of eggs, toast and coffee.

"Breakfast? In bed?" She scooted up into a sitting position against the headboard, blushingly covering her breasts with the bed linens. "I believe you mean to spoil me most dreadfully."

His grin made her heart do a funny little flip. "Alas, you have found out my dark purpose—and this is only the start." He set the tray on a low table and drew it close to the bed.

When Sarah hesitated, he plucked a parcel from the desk by the window and opened it to reveal a lacy lavender wrapper. "I took the liberty of buying this for you yesterday. I thought it might suit you."

"It's beautiful." Sarah took the delicate confection from him with awe, then slipped it on, reveling in the sumptuous feel of silk and lace against her bare skin. She had never owned anything one tenth so fine before. "Thank you again."

"My thanks is in seeing you in it. I believe I can claim that my taste is as flawless as ever," he said with a wink.

Blushing again, she swung her legs over the edge of the bed so that she could reach the breakfast tray. "Everything looks delicious," she said, picking up a fork as he seated himself next to her.

"I wish I could claim to have prepared it myself, but I fear cooking is not one of my skills. Mrs. MacKay anticipated our needs, however, and had this ready when I went down." He reached for the other fork.

They ate in companionable silence, punctuated by lingering glances that promised more delights in the hours, days, even years to come. Sarah had never felt more content, her few remaining problems dwindling almost to nothing.

Soon she would find a way to tell Peter the full story of her youth, and William's, and he would understand. Together, they would find a way to help William and some of the other unfortunates on the streets of London.

"I suppose I'd best go back downstairs and attend

to our correspondence," Peter finally said with obvious reluctance, waking her from her rosy dreams. "I'll send up a maid to help you dress, and then you can join me in the library."

"Of course," she said, smiling up at him as he rose. He leaned down to kiss her lingeringly on the lips, then departed.

With a happy sigh, she picked up her wedding gown and underthings, pulled her lovely new wrapper tight around her, and slipped through the dressing room her chamber shared with Peter's. Entering her room, she stopped, startled, for a maid already awaited her.

"Morning, milady," said the red-haired girl she remembered was named Polly. "Millie will be up in a moment to help you dress, but Mrs. MacKay asked me to add coal to your fire and bring up fresh water."

Then, glancing at the closed door, she lowered her voice. "Also, there's this. A lad, a friend of Renny's, brought it not an hour since, but he didn't want Renny to see it. He said it was for her new ladyship." She held out a folded piece of paper.

Sarah took the note in suddenly nerveless fingers. It had to be from her brother. Renny must have given the note to Paddy, who had turned around and sent it up to her. "Thank you, Polly," she said with forced calm.

What could William need from the Saint, so soon after his last note? Would it contain yet more names—some with such urgent needs that he might risk filling them if the Saint couldn't?

The moment Polly left, she broke the seal, only to discover the note was not from Flute at all. It was in fact two notes, one inside the other. The outer one was a mere scrawl, signed with a name that looked like "Stilt."

With shaking hands, she unsealed the inner letter. It was written in a slightly better hand, but its message sent her safe new fairy-tale world spinning.

To the so-called Saint of Seven Dials:

I have your little troublemaker, Flute. If you want him safe beyond Monday, send me five thousand pounds in coin or notes. If you don't, I'll turn him over to the Runners for the reward, and what's left of Twitchell's lads can answer to me.

—Ickle

Chapter 15

Sarah dropped weakly onto her bed. Five thousand pounds! It was an impossible sum. Why, the dozen guineas she'd taken at the Wickburn ball comprised the most money she'd ever had in her possession at once. What on earth was she to do?

She reread the first note, the one signed "Stilt."

Flute left this for the Saint. Don't know where he went.

At least, that's what she thought it said, though the handwriting was difficult to decipher. She remembered her earlier contentment, now gone beyond recall. If Peter knew of her troubles, she had no doubt he would offer to assist in whatever way he could. She could ask him—

266

No! He had already done so much for her, more than she could ever repay. She was certain he could not afford to pay five thousand pounds. And even if he could—if he were caught paying off this Ickle, he might be arrested as the Saint himself, for this could easily be a trap. If there was a reward posted for William, that for the Saint would be far higher.

A tap came at the door, and Sarah quickly hid the note before Millie could enter.

"That gown will be fine," she told the maid, pointing out one at random, her thoughts already back on her problem.

Even if William's kidnapping was not a trap, she could never ask Peter to run afoul of the law for her sake. Her brother was still wanted for his previous association with the Saint. Peter was already shielding her, but it was too much to ask him to shield someone who had helped the real Saint—the traitor Peter despised—for years.

No, she must rely upon herself, just as she'd always done. This problem was hers alone to solve, and she knew only one way to go about it. She must do what she'd thought never to do again, what she'd promised Peter she would not. She must resort to thievery—and she must do it without arousing Peter's suspicions.

"Is everything all right?" Peter asked when Sarah joined him in the library half an hour later, again wearing one of her secondhand gowns.

"Yes, of course," she replied, though he noticed with concern that she did not meet his eyes.

"Sarah, if there is something I can help you with, you know you need only ask."

Her eyes met his and for a moment he could almost see words trembling on her lips.

"I'm your husband," he reminded her gently. "It is now my job to solve any difficulties you might have. I've solved your biggest one already, have I not? You are safe now."

He knew instantly that he'd said the wrong thing. Her expression became shuttered, even secretive. "Yes, of course, and I've tried to convey my gratitude for that. Truly, there is nothing more I require."

Again, she spoke of gratitude! Was that all he was ever to have from her? He restrained his impatience, however, reminding himself that he'd essentially forced her into this marriage for her own good. Some lingering resentment was natural.

"Are you still concerned about those friends you mentioned to me?" he asked.

She looked startled. "No! That is, I believe what I have sent them already is enough. It will have to be."

"I should like to meet these friends of yours sometime," he said then, still hoping she might confide in him.

As he'd feared she would, she shook her head. "That would not be . . . wise. The less you know of them the better."

Gently, he cupped her chin, tilting her face up so that she had to look at him. "Sarah, just promise me that if you ever feel tempted to do anything that might put you in danger, you will tell me. Your safety matters more to me than anything."

"Of course," she whispered. "And thank you for . . . for caring."

Though it was clear she was hiding something, he

let the matter drop—for the moment. "Perhaps you would look over these invitations with me. Then, once we've decided which entertainments to attend, I thought we might visit Bond Street. I don't want the world to think I can't afford to clothe my wife properly."

Sarah should have been having the time of her life, as Peter bade her select from an array of beautiful fabrics, ribbons and trinkets at one shop after another. But with every shilling Peter spent on her, the more wicked she felt—and the more determined to keep the truth from him.

"Here, Madame, hold this blue satin up to her—it should just match her eyes," he said to the modiste whose shop they were currently patronizing. "Yes, I thought so. Have that one made up into a ball gown—split over a white gauze underskirt, I think."

As she'd done several times before, Sarah remonstrated. "Surely the three ball gowns you've ordered already are enough, my lord? I can wear only one at a time, after all."

The modiste hesitated, but at her questioning look Peter waved her away with a smile. "Come, my dear," he said to Sarah. "You must trust me to know what you need. I daresay Robert's wife has three or four dozen ball gowns."

"But she is a countess, one day to be a duchess," Sarah pointed out. "And no doubt she is accustomed to such things. I have simple tastes, and can be more than happy with what you have purchased already. There is no need for anything more."

"Nonsense. I plan to show off my beautiful wife

everywhere possible. Besides, I'm quite enjoying this, knowing how much lovely clothes will become you. You were made for this, Sarah."

Sarah was far from convinced. If she were made for this, surely she would not feel so ill at ease, so . . . degraded. Indeed, she felt as she imagined a courtesan must feel at being showered with gifts by her protector, with nothing but beauty and sex to offer in return. In vain she reminded herself that this was different, that she was Peter's wife.

"Would not a thin muslin do as well as silk gauze?" she could not help asking as the modiste unrolled a bolt of the latter, a confection in white.

"With the finest Florence satin?" Peter asked in mock horror. "Certainly not! You have no idea how much I've hated seeing you in castoffs, Sarah. From now on, you will wear only the best."

She glanced at the modiste, who was discreetly pretending not to hear. "But . . . the expense!"

Peter smiled indulgently, making her feel like an untutored child, a feeling she rather resented. "I'll worry about the expense. All you need to do is enjoy yourself, which will make it worth every penny to me."

As it seemed true that buying her things made him happy, Sarah tried to mute her protests. She only hoped his zeal would not lead him into debt.

By the time they left the modiste, Peter had ordered six ball gowns of various hues, at least a dozen morning and day dresses, and an assortment of tippets, spencers and cloaks, as well as one fabulously expensive Court dress for Sarah's presentation the following month. From there, they progressed to a nearby jeweler's shop.

"As the fourth son, I fear I don't merit any of the jewels that have been passed along our family, so we will simply have to start from scratch," Peter explained. "We will begin, of course, with a proper set of rings, as there was no time to ask your preference before our wedding."

Sarah glanced down at the modest gold band and diamond he had placed on her finger yesterday, more extravagant than anything she'd have ever dared wish for. "I'm quite content with these," she told him truthfully.

"Pish! It's an old set, and borrowed in any case. You'll want something of your very own, I know."

"I suppose . . . if it's borrowed. But please, nothing large or ostentatious." *Nothing I will be tempted to pawn for William*, she added silently.

He only smiled, stepping to the counter where the jeweler eagerly awaited them. "Show us what you have, my good man. Only your best, mind you."

The man proceeded to remove trays from the glass cases, displaying an array of gems that made Sarah's mouth go dry. A mere two or three of these would pay William's ransom! Not that she could attempt to steal anything with Peter at her side and the jeweler watching them both like a hawk. With an effort, she turned her attention to nudging Peter away from the largest baubles.

In the end, she was able to convince him to buy her a diamond only slightly larger than the one she already wore, though she suspected the quality was such that the price would still make her gasp. As at the modiste's, Peter had been careful not to discuss cost in front of her—something she was beginning to find a bit irritating.

"I have managed my own affairs since I was nine years old," she reminded him as they left the shop, the earrings he had insisted on buying her already on her ears. "There is no need to shield me from the particulars, or the state of your finances, for that matter."

He cast her a sidelong glance. "What is the most money you've ever managed at once?"

"That is beside the point," she replied loftily.

"I think not. How much? If you wish me to tell you what I am worth, surely you should be willing to divulge the same information. What were you paid for teaching, your last two years at Miss Pritchard's?"

"Four pounds per annum, but that is not . . . How did you know the name of my school? I never mentioned it to you."

"Mrs. Hounslow told me." His answer seemed a bit too quick. "You do realize that four pounds per annum is a criminally low wage, do you not?" Indeed, he looked outraged on her behalf.

She gazed across the street, pretending to watch a street vendor polishing the glassware in his cart. "I knew it was low, yes, but my room and board were provided, and I was among people I knew. Nor did I have the means to go elsewhere, until I had saved up a bit."

"At which point you traveled to London to seek your fortune," he said. "Fair enough. But if that is all the money you ever had to manage—"

"Then you can see why I am uncomfortable with the vast amounts you are spending on me," she finished, knowing that was not at all what he'd been about to say.

He didn't seem disposed to argue that point, however. "And you must see why it affords me such satisfaction to buy you things you've never had before," he said. "I'm not sure you realize just how deprived you've been, Sarah, but I mean to see that you never again go without anything you need—or want."

How could she possibly tell him that all she really wanted was his love? And William's safety, of course. These earrings—what might they fetch if she pawned them? But no, she would then have to explain their absence—and it would be just as though she'd stolen the money from Peter himself.

"You're very good to me," she finally said, feeling guiltier than ever.

Though he was careful not to show it, Peter was growing increasingly frustrated. He had been so sure that Sarah would delight in the silks, laces, furs and jewels he was buying her, but instead she seemed to grow more and more distant with each new purchase. Much as he longed to see her arrayed like a queen, he was more eager to see her happy.

"Come, let's go home," he finally said as they left a milliner's shop with an armload of bonnets.

"Oh, yes, please." Her smile held such relief that he suddenly felt like a brute for subjecting her to what most women would have regarded as the outing of their lives.

He helped her into the waiting carriage then settled himself on the seat next to her, the opposite seat piled with all of their purchases.

"I fear you did not enjoy yourself today, Sarah,"

he said as they started off. "I simply wished to demonstrate that I can take care of you—that you need never worry about the future again."

Her smile held a trace of mockery, though directed at herself rather than at him. "I am an odd sort of female, am I not? Though I have long dreamed of just such an afternoon as this, I found the reality more than a little disconcerting. I fear it will take me some time to adjust to my change in station. I hope you will be . . . patient with me."

"Of course." He wanted to say more, to say that he would do anything, wait as long as necessary, to win her love. But then she might feel obligated to express a love she did not yet feel, to please him, just as she had clearly tried all morning to pretend pleasure in his purchases, to the same end. That was not what he wanted from her.

"We'll take a light luncheon with our tea when we get home, before we dress for the Wittington ball," he said instead. "I had in mind for you to wear the shot lilac silk tonight." He'd agreed to an exorbitant sum to have Madame Fanchot pin up a half-finished gown or two for Sarah's immediate use.

"And what will you wear?" she asked, with the first show of humor he'd seen from her all day. "Have you a lilac waistcoat to complement my gown?"

"As it happens, I do," he replied with a grin. "We'll have to have Holmes work with your maid to coordinate our future ensembles. Which reminds me—you do not have a maid yet, do you?"

Sarah shook her head. "In truth, the idea of a maid of my very own will take getting used to as well. I suppose you are right that I will need one, however." She thought for a moment, then said, "Miss Fanny Mountheath's maid is cheerful and competent, but dreadfully put-upon. Do you suppose we might induce her to come to us?"

"It is certainly worth a try, if you like her. I'll look into it tomorrow."

They lapsed into silence and Peter glanced at Sarah's profile, thinking again about the life she must have led, orphaned, homeless, then shipped off to a school hundreds of miles from anyone she knew. Perhaps it was not luxury she had longed for so much as security.

On that thought, he signaled the driver to make a detour to Curzon Street. Sarah looked at him questioningly, but he only smiled, hoping that her reaction to this surprise might be all he he could desire.

Sarah hoped that Peter did not intend to take her to yet another shop. She had plans to make for the evening and had counted on an hour or so of solitude to give thought to them. Remembering her pleasant new chamber, she smiled. The colors weren't exactly what she'd have chosen, but already she regarded it as a retreat of sorts.

Peter called for the driver to stop, and she peered out. They were on Curzon Street, before a row of exceptionally fine town houses. "What—?"

"Come. I'll show you." The suppressed eagerness in his expression heightened her curiosity.

He helped her from the carriage, then escorted her to the door of a lovely house of mellow brick with diamond-paned windows. Someone must live here that he wished her to meet. With her free hand, she smoothed her secondhand skirts, hoping he would not be disappointed by their reception of her.

Then, to her surprise, instead of knocking at the door he pulled a key from his pocket and unlocked it. Pushing it wide, he motioned for her to enter. With an even more curious glance, she complied.

Their footsteps echoed in the empty foyer, bare of carpets or furniture, though still beautiful with its richly colored marble floor and graceful curving staircase.

"Do you like it?" Peter asked.

Sudden understanding broke upon her and she whirled to face him. His eyes held an almost boyish eagerness, tinged by a hint of apprehension.

"Is this—? Do you mean . . . *this* is the place you found for us to live?" She couldn't believe it, even when he nodded. Slowly, she turned to examine her surroundings more closely, taking in every exquisite detail.

"It's the most beautiful house I've ever seen," she finally said. "But . . . it must cost a fortune. How—?"

"Did I not ask you to trust me on such matters? I won't pauper us, Sarah, I promise."

Again she felt a prickle of irritation that he seemed not to trust *her* enough to reveal the details of his finances. Clearly he was much, much wealthier than he had led her to believe, if he was able to afford this house. Still, looking around, imagining herself mistress of this lovely place, she could not find it in her to be too angry at him.

"So it is really ours?"

He nodded, that trace of anxiety leaving his eyes.

"I've taken a long-term lease, pending your approval. I wouldn't, of course, force you to live in a place you disliked. But I take it you approve?"

"If, as you claim, we can afford it, I very much approve."

"Then come, let me show you the rest before it grows dark." Like a child anxious to show off a new treasure, he led her up the beautiful oaken staircase.

Ten minutes later, Sarah had to confess herself thoroughly satisfied, though still overwhelmed. The house was everything she could have dreamed of, and far, far more than she had ever expected. Not only that, it seemed to welcome her, inviting her to make it hers, to put her own stamp upon it. Never had any place felt so much like *home*.

"When can we move in?" she asked as they left the dining room. The sun was near to setting, but she had no trouble imagining the artistic chandelier filled with blazing candles, a long table centered beneath it, surrounded by a large family. . . .

"There is paperwork yet to complete, but I was told we may have possession at once. If you'd like, we can begin shopping for furniture tomorrow."

More money to be spent! Money that could pay for William's safety. Her heart twisted within her, a full confession trembling on her lips.

"I fear I have no furniture of my own," he continued. "Everything in the Grosvenor Street house was purchased by my father—or his father. I'm looking forward to a home of my own as much as you must be, Sarah."

She swallowed the words that had nearly escaped her. Of course! The money for all of this must be coming from the duke. Peter had no job, no lands. He had served in the army, yes, but half-pay officers did not live in houses like this one.

Now she remembered how the Duke of Marland had looked at her yesterday, as though forced to acknowledge her against his will and better judgment. Imagine if he'd known the whole truth! No, she refused to put herself in *his* debt, even if she was ready to accept being in Peter's.

Accompanying him back through the front door, watching him relock it, she longed to ask him how far they must depend on his father's goodwill, but of course she could not. He would not wish to confess his dependency—which no doubt explained his reluctance to discuss the details of his finances.

Peter helped her back into the carriage, his eyes searching her face. She smiled, striving to appear content. Perhaps, once she had redeemed her brother, they could work together to achieve true independence from the duke. Until then, she would do nothing to make Peter feel inadequate—to include asking him for money.

At least, not until she had tried all other means to help William.

On their return, they had a hurried tea, then repaired upstairs to change. Sarah was assisted by Millie, one of the upstairs maids, whose enthusiasm compensated for her lack of experience in such matters.

"What a lovely frock, my lady," she exclaimed as she helped Sarah into the new lilac gown. "Oh! I'm sorry—I did not mean to prick you. So many pins! You'll have a seamstress in to finish the seams before you wear it again, I'm thinking? Now, will you wear your hair up or down?"

Though Millie did not possess Libby's skill, she was able to pull Sarah's hair back into a simple yet elegant style, brushing her curls about her shoulders. Sarah herself arranged the silk lilacs in her hair, as the poor maid seemed at a loss.

Peter's eyes lit up most gratifyingly as she descended the stairs to where he awaited her in the front hall. "I see my taste in women's clothing is nearly as impeccable as my taste in women," he said, taking her hand when she reached the bottom. "You do me credit, my dear."

She dipped a quick curtsey to hide her sudden nervousness, for his words served to remind her that this ball would be her first public appearance as Lady Peter Northrup. Everyone there would likely be watching her, evaluating her, wondering whether she could live up to the role.

Sarah prayed she would not let Peter down.

"You look rather splendid yourself, my lord," she said, rising. And he did, with his silver-embroidered lavender waistcoat and jacket of such a deep purple it was almost black. "I will be honored to appear on your arm."

During the short drive to the Wittington house, Sarah's nervousness increased, for a greater challenge faced her tonight than the stares and whispers that were sure to be directed her way. If she were to have any chance at all of amassing five thousand pounds in less than a week's time, she could not afford to waste a single evening.

Nor could she worry about such niceties as

whether any given target "deserved" his or her fate.
No, she would simply have to seize whatever opportunities presented: an empty room, an un-
watched pocket or reticule, an unguarded carriage.
Without William, she had no way to convert jewels
or plate into currency, so it would no doubt be best
to limit her takings to cash.

She was so busy with such thoughts, the carriage
seemed to stop almost as soon as it started. Stepping
down, she took Peter's arm and gazed up at the
house before them, her looming social trial abruptly
crowding out thoughts of larceny.

As they followed the throng of guests through the
foyer, Sarah tried to distract herself by comparing
this house to her own home-to-be. This hall was not
so wide, nor the staircase they mounted so graceful.
The observation steadied her somewhat. Then they
were announced.

"Lord Peter Northrup, Lady Peter Northrup," in-
toned the majordomo as they reached Lord and
Lady Wittington at the entrance to the ballroom.

Sarah felt that every eye in the room was upon her
as she greeted her hosts with a curtsey. For a terrifying instant, she wobbled and nearly lost her balance,
but then Peter steadied her with a hand on her elbow and she was able to rise, the vision of landing
on her backside receding.

"We are honored to have you both here only a day
after your wedding," Lady Wittington was saying,
her expression kind, though she could not quite conceal her curiosity. "Weren't you the sly ones, keeping
your courtship a secret? Lady Peter, have you met
my daughter?"

She was introduced to Miss Chalmers, then she

and Peter progressed into the room. As she'd feared, more than a few ladies were regarding her with raised eyebrows or even hostility, though others smiled pleasantly enough.

"Would you care for a glass of something before the dancing begins?" Peter asked. "It promises to become quite warm in here."

Sarah nodded, grateful for his attempt to divert her attention. Now that the first hurdle was past, however, she recalled what must be her main goal for the evening. "I believe I will locate the ladies' withdrawing room while you fetch it," she said. "Shall I meet you here in five minutes?"

"Of course." With an encouraging smile, he went in search of a footman.

Taking a deep breath, Sarah headed toward an alcove off to her right. If she moved quickly, she might be able to take a first step toward her goal before Peter returned.

Chapter 16

As Sarah had hoped, everyone was still congregating in the small ballroom, ladies and gentlemen alike vying for dance partners for the evening. The short hallway beyond the alcove was deserted. The door on the right did indeed lead to the ladies' withdrawing room, judging by the two women who had disappeared through it a moment before. The French doors in front of her, however, opened onto a balcony overlooking the street below.

She glanced over her shoulder to discover more than one pair of eyes turned her way. Smiling, she moved to the balcony doors at a leisurely pace, as though simply exploring—which was exactly what she was doing. The door was closed against the October evening chill but not locked, so she stepped through to glance down at the busy street, then along the front of the house.

The balcony ran the length of the row of houses, with two other doors opening to the Wittingtons' before the low wall that separated this portion of the balcony from that fronting the next house along the row. A wall Sarah could easily climb.

Making a show of breathing the cool air, she then pulled her shawl tighter about her shoulders and headed back inside, mulling over the possibilities. Perhaps later, when people had tired of watching for any *faux pas* she might make, she would be able to slip back out here and use the balcony to gain entry to other houses.

So deep in thought was she that she failed to notice Lady Mountheath's approach. "Why, Sarah!" she exclaimed loudly, apparently unable to bring herself to use Sarah's new title. "How nice. I confess I did not expect to see you out in Society quite so soon. Have the novelties of marriage paled so quickly?"

Sarah made certain her smile encompassed both of the Mountheath daughters as well as their mother, whom they hovered behind, tittering. "Not in the least, my lady!" she replied at similar volume. "However, Lord Peter was embarrassingly anxious to show me off, *properly* attired."

Lady Mountheath reddened, her eyes flicking about at the dozen or more people within earshot, some of whom were showing signs of amusement.

"Yes, that is a most becoming gown," she said placatingly, before lowering her voice. "I am delighted, of course, that I was able to marry you off so creditably. I trust you will remember the role I played in helping you to your new status."

"I'm certain I will remember *every* detail of your charity to me, my lady," Sarah told her. "Never fear."

Her erstwhile benefactress seemed so satisfied with this response that she merely nodded her feathered headdress and turned away, beckoning her daughters to follow her.

"Here you are." Peter came up just then, carrying two glasses as Sarah basked in her unexpected victory. He glanced at the rigid, departing backs of the Mountheath ladies. "Were they rude to you?" he asked in an undertone.

"Only moderately," Sarah replied, taking a glass from him with a grin. "I believe they regret it now, however."

Peter chuckled. "That's my girl. You can take care of yourself, can't you?"

"As I reminded you today, I've done so for many years." She sipped from her glass. "Oh! Is this champagne? I've never tasted it before."

"Yet another new experience I can show you," he said with a wink. "Do you like it?"

She took another small sip. "I'm not certain yet. I believe so. It . . . fizzes."

"Drink it slowly," he cautioned. "It can sneak up on the unwary. Speaking of new experiences, I should warn you that I plan to teach you to waltz tonight."

Sarah choked as a few drops of champagne went down the wrong way. "What?" she croaked, trying to get her breath back. "You can't be serious. I am enough of a cynosure without that."

"People watch you only because you are so lovely," he assured her, patting her back while she cleared her throat. She quirked an eyebrow at him and he shrugged. "And because of our sudden marriage, I suppose. But not because there is anything the least bit wrong with you."

Thinking ahead to what she hoped to accomplish tonight, she could only wish that were true.

Soon, however, she discovered that Peter was at least partially correct. Her marriage seemed not to have hurt her popularity with the gentlemen. If anything, the opposite seemed to be the case, for those she already knew petitioned her for dances while those she did not asked Peter for an introduction. The ladies seemed marginally more cordial to her than they had been before, as well.

Though her inclination was to dance only with Peter, she agreed to a few with other gentlemen, realizing that it might be easier to slip away from one of them for "Saintly" business than from her too-perceptive husband. Her first two dances were with Peter, however, and she enjoyed them thoroughly.

"Remember," he said as Sir Cyril Weathers claimed her for the next set, "I mean to show you a waltz later. The supper dance, if not before."

Though still skeptical, she nodded, then turned to accompany Sir Cyril to the floor.

"That shade definitely becomes you, my lady," he said as they took their places. "It makes your eyes an even deeper blue. In fact, they look nearly violet, like Lady Pearl's eyes—or, I should say, Lady Hardwyck's. I have always been a great admirer of hers, you know."

"I have not yet had an opportunity to meet her," Sarah said, secretly amused at such a backhanded compliment. As at the embassy reception, he seemed to have drunk more than was good for him, even though it was yet early.

"Oh, she and Lord Hardwyck are out of Town." He bowed as the opening strains of the dance sounded. "Hope she'll be back before winter, however. It would be a fair treat to have the two of you grace the same room sometime. Why, you could almost be sisters."

That thought diverted Sarah's attention for the next few minutes while she went through the movements of the dance. Hardwyck was the name Peter had mentioned in connection with her brother—the nobleman for whom he had acted as valet, at least briefly. A friend of Peter's own brother Marcus.

No doubt, given that connection, she would meet this Lady Pearl at some point. Perhaps she could then convince Lord Hardwyck to give William another chance as his valet? But no—that might be inappropriate, now that William was brother-in-law to a duke's son. Still, it would be better than . . .

"You are a vision in the dance, my lady," Sir Cyril said as they met again to link arms and promenade. "Such grace!"

They reached the bottom of the set and he leaned in close. "Married women are the only ones worth knowing, in my opinion." Instead of releasing her arm as the dance required, he twined it against him, inclining his head toward her as though to steal a kiss.

Sarah stiffened, shocked. But even as she began to pull away, she realized her hand was against his coat pocket. Leaning her head away from his attempted kiss, fluttering her other hand in protest, she quickly dipped into that pocket and palmed the wadded papers she found there before pulling away from him entirely.

"Sir Cyril, you forget yourself!" she exclaimed, slipping the papers into her own pocket without a twinge of guilt.

He blinked. "My most abject apologies, my lady! You are right. I had no right . . . Pray do not mention this to Lord Peter. I'd be no match for him on the dueling field."

Now it was Sarah's turn to blink. Somehow, she could not imagine Peter in a duel, though of course he'd spent some years as a soldier and presumably had seen his share of battle. She could not quite imagine that, either.

"Very well, sir, but you must keep your hands to yourself," she said severely. "Mine is not the only husband likely to take offense if you persist in pursuing married women."

The dance ended a moment later and she took chilly leave of him, though in truth she was eager to find a quiet corner so that she could examine what she'd plucked from his pocket. Lord Ribbleton, her next partner, was not in evidence, so she retired to the edge of the room, where she pretended to look out of a window while she pulled the wad of papers from her pocket.

As she'd hoped, they were notes from the Bank of England—twenty-pound notes totalling £280. A fortune—but still less than a tithe of what she needed to free William from his captor.

"My lady?"

Stuffing the notes back into her pocket, she whirled to smile brilliantly up at Lord Ribbleton.

"My apologies, my lord! I wished to escape the crowd for a moment between dances. I am ready to resume now, however."

"Allow me to congratulate you again, my lady," he said as they took their places, as though their conversation at the embassy reception had never occurred.

Sarah inclined her head graciously. This was another man from whom she could steal without a qualm. Alert therefore for opportunities, she paid close attention to the accessibility of Lord Ribbleton's pockets as their dance progressed. During their first promenade she was able to explore his right coat pocket, but felt only a quizzing glass.

During the second she managed to slip her hand into his left pocket without his noticing and closed her fist around something that felt like more bank notes. The coins she left, realizing that it would take more than she could carry to pay William's ransom. Notes were both lighter and quieter.

A quick check at the conclusion of the dance showed that she had added another £165 to her collection, and then Peter was claiming her for the first waltz of the evening. Suddenly, all thoughts of money, or even of her brother, fled.

"You're . . . you're sure you want to do this?" she asked nervously. "I am bound to embarrass myself—and you, too."

"Nonsense," he said smoothly. "The waltz is quite a simple dance, really. Here, let's move to a corner of the floor, where we'll be less visible until you get the hang of it."

The prospect causing her heart to pound in a way picking pockets had not, Sarah allowed him to lead her along the edge of the assembling dancers. "What . . . what do I do?"

"I'll show you." His voice exuded such confidence that she felt herself relaxing despite her doubts. "Place your left hand on my shoulder, so, and your right one in my left."

She complied, trying to ignore the thrill that went through her at such close contact, bringing as it did memories of what had passed between them last night. Then he placed his right hand at her waist— dangerously close to the pocket beneath her dress holding the purloined bank notes—and heightened the contact further, so that she could scarcely think at all.

The music began, and he moved his lips to within inches of her ear so that he could be heard over it without those nearby overhearing. "Now, in time to the music, *one*, two, three, *one*, two three. No, the other foot. There."

She felt exceedingly awkward, certain that the whole room was staring at her, though a quick glance about—which made her stumble—belied that. No doubt they had all just looked away in embarrassment, pitying her.

"A bit faster," he murmured. "In time to the music, remember? Like this."

All around them, she saw couples turning, around and around, their steps flawless. Peter, she noticed, had wisely not attempted turning her yet. Silently counting, she quickened her steps to match his, acutely aware of his hand against her back, warm and firm. He would never let her fall, however badly she might stumble. She smiled up at him gratefully.

"That's better," he said. "A dance is supposed to be enjoyed, not endured. You're doing famously, Sarah."

By the end of the waltz, Sarah was almost enjoying herself. Her keen sense of balance and quick reflexes made her a quick study. She was even able to execute a few turns without disgracing herself.

"You see?" Peter said as the dance concluded. "You fit into this world far better than you expected, just as I knew you would. I am the envy of every man here."

Sarah's smile felt stiff on her lips, though she hoped it did not show. Fit in? When she was forced to steal from her dance partners? What would Peter say if he knew? At the thought, she felt color creeping up her neck and turned hastily away.

"I think you exaggerate, my lord, but I thank you." Her words sounded more formal than she'd intended. She tried to soften the effect with another, more genuine smile. "You seem to bring out the best in me," she added, forcing that other matter from her mind. In the ways that mattered most, it was true.

With Peter she felt pretty, polished, special. As though she was capable of all he could wish. Perhaps, with practice, that fantasy might become reality.

"And you bring out the best in me," he responded warmly, gazing intently into her eyes.

Her color deepened further, but now she made no effort to hide it. "Really?"

He nodded. "I was merely drifting through life until I met you, Sarah, trying to forget—to find meaning in the ordering of other people's affairs. But now I find my own life far more interesting."

She parted her lips to ask what he needed to forget, only to find herself wishing that he could kiss her, that she could will the crowd around them to disappear. His eyes darkened as he held her gaze, tightening his grip on her hand, pulling her fractionally closer. Her eyelids fluttered closed.

"My dance, I believe, Lady Peter?" came Mr. Galloway's voice at her elbow.

Sarah's eyes snapped open and Peter hastily released her, looking slightly embarrassed. "Of . . . of course, Mr. Galloway," she stammered.

He glanced from her to Peter and back, grinning. "Newlyweds shouldn't venture out in public so soon after the wedding. I'll return her the moment the dance ends, Lord Peter, never fear."

Blushing, Sarah accompanied him to the set just forming. If she was to pilfer any more money tonight, she needed to remain as inconspicuous as possible—and now half the room seemed to be grinning and winking at her, and at Peter behind her.

"I'd worried the Mountheaths forced you into this match," Mr. Galloway confided as she curtsied and he bowed. "But that's clearly not the case. I wish you every happiness."

Sarah abandoned the idea of picking his pocket during the dance. "Thank you. I hope we will be."

"Wish I could have beaten him to the punch," he continued. "Wish I could have afforded to try, at any rate."

The dance separated them then, and Sarah considered his words. Without her deception, she and Peter probably would have an excellent chance of happiness, despite the disparity of their stations. How could a marriage flourish without trust, however?

Feeling suddenly guilty again, she glanced over to where she'd left Peter, to see him talking with Lady Beatrice Bagford, her first victim. They appeared to be deep in conversation. About what? A prickle of what could only be jealousy went through her.

"I confess I was dismayed to learn of your marriage on two counts," said Mr. Galloway as they came face to face again just then. "Not only are you lost to me, but I'd hoped you might act as my confederate to further my suit with Miss Lucy Mountheath."

Sarah pulled her gaze from the picture presented by Peter and Lady Beatrice with an effort. "Why should you need my help?"

He shrugged. "It seems Lady Mountheath does not quite approve of me. I'd hoped you might intervene on my behalf."

In fact, Sarah could not blame Lady Mountheath for her caution, much as she disliked agreeing with her. Mr. Galloway had never indicated by word or look that he loved Lucy—quite the reverse, in fact. Clearly he was only besotted by her fortune.

"I'm sorry," she said firmly. "I fear I will have no opportunity to help you, as I've had not one private word with Lucy myself since my wedding, nor am I likely to have."

He bowed, only the slightest trace of frustration in his face. "Of course. I assumed as much. Again, I wish you all happiness, my lady."

Sarah watched him go with a frown, wondering if she should warn Lady Mountheath, or Lucy herself—

not that either was likely to listen to anything she might say. At any rate, she had more pressing matters to consider just now. Turning back to where Peter had been standing, she found both he and Lady Beatrice were gone.

When she turned to scan the room, however, she was immediately accosted by Mr. Pottinger, her next partner. As they took their places, she realized that Peter was in the same set—opposite Lady Beatrice. The music began and she was struck by the parallel to her first ball.

Peter caught her eye then and smiled—an intimate smile that reminded her of just how different things were, despite surface appearances. Tonight she would go home with Peter, secure in the knowledge that he desired her, that he cared for her. . . .

"A penny for your thoughts, Lady Peter," Mr. Pottinger said, recalling her abruptly to the dance—and just as well. She still had much to do before going home tonight.

"I was simply counting the ways in which my life has changed over the past week," she replied, more or less truthfully.

The older man smiled. "Your good fortune could not have been bestowed on a more worthy object. Lord Peter is a very lucky man."

People kept saying that, and she could only hope that when all was done, Peter would not violently disagree. Glancing down the line of dancers, she decided she dared not attempt anyone's pocket with Peter in the same set. His eyes were far too sharp.

Instead, she did all she could to make herself agreeable to each person she passed as the dance progressed. It was entirely possible, after all, that she would need every friend she could cultivate, should her plans go awry.

"You're doing splendidly," Peter whispered when he briefly partnered her as she moved down the line. "I'm proud of you."

His words caused a knife of guilt to twist in her belly. She had promised him not to steal again. If he knew, he would surely feel she had betrayed him. "Peter," she said urgently, but then the dance moved them apart again.

Of course she could not tell him—not here. Perhaps not ever. She must keep her focus on William until he was free. Then, and only then, could she work on making her marriage all it could be.

When the set concluded, she excused herself and headed toward the ladies' withdrawing room. She had kept the dance before the supper dance free, with an eye to her goal for the evening. Glancing back, she saw Peter joining another set. Good! That gave her fifteen minutes before she need worry about him seeking her.

On reaching the alcove, she was joined by two other ladies headed in the same direction. Smiling a greeting, she accompanied them into the withdrawing room—a small antechamber with a screen in one corner, shielding the necessary. Sarah stood before the mirror, pretending to adjust the flowers in her hair until the others were occupied, then she left. For a mercy, the hallway was empty, so she quickly slipped through the doors to the balcony.

It was now even chillier outside than before, but that did not concern her. Stepping away from the glass doors, she moved to the low wall separating this section of terrace from the next. Making certain no one could see her from the house or the street, she hiked up her skirts and clambered over it.

The windows of the next house were dark—perhaps its inhabitants were here at the Wittingtons' ball. She tried the terrace door and when the handle turned, she breathed a sigh of relief that the family had not bothered to lock such a seemingly inaccessible portal.

Once inside, she tiptoed through a large hall, similar to the one next door, to the passage beyond, wondering where bank notes would most likely be kept. The bedchambers, perhaps, but the risk of encountering a servant there seemed too great. Instead, she crept down the stairs to the dimly lit ground floor and into a room that appeared to serve as a sort of office or study.

Her heart in her throat for fear some footman or maid might come to tend the fire, she hurriedly searched the desk and the small table next to it. Opening drawer after drawer, she was about to give up in despair, all too conscious of the minutes ticking past, when she found a small key.

She held her breath as she turned back to the table, which contained a small, locked cabinet. Fitting the key into the lock, she opened it. Success! Next to a neat set of ledger books was a sheaf of bank notes. Not bothering to count them, she stuffed them into her pocket.

With trembling fingers, she relocked the cabinet, returned the key to its drawer, then retraced her steps as quickly as she could without making a sound. Climbing too hastily back over the low terrace wall, she grazed her knee so badly that tears sprang to her eyes. She dashed them away impatiently, then paused until she again felt in command of herself.

A glimpse through the window showed a steady stream of ladies going to and from the withdrawing room. How was she to get back inside without being seen? She waited . . . and waited, growing colder by the minute.

Not until she could hear the faint strains of the waltz signaling the supper dance did the hallway empty. Seizing her chance, Sarah slipped back inside, then hurried in search of Peter, who would surely be wondering where she'd gone.

"There you are." He greeted her before she'd taken three steps into the ballroom. "Where—? Why, your hands are like ice!" Taking her gloved fingers between his own, he chafed them.

"I, ah, stepped out onto the terrace for a moment," she said, realizing that excuse would also serve in case anyone had seen her leave or return that way. "I was feeling rather warm, but I fear I stayed out there overlong."

His look was so understanding her breath caught, but then he said, "You were bothered by the crowds again? You should have told me. Are you equal to this dance, do you think?"

"Of . . . of course." She allowed him to lead her to the floor, where the dance had already begun, again struggling with her conscience. Fortunately she was still too inexperienced at the waltz to attempt much in the way of conversation.

"We'll leave right after supper, if you'd like," he suggested as the dance concluded, his expression still concerned—which only served to make her feel more wicked than ever.

"I should prefer that, I think." Certainly, she had stolen enough for one night—more than she'd expected to manage. Unless she missed her guess, she already had close to six hundred pounds.

Other couples joined them for supper, helping to divert Sarah's thoughts from her dishonesty with their chatter. Once alone with Peter in the carriage, however, she again felt oppressed by what she had done.

Shaken by an intense longing to tell him the truth, she cast about for something, anything, else to say. "Earlier tonight you mentioned that you had been 'trying to forget.' Forget what?"

When he did not answer, Sarah glanced up to discover him frowning into the distance, a haunted look in his eyes. "Peter?" she prompted softly.

With a start, he seemed to recall himself. "My apologies. I suppose it is only fair you know, though it's not something I like to discuss—or even think about."

She remained silent, waiting for whatever he felt willing to tell her. After another long pause, he recommenced.

"War is a damnable thing, Sarah. Necessary at times, but damnable—and it changes a man. I've tried to fight that change, but it's there, whether I acknowledge it or not."

"What happened?" she whispered, not certain she wanted to know, but feeling instinctively that he needed to tell her.

"Too many terrible things. But the events that

haunt me most occurred near the end of the war—
indeed, after Paris had already fallen to the allies. It
should have been a simple matter, mopping up a
pocket of resistance, but we were ambushed. I lost
more than a dozen men—young men whom it was
my responsibility to bring safely home to their
mothers and sweethearts."

Sarah took his hand, longing to erase the pain in
his eyes. "Surely they knew the risks. It was war, after all."

"Yes, it was war. But as much as I regret those
losses, I regret even more the things I did to prevent
greater ones. Or so I justified my actions at the time.
In retrospect, I believe I was at least partially driven
by vengeance."

He sighed, then continued when she did not respond. "I'll not burden you with the details, but suf-
fice to say that I ordered—and participated in—the
slaughter of a group of raw French recruits we
should have been able to capture and disarm. And,
God help me, in my fury at my losses I reveled in doing so. Until it was over. The rest of my men were
safe, but at a dreadful cost."

This was a side of Peter she never would have suspected. Still, she tried to help him come to terms with
his guilt. "I doubt your actions were more excessive
than any other commander's would have been."

"Excessive?" He gave a short, bitter laugh. "I received a commendation and a bonus for my actions.
Actions that would never have been necessary had I
not led my men into the situation in the first place."

"But if it was an ambush, you can scarcely blame
yourself."

He shook his head impatiently. "Our prior victories had made me cocky. I should have been more on my guard. I had reason to suspect our movements were known to the enemy—that there was a traitor still operating."

Sarah felt a chill spread through her belly. "A traitor?"

"The very one I mentioned to you before," he said, confirming her fear. "The recently captured Black Bishop—and Saint of Seven Dials. Now, perhaps, you can understand why I was so determined to disassociate you from that name—why I won't be satisfied until he, and all who helped him, hang for their crimes. For my men. For . . . for what they made me do."

"Yes," she whispered.

Yes, she finally understood. She understood that she could never tell him the truth about William, or about herself. She understood, in fact, that she'd have done better to go back to a life on the streets than bind herself to this man, who could never sympathize with what her brother had done. With what she had done.

Yes, she understood—now that it was too late to draw back her hand from the course upon which she had embarked tonight.

Belatedly, she realized the carriage had stopped. Peter assisted her down the step, then escorted her into the house. "Would you care to join me in a brandy?" he asked. "I fear I have unsettled your nerves along with my own."

She shook her head, her main concern to hide the money she had stolen tonight as quickly as possible. "I am tired enough that I shall sleep well without it, I suspect."

Bending down, he examined her face with a thoroughness that brought unwilling color to her cheeks. "Sarah? Was I wrong to tell you what I did? Have I changed how you regard me?"

"No, of course not," she said quickly—perhaps too quickly. "I'm merely tired, as I said. Truly, I am glad you told me."

And she was. For now she knew she must keep the truth from him at all costs.

Finishing his breakfast with only a newspaper for company, Peter wondered for the hundredth time if he had erred in telling Sarah what he had last night. Had he given her an irrevocable disgust of him? It seemed all too likely. A light footstep heralded her arrival and he summoned a smile to hide his concern.

"Good morning, Sarah. You were so tired last night, I didn't wish to wake you this morning. I trust you slept well?"

She smiled back, a trace of reserve in her eyes, but no censure. "Yes, I feel quite rested," she said, going to the sideboard to fill a plate. Then, "My, what a lot of food! Never tell me that whatever we do not eat is thrown away?"

In his relief, he answered almost at random. "I believe leftovers that the servants do not want are often given away to beggars and such." He was struck again by how privileged his life had always been—a marked contrast to Sarah's.

Apparently satisfied, she spooned eggs, ham and creamed sole onto her plate and sat across from him, smiling up at the footman who poured her coffee. "I apologize for being so . . . dull last night. I have yet to get used to the whirl of Society."

"Dull?" He chuckled, the last of his worries dissipating. "Not a bit of it, I assure you. My life is immeasurably more interesting—and pleasant—with you in it."

"I'm glad." She sounded doubtful, but he knew he would convince her in time how much she meant to him. After a lingering look at her, he returned to his paper.

"There is a new melodrama opening at the Strand Theater next week," he commented after a few moments. "Perhaps we will go. Have you ever been to the theater?"

Sarah shook her head. "I've always wished to, however."

"Then I shall take you—as often as you like." He continued to the bottom, mentally ticking off which shows she might like most, then turned the page.

His eye was arrested by a headline halfway down the page: NOBLE GUEST OR ENTERPRISING FOOTMAN?

"What—?" he murmured, and began reading the story that followed.

Authorities believe that the Saint of Seven Dials has struck yet again. Some three hundred pounds, in notes, were stolen from Lord Harrington's home late last night. It is perhaps not coincidental that, this same night, two different guests attending Lord and Lady Wittington's ball, in the house next door to the Harringtons', had money taken from their very pockets.

"I can't imagine how he managed it," Lord Ribbleton was heard to say.

Peter slowly lowered the paper, unable to read on, a sick suspicion knotting his stomach.

Chapter 17

Sarah glanced up from her plate to find Peter regarding her strangely. "What?" she asked. "Have I smudged food on my face?" She picked up her serviette and dabbed at her mouth self-consciously.

He stared at her for another long moment, then belatedly shook his head. "No, no. That is, you have remedied it."

"Peter?" Clearly something else was wrong, but she had no idea what.

"My apologies, Sarah," he said, finally smiling. "I was merely distracted, thinking about a few matters of business I need to attend to today. If you'll excuse me?"

Though still startled by his odd manner, she nodded. "Of course."

"I'll be in the library," he said, picking up the paper he'd been reading and taking it with him.

Perhaps it was something to do with the house he'd leased, Sarah thought, returning to her breakfast. Perhaps, as she'd feared, it was indeed more than he could afford. She tried not to feel regret, for even though she'd loved the house at once, she knew she wasn't made for such riches.

When she finished eating, Sarah debated joining Peter in the library. Deciding that he might want more time to deal with whatever business he'd mentioned, she went upstairs instead, intending to tidy her chamber—only to find that a maid had already done so in her absence.

"I will never get used to this," she muttered, resenting the invasion of her privacy even as she appreciated not having to do the work herself.

Suddenly recalling the money she'd stolen last night, she hurried to her dressing table and pulled out the right-hand drawer. Yes, it was still there at the back, but better concealment would be prudent.

In another drawer she found an empty box, fitted to the drawer, no doubt intended to hold ribbons or something similar. She removed the lid, the same width as the drawer, and wedged it an inch or.two from the back of the right-hand drawer so that it served as a sort of false back.

There! Now any seeking fingers would only encounter wood and not her secret treasures. Satisfied, she stood and glanced around the room again. It seemed ungrateful to be bored amid such luxury, but she had nothing to do or to read. She decided to join Peter in the library after all.

He smiled when she entered, though she thought he still seemed distracted—or perhaps disturbed.

"Is everything all right?" she could not help asking.

"I hope so," was his cryptic answer. Then, focusing on her more keenly, he said, "Sarah, you know that you can trust me to provide anything you might need, don't you?"

Her earlier suspicion revived. "Of course," she said reassuringly. "As I've said, however, my needs are few. I hope you will not, ah, overextend yourself in an effort to provide *more* than I need."

"More . . . no, no. Pray do not trouble yourself on that head." If anything, he seemed confused.

"Then . . . we will still be moving into the house you showed me yesterday?" She was surprised to discover the answer mattered more than she'd thought it would.

His brows rose. "Of course. Why should you think otherwise?"

Suddenly embarrassed, she shrugged. "You seemed so distracted, almost worried. It was all I could think of to account for it."

To her surprise, he laughed, his expression suddenly relaxed. "So you imagined I'd spent my fortune at the shops yesterday and could no longer afford the rent? Sarah, please believe that I will never allow you to feel want again."

"Then what—?"

"Never mind. It was nothing, as it turns out. Now, go fetch your parasol. I thought we'd visit a few furniture shops, and then I'll see about hiring Miss Fanny's maid away from the Mountheaths for you. And tonight I will take you to see your first opera."

Peter examined Sarah's rapt face in profile as she watched the singers and dancers upon the stage. All day he had been alert for anything in her voice or expression that might indicate her guilt in last night's thefts, but he'd detected nothing but an occasional shadow in her eyes when he'd bought her one or two particularly expensive trinkets.

As she had yesterday, she had protested such excess, claiming not to need such things, but he had bought them anyway. If there was any chance that she *had* played the Saint again last night, he needed to convince her that she no longer had any need to steal.

Several times he'd come close to asking her outright, but then remembered the promise she'd given him. How would she feel if he were mistaken? She would see the question as proof he did not trust her, which would undermine the sense of security he was trying to instill in her.

No, he would keep his suspicions to himself until he had more evidence, one way or the other. If another theft occurred tonight, while she was safely with him, he would know it was someone else playing the Saint of Seven Dials, and not Sarah. He couldn't help hoping that some great house was being robbed even as they watched the show.

"That was amazing," Sarah exclaimed when the final curtain descended. "Thank you so much for bringing me."

Peter gazed down at her upturned face, all thoughts of thievery banished. "There are many amazing things I hope to show you," he said with a wink. "Shall we go home so I can begin?"

Though she blushed, her eyes twinkled. "If you insist, my lord."

"I do." Placing her hand in the crook of his elbow,

he led her from the box, already anticipating an evening of delights. When they reached Grosvenor Street, however, his eagerness received a setback when he found Harry Thatcher waiting for him.

"Need to have a word with you, Pete," he said apologetically, glancing past him at Sarah. "A . . . er, private word."

Peter reined in his frustration. He and Sarah would have all night, after all—and every night following. "Very well. Sarah, why don't you go on upstairs? Your new maid should be here by now. I'll be up shortly."

Though she shot Harry a curious glance, she went without protest. Once she was gone, Peter led Harry into the library, then turned to face him. "Well?"

"Sorry, Pete. I know you have more, ah, pleasant things to do, but I'm badly dipped and m' father won't advance me a groat. I was rather hoping . . ."

With an exasperated sigh, Peter pulled a few guineas from his pocket. "How much do you need?" Perhaps it was time he told Harry the truth and turned his fortune over to him. It was a responsibility he no longer had time for.

"Fifty. I lost a bet to Caperton. Stupid thing, really: how many times Sherbourne would use his quizzing glass in an hour."

"Fifty! And on something like that? I don't have fifty pounds at the ready, I'm afraid, Harry." That probably wasn't quite true, but he didn't want Harry to know otherwise.

"Don't you?" Harry regarded him shrewdly. "You haven't been completely honest with me, have you, Pete?"

Though he feared he knew what was coming, Peter said, "What do you mean?"

Before answering, Harry crossed to the sideboard and poured himself a generous measure of brandy. Peter thought longingly of Sarah, waiting upstairs, but knew he had to get through this first.

"Ferny saw you on Bond Street yesterday, going in and out of some of the more expensive shops. I wandered in today to chat up a few of the shopgirls—they're always willing to oblige a war hero, you know—and I discovered you've been showering quite a lot of lucre on your new bride."

Peter had known word would get around to Harry eventually, but he hadn't expected it to be so soon. "She's had little enough her whole life," he said, avoiding the real issue. "I enjoy giving her some of the things she's lacked."

"Not the point, Pete, and you know it. Never tell me the duke settled that kind of money on her—or that you'd be spending it all at once, even if he had. And I know the Mountheaths won't have provided her with any kind of dowry. Where's it coming from?"

"Very well," Peter snapped. "I've laid a bit by—more than I've let on. I knew if I told you, you'd be continually touching me for loans, just as you're doing now. Can you blame me for keeping it to myself?"

Harry scowled. "Thought I was your friend. Hell, I had your back at Orthez! Yet you don't trust me?"

Again Peter's thoughts went to Sarah, but this time he was considering the matter of trust. It was far more complicated a matter than he'd realized. It was quite true that he'd trust his life to Harry without hesitation—but not his money. How did that parallel his situation with Sarah?

Realizing that Harry was still frowning at him, he said, "That was different. I know your weaknesses, Harry, and money is one of them. I could give you two hundred pounds a week, and you'd still run through every bit of it and come back to me for more. Can you deny it?"

"Not the point," Harry said again. "You've—"

"I think it is," Peter interrupted. "What kind of friend would I be to let you run yourself into debt, even with me as your banker? It would have destroyed our friendship, at the very least."

Now Harry shifted uncomfortably in his chair, taking a gulp of brandy that should have burned his throat raw before answering. "So you think if I'd known . . ." He broke off, then sighed heavily. "Damn it, Pete, don't you ever get tired of being right?"

Peter relaxed, almost limp with relief. Only now did he realize how worried he'd been that he would lose his best friend over this matter. "It's served me pretty well so far," he said with forced lightness.

"I have to admit I'd never have made that bet with Caperton if I hadn't heard about you spending so freely," Harry said ruefully. "Counted on you to bail me out if I lost."

"And if I'd lent you so much you could never repay it, you'd have started avoiding me," Peter added. "Just as you avoided your father for years."

"You know me far too well—and a good thing it is, too, though I hate to admit it." Harry tossed off the rest of his brandy, making Peter wince. "But now, what about the fifty I owe Caperton?"

Though it went against his better judgment, Peter relented—partially. "I'll give you twenty-five. You can pay him the rest when your check comes in two weeks. I know you're expert at putting off creditors for at least that long."

Harry started to frown again, but then grinned. "Fair enough. And I won't come to you for money again, Pete. Or, at least," he amended, "I'll try not to. A leopard can't change his spots overnight, you know."

"It's enough to know you're going to try." Going to the desk, he pulled out a few notes and handed them to Harry. "I'm always here for advice, if you want it."

His friend chuckled. "And even if I don't. I'm well aware of it. But thank you, Pete—for everything. You really are the best of good fellows."

They shook hands, then Harry headed for the door, saying over his shoulder, "Go on upstairs to your wife, old boy. Now that you've gone and got yourself leg-shackled, you might as well enjoy the benefits."

Peter waited until the front door closed behind him, then headed up the stairs to take one of the best pieces of advice Harry had ever given him. When he reached Sarah's room, however, her new maid, Libby, was just leaving it, closing the door behind her.

"Her ladyship is sleeping," she whispered to him. "She wanted I should tell you she's sorry, but she was that tired."

Irritated afresh at Harry's timing, Peter nodded. "Very well. Thank you." Frustrated, he retired to his chamber, wondering as he divested himself of his coat why Sarah had given him no such indication earlier. He didn't feel at all sleepy, so sat down at his writing desk to answer some correspondence.

It must have been an hour later when a sound from Sarah's room next door caught his attention. Had she perhaps awakened? He moved to the door separating the rooms to listen at the panels. Yes, someone was definitely moving about in there. Would she tap at the dressing room door? Should he?

Then, to his surprise, he heard her chamber door open and close—softly, as though whoever had done it did not wish to be heard. The maid again?

Suddenly hopeful that he might get Sarah into his bed that night after all, he quietly opened his own door to peer into the hall—only to see Sarah herself, garbed in her old gray gown and cloak, tiptoeing toward the servants' staircase.

It was true, then, he thought with a sick lurch of his stomach. Quickly pulling on a dark furze coat, he crept into the hallway himself just as she disappeared down the back stairs. He thought for a moment, then hurried toward the front stairs so that he could slip around the house and cut her off. Then, they would have this matter out once and for all.

Sarah knew she was taking a terrible risk, sneaking out of the house so early, but if she waited, she would have to break into houses to which the inhabitants had already returned for the night. Now, while some would still be out at various amusements, was surely the best time.

Now, before she could lose her nerve.

She thought she heard a creak in the hallway above

her and glanced back, but no one was visible. Suppose Peter decided to come into her chamber, despite Libby's message? He'd seemed eager—deliciously eager—to be with her again.

A sudden surge of longing stopped her in her tracks. Surely tomorrow night would be soon enough for her next attempt at robbery? Perhaps she would just . . . No! Peter was surely asleep by now. Besides, she had only four more nights before that odious Ickle said he would turn William over to the Runners. She had to obtain more money toward his ransom.

Rather than risk going through the kitchen, she went to the garden door on the ground floor and quietly unlocked it, hoping no servant would notice and lock it behind her before she returned. Stepping into the chill night air, she pulled her cloak more tightly about her. She would go at least two streets away, she decided, so that no suspicion could possibly fall on Peter.

She hurried across the garden, pushed open the gate and turned to the right. She'd taken only a few steps along the mews, however, when a dark shape loomed up right in front of her. Frightened, she shrank back with a gasp, but not until the figure spoke did she realize her true danger.

"Out for an evening stroll, my lady?" Peter asked blandly.

Sarah stared, her mind a blank. "No! Yes. That is, I—"

"Why, Sarah?" The gentleness in his voice was far worse than anger.

She swallowed, frantically trying to devise an excuse. "There was someone I wanted to see. An . . . an old friend," she offered.

But he was shaking his head already. "I know, Sarah. I know what you did last night."

Impossible! Wasn't it? "I don't know what you mean," she said, her voice high and unnatural, a betrayal in itself. "I was with you last night."

"Not every moment. You had ample opportunity to pick a few pockets, to break into the house next to the Wittingtons'."

Now she stared. "How can you possibly—?"

"It was in this morning's paper," he explained, his voice now bleak, defeated. "I suspected, but I didn't want to believe it could be you. Why, Sarah?" he repeated.

For a long moment she hesitated, struggling with conflicting loyalties, the overwhelming urge to tell him all the truth warring with her fear of what might result.

When she did not reply, he said, "You must know that if you need money, you need only ask me. And if you're in any sort of trouble, I will take care of it for you."

"I know." And she did believe he meant it. But he had no idea that the person she was helping was one of the very ones he had sworn to see hang. Even if she could conceal that connection from him, or if he could bring himself to forgive it, he might attempt to rescue her brother—which could lead to Peter's death as well as William's. No, she dared not risk it.

"It's . . . it's nothing like that," she finally said, trying to speak lightly despite the leaden weight in her heart. "I, ah, simply enjoy the risk, the . . . novelty. I led such a confined life for so long, you see." She held her breath, unable to read his expression in the dark alleyway, praying he might believe her.

When he spoke again, his voice seemed strained. "So you are unable to help yourself? I knew men like that during the war, who insisted on taking greater and greater risks, for the very thrill, until they were killed. I considered it a sort of sickness, a derangement of the mind."

So now he thought her mad? Better that than the truth. "I have no wish to die," she assured him, "though I suppose it is not entirely natural—especially for a woman."

He moved so suddenly she flinched, to grasp her by the shoulders. "Sarah, you must resist this urge! It is just as dangerous, and could indeed lead to your death, or your imprisonment and deportation at the least. If you seek thrills, I can show them to you—without running afoul of the law."

Pulling her tight against him, he covered her mouth with his own, kissing her with urgent passion, awakening an answering passion within her. She clung to him, giving herself up to the sensations he aroused. No, she could never lack for thrills, married to such a man. Amazing that he had believed her fiction, as far as it was from the truth.

"What would thrill you most?" he murmured against her lips. "If it is risk you crave, I can take you here, in the alley. Or in the garden yonder."

"But we might be seen," she gasped as he trailed his lips down her throat.

"Isn't that the point? I'm willing to risk it if you are."

She wasn't, but what could she say after the claim she'd just made? "It's . . . rather chilly outdoors."

"Mmm. Somewhere indoors, then. Come." Pinning her to his side, he led her back through the gate and into the house, much to her relief. Instead of taking her upstairs, however, he opened the library door.

"Will this be unconventional enough for you, my lady?" Already he was shrugging out of his coat, his eyes ablaze in the dim light of the dying fire.

Mutely, she nodded. Surely he couldn't mean to lie with her here? she thought nervously. She longed for his touch, but would prefer it in a proper bed, behind locked doors. . . .

Free of his coat, he divested himself of his shirt, then pulled her to him again. "You seem reluctant. Why?"

"I . . . I suppose I never expected—"

"That I might be willing to accommodate your tastes? But I am." He pushed her cloak from her shoulders and began unbuttoning her gray gown. "You need only tell me what you want, Sarah."

Despite her nervousness, she found herself fascinated by the play of the firelight over the planes of his bare chest. Tentatively, she touched him, tangling her fingers in the crisp, dark hairs, enjoying the hard, masculine feel of him. *Mine*, she exulted, fully appreciating that fact for the first time. Yes, she could do this.

He finished undoing her gown, and then her chemise. Then he pulled them both down over her arms, baring her to the waist, even as he was bare. She pressed herself to him, enjoying the way his chest abraded the sensitive skin of her breasts, enjoying the way they complemented each other.

Again he captured her lips, probing, demanding, his arms tight around her, imprisoning her. His strength, so much greater than her own, inflamed her even as it frightened her a little. He was so much larger, so much more powerful than she.

On that thought, she slid her hands down his belly and began unbuttoning his breeches. She wanted that power within her, a part of her. In moments she had freed him from his nether garments and leaned back so that she could examine her handiwork. He seemed impossibly large, rampantly erect in his evident desire for her. Memories of the pleasure he'd given her their first night together flooded back and she experienced a fresh wave of desire.

He seemed to sense it, for he growled low in his throat. "Come to me, Sarah." Pushing her gown and chemise down over her hips, he stepped out of his breeches, then kissed her again, hard. When he bent to remove his shoes, she did the same, and then they were in each other's arms again, completely naked before the embers of the library fire.

Running his hands up and down her back, Peter turned his head to glance around the room. "Here on the hearthrug, think you, or shall we try a chair?"

Nervousness flowed back at this reminder of how exposed they were here, but she did not pull away from him, determined to preserve her fiction. "What . . . whatever you think best," she whispered.

"Hmm. Let's try this, then." Drawing her with him, he sat on one of the overstuffed chairs, pulling her down until she straddled him, her knees wide, her feminine mound pressed against his turgid shaft.

Unwilling to let him see her surprise, she kissed him, chaotic sensations sweeping through her.

Grasping her waist with his large, warm hands, he lifted her slightly, then lowered her again, sliding her along his shaft, heightening those sensations. She heard a creak from the direction of the library door and stiffened, glancing wildly in that direction. What if Mrs. Walsh, or one of the servants . . .

"Relax," he murmured in her ear. "Part of the thrill is the chance that we might be caught, is it not?"

Swallowing, she nodded, though in truth the sudden fright had dimmed her desire somewhat. She turned back to him, though still darting furtive glances at the door. It did not open, nor did she hear any other sounds. Willing herself to calmness, she leaned down to kiss him again, even as he resumed moving her against him.

Passion, briefly banked, flamed again and Sarah gave herself up to it, willing herself to forget for the moment that she still had a serious problem to solve.

Though Peter would not have chosen this setting of his own volition, he found Sarah every bit as exciting in the library as in his bedchamber. If this added novelty could help her overcome whatever drove her to steal, he was more than willing to risk any small embarrassment that might result should a servant discover them here.

He'd felt her stiffen at that creak in the hallway—doubtless just one of the random noises a house of this age occasionally made. The risk of discovery did not seem to excite her as he'd expected it to. But if the reason she'd given him for stealing was false, any nervousness she felt now was due to her own deception.

Lifting and lowering her again and again, he felt her tense in a different way, her nipples hardening against his chest. The sensation of her sliding against him was exquisite, the feel of her soft, feminine body between his hands intoxicating. He would make her his in every way possible, body and mind, whatever it took, he was determined.

Her breathing was coming in quick gasps now and she slickened against him as he moved her. Lifting her higher, he impaled her upon him, covering her mouth with his own to stifle both of their cries. She tightened around him until he thought he might explode, but he contained himself, determined to pleasure her fully first.

Steadying her with one hand, he slid the other between them, her upright position giving him easy access to the spot that held the key to her desire. Rocking his hips, using his feet against the floor to propel himself upward, he thrust into her deeply, again and again, even as he stroked her cleft.

She began to make small, mewling cries, arching her back, driving herself down upon him with each upward thrust he made. He felt his legs shaking and knew he would not be able to hold back much longer. Fastening his mouth on one of her perfect breasts, he stroked her again and again, until she gave a great gasp and convulsed about him, tighter and tighter, driving him over the edge into ecstasy.

Clutching her against him, he emptied himself into her, caring nothing at that moment for any lies she'd told him, any secrets she still kept. She was his, he was hers, they were together. That was all that mattered.

Slowly, slowly, reason returned as he spent his passion, as she relaxed atop him. Reason, and realization that this had been but a moment out of time, a brief snatching of enjoyment that in no way addressed the problems that still stood between them.

But though he knew he should be demanding answers, he only nuzzled her neck and asked, "Will that thrill hold you for the night, do you think, or do you need more?"

She responded with a shaky laugh. "I won't attempt to sneak out again, if that's what you mean."

"I'll take that as a promise." He thrust away the knowledge that she'd already broken one such promise to him. "Suppose we go upstairs and then you can tell me whether you'd care for more thrills of a . . . ah, domestic variety tonight?"

A shadow seemed to cross her face for an instant, but then she smiled. "Your thrills are the best I've ever known. I'm not sure I'll ever have enough of them."

"Then it seems I have my work cut out for me," he said, wanting desperately to believe that this time she was telling him the truth.

When Peter led Sarah down to breakfast the next morning, he felt more strongly than ever that he'd been wrong last night to take her to his bed—or, rather, in the library—while so much still separated them. It made what should have been beautiful almost sordid instead.

He would have to ask her about the money she'd

stolen at the Wittingtons', for it must certainly be returned. He'd put it off, in hopes she might broach the subject herself, but she had not. He would say something over breakfast, he decided.

While none of those she'd robbed would suffer any lack, he didn't wish to delay any longer than necessary—though there was the problem of how to return the money without implicating Sarah in the thefts.

Glancing down at her, breathtaking in her new, sky blue morning gown, her golden curls loose about her shoulders, it seemed impossible she could ever do anything criminal—even though he knew beyond doubt that she had. He felt suddenly shaken, doubting the very judgment upon which he'd always prided himself.

"I'm quite famished," he remarked, to distract himself from that unsettling thought. "So much exercise last night has stimulated my appetite."

"I am hungry as well," she admitted, blushing. Again he marveled at her seeming innocence.

He took a deep breath, steeling his nerves for what he must do, even if it drove another wedge between them. "Sarah," he began—and was interrupted by a knocking at the front door. "What the devil? Who would call at this hour?" Motioning Sarah to proceed to the dining room, he went to greet the unexpected visitor.

A footman opened the door as he approached it, to reveal his brother Marcus and his wife, Quinn, on the front step.

"We headed back to Town as soon as we heard," Marcus said, coming forward, "but we stayed with

Luke last night rather than risk disturbing the new-lyweds." He grasped Peter's hand, slapping him on the shoulder with the other. "Congratulations! Where is your new bride?"

Chapter 18

Sarah emerged from the dining room to see Peter greeting a couple she had not met before, though the gentleman bore enough resemblance to her husband that she guessed it must be one of his brothers.

"Good morning," she said, bracing herself in case this brother evinced the same attitude as the duke and Lord Bagstead. To her relief, the newcomers both smiled with apparent delight as they started forward.

Peter's smile seemed oddly strained, however, as he made the introductions. "Sarah, this is my brother Marcus and his wife, Quinn. They've only just returned to London."

Quinn, a lively, petite brunette, took both of Sarah's hands in her own. "Of course we returned the moment word reached us of your wedding. Welcome to the family, Sarah—though perhaps I'm not the one to say so, recent addition that I am."

Her smile was as irresistible as her American accent and Sarah felt herself relaxing at once. "Thank you. Peter speaks fondly of you both. I'm delighted to meet you."

"I presume you need your trunks taken upstairs?" Peter asked then, signaling to the hovering footman.

"Unless you'd prefer we wait?" Marcus asked. "I know how awkward it can be to have others about so soon. . . ."

Sarah thought Peter hesitated for an instant before saying, "Nonsense. In any event, this was to be our last night here. I've taken a house on Curzon Street and we're anxious to move into it, are we not, Sarah?"

She readily agreed, though she'd have liked more opportunity to get to know Quinn. However, staying here with Lord and Lady Marcus would only make it that much more difficult to achieve her vital goal of ransoming William—not that it would be easy to slip away from Peter again, after last night.

"Is something wrong?" Quinn asked softly as Peter and Marcus headed to the dining room, discussing Mr. Thatcher and other mutual friends.

Sarah started. "No! That is, I am still adjusting to the idea of having a family—particularly such a family as this. Everything is so different from what I have been used to."

Quinn took her arm and led her into the dining room behind the gentlemen. "Ah! I see you have not yet eaten either. Let's have a nice chat over breakfast. I've always wanted a sister, you see, and I have a feeling we're going to become the very best of friends."

Warmed by the thought, Sarah admitted that she'd always wished for a sister as well. Quinn peppered her with questions, and she related her past as truthfully as she could without giving away too much. If Quinn suspected she was holding things back, however, she made no sign.

"It's hard to be suddenly on one's own in a new world, so to speak," she said when Sarah finished. "I experienced much the same, marrying Marcus only a week after arriving in England, though I never endured the privations you did. You have my heartiest sympathy, having to live dependent upon that odious Lady Mountheath—though I suppose I should be grateful to her, all things considered."

"Grateful?" asked Sarah in surprise. Peter had mentioned something. . . .

Quinn's eyes twinkled. "It is her fault that Marcus and I are married, you see. She created scandal out of an innocent meeting—though I admit I did behave rather foolishly—and he felt obliged to marry me as a result. Lady Mountheath, I later discovered, positively thrives on scandal."

"As long as she is not touched by it," Sarah said wryly.

"Yes, I'm sure half of London would love to turn the tables on her, if the opportunity arose," Quinn agreed with a laugh.

And Peter surely knew that, Sarah thought. His plan to trap her into marriage had been foolproof. But did he now regret it?

"There was some initial awkwardness between Marcus and me, of course," Quinn continued, "but we managed to get past it." The smile she sent her husband across the table spoke of intimacy, deep love—and trust.

Sarah couldn't suppress a pang of envy. Would she and Peter ever reach that level of understanding? Not while she kept secrets from him. Once William was free, she would try to find a way to confess the whole—unless Peter's trust had been permanently destroyed by then.

"So, how did you secure Lady Mountheath's consent to your marriage?" Quinn asked then.

Caught off her guard, Sarah blinked, but then Peter came to her rescue.

"We will doubtless have time to trade stories later," he said. "But now, if you are finished, my dear, I thought we would visit Wardour Street and finish the furnishing of our new home."

Sarah rose at once. "Of course. Just let me fetch my bonnet and parasol." When she rejoined Peter a few minutes later, they took cordial leave of Lord and Lady Marcus, then went out to the waiting carriage.

"Clearly we must come up with a plausible story to account for our hasty marriage," he said as they started off. "My father never inquired—preferring not to know, I presume—but Marcus and Quinn won't be so easily put off, particularly as their own match was so unorthodox."

"Can we not tell them the truth?" Sarah asked. Then, at Peter's frown, she hastened to add, "Not all of it, of course, but that I was abroad on my own at night, that you assisted me, and that Lady Mountheath came to hear of it and insisted upon our marriage."

"Quinn will ask why you were abroad."

"I can say that I was attempting to visit old friends of mine," she offered.

He regarded her for a long moment. "And will you tell her more of these friends than you have told me thus far?"

"It . . . it was merely an excuse," she explained, wondering how much he suspected of the truth. "I really don't . . . that is—"

"You did mention those friends the night I caught you leaving the Llewellyns' house," he reminded her. "You implied there were others, besides the boy, Flute. Tell me, Sarah, was it one of them you were going to see last night?"

"No! I . . ." Sarah realized she was trapped. If she confessed that no such people existed, she would be implicating William as her only accomplice. But if she did not, Peter might think . . . "There is no one else, Peter. You must believe me."

"Must I? And what of the money you took the night before?"

Because William's life was at stake, Sarah forced herself to meet Peter's eyes squarely. "I have no idea what money you mean."

She caught a glimpse of disappointment in his eyes before he turned away from her. "I see. Ah, here we are." His tone changed abruptly. "Let's buy some furniture, shall we?"

"I'm glad you could make it, Noel," Luke, Lord Hardwyck, said as he ushered the chestnut-haired young man into his library that afternoon. "Marcus and I thought it best that all three former Saints put our heads together to decide how best to deal with this situation."

"Your letter was rather cryptic," Noel Paxton replied, taking a seat in one of the deeply upholstered chairs arranged near the fireplace. "But it sounded urgent, so I thought it best to travel down from Derbyshire without delay."

Luke nodded. "I didn't dare write anything plainer, lest the letter fall into the wrong hands, but it would seem that another Saint of Seven Dials has appeared. I presume you didn't nudge anyone in that direction, any more than Marcus did?"

Noel shook his head.

"I read the accounts in the news sheets you gave me last night," Marcus said. "If the stories are to be believed, this fellow is nearly as talented as you were yourself, Luke, stealing a pendant from Lady Beatrice's very neck. Did you speak with the lads on the street, as you'd planned?"

"I tried. Flute seems to have disappeared, and Stilt doesn't know where he's gone—a matter of some concern to me."

"Do you think this bogus Saint may have spirited him away?" Marcus asked with a frown. "Or—forgive me, Luke—could Flute himself be our man?"

"That was my first thought as well, actually," Luke said, "but Stilt insists he can't be. In addition, Flute apparently left a note for this new 'Saint' before he disappeared, which may have explained where he was going. The note was, alas, delivered unread."

"Delivered?" Noel asked sharply. "By whom? To whom?"

Luke shrugged. "That's the difficulty. Stilt doesn't know the ultimate recipient, and the lad who does isn't telling. This latest Saint appears to have inspired loyalty in at least one follower already."

"Are you sure we need to do anything, then?" Marcus asked. "If he's carrying on the work properly, does it really matter who he is?"

"I'd say not, except that I'm not at all certain he is doing the thing properly, as you say. Stilt says that Flute did give money to one poor family after the first known robbery, as well as a bit to some of the lads. But there have been thefts since then, with no apparent delivery of the proceeds."

"Then you think this new fellow may be using the name to line his own pockets?" Noel asked.

"It's a possibility," Luke said. "Not that I have a problem with that, so long as he shares with the poor as well. I did the same, when it was my only means of survival. But apart from his motives, and the question of Flute's whereabouts, I find myself seized with a consuming curiosity as to his identity." He grinned at the others.

Marcus grinned back. "Then the question becomes, how do we catch him? Noel? You're our expert there."

Though he snorted, Noel knit his brow for a long moment, then nodded. "A line of communication is already in place. We simply need to make use of it."

"To set a trap, do you mean?" Luke's dark eyes brightened.

"Exactly," Noel replied. "What would this fellow find irresistible?"

"An easy haul," Marcus suggested. "Preferably in cash. According to the papers, the last robberies were all in notes—pockets picked at a ball and a deal of money taken from the house next door. That seems to be his new preference."

"Then we may not have much time," Noel said.

Luke and Marcus exchanged startled glances. "Why do you say so?" Luke asked.

"He may be trying to amass enough money to leave Town, or even England, and then live comfortably," Noel explained. "Perhaps he began with the intention of helping the poor, or perhaps that was merely a deception. Now, however, it sounds as though his purpose has altered."

Luke nodded now. "It could be that he's realized what kind of risk he's running, what with all of this publicity, and it's scared him. I can remember walking that line once or twice."

"But you always came down on the side of the poor," Marcus pointed out. "You're right. We need to catch this fellow and, ah, redistribute his recent takings. We don't want the Saint's reputation besmirched, after all."

They all chuckled, then Luke asked, "Noel, do you still have that flat on Long Acre, near Bow Street? Good. I have an idea."

For more than three hours, Peter and Sarah discussed types of wood, styles, fabrics, colors—but nothing more personal. Peter knew, with a sick certainty, that Sarah was still keeping secrets from him. As long as she was unwilling to trust him with the truth, it was clear that he could not trust her, either. Perhaps this marriage had been the mistake she had insisted it was from the first.

"Can it be delivered by the end of the day?" he

asked the salesclerk who had been following them around the Sheraton warehouse. They had already selected a few Hepplewhite pieces and a Chippendale or two from one of the nearby stores.

"Certainly, my lord," the man answered, ducking his head deferentially.

Peter gave him the direction of the house on Curzon Street, then turned almost reluctantly to Sarah. "That should be sufficient for a beginning, don't you think?"

She was looking rather dazed, much as she had on Bond Street. "Yes, more than sufficient," she replied.

Despite his inner conflict, Peter could not deny a stab of concern. "Come, let us stop somewhere for ices, and perhaps some chocolate," he suggested. "That will put you back into curl."

"I'm not . . . Thank you, my lord." Her smile seemed to take some effort. "As you know, this sort of thing is rather outside my range of experience, but no doubt I shall grow accustomed to it."

"No doubt." The warmth in his voice surprised him. What was it about Sarah that stirred him to such protectiveness, even when he did not trust her? She stirred him in other ways as well. "Come. We'll go to Gunter's, and then to Curzon Street so that we may supervise the placement of the first deliveries."

By late afternoon, their new house was furnished enough for livability. The library boasted four Hepplewhite chairs, the dining room a polished mahogany table with Adams-style detailing, the parlor several light Sheraton chairs and small tables. There were also new oaken bedsteads and matching wardrobes in two adjoining rooms on the second floor, along with small writing desks in each room and a lovely rosewood dressing table with a built-in glass for Sarah.

"We still need a hall table and a desk for the library, a pier glass or two upstairs, and chairs for the ballroom, among other things," Peter said, surveying said ballroom on the first floor. "And, of course, we've no servants beyond your maid and my valet. We will remedy that tomorrow."

"Can we stay here tonight?" Sarah asked, gazing around with wide eyes. "It's . . . it's so beautiful."

Peter felt his heart contract. He wanted to give her so many beautiful things, to give her every happiness she could desire. If only . . .

"I'm afraid we really can't. Not only have we no cook as yet, but the feather mattresses for our beds won't be delivered until tomorrow. I don't fancy sleeping on bare boards."

She shrugged, still smiling. "I've slept on worse. But I suppose you are right." She turned away from the ballroom with a small sigh. "Tomorrow, then."

As they drove back to Grosvenor Street, Peter reminded himself that she'd had little reason in her life to trust others. Or was he merely making excuses for her? He didn't know anymore.

"We were beginning to wonder whether you meant to return at all." Quinn greeted them on their return. "Come, Sarah, you must tell me every detail of what you have bought, and tomorrow I insist on seeing your house for myself." She led Sarah to the sofa and the two were soon chatting comfortably together.

Peter watched them for a moment, remembering when he and Sarah had been able to talk like that—

before they were married. Would they ever recapture that easy camaraderie?

"You seem pensive," said Marcus, at his shoulder. "Care to talk about it?"

"I seem to recall you rebuffing my attempts to advise you early in your own marriage," Peter replied with an attempt at a grin.

Marcus's grin was more genuine. "Ah, but you were a bachelor at the time. Now, however, I have the advantage of you, with four months of married life to draw upon. Perhaps I can offer some sage wisdom from my vast experience."

"I doubt it. My situation is rather unique."

"So was mine," Marcus said. "Yet something you said at a critical juncture proved helpful. Something about mutual respect and kindness being necessities for a happy marriage."

Peter blinked, trying to recall having said such a thing. Marcus and Quinn had always seemed so happy . . . but no, during their first few days of marriage, there had been definite signs of strain between them, as there was now between himself and Sarah. The cause, however, had surely been quite different.

"I was quite the meddler, wasn't I?" he said, remembering how he'd tried to force his advice on Marcus at the time.

Marcus shrugged. "I thought so then, but I know now you had our best interests at heart. As I do for you and Sarah."

Stifling a sigh, Peter nodded. "I know you do, Marcus, but I fear we will have to work out our difficulties on our own."

"So you admit there are difficulties?" Marcus was grinning again. "Sorry, old chap," he said in response to Peter's frown. "But it's rather gratifying to see that my big brother is no more perfect than I am."

No, Peter thought, nowhere near perfect, or he wouldn't find himself in this untenable situation. And while "mutual respect" sounded well enough, how was it to be achieved when Sarah persisted in keeping secrets—perhaps criminal secrets?

"Still—" Marcus glanced over at Sarah, still chatting happily with Quinn "—it's obvious the two of you dote on each other, so I've no doubt you'll work through whatever small problems you might have. Marriage is rather a large adjustment, but well worth the effort, I've discovered."

Peter followed his brother's gaze, carefully concealing his surprise. Marcus thought Sarah doted on him? Would that it were true. Even watching her from across the room, he felt his pulse accelerate, his vitals tighten. Dishonest or not, she meant the world to him.

But would she ever let him enter fully into her world? He hoped so, because he would never settle for half measures again.

Sarah found that attending an entertainment with a party made her far less conspicuous than attending with only Peter—or perhaps it was simply that Society had already moved on to newer gossip than their abrupt wedding.

In any event, Quinn and Marcus were amusing companions and their chatter helped to distract her from the awkwardness that had sprung up between Peter and herself—an awkwardness of her own making, but which was beyond her power to undo.

"Lady Ribbleton certainly has outdone herself,"

Quinn commented, gazing around the large ball-room. "Do you suppose she is mimicking the mamas of debutantes with this ball, hoping to marry off her son?"

"I should think most women would be too intimidated by the dowager to dream of taking her place as hostess here," Sarah replied, trying to stifle a sudden memory of the money she'd stolen from Lord Ribbleton two nights ago.

"Perhaps that is her intention," Peter said. "I have heard that she is unfailingly critical of any lady in whom Lord Ribbleton shows the slightest interest. She watches his dancing partners like a hawk, alert for any error." The glance he sent Sarah showed that he, too, had that theft on his mind.

She quickly looked away. "I'm glad I didn't know that before, or I'd never have dared accept his invitation to dance," she said. Peter had still not questioned her in any detail about the money she'd taken that night, though she knew he must want to.

"Oh, I'm sure she is not so critical when he partners a married lady," Quinn said reassuringly. "She would not see you as a threat to her position, Sarah. Still, Lord Ribbleton is rather off-putting, is he not?" She glanced over at the marquess, still in the receiving line, with an odd little grimace.

Sarah nodded, remembering his remarks to her before she'd married Peter. "I confess I do not much like him. I find him both arrogant and pompous."

"That, too," Quinn agreed. "Have you met the Misses Melks yet? No? Come, I will introduce you."

The evening seemed endless to Sarah, though if she and Peter had been on easy terms no doubt she would have enjoyed it. As it was, he stayed close, watching her constantly, though never engaging her in private conversation. He insisted on dancing more than half the dances with her, and for those where she partnered other men, managed to be in the same set.

Raising William's ransom had seemed an impossible task before, but now, with Peter alert to her every move, she would never have opportunity to add to the six hundred pounds she had accumulated so far.

"The supper dance is mine, I believe," Peter said then, moving to her side as the previous set finished and a waltz began.

"When tomorrow will we move to our new house?" Sarah asked after several moments of silent dancing, merely for the sake of saying something.

"As early as you like," he replied with the same stiff reserve he'd used toward her all night.

Sarah longed to thaw that reserve, but saw no way to do so—or no safe way. Only a complete understanding between them would heal the breach that divided them now, and it seemed impossible that such understanding could ever be. Perhaps she could reclaim one aspect of intimacy, however.

"Can we leave after supper again tonight?" she asked, a hint of seductiveness in her voice.

He glanced at her, surprise and a glimmer of warmth in his eyes. "Are you tired again?"

She winced, for he had not been able to keep a trace of sarcasm from his tone—not that she could blame him.

"No. I wish to be alone with you," she replied, refusing to look away, even as she felt her color rising.

"I can't . . ." He broke off whatever he'd been

about to say with a frown. "Very well, Sarah. We may leave early if you like."

But as Quinn and Marcus accompanied them home after supper, Sarah had no opportunity to gauge Peter's feelings or give him a hint of her own. As at supper, the conversation was general, touching mainly on social news. Sarah's attention wandered to the line of Peter's jaw, the breadth of his shoulders concealed beneath his burgundy coat and rose waistcoat.

"—did you, Sarah?" Quinn asked, making her start.

"I beg your pardon?"

Quinn's smile was indulgent, implying she guessed the cause of Sarah's abstraction. "I was merely asking whether you had noticed how foolish Lucy Mountheath appeared tonight, mooning after Mr. Galloway, who was pursuing Miss Cheevers."

"Oh. Ah, no. I fear I did not, though I have observed her interest in the past, despite her mother's objections."

Indeed, Sarah had noticed little beyond Peter tonight. She feared she was in danger of becoming rather obsessed with her husband—an obsession that could put more than her peace of mind at risk. The carriage rolled to a stop and her pulse quickened at the thought of what surely lay ahead.

None of the four seemed inclined to linger below, so they all made their way upstairs and said their good nights. Marcus and Quinn disappeared into their chambers, and Sarah turned toward her own, trying to frame an invitation before Peter could disappear.

"I'll join you in a moment," he said before she could speak.

Her heart suddenly far lighter than her circumstances should warrant, she nodded. Whatever lay ahead, at least she would have tonight.

"No, not the flannel," she told Libby when the maid had divested her of her ballgown and held up a nightrail. "Just the lavender wrapper, I think. Then you may leave me."

With a knowing wink that Sarah scarcely noticed, Libby draped the lace and silk confection about her, then silently departed. This wrapper, Peter's first gift to her, was a reminder of their first blissful night—before Ickle's note had arrived to shatter Sarah's world. Perhaps, wearing it, she could recapture some of that former magic.

For a moment she considered the problem she still faced, of somehow coming up with the rest of William's ransom. She would have to slip out again, though she wouldn't attempt it until much later. Perhaps when Peter returned to his chamber, after . . .

A tap came at the dressing room door and her breath caught, every other thought fleeing. "Come in," she called softly.

Peter stepped through the door, utterly gorgeous in his midnight blue dressing gown. Sarah felt her heart accelerate, her nerves tingling with anticipation. She took a step toward him, reaching up to untie the ribbons of her wrapper.

"I've been looking forward to this all evening," she confessed, letting her love for him show in her eyes.

He reached for her, but only to cover her fingers with his own, halting them. "That's not why I'm here, Sarah. We both know you have not been entirely honest with me. Until you are, I believe it is best we refrain from activities intended for couples who enjoy each other's full trust."

Sarah took a step back, feeling as though he had dashed cold water on her. He released her hands at once. "But I . . ." No, she would not compound the problem by reiterating the lie she'd told him last night. The truth, however, was out of the question.

"Yes?" he prompted, and there was no mistaking the hunger in his eyes—hunger for her confidence as well as her body. But while she was willing—eager—to give him the latter, she did not dare surrender the former.

"I'm sorry, Peter," she finally said. "I have told you all I can. I'll . . . I'll see you in the morning."

Perhaps it was for the best, she thought. It was almost a relief to have his lack of trust in the open, along with her admission that she merited it. At least that much was honest. And without him here, it would be much easier for her to slip away, to do what she must to save her brother.

But he was shaking his head. "I'll be staying here, Sarah, though not in your bed. Whether you'll trust me with the truth or not, I mean to protect you, even from yourself. I won't allow you to leave the house again tonight."

Chapter 19

⌒⌒

The alarm, quickly concealed, that flared for an instant in Sarah's eyes told Peter she had intended to do exactly that. Again he felt the bitter bite of jealousy. Who was it she wished to meet? He simply could not believe she planned to steal again. He had proven how unnecessary that was, no matter what the cause.

"Who are you protecting, Sarah?" he asked urgently. "Why won't you tell me?"

She stared at him helplessly, lovely in her sheer wrapper, her golden curls loose on her shoulders. "Oh, Peter, I wish I could." Her beauty clouded his mind, making him desperately want to believe her.

"If you want to, you can," he insisted. "I told you about the darkest moment of my past. Surely this can

338

be no worse. You haven't murdered anyone, have you?"

"No, of course not."

"Then are you protecting a murderer?"

"No." She did not meet his eye as she spoke the word, however. He must be getting close to the truth.

"Then you can tell me without fear, Sarah. It cannot be worse than that, can it?" What had this Flute, whom he believed to be her brother, done?

But she turned away from him. "I don't believe so, but you may not agree. Oh, Peter, if I were the only one at risk, I would tell you in an instant." She turned back to stare pleadingly up at him. "You must believe that."

He swallowed the bitter bile that rose in his throat, the suffocating suspicion that perhaps it was not her brother but someone else she was protecting. What else might she think he would regard as seriously as murder, if not adultery? He reminded himself of how innocent she'd been on their wedding night . . . and how innocent she had acted the day after her last thefts.

Suddenly weary, he moved to the chaise longue and stretched himself upon it. "Go to bed, Sarah."

For a long moment she hesitated, then turned toward the four-poster and removed her wrapper to reveal a near-transparent chemise before climbing beneath the sheets. Disappointed, angry, even disgusted as he was, Peter could not control his body's response to that glimpse of the delights he was deliberately denying himself.

Sternly, he willed his body to quiescence, for to give in now was out of the question. She had all but confirmed his worst fear—that she was indeed meeting another man. Clearly, she believed that if Peter knew all, he would feel obliged to kill the man—and just now he felt he could happily do just that. But where did that leave his feelings for Sarah—or hers for him?

He dared not dwell on that, for to do so might well send him over the edge into despair—or violence. Trying to ignore the soft sound of her breathing only a few feet away, he closed his eyes and began slowly counting to one thousand. When he reached it, still awake, he began again.

"Our new cook shows promise, don't you agree?" Peter asked.

Sarah put down her fork and nodded, though in truth she couldn't claim to have enjoyed her first dinner in their new house on Curzon Street. That was scarcely the cook's fault, however.

"He did say he had studied under a French chef," she pointed out, her mind not really on her words.

It had been a trying day.

Breakfast had been an ordeal of concealing from Quinn and Marcus the friction, heightened since last night's conversation, between Peter and herself. Then Quinn and Marcus had come to see the new house, prolonging the difficult charade of happy newlyweds. Once his brother and sister-in-law had left, Peter was all business, directing the placement of new deliveries while Sarah met with the new housekeeper, cook and under-servants.

Dinner had been their first opportunity for private conversation, but Peter had never dismissed the footman—rather to Sarah's relief, as she had no idea what she would say to Peter anyway. Perhaps he felt the same. But now, the meal over, she wondered whether he would finally reopen the subject he had broached last night.

He stood, and she looked up expectantly. "I'm going out briefly," he said. "You will no doubt wish for a bath before bed, as hard as you have worked today. I will have mine when I return."

Sarah swallowed, wanting to make some sort of peace offering, but knowing the only one he would accept was the truth—the one offering she dared not make. "When—?" she began, but he had already turned away.

With a silent sigh, she let him go. Today was Saturday. The day after tomorrow, Ickle would turn William over to the authorities if she did not deliver the ransom—clearly an impossibility now. Did she really have anything to lose by telling Peter the truth? However angry he might be, he was more likely to show her brother mercy than the Bow Street Runners were.

Defeated, she left the dining room, heading to the kitchen to request bathwater before going upstairs. When Peter returned, she would tell him everything, beg him to somehow pay William's ransom, while dissuading him from attempting a rescue. It was her only remaining chance to save her brother, even if it destroyed her marriage.

Or what was left of it.

Deep in her melancholy thoughts, she was distracted by a minor commotion when she reached the kitchen.

"Away with you, boy," the cook's assistant was saying to someone just outside the kitchen door. "Her ladyship can't be bothered to talk with the likes of you. If you come back Monday, the house-keeper might see you. She's the one interviewing for positions."

"But this is important," came a familiar voice. "Can I at least leave a message tonight?"

Quickly, Sarah stepped forward. "Thank you, Mrs. Fenster. I'll handle this."

The cook's assistant started, then obediently moved away from the door. "Of course, milady! Now you're for it, boy," she added ominously to the unseen visitor outside.

Crossing the kitchen, Sarah stepped through the back door and closed it behind her before turning to Paddy. "You have a message, you say?" she asked. "How did you find me here?"

The boy grinned up at her, tugging his forelock. "Polly, the maid what took the last note for you, told me how you'd moved out o' the other house. Weren't but a matter o' asking a few questions on the street to find out where."

"And the message?"

He reached into his pocket. "Another letter. It was give me by Renny, like the last one. D'ye know, mi-lady, Renny thinks you're the Saint o' Seven Dials?" He chuckled at the joke. "Tried and tried to get me to tell 'im who you were, but o' course I wouldn't say nothing."

Sarah forced a small laugh. "How silly! But thank you, Paddy, for not telling him anything about me. I greatly appreciate that." Though she itched to open her letter, she voiced a sudden thought. "Would you be interested in regular employment—something safer than sweeping crossings?"

His eyes widened. "You mean here, milady?" But then his face, which had brightened briefly, clouded. "I ain't really fit for much, you know."

"No one is, until they're taught," she replied. "Come back Monday, as Mrs. Fenster said, and we'll find something for you to do. We still have several positions to fill."

A wide smile broke across his face, reminding Sarah painfully of her brother when he was younger. "Oh, aye, milady! I'll do that, certain! Thank you!"

Sarah watched him across the garden, then, tucking the letter into her sleeve, reentered the kitchen.

"Mrs. Fenster, when that boy returns Monday, send him to the housekeeper. I'll have a word with Mrs. Bing before then about his position here." Whether she managed to save William or not, she could at least help poor Paddy.

The cook's assistant looked as though she'd have liked to protest, but didn't dare. "Aye, milady. Will there be anything else?"

"Yes. Please have a bath and water sent up to my chamber. And convey my compliments for an excellent dinner to Mr. Ogden."

Now Mrs. Fenster beamed. "I will, milady. Thank you, milady!"

Hurrying up to her room, Sarah sent Libby downstairs to supervise the preparing of her bath and then opened her letter. It was written in Stilt's untidy scrawl.

Dear Saint,

We've heard there's a smuggler keeping a large amount of money at his flat on Long Acre, the right-hand one on the second story at number 12. He'll likely be gone tonight, should you want to relieve him of it. Let me know if you need the lads to help.

—Stilt

Sarah read through the note three times with growing excitement. Surely, this was an answer to her prayers! A smuggler might well have enough money to pay William's ransom, and it would be just in time to satisfy the odious Ickle. It was perfect!

But then her excitement ebbed.

It was too perfect. Suppose this was a trap of some sort? She knew nothing of this Stilt except that he had delivered Ickle's note to Renny. Suppose he was working for Ickle himself?

Or . . . perhaps he had learned of William's kidnapping and this was his way of helping the Saint to raise his ransom? That might account for the too-convenient timing of this note. Nor could he suspect that the "Saint" was a woman. If she were careful . . .

No, Peter would never allow her to slip out of the house. He'd made that clear last night. She'd awakened several times to hear his breathing across the room. Somehow she had no doubt that he was a very light sleeper. Wouldn't his years as a soldier ensure that?

Still, it was all she had. If she could not somehow evade his watchfulness by, say, two o'clock in the morning, she would finally tell him the truth.

She devoutly hoped, however, that would not be necessary—not until William was safe.

A tap at the door interrupted her musings, and an instant later Libby and two footmen entered, carrying the brand-new copper tub and a pair of steaming kettles. The footmen left and Libby helped her to undress for her bath. Settling into the bath a few minutes later, Sarah heard the door to the next room—Peter's room—open and close.

She tensed, waiting, her eyes fixed on the dressing-room door that separated their chambers. If Peter came to her now, could she tempt him into her bed, despite his resolve? Then she might summon the courage to tell him the truth—or he might fall deeply enough asleep for her to creep away without waking him.

She heard his voice through the panels, no doubt giving instructions to his valet. Then, after a long pause, the handle of the dressing room door turned.

Not until he saw her naked in the tub did Peter remember he'd suggested Sarah take a bath. Though he knew he should retreat, he somehow couldn't wrest his gaze away from her glorious body.

"Peter?" she said softly, making no attempt to cover herself.

He swallowed. "My apologies. I'll, ah, return later." If he was going to carry out his plan for the evening, he needed his wits about him, and the sight of Sarah unclothed was not conducive to that end at all.

"You can stay, if you like."

Her voice was seductive, but also rather stilted. Was she nervous? Or . . . was this some plan to put him off his guard? The idea helped him to gain a modicum of control over his rioting emotions. He took a step into the room.

"I thank you for the offer, but no." His voice surprised him with its firmness, for in truth he felt like doing nothing so much as stripping off his own clothes and joining her in that tub. "It happens that I must go out again, and I simply wished to inform you of it before leaving."

Now she did cover herself, leaning forward to reach for a towel. He risked another glance and saw disappointment on her face. Could it be he was wrong? He took another step forward, then stopped. No, he would carry out his plan. Then he would know once and for all whether his suspicions were correct.

"Where are you going?" she asked, standing and wrapping the towel around her dripping body.

Peter had to again subdue his involuntary reaction, force himself to stay where he was. "I have learned that a friend needs my assistance," he said, glad he had rehearsed the words earlier. "He may require my presence for several hours, so you needn't wait up for my return."

He watched her face closely as he spoke, and thought he detected a slight widening of her eyes— but that was all. Not enough for proof. "It goes without saying that you're not to leave the house," he added.

Now she evaded his glance—as he'd both expected and feared she would. "Of course. My . . . my best wishes for your friend."

"Thank you." Before he could give in to the almost overwhelming temptation to take her in his arms and force the truth from her with his touch, his lips, he turned and went back to his room.

There, he leaned against the dressing-room door and took several deep breaths. The very fact that Sarah had not asked the name of his friend was damning, he realized now. Clearly, all she cared about was that he would be out of the house, freeing her to meet whoever it was she was protecting.

He motioned to Holmes, and the valet divested him of his brightly colored coat and waistcoat to replace them with black garments that would be much less noticeable on the dark streets of London. Once ready, he left his room again, closing the door audibly before heading downstairs.

Taking his hat and greatcoat from a waiting footman, he departed through the front door and headed down Curzon Street in full view of Sarah's window—though he managed to restrain himself from glancing up to see if she was watching him. He turned onto Down Street, then slipped into the alleyway behind the houses and headed back the way he'd come, to keep watch on the back door of his own house.

Half an hour passed with no sign of Sarah. Three quarters of an hour. Peter began to hope that he'd been mistaken, though of course it was still early. An hour. An hour and a quarter. His hope grew stronger.

A movement caught his eye and he sharpened his gaze, now well acclimated to the darkness of the alley. With an almost physical shock of disappointment, he recognized Sarah, again clad in her nondescript gray cloak and hood, emerging into the back garden and creeping toward the gate. He took a cautious step forward.

This time he did not intend to stop her. Not until he discovered who she was meeting, and why—even if the knowledge destroyed his happiness forever.

* * *

Sarah closed the gate silently behind her and breathed a sigh of relief. She'd done it! Even if Peter should return, he would not know where she'd gone, would not be able to stop her. Not until she'd obtained—and delivered—William's ransom.

Once William was free, there would be time enough to worry about repairing her marriage and rebuilding Peter's trust. Surely she and William together could concoct a story to account for her keeping her brother's existence a secret, and she could finally take care of him, with Peter's help.

In fact, if all went as she hoped, Peter would never even know she had gone out tonight. First, however, she had to achieve her goal. Long Acre, she knew, was only two streets from Seven Dials, and adjacent to Bow Street. Again she wondered whether this might be a trap—set by the Runners, if not by Ickle. And again she reminded herself that she had no choice but to try.

She set out at a brisk walk, as her destination was more than a mile away. The streets were still busy, filled with carriages and pedestrians on their way to the theater or other evening entertainments or employments.

Turning onto Coventry Street, Sarah felt a prickling at the back of her neck. Glancing back, however, she was unable to pick out anyone who seemed to be paying her undue attention. She continued on her way, trying to shake the feeling she was being watched. Even if this were a trap, no one could have known where she would be starting from. She trusted Paddy completely.

As she left Mayfair for less exalted parts of Town,

the makeup of the crowds changed, though they did not thin appreciably. Top hats and greatcoats were replaced by furze coats and woolen caps, though groups of young bucks in more formal attire, on their way to the theater district, still dotted the streets.

After twenty minutes, Sarah reached Long Acre. The shops lining the street were closed at this late hour, and the pedestrian traffic therefore thin. The letter had said Number 12, which proved to be a chandler's shop, with living apartments above.

Trying to appear innocently purposeful, as though she belonged here, Sarah stepped through the narrow doorway leading to the stairwell. The second story had only two doors off the short hall, so she crept to the one on the right, as Stilt's letter had advised. No one was around, so she pressed her ear to the door in an effort to verify that the apartment's occupant was indeed away.

Silence. But—was that a step on the stairs behind her? Sarah straightened and lifted her hand, as though to knock at the door, waiting for whoever it was to come into sight. No one did. Perhaps she had been mistaken—or perhaps it was someone moving about in another apartment. Heart pounding, she again bent to the door before her, to try the handle.

Locked, of course. She frowned at the keyhole, then pulled an assortment of keys from her pocket, which she had brought for just such a problem. None fit exactly, of course, but she diligently jiggled a small key in the lock until she was rewarded by a faint click. With a last glance over her shoulder, she opened the door and slipped inside.

Closing the door behind her, she paused to allow

her eyes to adjust to the dimness. The apartment appeared to be of moderate size, consisting of at least two rooms, judging by a closed door that doubtless led to a bedchamber. This main room held a small table, three chairs, a writing desk and a sofa. A bookcase near the door held only a few volumes, their titles unreadable in the dim light.

Cautiously, she moved across the room, wondering where the smuggler might have hidden the money Stilt mentioned. The desk? It seemed the obvious place to start. Quietly, she opened one drawer, then another, feeling all the way to the back. Nothing. Nor did any of the cubbyholes hold anything, not even pens or ink.

Frowning, she surveyed the room again and realized there was no evidence that anyone had lived here recently. As it had earlier, her skin began to prickle, her suspicion that this was a trap sharpening to sudden dread. Surely, though, even if she were caught here, she could explain that she had meant to meet a friend, that she had simply entered the wrong flat.

Torn between need for the money that might be here and an urgent desire to escape, she tiptoed to the bedroom door and again put her ear against the panel to listen. Was that a whisper? She was almost certain she'd heard *something*. Though every instinct screamed at her to hurry, she backed slowly, silently away.

And tripped over a metal ash can.

Both can and Sarah fell to the floor with a resounding clatter. With a gasp, she leaped to her feet, but before she could take so much as a step toward the outer door, the inner one flew open with a crash.

"We have him!" exclaimed a cultured but unfamiliar voice. "Quickly, before he can escape!"

Two other men emerged from the bedroom, one moving to stand between Sarah and the outer door while the other joined the first one in seizing her by the arms. Sarah struggled wildly, a vivid memory of her near rape in Seven Dials rising up to suffocate her. This time there was no chance of William appearing to rescue her.

"By Jove, it's a woman," said one of the men holding her. His voice was vaguely familiar, though in her panic Sarah could not place it.

"Who are you working with?" demanded the first voice. "Who is playing at being the Saint of Seven Dials?"

Sarah tried to think quickly. As she'd guessed would happen, they did not assume that she, a woman, could be carrying out these thefts herself. " 'E's the Saint, right enough," she gasped out, using her street accent in a wild hope that might help somehow. "Why'd ye think 'e's not? An' I give me oath I'd not betray 'im."

All three men chuckled grimly and Sarah felt a cold chill run up her spine. Were these Bow Street Runners, then, who knew that the real Saint had been arrested? What if they somehow connected her to William?

"Why should we think he's not?" one of them echoed. "You might say we're all intimately involved with the real Saint of Seven Dials."

This reinforced her suspicion, though they sounded more like gentlemen than the one or two Runners she'd had brushes with in her youth. "Then ye'll know he don't work wi' women," she retorted, still trying to brazen it out.

"Not usually," said the familiar voice, with a hint of laughter. "At least, I never intended to."

Sarah gasped, forgetting to disguise her voice. "Do you mean . . . *you're* the Saint of Seven Dials?" If Peter was right, and the Saint was a traitor, her life was now in grave danger. Had he escaped?

Then the first man spoke again, and she realized it was even worse than she'd imagined. "In fact, you could say that we are all three the Saint. But tell us: Who are you?"

Chapter 20

Peter stepped from the landing into the second-story hallway, struggling against disbelief. To avoid being seen, he'd had to rely more on his hearing than his sight, but it appeared that Sarah actually had a key to this apartment—which must mean she was a frequent visitor. The location also meant she definitely wasn't visiting an indigent younger brother who lived on the streets.

He moved quietly to the door and heard the unmistakable sound of voices within—an adult male voice, then Sarah's. Though he could not decipher the words, the tones were not precisely loverlike. Then he heard another male voice, distinctly different from the first, then Sarah again. She sounded frightened.

In an instant he forgot his suspicions, his heartache,

everything but Sarah's safety. Wishing he'd thought to bring along a pistol, he kicked open the door, hoping surprise would be advantage enough.

That the occupants of the room were surprised was evident, for all of them wheeled around to face him. Three men, two holding Sarah—that much he could distinguish by the dim light from the hallway. With a roar, he launched himself at the one on Sarah's right. If she'd been hurt, he would kill him—kill them all.

"It's him!" one shouted.

"I knew it!" cried another. "Hold him!"

Then they were all engaged in a melee of fisticuffs, Peter drawing on every bit of his nearly forgotten skill. He knocked his first target to the floor and sensed rather than saw that Sarah had broken away from the other man holding her. As that man turned to pursue her, Peter lashed out with a foot, tripping him.

"Run!" he gasped at Sarah as the third man grappled with him from behind.

She started for the door, but before she could reach it, the first man Peter had tackled lunged to his feet and slammed it shut. At the same time, the man he had tripped rose to help the one behind him pinion his arms to his sides. He lashed out again with his foot, connecting with the man's shin, but though he grunted, he did not go down. The two men forced him into a chair.

"A light!" one of them shouted. "Someone strike a light!"

There was a scraping sound, and a moment later a match flared, followed by the steady flame of a candle. By its light, Peter saw the faces of all three men:

Lord Hardwyck, Noel Paxton and . . . Peter's own brother, Lord Marcus Northrup.

"Peter?" Marcus said in obvious amazement, releasing him. "Never tell me it was you?"

"Marcus? What the devil—?" Peter said at the same time.

Lord Hardwyck, the one who had lit the candle, stared around at the stunned faces. "Now this is interesting," he said. "Lord Peter, I take it you know this woman?"

Peter blinked, then looked at Sarah—frightened, bewildered, disheveled, but still beautiful. "She is my wife," he said. "But why she is here—why any of you are here—I haven't a clue."

"Then you are not this most recent Saint of Seven Dials?" Marcus asked, glancing curiously from Sarah back to Peter. "I'm relieved, as it would seem completely out of character for you, Brother."

Lord Hardwyck moved to light more candles, then said, "I suggest we all sit down and figure this out. Lady Peter, you take the sofa—and please accept my most profound apologies."

While Sarah moved dazedly to the sofa, Peter turned to Noel Paxton. "I thought you, at least, knew who the Saint was. Were you not responsible for the Black Bishop's arrest?"

Noel raised an eyebrow. "Someone has been talking out of turn, I see. But yes, the traitor faces trial at the end of this month. He was not, however, the Saint of Seven Dials."

"Then," Sarah said shakily from the sofa, "you have not escaped from prison? But you said—" She turned toward Lord Hardwyck.

"That we were all Saints," he concluded. "But not traitors, my lady. Never traitors."

Sudden understanding broke upon Peter. "You acted as the Saint to catch the Black Bishop!" he exclaimed to Noel. "That is why there were no more thefts after his arrest."

Noel nodded. "I've always known you had a formidable intellect, Peter. It rather amazed me, in fact, that you never suspected Marcus during his brief stint as the Saint."

Now Peter turned to his brother in amazement. "You? I recall when Noel was questioning you last summer, but I thought his suspicions completely absurd. You were just getting married, after all, and it didn't seem . . . that is . . ."

"Too heroic for your feckless little brother?" Marcus suggested with a grin. "I won't say it didn't complicate my life—and my marriage—for a while. Of course, when I took over from Luke, I had no idea I'd be getting married so soon."

Peter scanned all three faces. "Then . . . Luke—Lord Hardwyck—you were the first Saint? The original one?"

He nodded.

"And Marcus, you were next?"

"Took over when Luke married," Marcus affirmed.

"And then Noel?" Peter asked, putting the final pieces of the puzzle together. "Is there anyone else?"

"That's what we were here to determine," Luke replied. "Someone has been stealing, and has sent money to Flute—my onetime manservant—claiming it was from the Saint, or so Stilt tells me. But now

Flute has disappeared and the thefts continue, though London's poor are not seeing the benefits."

Peter glanced at Sarah, who was staring at the floor, her face pale and scared.

"When you burst in here, Lord Peter," Luke continued, "I assumed it must have been you, for we set this trap specifically for the person sending messages to Flute. However—"

"It was me," Sarah quietly interrupted him. "Peter had nothing to do with it."

The others stared in amazement, but Peter moved to her side and took her hand. "Why, Sarah? Can you finally tell me why?"

Instead of answering, she looked at Noel. "You say the Saint was never a traitor? Nor any of the boys helping him?"

Noel shook his head. "Never, though I can understand Peter's leaping to that conclusion. I hope no one else has."

"Not to my knowledge," Peter told him, then turned back to Sarah. "Why do you ask that?"

Now she met his eyes, her own wide and pleading. "It is why I never told you the truth before. The risk seemed too great, considering the penalty for treason—and then you told me of your personal animosity toward the Black Bishop, for what he did to your men, and—"

"And you were afraid I would never forgive you for helping someone who had helped him," he concluded, a most welcome light dawning. Unless— "But who was it? Who were you protecting? For I know you have played the Saint only in recent weeks."

"My brother," she confessed. "I know you once suspected that the boy I sought was my own brother, and you were right." She turned to Lord Hardwyck. "Flute, the boy who has been kidnapped, who helped the Saint—who helped you, my lord—is my brother."

Luke blinked, but picked up on just one word of her confession. "Kidnapped?" he asked sharply.

Sarah nodded. "That is why I needed money so desperately." She sent Peter another pleading glance. "A thief-master named Ickle is threatening to turn him over to the Runners unless I give him five thousand pounds by Monday. But . . . I presume there never was any money here?"

Noel shook his head. "This flat was mine, and I still hold the lease. It was all a ruse to lure in the bogus Saint—begging your pardon, Lady Peter."

"What sort of ruse?" Peter asked, his heart seeming to expand in his sudden relief.

"I received a note tonight," Sarah said. "It said I would find a great deal of money in this apartment—that a smuggler lived here."

Luke nodded. "We had Stilt send it via Renny, who gave it to a young crossing sweeper. A very loyal crossing sweeper, I might add," he said with a wink at Sarah. "Renny did his best to wring your identity out of him, and tonight I offered him quite a bit of money as well, but he gave us not a clue."

"Dear Paddy. I don't know what I'd have done without him." A brief smile crossed Sarah's face, but then her eyes filled with tears. "But what about my brother? I have only six hundred pounds toward the ransom. Can . . . can you gentlemen lend me the rest?"

Peter tightened his grip on her hand, aching for what she had gone through, understandably afraid to trust him with her secret, trying to handle all of this alone. "Of course," he began, but Luke cut him off.

"We'll do better than that. We'll rescue Flute from the dastardly Ickle this very night. Marcus, Noel, are you with me?"

The other men nodded.

Sarah scrambled to her feet. "Let me help. Please."

"And me," Peter said, standing beside her, her hand still in his. He looked down at Sarah and she gazed back, her eyes wide and grateful, a tremulous smile on her lips. That look made any risk worthwhile.

Luke frowned at them both, then shrugged. "Very well. Let's go."

If Sarah hadn't been so worried about her brother, she would have been euphoric as the group headed toward the heart of Seven Dials. Her secret was out, Peter had forgiven her, and the look in his eyes, the grip he kept on her hand as they walked, told her he truly cared for her.

"Look sharp, now," Lord Hardwyck said, bringing her abruptly back to the problem at hand. "Ickle's flash house is in the rear of that inn up ahead, the Three Larks. This area will be thick with his lads, and some of us don't exactly look as though we belong here." He cast a quizzical look at Peter's sober but still fine ensemble.

Peter shrugged—a grin tugging at his mouth—looking more cheerful than Sarah had seen him lately. "At least I didn't wear my gold waistcoat."

The others chuckled, but quietly, as they were nearing their destination. "Around this way," said Lord Hardwyck, turning down a narrow alley one building away from the Three Larks. "Stay close together, and stay alert."

Sarah was amazed to see how well all four men— even Peter!—were able to affect a slouching, shambling walk, completely different from their usual firm, authoritative strides. In fact, had she not known otherwise, she'd never have guessed that Lord Hardwyck or Mr. Paxton, in particular, had ever lived among the wealthy, much less were members of that class themselves.

As for herself, she was able to slip back into her girlhood character. An old woman peered out of a doorway as they passed, and a younger one leaned out of a window above, but neither raised any sort of alarm. Perhaps they could carry this off after all!

At the intersection of the alley with another, they paused. "That's it, there." Lord Hardwyck motioned toward a ramshackle two-story addition to the inn. "The entrances will be guarded."

"What . . . what if this Ickle kills William rather than allows him to be rescued?" Sarah couldn't help asking, despite the comforting pressure of Peter's hand on her shoulder.

Lord Hardwyck grinned, his white teeth flashing in the darkness of the alley. "That may be his plan, and I've no doubt he has Flute heavily guarded, as it's known I broke the lad out of Newgate last spring. However, Ickle will be expecting an attempt by one Saint, not three. Or, I should say, four." He bowed in Sarah's direction.

She was glad for the darkness, which hid her

blush. "No, I was never a true Saint," she began, but Lord Marcus cut her off.

"If what I've heard is true, you merit the name as well as any of us. Sometime you must tell me how you managed Lady Beatrice's necklace."

"But not now," said Lord Hardwyck. "Come, let's lay out our plan. There are two ground-floor windows and one door, if memory serves. I propose we fan out and secure all three at once. Allow no one who comes out to go back in—no alarm must be raised. Marcus, you're with me. Noel, you go with Lord and Lady Peter."

Breaking into two groups, they moved with seeming aimlessness toward the back of the inn. As they drew nearer, Sarah saw that Lord Hardwyck had been correct. There were teenaged urchins outside the window visible from this side, while an ill-favored middle-aged man lounged in the narrow doorway, picking his teeth with the point of a wicked-looking knife. Mr. Ickle, no doubt.

Lord Hardwyck and Marcus angled toward the nearest window, laughing together and stumbling as though they were drunk. The other three veered to the far side of the narrow alley as though they meant to pass by the inn entirely.

"I'll take Ickle," Mr. Paxton breathed as they drew opposite the door and its leering guardian. "You two take the other window."

"No," Sarah whispered on sudden inspiration. "I have an idea." Not waiting for a reply, she stepped from beneath Peter's protective arm and headed boldly toward Ickle himself. She heard a furious whisper behind her, quickly hushed, but did not look back.

Already the pock-faced man in the doorway had noticed her, his leer becoming more pronounced. He looked sturdily built but not overlarge, she noted with relief. Praying that Peter would not act prematurely, Sarah threw back her hood to reveal her golden curls and sauntered forward.

"Gorblimey! An' what 'ave we 'ere?" Ickle growled, a wolfish grin splitting his ugly face.

"Come *on*," Noel hissed at Peter as he stopped, aghast, to watch his wife approaching their nemesis. Belatedly, he realized Noel was right and followed him to the corner of the building before glancing back again. They dared not draw attention to themselves yet.

"You're out of his line of sight here," Noel whispered then, "so you can stay in the shadows and keep an eye on her. I think I know what she has in mind. I'll secure the other window."

Peter nodded, not taking his eyes from Sarah as she reached out with one delicate, ungloved hand and touched the foul Ickle's shoulder.

"Folks 'ereabouts call me Sally," he heard her say in an accent as rough as Ickle's own. "I 'ear tell you're a man worth cultivatin', Mr. Ickle."

The thief-master's grin widened in a manner that made Peter's fists clench. Slipping his dagger into a pocket, Ickle put a filthy finger against Sarah's face. "Aye, that I am, Sally lass. I'm in a position to be real nice to them what please me."

Peter was about to throw caution to the winds and burst from hiding when he noticed Sarah's hand sliding caressingly down Ickle's arm—and into his pocket. "Oh, I think I can please you," she said, her hand reappearing with the knife.

From behind him, Peter heard the sounds of a scuffle and a quickly muffled shout. Noel must have dispatched the guardian at the window. Unfortunately, it appeared Ickle had heard it as well.

"Eh? What's that?" he said, turning his head. Peter shrank into the shadows before he could be seen.

Sarah dropped the knife into her cloak pocket and slid her hand back up the man's arm. "Probably those sots I was with. They was arguin' over me and I told 'em neither could hold a candle to you, and sent 'em on their way. Like as not they're fightin' now."

Ickle nodded. "Mebbe so, but I'd best have a look. Man in my position can't be too careful, you know." He took a step toward Peter, but Sarah blocked his way. "You're goin' to walk away from me, then?" she asked with a convincing pout.

Not convincing enough, apparently. Ickle's thick brows drew down in a sudden frown. " 'Ere, I know this game! Staged it meself enough times, I have. You're shillin' for them fellows while they bust into me place!" Grasping her roughly by the arm, he turned back to the door.

Recognizing his cue, Peter leaped forward, cutting Ickle off. "I don't think so," he said smoothly.

Quick as a snake, the man wrapped an arm around Sarah's neck, while thrusting his other hand into his pocket. If he hadn't been so worried for Sarah's safety, Peter would have found his expression comical.

"Looking for this?" Sarah gasped, pulling the dagger from her pocket. Before Ickle could snatch it from her, she tossed it to Peter, who caught it neatly by the handle.

"Ye lying bitch!" Ickle roared. "I'll snap yer neck." He tightened his stranglehold on Sarah, turning whatever retort she tried to make into a breathless squeak.

Suddenly, Peter was back on the battlefield, a life he'd been charged to protect in the balance. Without hesitation, he closed with his enemy, his training telling him exactly where to strike. As the knife slid between the villain's ribs, Ickle's hold on Sarah suddenly slackened. With one surprised grunt, he slumped to the ground.

Peter spared him scarcely a glance, but gathered Sarah into his arms. "Are you all right?" he asked urgently.

But she was staring at the man at their feet. "He would have broken my neck in another instant," she rasped, her voice hoarse. "You killed him . . . to save me. I'm sorry, Peter. I should never have put you in such a position, after—"

"Shh! Don't talk now. Let's see if the others need help." Oddly, Peter felt no remorse for what he'd just done, despite the vows he'd once made never to use violence again. Sarah had been in danger and his course had been clear. It was as simple as that.

They rounded the corner to see Noel gagging one lad while another already lay bound at his feet. "Everything under control, then?" Peter asked.

Noel nodded, grinning. "See how the others are doing."

They headed back the way they'd come and found Marcus guarding two more bound urchins. "Where's Luke?" Peter asked.

"Right here," came a voice from behind them.

Turning, they saw Luke emerging from the doorway, a lanky teen at his side.

"Oh, William!" Sarah cried, flinging herself at the boy. "You're safe!"

"Sarah?" the boy said in amazement. "What the devil are you doing here?"

Luke glanced behind him at the doorway. "Explanations will have to wait. Let's get out of here."

Peter stepped forward and put one arm around Sarah and the other around her brother, grinning down at the boy, who stared up at him in baffled awe. "Yes. Let's go home."

"So let me get this straight," Flute said. "Sarah was the one who sent me those jewels and such, sayin' they were from the Saint?"

The six of them sat around the fire in the library at Peter and Sarah's house on Curzon Street. Sarah leaned against Peter on the sofa, Flute on a stool at her feet. She had never been so happy in her life.

"I had to keep you from attempting to play the Saint yourself," she told her brother. "I confess my solution was rather unorthodox, but it seemed the risks to you would be greater than for me. Besides, no one would suspect a woman."

"Almost no one," Peter corrected her, even as the others voiced their agreement with her statement.

She gazed up at him, drinking in the planes of his face, now softened by his obvious affection for her. "I knew you would be my greatest challenge, for almost from the moment I met you, you always seemed to know my very thoughts." He smiled down at her, his brown eyes kindling.

"And you're married to this gent," Flute said, bringing them back to their surroundings. "When were you planning to tell me about that?"

Sarah tried to look apologetic, but was too content to have much success. "It all happened so quickly—there really wasn't time. And it was only the day after we were wed that I received that ransom note from Ickle."

"Well, that's one problem that will no longer plague the London streets," Marcus declared. "Sorry you had to be the one to take him out, though, Pete."

At that reminder, Sarah glanced up at her husband with concern, but Peter shrugged. "I had no choice. Certain situations demand difficult solutions—and a man can't live his life in regret for having done what was necessary."

Sarah squeezed his hand, tight in hers, to convey that she understood just how important that realization was for him. He squeezed back. Suddenly, she couldn't wait to be alone with him.

"Well said," Noel Paxton declared, rising. "And quite true. It's a lesson with which I had to come to terms some time ago. But now, I'd best take my leave, as I'm heading back to Derbyshire at first light. I only hope Rowena won't be too upset that she missed our little adventure when I tell her about it."

The others rose as well. "Tomorrow we'll see how many of Ickle's lads we can convince to go to your school, Marcus," Lord Hardwyck said. "Flute, suppose you come home with me tonight, and bring me up to date on all that's happened in my absence."

The lad glanced at Sarah, who nodded. "We'll have your room ready tomorrow," she promised.

"And when you get back, we'll talk about you going to school yourself."

He frowned. "I ain't goin' back to Westerham! That place—"

"Of course not," she agreed. "I had something quite different in mind. What would you say to Oxford?"

Now surprised delight spread across his face. "Oxford? Really?"

Lord Hardwyck put a hand on his shoulder. "I'll write you a letter of recommendation myself."

"And tell me more tales of it?" Flute asked hopefully, making everyone chuckle.

"Of course—but only the decent ones," Lord Hardwyck replied, with a wink at Sarah.

A few minutes later they had all gone, leaving Sarah and Peter alone in their beautiful marbled front hall. Peter twined his arm around her waist, pulling her to him. "It occurs to me," he murmured, "that while you had your bath this evening, I never had mine. Perhaps you would care to assist me?"

She tilted her head up to kiss his jaw, lightly stubbled with a day's growth of beard. "I'd be delighted," she said.

Together, they mounted the stairs. On reaching Peter's chamber, he sent Holmes, his valet, downstairs to request a bath, then turned back to Sarah. Suddenly clasping her tightly to him, he buried his face in her hair.

"I'm so glad to have you safe," he whispered. "So glad you never need put yourself into danger again, for I think it might kill me to lose you. I love you, Sarah."

She clung to him, reveling in the words she'd wanted to hear for what seemed an eternity, though in truth it was little more than a week. But what a week! "I love you too, Peter. More than life itself. I will never keep secrets from you again."

"I will hold you to that promise, and pledge the same. I believe we both learned something about each other, and about ourselves, tonight. You are a clever, resourceful woman, Sarah, and all I could ever have hoped for in a wife—even if you have worried me half to death as a result."

She stared up at him, her eyes wide. "Truly, Peter? I so want to be worthy of you."

"You are a treasure beyond price," he declared, the intensity of his gaze underscoring the sincerity of his words. "I believe I may well be the luckiest man alive."

He bent to kiss her, but Holmes returned then, with footmen who quickly prepared Peter's bath. Sarah and Peter stood side by side, arms entwined, until they were again alone. Then she turned to him and began unfastening his shirt.

"This is much easier when you're not wearing one of those complicated cravats," she commented lightly, though her heart was full to overflowing.

He grinned, undoing the top button of her old gray dress. "This gown does not pose as much challenge as your finer ones, either," he said. "Perhaps we should dress down more often. But I must say, it was rather unsettling to see how easily you slipped into the role you played tonight."

Sarah leaned forward and pressed her lips against his now-bare chest. "It is a role I never intend to play again—a past I wish to forget as much as you wished to forget your time in the war. Indeed, I feel quite sullied by my contact with that nasty Ickle. I believe I will need another bath."

Chuckling, he stripped off her gown until it lay pooled on the floor at her feet in a gray heap. "I was hoping you would say that." Stepping into the bath, he picked up a cloth and wet it. "Come here."

Her heart hammering with anticipation, she came to him. "I fear we won't both fit into the tub."

"No matter. Once we're clean, we'll move to the bed—unless you would prefer the library?"

She shook her head. "As I think you guessed, security makes for a more enjoyable . . . experience."

He began washing her breasts, the rough cloth sending tremors through her body. Stooping to seize another cloth, she rubbed it slowly down his chest, delighting in the way his flat nipples hardened at her touch. Then she progressed lower, lower.

He growled, then covered her mouth with his, pulling her tight against him. At the same time, he laved her back, a lovely sensation of its own.

"Now this is the sort of novelty I can enjoy," she said when he finally released her lips. "Ah! Here is the soap." Bending down again, she retrieved it and quickly worked up a lather between her hands. "No, my lord."

Though he twitched as she washed him, he made no attempt to stop her and she marveled yet again at the size of his maleness. She ran her fingers up and down its length, then covered its tip with the palm of her hand, massaging it.

He swallowed convulsively and gasped, "If we're to make it to the bed, we'd best rinse off." He knelt, and she followed him down, gasping herself as the warm water—and then his hand—contacted the juncture of her thighs. "My turn," he murmured, making her twitch as he'd done, until the water slopped over the sides of the tub.

"Oh, my," she said. "Holmes won't like that at all."

"Mmm. Let's dry off, then." Pulling her to her feet, he stepped from the tub and wrapped a thick towel around her, again roughing the sensitive skin of her breasts. "We'll have to share, as there is but one towel," he said.

Sarah grinned, gave him a quick kiss, then rubbed the towel, still around her own body, against his. Then, as he'd done, she wrapped the rough material about him, drying his back, pressing her breasts against his chest.

"Dry enough, I think," he said, and, to her surprise, he scooped her up in his arms to carry her to the bed. "Now, my lady wife."

Already her body clamored for his, and he did not make her wait, for he was clearly as eager for this, their first completely honest joining, as she was. Parting her with his fingers, he entered her with a groan, suckling at her breasts as he drove into her. She arched her head back, exulting in the knowledge that he was hers and she was his—completely.

"I love you, Peter," she gasped, as he drove her over the edge of ecstasy. "I love you with all my heart."

"And you are my heart, Sarah, my love, my life." With a final thrust, he emptied all he had into her, then collapsed beside her on the bed.

"I hope you now feel completely secure with me,

Sarah," Peter said when their breathing had slowed enough for more speech. "It's what I've wanted for you all along."

"Completely," she assured him, pressing her lips to his to reinforce her answer. "In fact, the very day I met you I fantasized that you might sweep me off my feet and take care of me forever."

He grinned, delighted. "Indeed? Then you'll be pleased to know I've taken steps to do just that, whatever should happen to me. You never asked, but I arranged to have thirty thousand pounds settled upon you the day we married. You need never worry about your future—or your brother's—again."

Sarah gaped at him. "Thirty . . . *thousand* pounds? Just how rich *are* you, my lord?" she asked sternly, "And why did you not tell me?"

"I had to be sure you didn't want me for my money," he said, enjoying her amazement. "I've done well with some investments, and can now claim to be one of the weathier men in England. Not until I met you, however, did I know how to use it properly. I donated a similar sum to Mrs. Hounslow for her kindness to you. She assures me she intends to put it to very good use helping other poor orphans."

Sarah flung her arms about him. "Oh, Peter, you are the most generous man I have ever known. I can't think why Marcus doubted you could have been the Saint, for you are certainly heroic enough."

"You flatter me, my love. But now you are retired, I have no intention of taking your place as Saint. I'll be far happier simply being your husband."

She kissed him again, and even as he felt his body

stirring in response, he realized he might know someone who would enjoy playing the Saint. Perhaps with a mission to give his life meaning, Harry would finally develop the responsibility to take over his own fortune.

"And I'll be eternally happy to be simply your wife," Sarah murmured against his lips. "Believe me, I have put my wicked ways behind me forever."

"Not all of them, I hope," he replied with a grin, pulling her tightly against him.

Eagerly molding herself to his body, she chuckled. "Very well, I'll be wicked for you—but only for you." And she proceeded to show him exactly what she meant.

Lose yourself in enchanting love stories from Avon Books.
Check out what's coming in December:

HOW TO TREAT A LADY by Karen Hawkins
An Avon Romantic Treasure

Harriet Ward invented a fiance to save her family from ruin, but when the bank wants proof, fate drops a mysterious stranger into her arms, a man she believes has no idea of his own identity. And so she announces that he is her long-awaited betrothed!

A GREEK GOD AT THE LADIES' CLUB by Jenna McKnight
An Avon Contemporary Romance

What if you had created the perfect replica of a gorgeous Greek god, and right before you're about to unveil it to a group of ladies, it comes alive in all its naked glory? What if your creation wanted to reward you by fulfilling your every desire? What if you're tempted to let him . . .

ALMOST PERFECT by Denise Hampton
An Avon Romance

Cassandra wagered a kiss in a card game with rake Lucien Hollier and willingly paid her debt when she lost. Then, desperate for funds, she challenges him again . . . and wins! Taking Lucien's money and fleeing into the night, the surprisingly sweet taste of his kiss still on her lips, Cassie is certain she's seen the last of him . . .

THE DUCHESS DIARIES by Mia Ryan
An Avon Romance

Armed with advice from her late grandmother's diaries, Lady Lara Darling is ready for her first Season. But before she even reaches London, the independent beauty breaks all the rules set forth in the Duchess Diaries when she meets the distractingly handsome Griff Hallsbury.

Avon Romantic Treasures

*Unforgettable, enthralling love stories,
sparkling with passion and adventure
from Romance's bestselling authors*

Have you ever dreamed of writing a romance?

*And have you ever wanted
to get a romance published?*

Perhaps you have always wondered how to
become an Avon romance writer?
We are now seeking the best and brightest undiscovered
voices. We invite you to send us your query letter to
avonromance@harpercollins.com

• *What do you need to do?*

Please send no more than two pages telling us
about your book. We'd like to know its setting—is it
contemporary or historical—and a bit about the hero,
heroine, and what happens to them.

Then, if it is right for Avon we'll ask to see part of the
manuscript. Remember, it's important that you have
material to send, in case we want to see your story quickly.

Of course, there are no guarantees of publication,
but you never know unless you try!

*We know there is new talent just waiting
to be found! Don't hesitate . . . send us
your query letter today.*

*The Editors
Avon Romance*

Discover Contemporary Romances at Their Sizzling Hot Best from Avon Books

STUCK ON YOU   by Patti Berg
0-380-82005-6/$5.99 US/$7.99 Can

THE WAY YOU LOOK TONIGHT   by MacKenzie Taylor
0-380-81938-4/$5.99 US/$7.99 Can

INTO DANGER   by Gennita Low
0-06-052338-7/$5.99 US/$7.99 Can

IF THE SLIPPER FITS   by Elaine Fox
0-06-051721-2/$5.99 US/$7.99 Can

OPPOSITES ATTRACT   by Hailey North
0-380-82070-6/$5.99 US/$7.99 Can

WITH HER LAST BREATH   by Cait London
0-06-000181-X/$5.99 US/$7.99 Can

TALK OF THE TOWN   by Suzanne Macpherson
0-380-82104-4/$5.99 US/$7.99 Can

OFF LIMITS   by Michele Albert
0-380-82056-0/$5.99 US/$7.99 Can

SOMEONE LIKE HIM   by Karen Kendall
0-06-000723-0/$5.99 US/$7.99 Can

A THOROUGHLY MODERN PRINCESS
                                     by Wendy Corsi Staub
0-380-82054-4/$5.99 US/$7.99 Can